AFRICAN COVENANT SERIES
2

Quest
FOR THE
Promised
Land

AFRICAN COVENANT SERIES
2

Quest FOR THE Promised Land

Oppressed by British rule, the van der
Kemps cross a hostile wilderness
to find a home.

JACK CAVANAUGH

MOODY PRESS
CHICAGO

ISBN: 0-8024-0863-X

1 3 5 7 9 10 8 6 4 2

Printed in the United States of America

To Clarice Maben and John Howerton
who infected me with their love of history

Acknowledgments

To John Muller—a constant friend, faithful encourager, and insightful critic. Thank you again.

To Julie Ieron, Ella Lindvall, and the Moody staff—I could fill this page with the number of ways you have been patient with me on this project. My hope is that your faith in my abilities is justified.

1

This wasn't the first time they had faced death. Death on the South African frontier was as common a sight as a herd of fleet-footed springboks or a flock of blue cranes. Swift and often cunning, the ultimate predator could leap from a bush with the caterwaul of a leopard, splash out of the river with crocodile jaws, or drone annoyingly with the ominous buzz of a tsetse fly.

Today, the specter of death rose up from the grassy knoll that separated the van der Kemp settlement from the muddy-brown Fish River. It appeared in the form of a host of glistening black Xhosa warriors. Hundreds of them.

They stood in defiance, shoulder to shoulder, shield to shield, their erect spear points glistening in the sun as a few of their number drove Christiaan van der Kemp's cattle across the river that served as the official boundary between the Cape Colony settlers and the Xhosa tribes.

Christiaan van der Kemp, his gun at the ready, watched from an open window of his house as his cattle disappeared over the ridge. He could hear their bellowing and the splashing of their hooves as they were herded across the river.

"Aren't we going to stop them?" Oloff Klyn shouted.

Christiaan's seventy-two-year-old neighbor was crouched beneath a second window facing the ridge. His tan, leathery face wrinkled into an expression of disbelief at his neighbor's inactivity. Oloff's eighteen-year-old son, Henry, lay on the floor next to him, nervously gripping and regripping the rifle he'd just loaded for his father.

"They're only cattle," Christiaan said, wincing at the absurdity of his own statement.

"Only cattle!" Oloff bellowed. Meaningless syllables sputtered from the old man's lips. Apparently he could find no adequate words to confront such heresy. Instead, he raised his musket and pressed the stock against his cheek. "Of all the fool-headed . . ." he muttered. "This is the only thing they understand." Squinting his left eye, he aimed down the barrel, doubtless leveling the sight on the chest of a Xhosa warrior.

"Oloff—don't shoot that gun!" Christiaan warned.

The old man hitched his shoulders and settled himself. The blast of the musket was imminent.

"I said don't shoot!" Christiaan thundered. His voice boomed so loudly it not only rattled everyone in the house, it caused a rippling stir among the ranks of Xhosa warriors on the knoll.

Oloff lowered his gun. His patchy white beard bristled as he set his jaw. Bloodshot eyes fixed firmly on Christiaan. Shaking the musket, he said, "If we don't kill them today, they'll be after my cattle tomorrow and Pfeffer's cattle the day after that!"

At the far end of the large room a meek-looking Adriaan Pfeffer sat lodged against the interior wall beneath an open window in similar fashion to Christiaan and Oloff. His pockmarked son crouched next to him, having paused in his loading with a measure of powder in his hand. The muzzle of a gun barrel gaped open in anticipation of receiving the charge. Pfeffer's wife and infant twin daughters huddled on the floor nearby.

"Oloff's right," Pfeffer said softly. "If we don't stop them today, sure as the sun rises they'll be back tomorrow."

The room fell silent. All heads turned toward Christiaan, awaiting his response.

He wished he were out plowing his field, and Christiaan hated plowing. But he hated being thrust into a position of leadership even more. A powerful man with thick arms and broad shoulders, Christiaan stood taller than most men. And for some reason, people associated his size with leadership. It was an association he despised.

However, this was his house, and these were his neighbors. Pfeffer was a good man but timid to the point of indecisive; and indecision on the frontier was one step away from death. Oloff, on the other hand, was hard and bitter. His solution to the frontier problem was simple—exterminate the Xhosa and anyone else who challenged the colonists' right to live as they pleased.

With a sigh the forty-five-year-old descendant of Dutch immigrants scratched his bearded chin and looked to his wife and children sitting on the floor next to the Pfeffer family.

Johanna's eyes met his. A heavy woman, she looked unnatural and uncomfortable on the floor. She fidgeted this way and that, but her restlessness had less to do with her seating arrangement than it did with the struggle taking place within her.

Christiaan recognized his wife's discomfort: pursed lips, sharply focused eyes darting from side to side, rising color in her neck and cheeks. He also knew the source of her pain. Johanna was bursting internally because she wanted to speak her mind. Under normal circumstances, she would have done so without hesitation. However, given the fact that they were under attack and Oloff was challenging her husband in his own household, she restrained herself.

Christiaan smiled slightly. He loved her all the more for her restraint, knowing it did not come easily.

To put Johanna van der Kemp and the word *forthright* in the same sentence was to be redundant. Not only did she epitomize the candid nature of frontier women, she was their chief. Her tongue was a wild stallion that refused to be tamed. When the occasion warranted, as it presently did, she could corral it for a time; but inevitably it would bolt with power and pent-up fury.

But Johanna was also a practical woman. And in a crisis such as this, practicality dictated that there should be but one leader. So she held a tight rein on her tongue and waited on her husband to set their course of action. She only hoped that before he did anything they all might regret, he would ask her opinion.

Sitting next to Johanna and leaning against her was Sina, their daughter. At sixteen years of age she was brown-haired, fair-skinned, and slender, much too slender for a frontier girl. In spite of the fact that a host of Xhosa warriors were lined up outside her house, she seemed more concerned with the nearness of young Henry Klyn. Several times, when she thought no one was looking, Sina cast amorous glances his direction.

Her younger brother, Kootjie, squatted on his heels on the other side of their mother. At barely twelve, he locked his wide eyes intently on his father. He was looking for any sign he might interpret as permission for him to join the men at the windows. Although he was big for his age, Kootjie was still too immature for his father to think of him as a man. However, in Kootjie's eyes he was already a man. He was a good shot and good in the saddle, though he had not yet mastered the art of loading and shooting while riding, a skill Boer men did better than any other.

Christiaan recognized the eagerness in his son's eyes. The years were not so distant that he did not know what the boy was feeling. He was eager to fight the Xhosa. To shoot them. To kill.

Too eager.

And if recent frontier history was any indicator, Kootjie would have plenty of opportunities to kill Xhosa warriors. But not today. Not if Christiaan had any say in the matter.

Turning to Oloff, but speaking in a voice loud enough for everyone to hear, Christiaan said, "There will be no killing today."

"You're a fool!" Klyn bawled. "Mark my words, van der Kemp, if we just let those heathen prance across the river with your cattle, they'll come back and kill us all in our sleep before the week's over."

Hearing his bellow, the Pfeffer twins burst into tears. Angenitha Pfeffer busied herself with quieting the girls.

A voice beside Christiaan said, "As much as it pains me to agree with *Mynheer* Klyn, we must not let the Xhosa take the cattle unchallenged."

Christiaan looked with surprise at the black-skinned man hunkered next to him.

Jama's skin was actually chocolate brown in color, but that fact made little difference to anyone in the Afrikaner settlement. Nor did it matter that he was the descendant of a long line of free men that extended back to early Cape Town. Among the colonists, Jama was known as Christiaan's black.

Between Christiaan and Jama, however, there was no sense of superiority or inferiority. The two men had known each other all their lives, as had their fathers and their grandfathers before them. Friendship between the families extended back as far as anyone could remember. And there was no one on the frontier Christiaan respected more than Jama. Despite the visible contrast of their skin, they were brothers.

"To the Xhosa personal possession is not sacred," Jama said. "Theft is honorable as long as the thief is not caught. And the person whose possessions are stolen is regarded as a fool."

"What are you saying?" Christiaan asked. "Do you agree with Oloff that we should shoot them?"

Jama shrugged. "If we shoot at them, they'll attack."

"Let 'em attack!" Klyn thundered.

"But there are hundreds of them out there!" Christiaan protested. "At best we have six guns, and that's if you count the boys."

"Seven if you count me!" Kootjie cried enthusiastically.

The boy's enthusiasm withered under his father's disapproving glare.

"It matters not how few we are," Klyn replied, his voice as deep as a prophet's. "God favors the righteous. As it says in the Scriptures: 'And stay ye not, but pursue after your enemies, and smite the hindmost of them; suffer them not to enter into their cities: for the Lord your God hath delivered them into your hand.'"

Christiaan stopped listening to Oloff's recitation midway through the Scripture. Jama was right. And, Christiaan reluctantly concluded, so was Oloff. Something had to be done to stop the Xhosa. It seemed that once again life on the frontier had been reduced to a simple equation: Kill or be killed.

Why must it always be this way? All he wanted was a portion of land upon which he could build a home, rear his children, raise his livestock, and live in peace. Was that asking too much?

In the corner of the room the Pfeffer twins sniffed back tears. Beside him, Jama looked to him for a response, as did Adriaan and Conraad Pfeffer. Klyn glared at him like an old schoolmaster waiting for the correct answer. Even Sina had stopped fawning over Henry Klyn long enough to await her father's decision, which was just as well. Christiaan wondered what his daughter would think of Henry if she saw how uncontrollably his pants legs were shaking. Kootjie's expression remained unchanged; he was eager to fight. Johanna looked ready to burst.

"My love," Christiaan said to his wife. "Do you have a word of advice for your husband?"

Johanna straightened herself before speaking. Now that relief was at hand, she did not want to appear too eager. "My dear husband," she said, "no one knows your heart better than I. And you have proven yourself on too many occasions for anyone to believe that your reluctance to fight is founded on fear. But this I would ask you—would you save your family from the Xhosa spear only to condemn them to starvation for want of a herd?"

Christiaan smiled. Practical, as always. It was Johanna's gift. While emotion and passion clouded others' minds, his wife had the ability to penetrate the clutter and find the nugget of truth. But while he valued her advice, it also grieved him.

She had sided with the others.

"Smart woman!" Oloff boomed. "Enough talk! Our course is clear." He repositioned himself to shoot at the Xhosa.

"Lay down your weapon, Oloff!"

A dumbfounded Oloff Klyn gawked at him. Making an appeal to the others in the room, he cried, "The man's mad! Completely addled!"

Christiaan ignored him. Standing abruptly, he laid aside his musket. "Jama," he said. "Come with me."

Jama's eyes narrowed questioningly as he started to put down his gun too.

"No, bring it," Christiaan said.

"What fool thing are you up to now?" Klyn exclaimed.

Johanna's brow gathered in worried furrows. "Christiaan . . ."

13

Without explanation, Christiaan van der Kemp pulled open the front door of his house and stepped out to face the Xhosa warriors.

"Train your gun on my back," he whispered behind him to Jama.

"What?" Jama sputtered.

"You heard me! Jam the barrel into my back and push me forward."

Christiaan felt a gun barrel ram into his kidneys.

"Not so hard!" he complained.

"It would help if I knew what we were doing," Jama whispered.

"We're getting their attention."

"Well, we're doing a good job of it," Jama said.

It was true. The line of Xhosa warriors, to the man, wore expressions of puzzlement. They watched cautiously as the unarmed white man was pushed toward them at gunpoint. When Christiaan and Jama were a few hundred feet away, three warriors stepped out to intercept them.

One of the three, a young man adorned lavishly with leopard skins and wearing an ostrich feather headdress, said something loud enough for all the other warriors to hear. The ranks of Xhosa laughed at the comment, as did Jama.

"What did he say?" Christiaan asked with a half-smile.

Jama translated: "He said he knew it was only a matter of time before the colony blacks enslaved the whites."

Christiaan grinned and nodded.

The Xhosa chief sobered instantly, seeming to take exception to Christiaan's sharing the humor. His white eyes focused and grew hard. Beads of sweat glimmered on his temples and cascaded down black, hollow cheeks. His chest rose and fell with measured breaths.

The laughter of the warriors ceased so abruptly it was unnatural. Their demeanor reflected the anger of their chief. Some shifted nervously from foot to foot; others stood deathly still, looking like panthers ready to spring.

"Jama," Christiaan said softly, "tell them we mean them no harm."

Jama translated.

The chief snorted. "Empty words when we fear no harm," he said. "Does the elephant fear the jackal?"

"We cannot allow you to take our cattle," Christiaan said.

Jama translated.

The Xhosa chief's eyes narrowed. He looked from Jama to Christiaan to the gun, then to Jama again. To Jama he said, "This man is not your captive."

"No," Jama said, lowering his musket.

14

The chief grew agitated. His eyes darted from side to side, searching the terrain behind the two men. "More white treachery!" he cried, stepping backward. "Like tobacco on the ground."

Feeding on their chief's anxiety, the ranks of Xhosa warriors rattled to the sound of spears striking shields.

"No!" Jama cried. "Not like tobacco! Not like tobacco!"

His words fell on closed ears. The tobacco incident had been a blistering boil between the Xhosa and the settlers for years. According to the Xhosa version, when the first colonial farmers arrived in the Zuurveld region, one settler scattered tobacco on the ground as an offer of peace to a Xhosa party. Then, when the Xhosa stooped down to pick it up, they were mercilessly slaughtered. The settler family to whom this treachery was attributed insisted the story was without merit—that it was a missionary fabrication to gain the favor of the Xhosa tribes.

For Christiaan and Jama, the truth of the incident mattered little at the moment. What mattered was that the Xhosa believed the story to be true.

"No treachery!" Jama insisted. "You have taken our cattle. We could have shot you from the house. Instead, we have come in peace to talk."

"Talk?" The chief sneered. "The words of the settlers are as slippery as serpents. They cannot be trusted."

Christiaan stood by helplessly. He understood very few of the words that passed between the chief and Jama. However, it was clear from the Xhosa's tone and threatening gesticulations that it would take an extraordinary gesture to win his favor.

"Look at my skin!" Jama cried. Wiping his forearm with a hand, he said, "I am the same color as you! You can trust my words."

"You are his slave!" the chief scoffed. "Your lips move, but it is his words that come forth."

"You are wrong!" Jama insisted. "We speak as one. We speak as brothers."

Though Christiaan did not fully understand the exchange, he saw that Jama's hand movements attempted to link the two of them in some way. He parroted the last Xhosa word he heard: "Brothers," he said, pointing to Jama and himself.

The chief laughed mockingly.

Jama pressed forward. "Does not the Xhosa proverb say, 'People are people through other people'?"

The chief appeared surprised at Jama's knowledge of the saying. Warily he said, "That is a Xhosa truth."

Jama concluded, "Then believe me when I say that this man treats me as his brother. You can know that he and his family are good people by the way they treat me."

Christiaan suppressed a grin. The last time he grinned, he had offended the Xhosa chief. But Jama was making progress.

The rigid lines on the chief's face began to soften ever so slightly. He said something that brought a smile to Jama's face.

Jama translated for Christiaan. "He just said, 'You talk. I listen.'"

Christiaan nodded solemnly at the chief. His nod was not returned. The next several moments passed in silence as the three looked at each other.

"Well?" Jama whispered to Christiaan. "What do I say now? This was your idea!"

"Makana," Christiaan said directly to the chief. He paused for a reaction.

It was immediately forthcoming. The Xhosa's face clouded with outrage and fury. It was as though Christiaan had spoken a Xhosa god's name in vain.

Christiaan had hoped for a reaction, but not one as openly hostile as this. He said to Jama quickly, "Tell the chief we come in the spirit of Makana."

Jama conveyed the message.

"What do you know of Makana?" the chief thundered. He spoke directly at Christiaan.

Christiaan replied, "I hold in honor the name of Makana for what he did for the Xhosa people. I present myself to you in the same spirit with which Makana presented himself to white settlers. My hope is that the Xhosa are wiser and more compassionate than those to whom Makana delivered himself."

Jama's eyes grew frightfully wide as he listened to the words Christiaan wanted him to repeat. He whispered to Christiaan, "Are you sure you want me to say this?"

"Tell him," Christiaan said.

As the words passed between them, the Xhosa chief stared intently at Christiaan. The fury in his eyes gradually diminished—Makana the Left-Handed, as he was known—was a highly regarded Xhosa religious and military leader. Earlier, he had led his people in several wars against the British and the colonists at Port Elizabeth and Grahamstown. However, the Xhosa warriors were no match for British weapons. Thousands of Xhosa men were mowed down in swaths by grapeshot. Then, in retaliation, the British mounted several raids in Xhosa territory, killing the populace and burning their homes. There was nothing the Xhosa people could do to stop them. Makana watched helplessly as his people were slaughtered.

In a desperate gamble to stop the bloodshed, Makana surrendered to the British, hoping that by delivering himself up to the conquerors he might be able to restore peace to the country. Makana was shackled, thrown into the back of a wagon, and transported to Robben Island Prison. He drowned years later, helping prisoners escape from the wretched place.

"I present myself to you," Christiaan said, "just as Makana gave himself up to the British, in the hope that, by doing so, the fighting between your people and my people might stop."

For what seemed eternity, the chief stared at Christiaan as Jama translated. The two warriors flanking the chief, when they heard Christiaan's words, stared at him in disbelief.

Finally the chief spoke. "What would I do with a white man?" he said. His tone was humorous. The two warriors beside him laughed. Sobering, the chief said, "Our land is dry. Our cattle have died. My people are weak and hungry. We must have cattle and food to live."

Christiaan nodded solemnly. So the raid had nothing to do with tradition or a young man's need to prove himself to his superiors. It was a desperate attempt to survive. All at once, Christiaan felt foolish. Why had he been so quick to assume that the Xhosa's actions were any less noble than his own? He knew the effects the drought was having on the farmers on this side of the Fish River; he had never given any thought to the likelihood that the people on the other side would be having the same struggle.

He turned toward the house. "Kootjie!"

The boy's eager face appeared in a window.

"Come out here!"

Kootjie's head disappeared. Christiaan waited a moment for the front door to open and his son to join him. The door remained shut tight. Then Kootjie reappeared at the window. This time his mother appeared behind him.

"What did you say?" Kootjie yelled.

"Come here!" Then as an afterthought, Christiaan added, "And bring Conraad and Henry with you."

Kootjie's head jerked back into the house. Something was said behind him. Turning to his father again, he cried, "Should we bring guns?"

"*No!*" Christiaan yelled.

Kootjie turned back, listened, then called to his father again, *"Myn-heer* Klyn won't let Henry come out if he can't bring a gun."

"Then you and Conraad come!"

A few moments later, the door of the van der Kemp house tentatively swung open, and the two boys appeared. The elder Pfeffer and Klyn appeared in the windows with muskets in their hands.

Kootjie approached without apparent fear, Conraad tentatively. A couple of times Kootjie reached back and pulled at Conraad's arm to get him to walk faster.

Christiaan met them halfway between the house and the Xhosa chief. While the boys stared past him at the warriors, Christiaan told them what he wanted them to do.

"Go on," he said. "The day's nearly gone."

The boys took off running in two different directions. Then Christiaan informed the chief of his instructions to the boys. The chief's response was a skeptical glance. He retreated to his line of warriors and spoke quietly to them.

Before long, Kootjie reappeared with a horse-drawn wagon. In short order, so did Conraad. The wagons they drove were loaded with foodstuffs.

As Christiaan presented the food to the chief, the boys jumped from the wagons and stood back as Xhosa warriors descended upon the supplies and loaded their arms with food.

"Kootjie," Christiaan said, "did you get what I told you to get?"

The boy nodded. He wove his way back to the wagon, past one warrior after another. In amusement Christiaan watched the Xhosa and Kootjie eye each other as they passed. From under a blanket beneath the seat, Kootjie pulled out a copper pot.

A cry came from the house. "Kootjie! What are you doing with my best pot?" Johanna filled the doorway with her hands on her hips.

"Bring it here," Christiaan said, ignoring his wife. He handed the copper pot to the chief. "A gift," he said. "From a friend."

Jama translated.

The Xhosa chief took the copper pot. He stared at Christiaan, still unsure what to make of the white man's gesture. He turned then and shouted an order to his men. Within a few minutes the chief and his warriors crossed the Fish River and disappeared into their own territory.

Oloff Klyn burst through the door and into the field. "You gave them food?" he roared.

"They're hungry," Christiaan said. He motioned for Kootjie to come to him. Placing his arm around his son—in doing so, he was reminded how tall the boy was getting—the two of them walked back toward the house, followed by Jama and Oloff.

"Since when is it our duty to feed the heathen?" Oloff bellowed. "And what happens when the food runs out? They'll be back! And if you don't give them more, they'll take it from you!"

"They're hungry," Christiaan repeated. "All we did was lend assistance to a hungry neighbor. It seemed the right thing to do." Then, with a twinkle in his eye, he said, "I would have done the same thing for you."

As Christiaan expected, Oloff took exception to the comparison. "You won't think this is funny when those savages return! And what about your cattle? Did you give your cattle to them too?"

Christiaan's smile faded. "No, I didn't."

"Then they're going to return the cattle?" Johanna asked.

"I don't know. I didn't ask."

"You're a fool!" Oloff scoffed. "You'll never see your cattle again!" At the house, he called to Henry to leave. "When your family's starving because of your foolishness, don't come begging at my place, hoping for sympathy! Go to your Xhosa friends. Then you'll see how grateful they are!"

Oloff Klyn and Henry mounted up and rode toward home. Sina watched them ride off.

The Pfeffers gathered their children and things to take their leave. "At least we're all safe," Adriaan said with a sigh. "I guess we should be grateful." To Conraad he said, "Take the twins with you in the wagon. Your mother and I will follow."

As the Pfeffers rode out, Johanna turned to her husband. "You gave that Xhosa warrior my best copper pot!" she cried.

"The Xhosa value copper highly," Jama said brightly, defending Christiaan's actions.

"So do I!"

Christiaan released Kootjie to retrieve the wagon. To Jama he said, "Do you think they'll return our cattle?"

Jama shook his head and shrugged.

Johanna turned and went back into the house.

The copper pot issue wasn't dead. Christiaan knew he would hear about it again when they were alone. He also knew she would forgive him. In time.

For the moment, Christiaan was content. He watched as Kootjie lumbered awkwardly toward the wagon; half boy, half man. Christiaan was proud of the way his son handled himself today.

Turning to Sina, he watched her stare after a cloud of dust that neared the horizon, all that was left of the departing Henry Klyn. He wondered what it was about the Klyn boy that attracted her. He shuddered at the thought that he and Oloff might one day be family.

"I'll check on the workers," Jama said, ambling away.

From inside the house came the angry banging of pots and pans that had been left behind.

Christiaan stared in the direction of the Fish River. He wondered if he had done the right thing. There had been no promises that the cattle would be returned. So what possible reason did he have for hoping the Xhosa would return them? And even if they did, what then? The food he gave them wouldn't last long. When it ran out, would the warriors return for more food as Oloff Klyn predicted?

Christiaan smiled broadly at no one in particular. Closing his eyes, he lifted his head heavenward and thanked God for His care. Time would tell whether or not he did the right thing today. But of one thing he was sure—Sina and Kootjie and Johanna and Jama were still alive. And that was no small blessing.

Not for people who lived on the frontier.

2

Sina van der Kemp leaned against the rough, whitewashed thatch of the house with arms folded contentedly across her narrow frame. She stared at the dissipating dust cloud on the horizon. It was Henry's dust cloud. Its edges were tinged with pink from the sun, which hung low in the sky. Feathery. Romantic. Enchanting. An almost perfect dust cloud in every way. As was he who made it.

Just thinking that a short time earlier Henry was in her house—armed for battle, bravely taking a stand, ready to die rather than let the fearful Xhosa warriors hurt her—turned her arms to gooseflesh. She rubbed the bumps, savoring the tingling sensation.

A random thought caused her to close her eyes, lean her head back, and smile. An image formed behind the darkness of her lids. She saw Henry on the floor of her house, cradling his father's gun. *Mynheer* Klyn had said something. She couldn't remember exactly what—she wasn't listening to him anyway. Then, for some reason, her father took exception to his comment. He shouted a response, and everyone's attention turned to him. Sina remembered thinking this was a perfect moment for her to steal a glance at Henry. She did. However, her gaze lingered longer than it should . . .

Henry had looked up at her! He'd caught her staring at him!

Even now she could remember the warmth of the blush that crept up her neck. Then, just as she was about to turn away, he smiled at her! It was that adorable boyish grin of his, the one where just the corners of his mouth turned upward ever so winningly. Sina fought her natural impulse to lower her gaze as Henry's eyes seemed to reach out to her, to embrace her . . . tenderly, lovingly . . .

"Sina! Why are you standing there doing nothing? Help me with this table." Her mother's voice had the sharpness of a cock's crow to it, puncturing a pleasant dream.

Turning, Sina saw her mother by the door, bending over, gripping one edge of the toppled small table that served as her daily command post. Her eyes looked at Sina expectantly as she gave a nod to the far edge of the table. "I'm waiting," she said.

Grabbing the edge of the table, Sina helped right it.

"What were you doing over there?" her mother asked.

Sina shrugged. "Pondering."

"It looked to me like you were making cow eyes at Henry Klyn again."

"I was doing no such thing!"

Using her apron as a dust cloth, her mother wiped the top of the table. "Staring at a dust cloud will not make the boy more attracted to you."

Sina's lower lip protruded.

"And it's unbecoming the way you stare at him. In fact, it's indecent."

A frown accompanied Sina's lower lip, turning pouting to angry defense. "I don't stare at him!" she protested.

Her mother's hand stopped its sweeping motion. She looked up. Her eyes challenged Sina with a clear, no-nonsense stare. There was no anger in them, but it was clear they would not tolerate falsehood.

Sina lowered her gaze. "I thought no one was looking," she said softly.

"It's unbecoming a Christian lady," her mother said. Her hand resumed its circular scrubbing.

Glancing over her shoulder, Sina took a last look at the horizon. The dust cloud had dissipated. No longer was the landscape outlined with the sun's pinkish-orange coloring. In the twilight, the tangle of bushes stretching across the frontier landscape was flat and gray. A slight breeze stirred the pungent smell of dirt. In the distance, Kootjie could be heard yelling at his dogs. Sina's shoulders slumped. Her heart, which had beat with romance, now resumed its monotonous daily rhythm.

"Grab the broom and sweep the floor," her mother said flatly. "It's hard for me to understand how those men can track so much dirt into one house with so little effort."

Sina shuffled into the house. Pulling the broom behind her, she went to a far corner and began sweeping her way toward the door. The stroke of the broom lacked any hint of enthusiasm.

Alone in the barnlike structure of the darkening house, Sina tried to quell her rising anger toward her mother. In her mind, she knew it wasn't her mother's fault. Blaming Mother for the reality of life on the frontier was like blaming the crowing cock for the rising of the sun. And in her heart, Sina knew her mother loved her. But must she always be so unromantic?

"Sina!"

At the sound of her mother's voice, the broom stopped mid-stroke. Sina closed her eyes. "Yes, Mother?"

"It's Karel!"

Sina's eyes opened, brightened. Her smile shrugged off the gloom of the darkening interior. Dropping the broom, she rushed out the front door just as a rider drew within hailing distance.

"Is everyone all right?" a youthful male voice shouted.

Sina and her mother exchanged glances. Then her mother went inside the house, leaving Sina to answer. Running to greet the approaching rider, she waved happily.

He dismounted a short distance from her and covered the last bit of his journey on the run. Strong hands gripped Sina's shoulders. "We heard that the Xhosa were attacking you!"

Sina smiled up warmly at the tall figure.

His chest rose and fell in gasps from riding hard. Brown eyes beneath a large-brimmed hat were charged with concern.

"They're gone now," Sina said. "But not before taking our cattle."

Still holding her shoulders, Karel glanced beyond her at the house. "Was anyone hurt?"

Sina shook her head. "Father and Jama talked to them, gave them some food, and they left."

A puzzled expression crossed Karel's face.

"Henry and his father rode in to help us!" Sina said excitedly.

Karel's face screwed up as though he were chewing on something distasteful. "With protection like that, I'm surprised you're still alive," he said.

Sina slapped his chest in playful anger. "Karel De Buys, shame!" she cried. "I think it was sweet of Henry to come to my rescue."

"*Ja*, sweet," Karel said. "Where's your father?"

Side by side, Sina and Karel ambled toward the house.

As the first of the night's stars dotted the sky, her heart beat happily again. For as long as she had known him, which stretched back to the days of her earliest memories, Karel had made her feel special. It was a good feeling, different from the way Henry made her feel. Instead of exciting her to the point of feeling flustered, Karel made her feel comfortable, accepted, secure. With Karel there was no need for pretense or airs. They knew each other too well; there was no need for masks.

Her father emerged from the far side of the house. "Karel!" he boomed.

Sina beamed as her father and this eighteen-year-old exchanged greetings. To see her father treat one of her friends as an equal was still a

23

relatively new experience for her. There was a genuine glint of respect in her father's eyes as he spoke to Karel. Sina liked that but at the same time was disturbed that she had never seen him greet Henry in similar fashion.

"I'm sorry you rode all this way for nothing," Christiaan said.

"You would do the same for us," Karel replied. His brow furrowed. "Sina tells me they took your cattle . . ."

Her father nodded sheepishly.

"Sina!" It was Mother again. "Karel is hungry. Help me prepare a meal for him while he and your father talk."

Sina looked at Karel, who smiled back at her. Her father led him away, recounting their confrontation with the Xhosa warriors.

Karel sat close by Sina's side on a bluff near the house. The meal was finished, as was the evening reading of the Bible and prayers. From their elevated view they could see the thatched roof of the house to their left; pale yellow light streamed out the doorway and windows. Immediately in front of them, the Great Fish River looked like a silver snake with the moonlight glistening on its scales. A dark, spotted canopy stretched overhead from horizon to horizon.

The bluff was not far from the house, so for privacy they had to speak in soft voices. Even then, Sina sometimes wondered how much of her private conversations her parents had heard over the years. Beside him lay Karel's gun in the dirt. As close as they were to the house, it was still wise to have a firearm within reach, especially at night.

"Henry was wonderful!" Sina gushed. "When everyone else left the house, he stayed behind to protect me!"

Karel rolled his eyes. "That's not what your father told me."

"It's true!" Sina cried. Her voice echoed against the wall of the house. She drew up her shoulders and covered her mouth in embarrassed fashion, then repeated in a whisper, "It's true!"

Karel nodded.

They sat in uneasy silence. Sounds of clanking pans could be heard from inside the house. Jama's silhouette appeared in the light of the front door. He stretched, then wandered around toward the back of the house. Either he didn't see the two of them sitting on the bluff, or he paid no attention to them.

When he was gone, Sina said softly, "Why don't you like Henry?"

"I don't want to talk about this," Karel replied.

"Why can't you see Henry as I see him? Henry is a kind, brave—"

Karel stiffened. "I didn't ride all this way to talk about Henry Klyn," he said. "Let's change the subject."

The dim light of night glistened on Karel's set jaw. Sina had seen that look on him before. It hadn't changed since he was a little boy. The jaw itself had changed—it was much stronger now and had the blue-gray shadow of a man needing a shave—but the expression had not changed. When Karel got that look on his face, there was no reasoning with him.

From experience, she knew it was best to let the subject drop. When she was younger, she would have pressed the matter stubbornly and irritated Karel to the point where he would stomp away and she wouldn't see him again for weeks. But now she was wiser. She changed topics . . . to another one she knew would irritate him.

"Fine," she said. "If you don't want to talk about Henry, what do you want to talk about? Deborah van Aardt?"

Her question was met with stony silence.

Sina smiled inwardly, satisfied that she had goaded him even as she had been goaded. Contentedly, she grabbed her knees, rocked back and forth, and awaited his response.

"No, I don't want to talk about Deborah, either," Karel said in a carefully measured tone.

"Oh?" Sina sat up hopefully. "Have you finally given up on her?"

A spark of angry fire lit his eyes, then went out. "No, I haven't given up on her," he said. "I don't want to talk about Deborah or Henry Klyn because every time we do we end up arguing. If I wanted to argue, I would have ridden home tonight and argued with my younger brothers."

Sina lowered her head contritely. Karel *had* ridden half a day's ride because he thought her family was in danger, and here she was treating him horribly. She knew she was wrong to treat him this way; it was just that it angered her that nobody was willing to give Henry a chance. Why couldn't they see him as she saw him? Especially Karel. It would mean so much to her if Henry and Karel could one day be friends.

"I'm sorry," she whispered, chastened. "You're right. Let's change topics. What do you want to talk about?"

He didn't speak immediately, but from the way his shoulders relaxed, Sina knew that he had accepted her apology and they were friends again.

All was silent, but it was an easy silence. Even as children, Sina and Karel had never felt it necessary to fill every minute with words. Sina could remember days when the two of them would lay atop this same bluff and stare at the clouds passing overhead, sometimes for nearly an hour without a word being spoken.

Karel cleared his throat.

Sina turned toward him, awaiting his comment.

A smirk curled the corner of his mouth upward. "Do you remember," he said, "the time we were on this bluff and we kissed?"

A surprised squeal escaped Sina's lips before she could catch it. Her face and neck flushed red and glowed so warmly she just knew she looked like a lighthouse atop the bluff. "Karel!" she squeaked breathlessly.

"What?" he cried. But he knew. His face wore that impish grin boys get when they know they've done something shocking.

The incident had lain dormant between them since the day it happened, nearly eight years before. They had never spoken of it, nor had they ever kissed again.

"What?" Karel cried again. "We were children!"

"Well . . . yes, we were children . . . but . . ." she sputtered. "But . . . what made you think of that now?"

Karel shrugged. "I don't know . . ." He smiled. "It just came to me."

"Well, it can just leave you as abruptly as it came!"

"Fine with me," Karel said placidly. "You're the one that asked me what I wanted to talk about."

"I never thought it would be *that!*"

Realizing how loud her voice had become, she glanced down at the house. The figure of her mother was lit by the light escaping the doorway. She was wiping her hands on her apron and staring into the darkness at the bluff.

Sina clenched her teeth, then whispered, "Now look what you've done!"

Karel grinned a satisfied grin. "So when are you and your family leaving for Nachtmaal?" he asked in a voice loud enough for Johanna van der Kemp to hear.

3

"You needn't look so smug." With a disapproving glare Johanna looked at her husband sitting next to her.

"Smug? Do I look smug?" Christiaan chuckled.

The two sat side by side in the wagon as it rocked back and forth on the journey to Graaff-Reinet for Nachtmaal. Christiaan's hands were folded in his lap. He was indulging himself in a rare bit of self-satisfaction. Behind them, Sina lay sheltered from the sun beneath the canvas covering stretched over rib-like bows that arched from one side of the wagon bed to the other. Kootjie walked in front of the wagon, leading the oxen.

"Your attitude is not befitting a Christian man," Johanna said.

"I have done nothing wrong!" Christiaan protested.

"You can't fool me, Christiaan van der Kemp. I've lived with you too many years. It's plain from that silly expression on your face that you can't wait to get to Graaff-Reinet so you can tell Oloff Klyn how the Xhosa returned your herd."

"To the cow!" Christiaan gloated. "To the cow! Not one was missing."

"It's not a very Christian attitude."

"Aren't you happy our cattle were returned?"

"Of course I am!" Johanna replied. "But not as happy as you are at the prospect of letting everyone at Nachtmaal know that you were right and Oloff Klyn was wrong."

Christiaan bowed his head in subdued contrition. "You're right, as usual, Baas," he said. Christiaan began calling his wife *Baas,* a word most often used by slaves for their masters, shortly after they were married when he witnessed the way she issued a flurry of directives that sent workers scurrying in every direction. Continuing in a tone of mock penitence, he said, "And I will pray that I might be humble . . . while I tell everyone at Nachtmaal that Oloff Klyn was wrong and I was right."

"You're shameful!" Johanna said. She added, "In all honesty, I must admit that I too thought we had seen the last of that herd."

With only eight oxen pulling the wagon, the journey to Nachtmaal was tedious. At best they traveled six to eight miles a day, oftentimes in rather circuitous routes to circumvent ravines. Each night Christiaan thanked his Maker for the Southern Cross so prominent in the sky. It was that constellation that kept them on a northwest heading as they traversed open countryside. The journey to Graaff-Reinet, the area's district headquarters, took several days. It was a trip the van der Kemps, and all other God-fearing families who lived on the frontier, made at least once a year for Nachtmaal.

Nachtmaal, "night meal," was Holy Communion for the Dutch Calvinist community. Families living nearby were expected to attend every year. Those who lived farther away might attend only once every three or four years, and when they did make the long journey they often stayed for a month.

It was their most important religious and social gathering. Parents brought children to be baptized. Young lovers came to get married. New church members were welcomed into fellowship. And there were singing parties at night for young people. A good number of married couples remembered fondly the singing parties as the place where they met and fell in love.

The events of Nachtmaal centered on the church service, which lasted for four days. The Sunday ceremonies alone lasted four hours. It was a time of remembrance and thanksgiving as the people gathered to give thanks to God for their farms, their families, and one another.

It was a time when the people were reminded of their spiritual heritage, of how God had led their ancestors to Cape Colony that they might forge a covenant nation based upon His Word, the Bible. It was a time when the community was strengthened as wives comforted one another in their annual pregnancies and as men swapped stories about their struggle against the land, the elements, the British, and the Xhosa.

And it was a time to mourn the dead and comfort the suffering. There was not a family among them that was not acquainted with suffering—women who had lost babies, wives who had lost husbands, parents who had buried one or more children.

"*Kyk daar!*" Sina cried, leaning between her parents. "Look there! Wagons!" Her finger pointed toward a small puff of dust near the horizon and to the left.

Christiaan squinted that direction. "Looks like we have traveling company," he said.

For the better part of the day the van der Kemps kept track of the distant wagons. Meeting other travelers this far from Graaff-Reinet was indeed good fortune. The chance for conversation and social exchanges would make it seem that Nachtmaal was starting that much sooner.

"Three wagons!" Sina squealed. "It's Karel!"

Christiaan winced at her shout so close to his ear. "Just because there are three wagons doesn't mean it's the De Buys family."

"It's Karel," Sina cried. "I know it is."

As the wagons drew within hailing distance, Sina was proved right. Walking beside the lead wagon and driving the oxen was Karel. His aunt and uncle had raised Karel, having found him bundled and hidden in a bush following a skirmish with the Xhosa in which both his parents were killed. He was the oldest sibling in a family with seventeen children of their own.

The De Buys farm lay just beyond the Pfeffer settlement. So, in a sense, they were neighbors. But living among a people who felt claustrophobic if they could see the smoke of their neighbor's chimney meant that the van der Kemp family and the De Buys family saw each other infrequently. However, that hadn't prevented Karel and Sina from becoming close friends—closer than a boy and girl ought to be who are not romantically inclined, according to some of the resident wagging tongues.

When the wagons met, the two clans set to socializing at once. The two men greeted each other and immediately began comparing travel notes—the condition of their oxen, how far they traveled each day, and the best route between their present location and Graaff-Reinet. Johanna joined *Mevrou* De Buys in her wagon, and the two began chattering about children and clothes and recent gossip.

Karel and Sina, both of them all smiles, were immediately drawn to each other. They walked a short distance from the wagons to gain a small measure of privacy, heeding their parents' warning not to go off too far.

That left Kootjie with the seventeen De Buys children, all of them younger than he. As they scurried about him like chickens to grain, he wished he were back home with his dogs and Jama.

After coffee—and for Louis De Buys, a pipe—the two parties merged and continued their journey. The men walked beside the van der Kemp wagon while the women rode in the De Buys wagon. Sina and Karel walked behind the van der Kemp wagon at a discreet distance, talking and laughing. Three of the De Buys boys were granted permission to walk with Kootjie, who resumed his duty of leading the van der Kemp oxen. He stood a good foot taller than the tallest of the De Buys boys.

"Like little chicks following their mother," Louis De Buys said with a grin, pointing to his boys and Kootjie.

Christiaan laughed. He was struck by the size difference between Kootjie and the other boys. The breadth of his shoulders, compared to theirs, made him look like a man. So why did he find it so difficult to think of Kootjie as anything other than a little boy?

"And what about them?" Louis said with a wink. He pointed over his shoulder with his pipe.

Christiaan turned.

Sina was laughing. She reached over and touched Karel's arm. Their heads tilted toward each other.

"You'd think they were lovers," Louis said.

"Sina has her eye on the Klyn boy."

"Is that a fact? My condolences."

Christiaan and Louis exchanged glances and laughs.

Christiaan liked the man. Beneath his broad-rimmed hat Louis was brown and weather-beaten, like most other men who daily battled the frontier. But despite hardships, he had a quick smile, which displayed an array of gapped teeth. And he seemed to have brought up Karel well.

Taking another glance behind him, Christiaan liked what he saw—a young man of medium build, whose walk was confident without being cocky. A shock of bush-brown hair was hidden beneath his hat, the rim of which cast a shadow over brown eyes and a clean-shaved, strong jaw.

"He still seeing that van Aardt girl?" Christiaan asked.

Louis nodded, none too happy.

"Think there's any chance you could talk him into marrying Sina?"

"I've spent a good number of evenings trying to do just that," Louis said.

"And?"

"He says they've been friends so long, they could never fall in love."

"I get the same thing from Sina." Christiaan sighed.

They walked in silence for a while.

"Karel is going to ask van Aardt for his daughter at Nachtmaal," Louis said, relighting his pipe.

Christiaan looked at the lowering sun. It was nearly time to make camp. "Will there be a wedding next year?"

"He says Deborah insists on it. You know how she is. Everything has to be done in a grand sort of way."

"She gets her pride from her father." Looking over his shoulder one more time, Christiaan sighed again. "Too bad. Karel and Sina would make a good couple."

"*Ja,* a good couple," Louis replied.

Just ahead of them, Kootjie turned his head. He was more interested in watching Karel and Sina than he was in the oxen. The three De Buys boys pummeled him with questions, which he ignored.

While he was busy looking behind him, his foot struck a rock. Arms and legs sprawled awkwardly as he tried to keep himself from falling. His effort was unsuccessful. He fell in a heap, having to roll to one side to keep from being stepped on by the oxen.

The three De Buys boys howled with laughter. So did Karel and Sina.

Christiaan yelled at his son. "Kootjie! If you were paying attention to your work that wouldn't have happened! What if you had knocked one of the boys under the feet of the oxen? You could have killed someone!"

From the ground, an embarrassed Kootjie stared silently upward at his father.

"Come on, get up!" Christiaan shouted. "It's time we made camp anyway."

With everyone looking at him, Kootjie picked himself up and brushed himself off. For the rest of the night he kept to himself and said not a word.

4

The level of excitement among the four-wagon party rose considerably when Spandau Kop came into view. Like God's pillar of fire in the desert, the mountain heights of Graaff-Reinet led His covenant people to Nachtmaal.

To a people who knew only the flatness of the veld, the physical appearance of the chain of mountains that made Graaff-Reinet a natural amphitheater was awe-inspiring. As the mountains first came into view, it was not uncommon to hear a score of testimonies that began, "I remember the first time I saw Spandau Kop . . ."

The van der Kemps now joined a city taken over by canopied wagons bound for Nachtmaal. Canvas tents pitched next to wagons housed the religious travelers. Oxen grazed in nearby meadows, and sheep as well that had been driven to market. Everywhere, backs were slapped and hugs exchanged as the settlers greeted one another.

Christiaan deferred to the "Baas" as Johanna directed each of them in the necessary chores to make camp. Calling the oxen by name, Kootjie headed them to pasture. Christiaan erected the canvas tent while Sina and Johanna prepared the fire and started the coffee. It would be unthinkable to have friends stop by and not have a cup of coffee with which to greet them.

A festive air permeated the sea of canvas shelters. Sina's heart beat excitedly as she started the fire, glancing up with great frequency to see if she could catch a glimpse of Henry Klyn.

On the night before Nachtmaal, the men gathered around a community fire in the large square before the church.

"The Xhosa are not the enemy," Louis De Buys said. "They're a nuisance. The enemy is the British."

A murmur of agreement rippled around the circle of men. Swirls of smoke and the predominating odor of pipe tobacco pervaded the assembly.

Christiaan sat back and listened, as he often did at such gatherings, preferring to take in the opinions of others rather than express his own.

His quiet approach wasn't a matter of shyness but one of learning. A thoughtful, introspective man, he sought to learn by listening to others. How could he learn anything if he was the one speaking?

"Nonsense!" Oloff Klyn bellowed. "Not a one of us here has not been deprived of a loved one—for me, my beloved wife, as all of you well know—by a Xhosa assegai. How can you say they're not our enemies when they've killed our loved ones and burned our farms?"

A louder rumbling agreed with Klyn.

"All I'm saying," De Buys defended himself, "is that if the British were providing adequate protection, the Xhosa wouldn't be a problem."

"The British will never provide us anything worthwhile!" Klyn cried. "They are nothing but braggarts, liars, and tyrants!"

A loud chorus of assent arose. Though the Boers were considered a quarrelsome people—even among themselves—if there was anything upon which they could agree, it was that the British were incompetent rulers.

The settlers first came under British colonial rule in 1795 when Britain seized Cape Town colony. The British defended their actions, declaring that they were merely taking the Cape into protective custody. While Napoleon ravaged Europe, they wanted to insure that this strategic port of call on the way to the Indies did not fall under French control. When Napoleon was subdued, they returned the Cape to Holland only to seize it again a few years later when Napoleon resumed hostilities with Spain. This time they were there to stay.

For a short while, the British and the Boers managed to endure one another. They even united to defeat a few impoverished trekboers who fomented rebellion in the colony. However, the autonomy that the farmers had enjoyed under the Dutch East India Company came to an end. The British gradually asserted control over the entire colony, emphasizing British culture and institutions.

The Dutch system of district administration, using men appointed from the farming population, was replaced by British magistrates who had no local affiliations. In place of amateur Dutch courts, the British appointed their own lawyers from Britain and introduced British legal procedures.

And while the government continued to support the Dutch Reformed church, it asserted supervision over it. In addition, English became the official language of government offices, law courts, and public schools, even though the majority of the Afrikaner population could not speak it.

In an attempt to escape the stranglehold the British had on them, hundreds of Afrikaner families—the van der Kemps among them—fled the Cape for interior coastal lands. However, the British followed, and a district government was established at Graaff-Reinet.

The heavily bearded man sitting next to Klyn rose slowly to his feet. "The British lie to their own kind; how can we expect them to be honest with us? Consider what they did in eighteen twenty!"

"*Ja!*" Klyn agreed. "I know a British wheeler and cobbler who'd join us willingly if we were to take up arms against the British!"

Christiaan winced at Klyn's talk, and the mention of rebellion created an instant uproar with opinions expressed loudly from both sides.

In 1820, in an attempt to put down hostilities between the Boer frontiersmen and the Xhosa, the British tried to create a buffer between the two. They annexed a large portion of land and attempted to settle it with Englishmen. To do so, they promoted the area as a veritable Eden.

The men and women who responded were, for the most part, not farmers but tradesmen who were looking for a fresh start. When these new settlers arrived, many of them wept at the first sight of the land. It was anything but Eden. The land was barely useful for grazing and totally unsuitable for crops. The rainfall was unpredictable—years of drought were followed by floods. And most of the year the spring water was beyond brackish; it was simply undrinkable. No amount of English support could make the annexed buffer a success. The disillusioned tradesmen-turned-farmers migrated to the nearby towns and took up their trades once again.

And the Xhosa problem continued.

"How do they expect us to work our herds and the land without slaves?" one settler cried.

In response, a slight man with a large mouth stood up uncertainly and shouted with a mock British accent, "Didn't you journey to London to get your just compensation?"

A roar of laughter followed.

At the urging of London missionaries residing in the area, the British government had adopted a plan to emancipate the slaves. In return, the government would provide compensation equal to one-third of their assessed value. Claims for compensation had to be made in London.

Oloff Klyn pounded an empty ale tankard on a table. "I have only one more word to say," he thundered. "*Slachtersnek!*"

A near riot ensued. Men jumped up. Shouts and whistles echoed up and down the tree-lined street.

The incident that incited such a volatile reaction had occurred in 1813. In violation of British law, a headstrong Boer farmer by the name of Bezuidenhout refused to release a Khoi laborer when his work contract expired. In addition, he held back the man's pay and cattle for compensation due to losses sustained by the worker's ineptness.

According to Bezuidenhout, the slave was more trouble than he was worth, having lost twenty-one of his master's sheep due to negligence, having broken farm equipment, and having caused other damage.

The Khoi slave brought the matter to the British officials, who called Bezuidenhout to give an accounting to them. Bezuidenhout ignored the summons. To him, and to the Boer community as a whole, it was intolerable that a white man should be haled into court to answer to a servant's complaints. So for two years Bezuidenhout failed to respond to the citation sent him.

On a hot October morning a military detachment of two white officers and sixteen colored soldiers arrived at Bezuidenhout's farm to arrest him.

But the stubborn Boer farmer was ready for them. He had stashed food and ammunition in a cave on a hillside, and when the detachment arrived, he opened fire on them with a long-barreled elephant gun. The battle raged for several hours until finally Bezuidenhout was hit and killed.

Outrage over his death swept the Boer community. A few days later a group of farmers swore vengeance against those who caused their neighbor's death. However, news leaked to the British authorities. A force of dragoons was sent after the conspirators and captured them at a pass called Slachtersnek.

While the other conspirators surrendered, Bezuidenhout's brother opened fire. With his wife and twelve-year-old son loading and reloading seven muskets for him, he managed to keep the soldiers at bay for a time. Eventually, he too was gunned down, and his wife and son were badly wounded.

Forty-seven of the rebels stood trial. Thirty-three received sentences ranging from banishment to terms of imprisonment and fines. Five were sentenced to death by public hanging.

When the day of execution arrived, the hangman, having received the impression that only one man was to be hanged, failed to bring enough rope. Four more pieces of rope were quickly obtained, but these were rotten. So when the lever was pulled to release the trapdoor and hang the conspirators, only one man died. The other ropes broke, and the men dropped to the ground, still alive.

Amid scenes of anguish and hysteria, the men jumped to their feet and pleaded for mercy. Tearful family members argued that God in His goodness had somehow intervened to save their lives. However, the pleas fell on hardened hearts, and, one by one, the men were each hanged with the good rope.

"Remember Slachtersnek!" Henry Klyn shouted.

All around Christiaan, men stood to their feet and shouted for rebellion against the British tyrants. The longer the shouting lasted, the more strength it seemed to gather, and Christiaan thought for sure that a revolution was about to break out on the eve of Nachtmaal.

5

Sina van der Kemp's recurring nightmare was that she would die before ever being truly loved by a man. The nightmare was more an intangible fear than it was a dark visual representation of her premature demise, but it was haunting nonetheless.

"He'll never notice me!" she complained to Karel in a whisper. "I'm going to die. I just know it! I'm going to die!"

Seated next to her, Karel peered through the young people who had gathered outdoors on an assemblage of wooden benches for a singing party. He spotted the object of Sina's affection—Henry Klyn. He was regaling three other fellows with a story that prompted robust laughter that could be heard clearly over the growing din of gatherers.

Karel leaned into Sina, playfully shoving her with his shoulder. "Do you want me to invite him over?"

Sina's eyes shot open. Her pupils were black dots in a sea of white. "Don't you dare! He would think I was forward! Henry would never marry a forward woman!"

Karel snorted. "Henry Klyn would marry any woman who loved him half as much as he loves himself."

Sina slapped him on the shoulder. "You said you'd be nice!"

"I was being nice!" Karel protested. "That was the nicest thing I could think of to say about him."

"Oh!" She shoved Karel, knocking him off balance and off the end of the bench. He hit the ground with a grunt and a thud. His flailing arms and the surprised scream of a girl standing behind them combined to draw everyone's attention.

The gathering became embarrassingly silent. With everyone gawking at him and several sniggering, Karel picked himself up. Spreading his arms wide and bowing, he said, "For your further enjoyment, I can also do bird calls."

His good-natured handling of the situation brought laughter and a spattering of applause. He took his seat next to Sina as the multitude of conversations resumed. Lowering his head, he leveled a mock frown at her.

"Don't give me that look—you deserved it, and you know it!" she defended herself. "You promised that you would not say anything mean about Henry if I didn't say anything mean about—" she changed her voice to produce a deep, sultry tone "—Deborah van Aardt!" For added dramatic effect, she held folded hands over her heart and batted her eyelashes.

The smile on Karel's face vanished. His jaw set in anger, but only for a moment. "You're right," he conceded. "If you'll keep your opinions to yourself about Deborah, I'll keep silent about the fact that Henry Klyn is a pompous—"

Sina shot him a warning glance.

Two open palms shot up as Karel said apologetically, "Sorry, it just slipped out."

The two friends sat in silence. Wearing a plastered-on smile, Sina glanced around gaily, attempting to give the appearance of a contented young woman who came to the event for nothing more than an innocent evening of fun and singing. In reality, her every sense was acutely aware of Henry Klyn's slightest movement.

The concentration of her senses was not unlike that of a hunter, the only difference being her surroundings. She peered at her prey through a cluster of people instead of through the branches of a bush; and her intended target was a man, not a wildebeest—though Karel would certainly be amused at the association of the two.

To Sina, the target of her affection was a striking figure. Tall, not too thin, but not stocky either. Night's canopy of stars made his brown hair look darker than it was. Sina preferred the way Henry looked in daylight, when the sun flashed upon his hair's blond highlights. He had a cocky confidence about him that she found attractive. It made him stand out among the other young men his age who were uncomfortable with their looks, their voices, even the way they stood.

Another way in which Henry Klyn was set apart from his peers was his clothing. Like his father, Henry was a Dopper, a member of the strictest, most fanatical Calvinist sect in South Africa, which held closely to the old ways. Unlike other Boers, Doppers wore no belts and had no use for newfangled braces. Their trousers were fastened with a buckle in the back. In addition, their coats were shorter. Thus, the combination of sagging trousers and shorter coats created a definite gap between the two, which exposed their white shirts. Some people compared the Doppers, unkindly, to the white-rumped springbok because they were easily spotted from afar. Henry's coat was made of blue nankeen with a red stripe. Matching trousers of smooth corduroy stretched down his leg but stopped short of his leather shoes, exposing bare ankles.

The other young men at the festival wore trousers—mostly made of moleskin, the poorer wearing leather—that buttoned up the front, that stretched all the way down to their shoes, and that were held up with belts. Their coats and waistcoats were of woolly duffel, brown or tawny. Without exception, all wore their best white linen shirts.

For the young ladies, Nachtmaal was a chance for them to set aside their usual plain, sober clothing for more colorful creations—within the bounds of proper taste, of course. Sina smoothed the green silk of the dress that covered her lap. The dress had been nearly six months in the making for this all-important occasion. It had a turnover collar, fairly wide sleeves fastened at the wrist, and flounces round the lower part of the skirt. The dress was complemented by white stockings, shoes, and gloves. A little green hat with long streamers sat atop hair that was parted down the middle, smoothed back, and fastened into a bun with a tortoiseshell comb.

Likewise, the other young ladies wore dresses ranging from silk and linen in quiet colors to flannel, thick woolly baize, or leather. Petticoats ran along modest lines with equally quiet colors. Hats were small for festive occasions, in contrast to the large, sunbonnet *kappies* of fine white linen of everyday use, which shaded them from the sun's aging rays. For this occasion, gloves were not uncommon, and some of the ladies carried matching parasols. No one wore her hair loose, not even little girls. Loose hair was a sign of loose morals.

"There's Deborah," Sina whispered, leaning close to Karel.

Flanked by two girls who were shorter and not as pretty as she was, Deborah van Aardt made her entrance into the area. When Karel saw her, he melted a little, smiled, and sighed. Sina, on the other hand, bit her tongue to keep from saying what she was thinking.

It wasn't so much Deborah that Sina didn't like, but girls like Deborah—openly flirtatious and beautiful. Scratch the surface of Deborah, and you would find not an evil person but no person at all. A first impression of the girl plumbed the depths of her being.

One problem Sina had with Deborah was that Deborah was so good at being Deborah. Her every action was instinctual. Surrounding herself with girls of lesser attraction was not a calculated plan to heighten the beauty of her presence. Deborah couldn't calculate the number of shoes she was wearing. She operated on pure instinct. Somehow she just knew that a single rose looks most beautiful not in a garden among other roses but in a sea of ragweed.

But what upset Sina most with Deborah was that Karel, along with half the male population of the eastern South African settlement, was attracted to someone like her. She thought Karel had more sense than to allow himself to be beguiled by outer beauty. Apparently she was wrong.

"Excuse me," he said, without taking his eyes off Deborah. He stood and floated her direction, like a bee to pollen.

Disgusting.

"Tell me he's not coming back."

Sina swung toward the deep voice asking the question. Her heart stopped cold. The voice belonged to Henry Klyn, and he was standing inches away from her, gazing down at her with those alluring blue eyes of his.

"Who . . . um . . ." Sina stammered, glancing at the departing Karel, then back at Henry, where she was struck again by the clearness of his eyes and the closeness of his presence. "Um . . . Karel? No, probably . . . at least, I don't think . . . um, no, he's not coming back." She silently scolded her tongue for failing her at this crucial moment, as her romantic future hung in the balance.

"Good!" Henry said, looking after Karel none too kindly. "Mind if I sit here, then?"

"No!" Sina cried. "That is, no, I don't mind. I didn't mean, no, you can't sit here. Sit!" The word sounded like a command. Of all the times for her faculties to fail her! This time it was her brain. "Please . . . um . . . sit. If you want to sit, I mean."

Mercifully, Henry seemed not to notice her stammering. He lowered himself beside her. Close. As he settled in, his arm touched hers. He made no effort to readjust and put distance between them. Neither did she. Sina could feel his warmth through her sleeve.

Henry casually surveyed the gathering. The sound of instruments tuning indicated that the singing would begin momentarily.

Imitating Henry's casual attitude, Sina adjusted the plastered smile on her face, the smile that had served her so well earlier in the evening, and let her gaze wander. However, her eyes refused to settle on anything, nor did they focus. They, and all her other senses, were operating at diminished capacity in order to give priority to her tactile awareness.

Her arm and Henry's arm were touching. Everything else dimmed as she sensed the warmth of his arm against hers. At this moment, nothing else in heaven or earth mattered.

The singing began. Beside her, Henry sang one hymn after another lustily. Sina's lips moved. Maybe she produced a sound—she didn't know for sure. All she knew was that her arm and Henry Klyn's arm were touching.

6

Like a colossal stony hand, mountains cupped the village of Graaff-Reinet, cradling the assembled Nachtmaal pilgrims in its palm. Seated on a wooden bench next to the docile Adriaan Pfeffer, both men nursing mugs of coffee, Christiaan listened with mounting anxiety to the storm of vitriolic diatribes that swirled around him and echoed against the ominous black peaks. The cries of "Remember Slachtersnek!" still rang in his ears. To his chagrin he had somehow managed to position himself in the center of the men's gathering.

As speaker after speaker stood to denounce British rule, Christiaan and Pfeffer craned their necks first one way than another—behind them, to one side, then to the other, behind them again, then in front. After a time the two men got to chuckling over their shared contortions, and Christiaan resigned himself to listening only.

Closing his eyes, he rubbed the back of his aching neck. When he opened them again, the scene before him stirred a sickening pool of dread in the pit of his stomach. The strength of his reaction surprised him. Having focused on each speaker, he hadn't really noticed it before now.

Beginning just a few feet in front of him and stretching across the entire church courtyard was an undulating sea of crimson faces. It was an angry sea—V-shaped brows, bitter lips, fiery eyes, clenched teeth—black expressions all.

And so many of them! Never in all his years at Nachtmaal had Christiaan seen so many settlers in attendance. The mass of men before him not only filled the square, it spilled over the edges and into the streets and alleys.

To a man, their attention was focused on Oloff Klyn behind him. Christiaan knew it was Klyn they were looking at by the ranting sound of the man's voice. It had a disagreeable edge to it, as did the man's Dopper radicalism.

The storm of protest was gathering momentum, feeding off itself. While Klyn drew greater boldness from the intensity of their anger, he stoked their escalating emotions with inflammatory rhetoric.

The intensity of the emotional whirlpool caused Christiaan to feel incredibly tired. He lowered his head. At first he thought it was just the trip catching up with him with its change in schedule and diet and having to sleep on the ground. But this was only the eve of Nachtmaal! He'd never felt tired this early before. Maybe he was just getting old.

Then a chilling revelation seeped into his thoughts. It wasn't the journey that was making him tired. Nor was it his change in diet or sleeping accommodations. It was sitting here for hours, immersed in vitriol, that was draining him. Here, in the center of this vortex of anger and hatred, sapping his strength like some demonic parasite.

Closing his eyes again, Christiaan forced himself to disengage from his surroundings, if only for a few minutes, hoping to shelter himself from the effects of the emotional storm.

He sipped his coffee. His tongue worked the earthy liquid inside his mouth, extracting its flavor. A distinctive oily residue coated the roof of his mouth and his tongue. He exhaled. Coffee breath. The aroma prompted a smile. It made him think of Sina. At the dinner table one evening she had confided that coffee breath was her earliest and fondest memory of her father, something she would always associate with him. Of all things for her to remember—Christiaan chuckled—she remembered coffee breath.

Silence brought him back to the moment. Although in the distance could be heard youthful singing, the storm around him had grown suddenly and eerily quiet. Opening his eyes, he glanced up. A multitude of eyes were still focused on something in back of him.

Christiaan twisted his body to get a look behind him. As he did, the stillness was punctuated by a hacking cough. He saw Oloff Klyn, doubled over, racked by coughing spasms. A man was helping him, bending over with him, one arm around Klyn's back, the other holding him up. Another settler handed Klyn a mug. The Dopper accepted it, lifted it to his lips, and tried to drink. After two attempts, his coughing eased long enough for him to take a swallow.

Klyn nodded his thanks to the men who had attended him. Then, straightening himself, he signaled to everyone that he was fine. After one more cough and a throat-clearing, he attempted to continue speaking. When he did, his voice was raspy.

"Land, labor, and security—an inseparable trinity." Klyn coughed, then took another swig from the mug. The man who handed him the coffee said something to Klyn that Christiaan couldn't hear.

Klyn shook his head. Leaning over and speaking to the man, he said loud enough for everyone to hear, "I must say this!" Addressing the assembly then, he repeated, "Land, labor, and security. As for land, the

British have given it away to our enemies. As for labor, they have sided against us and with the heathen. As for security—"

"What's that?" a mop-haired wag yelled.

The entire courtyard erupted with laughter.

"My point exactly!" Klyn shouted, pointing at the jokester. His yell set him to coughing again. After a time he said, "At the moment, I can't go on . . ." He took one last swig from the mug, then handed it back. "But before I sit down . . . all I'm saying is that we will never have land, we will never have liberty, nor will we ever have security until we have our own government!" He sat down, coughing.

The assembly exploded with shouts and applause.

"Revolution!" the wag shouted. "The Americans threw off the yoke of English slavery—so can we! It's time for a revolution of our own!" Thrusting his fist into the night air, he began to chant, "Revolution! Revolution! Revolution! Revolution!"

The voices of chanting men reverberated against the walls of the surrounding buildings.

The cry for revolt came so quickly and neatly following Klyn's closing statement that Christiaan wondered if it—and the humor—had been staged. He looked toward Klyn but couldn't see the wily old man. A mass of bodies blocked his view.

All around Christiaan the square had come alive, bursting into a tempestuous sea of motion and noise. Chanting. Shouts for revolution. Curses directed at the king. Slogans promoting freedom.

Then, to Christiaan's surprise, in the midst of the demonstration, quiet Adriaan Pfeffer slowly set aside his coffee mug, stood up beside him on the bench, and waited to be recognized by the assembly.

It was the oddest sight Christiaan ever recalled seeing. There Pfeffer stood, hands folded serenely atop his paunchy midsection while a storm of protest whirled about his knees and feet. He stood motionless, without expression. And with the dim light of the moon giving his skin a grayish cast, he looked like a courtyard statue honoring some nondescript government accountant. He was still standing on the bench when, for lack of a specific course of action, the protest began to abate.

Pockets of men soon took notice of Pfeffer. They too appeared struck by the oddity of the man's statuelike, if not humorous, pose. Nudging their compatriots who had not spotted him yet, they pointed him out. A hush fell over the crowd as the number of curious and amused Pfeffer-watchers grew. Soon they were a majority, presumably wondering what, if anything, he would do.

They stared. He stood—for what seemed to Christiaan an inordinately long time but which in reality was probably only a minute or slightly more. The human statue did not seem to notice that he had the attention of everyone in the courtyard.

Christiaan tugged at Pfeffer's pants leg. He whispered, "Everyone is looking to you. Say something!"

There was no indication Pfeffer heard him. He said nothing in response, nor did he gesture, or blink, or even appear to breathe.

"Pfeffer!" Christiaan tugged again. Still no response. Christiaan grew concerned now. "Adriaan?"

For the first time, the statue showed signs of life—specifically, fear. His rigid hands trembled. Beads of perspiration popped out on the backs of them. His pants legs quivered. Christiaan looked up at him. The bottom ridge of Pfeffer's jaw ran with sweat, like rain falling from a roof ledge.

Christiaan spoke softly to him. "Adriaan, it's all right. You don't have to speak. Sit down."

Pfeffer's head shuddered, flinging drops of sweat from his jaw. He cleared his throat. While the rest of him remained stiff and his eyes stared straight forward at nothing, his lips and tongue began to formulate words, or at least to make the effort.

After two self-aborted attempts to begin, he managed to say softly, "I remember a prayer my father used to say . . ."

"Louder!"

"We can't hear you!"

The lips froze. Would Adriaan be able to force them to move again? After a moment, he did. This time his voice was louder. "I remember a prayer my father used to say. Maybe it would be appropriate at this juncture." He cleared his throat. His eyes fluttered nervously. Heaving a chest-rattling sigh, he began to recite the prayer, his shaky, high-pitched voice wafting over the heads of the assembled men:

> "O Lord of Lords!
> Who will again rule here in Africa,
> All those who are exiled from England
> Become great men here;
> And we poor Dutch fellows,
> Can count the ribs on our bodies.
> Lord, will you not deliver us,
> From all the English oxen
> And lead us to our wishes,
> We poor Dutch Christian people,
> Amen."

Pfeffer did not rush to sit down. He continued to stand—in silence. The men waited for more, but Adriaan was finished.

Christiaan watched as the stony figure returned to flesh. Then, with the same unassuming manner in which he had climbed upon the bench, Pfeffer stood down and took his seat.

A smattering of soft amens from the crowd accompanied him, which prompted a couple of louder, renewed calls for rebellion.

Klyn was on his feet again. "That's a lovely prayer, Adriaan," he said hoarsely and without any trace of sincerity. The Dopper had regained a portion of his voice and seemed eager to use it. "But there is a time to pray, and then there is a time for action!"

A louder chorus of amens backed Klyn.

He acknowledged the boisterous response before continuing. Addressing Pfeffer, he said, "So what do you think we should do, Adriaan? I mean, now that your prayer is ended. What do you think we should do?" With a smirk, he awaited a reply.

Christiaan scowled. This was typical Klyn. He was baiting Pfeffer, indulging his own mean-spirited sense of humor at Adriaan's expense. And it wasn't the first time. Christiaan had seen Pfeffer take the bait before, realizing only too late Klyn's intentions. Tonight, however, to Pfeffer's credit, he didn't jump at the hook. Rather, he sat wordlessly with bowed head. For once, he seemed to sense Klyn's intent in time to save himself from embarrassment.

Then, to Christiaan's astonishment, Pfeffer rose from his seat. He climbed atop the bench as before and faced Klyn. Clearing his throat, he spoke in the same exaggerated voice he'd used when reciting his father's prayer. "Since you asked," he said, "I'll tell you." He paused and looked at his shoes. His hands, which dangled at his side, were shaking. He pinched his pants between thumb and forefinger to still them.

Christiaan's heart went out to the quiet man. It was one thing to recite a memorized prayer before a crowd, quite another to take a public position on a volatile issue in the midst of one's peers, especially when the opposite point of view was touted by the brash, unfeeling Oloff Klyn. Christiaan didn't envy Adriaan Pfeffer his present circumstance.

With a deep breath, Pfeffer said, "Since the early days when my family first settled on the frontier, I have been guided by the Bible and a single maxim. For twenty years . . ." He looked down at Christiaan and whispered, "It *has* been twenty years since I settled near you, hasn't it?"

Caught completely off guard, Christiaan was rendered dumb. His mind went blank. Had it been twenty years? It didn't seem that long. Sina wasn't born yet when the Pfeffers first arrived, or was she? He couldn't remember! Feeling the ponderous weight of public scrutiny pressing down upon him in the silence of the moment, Christiaan nodded, not really sure if it had indeed been twenty years or not.

Pfeffer took his word for it and continued. "As I was saying, for twenty years the Bible and one maxim have guided me. I have not strayed from them, nor would I want to stray from them. For through them God has blessed my family mightily. So now you ask me what I will do in the face of increased British persecution? I'll tell you. I will do what I have always done. I will trust God's Word and my maxim to guide me."

Klyn was intrigued but cautious. The one who had baited now ostensibly felt the tug of the lure. "And what is your maxim?" he asked.

Pfeffer did not answer immediately. For one brief moment, his fear seemed to vanish, and he actually looked as if he were enjoying the fact that he had a secret which Klyn wanted to know.

And Klyn was not alone in his curiosity. The entire courtyard stilled as men waited to hear Pfeffer's maxim, perhaps hoping that in it they might discover some nugget of wisdom that might ease their frontier struggle. Christiaan, too, found himself leaning toward his neighbor to learn Pfeffer's secret truth.

"My maxim is this," Pfeffer finally said, "whenever there is a decision to be made, I do whatever my good friend Christiaan van der Kemp here does." With that, he slapped Christiaan heartily on the back, took his seat, and folded his hands in his lap with a satisfied grin.

The eyes of every man in the square turned to Christiaan van der Kemp.

Nachtmaal served as the highlight of the altogether rare social gatherings for young people, separated most of the year as they were by miles of dirt and scrub brush. Though most of the songs sung at the festival were hymns, all were sung lustily as befitting the nature of the youthful gathering. In keeping with the excitement such a social event would inspire, boys vied wildly for attention, attempting to outdo each other with one immature prank after another, while exaggerated girlish giggles and squeals egged them on.

At the moment, Sina was oblivious to it all. The music. The pranks. The giggles. Her every sensory faculty was concentrated on one thing and one thing only—Henry Klyn, sitting next to her. When their arms touched —not a fleeting brush but a sustained pressure of flesh against flesh, clothed, of course, but what did that matter?—Sina's heart started galloping. Giving her emotions free rein, she suffered what she thought might be a terminal case of light-headedness.

At one point, the entire group stood for a song, and Henry's and Sina's arms were no longer touching. Her emotions plummeted correspondingly and would have crashed had they not been buoyed by a quick, sideways, flirtatious glance from Henry.

When the song ended and everyone took their seats, a gap formed between them. It was a small gap, mere inches, but it might as well have been a canyon, because any gap meant that she and Henry were separated. The thought was unbearable. Sina considered leaning against him, accidentally, of course. Her own boldness horrified her. What would Henry think if he knew she was thinking such indecent thoughts?

A new song was struck up by the instruments with verve. It was a lively tune this time. The fiddler's arm set into motion and picked up speed until it was nearly a blur.

At any other time, such an upbeat rhythm would have invigorated Sina. Her fondest memories of previous Nachtmaal celebrations were of the music. Things were different now. No music in heaven or earth was so grand that it could stir her emotions as deeply as Henry's presence had stirred them. She had been touched by the one she loved. And try as she might to maintain some semblance of control over her feelings, to stem the rising amorous tide within her, she found it unacceptable that a gap existed between her and her man. Two inches of space. Maybe three. She had to think of a way to close the gap without appearing to be forward.

Beside her, Henry started clapping, joining in with the other celebrants who were merrily keeping time with the rhythm of the tune.

Sina joined in too. She clapped to keep from being conspicuous. Karel and Deborah were clapping. Conraad Pfeffer was clapping. So Sina smiled her festive smile and clapped gaily with them. She clapped and smiled and smiled and clapped as though nothing else in the world mattered but clapping.

But her hands and her smile were nothing more than a diversion to keep everyone from guessing what truly occupied her mind. She had decided to be bold, to sway from side to side as she clapped and—accidentally, of course—brush up against Henry's arm.

Then it happened! More than she could have hoped for. Henry leaned forward. He rose from the bench ever so slightly to adjust himself. When he settled back, he settled back closer to her. The gap vanished. He had settled down next to her so that his arm was touching her arm again. Not just touching but pressed up against her!

The sensation drained Sina's festive smile from her face, melting it like lard in the summer sun. Her insides responded in similar fashion, and she would have been reduced to a pool of satisfied emotion had she not caught Karel's eye. His hands were clapping cheerily, but his face was a dark scowl leveled her direction. From the look on his face it was clear he had guessed that something was going on between her and Henry. Clearly, he disapproved.

Sina looked away. She didn't care what Karel thought.

She closed her eyes and focused on the warmth and pressure of Henry's arm against hers. Oh that she might prolong this feeling, this night forever. She even considered praying. After all, if God could halt the course of the sun in the heavens to extend the length of a day, allowing the Israelites to gain a military victory, could He not halt the course of the moon and extend the night so that she and Henry could be together?

On further reflection, Sina decided not to offer the prayer. It just didn't seem right to pray to God about sensual things. Consequently, the remainder of the evening sped by, and all too soon the music ended. While others stood, stretched, milled about, and took their leave, Sina remained on the bench, her head bowed coyly, her arm pressed against Henry's.

"Sina?"

She loved the way her name wafted from his lips, like a whisper riding a cloud. She had never been fond of her name—it was a little girl's name, not the name of a maturing woman. But somehow, Henry made it sound alluring. She deliberately ignored him and, by doing so, caused him to speak her name a second time.

"Sina?"

With her eyes lowered, still savoring the sound, she said, "Yes, Henry?"

He broke contact with her, scooting away. Their arms no longer touched. The gap not only reappeared; it loomed larger than at any time since Henry first sat down. But Sina's impending agony was short-lived. He reached for her hand.

It was such a simple movement, one hand taking another. But to Sina it was a ballet of two extremities performed in exquisitely slow, memorable steps. The initial shock she felt when she caught sight of his hand approaching, unaware of its intentions; felt the hot touch of his flesh against hers as he gently scooped her hand from her lap. Her pleasure mounted as he conveyed her hand across the gap where it was met and cradled tenderly by his other, waiting, hand.

"Sina?"

"Um . . ." She was staring at her hand in his, her mind refusing to comprehend that such a thing was actually happening to her. "Um . . . did you . . . yes?"

"You seem distracted."

If you only knew, she thought, still staring at her hand. It was the most pleasurable distraction she had ever experienced.

"Distracted? No . . . well, actually yes . . . I mean . . ." She pressed her lips shut to stop the flow of babbling sounds. Not until her mind formed an intelligent sentence did she speak again. "It's just that I don't want the evening to end," she said.

"Neither do I."

Had she heard him right? Could it be that he had similar feelings for her—albeit not nearly as strong, since he was a man and men simply weren't capable of feeling as deeply about things as women? But given the limitations of his gender, was he saying what she thought he was saying?

Sina lifted her gaze upward, past Henry's chest to his dimpled chin, to his delightfully thin mouth, and upward along the strong ridge of his nose to the crystal-blue waters of his eyes. She nearly lost herself in those eyes. Without a second thought she could dive into those eyes and not surface for days.

She didn't know how she did it, but she managed to find her voice. "You don't want the evening to end either?" she said breathlessly.

Lifting his eyebrows innocently, Henry smiled and shook his head. "I've been a fool not to notice you sooner."

Sina's heart fluttered, as though it had captured a wren.

"For some reason," Henry continued, "on that day at your house when the Xhosa attacked, you looked at me and I saw you differently than I'd ever seen you before."

"Differently?"

Henry looked down at her hand in his. He nodded slightly. "Differently, as in romantically."

"Really?"

Sina was so astonished by Henry's confession—and his evident embarrassment over his romantic feelings—that she was reduced to single word sentences. Any other time she would have berated herself for her bumbling tongue. But right now she didn't care. She was overwhelmingly overwhelmed.

"And it's really a shame too," Henry said.

"Shame?"

Sina's heart seized. So here it was, the rose's thorn, and she was about to feel its prick. At that moment the world stopped turning on its axis, ocean tides froze, the Great River ceased its flow, raindrops dangled in mid-air refusing to fall, stars stood in their courses, animals turned into statues, birds halted in flight, and angels held their breath. All creation waited on Henry Klyn's next words.

"A real shame," Henry repeated. Looking around at the depleting crowd, he added, "And I wish I could tell you why, but not now, not here."

"Henry, you must tell me!" Sina pleaded. Her free hand was on top of his before she knew what she was doing.

Henry looked down at their entwined hands. "I really want to tell you," he said, his voice tinged with agony, "but not with so many people around. Is there some place we can go where we can be alone?"

It was an age-old question that had haunted young couples at Nachtmaal for decades. The congested festival was itself an incongruity for the independent Boers, who valued privacy above all else, for there was no privacy at Nachtmaal. And no one felt the lack of privacy more deeply than young couples in love who wanted to be alone.

There was one place that afforded a measure of privacy if the night was sufficiently dark—the peach orchard. Over the years the orchard had gained a reputation as a place where couples could go to be alone. Its reputation carried with it a score of stories of young men and women who were tempted amorously beyond their ability to resist; so much so that married adults joked about the grove and mothers warned their daughters against going there.

"There is one place . . ." Henry said tentatively.

Sina's eyes brightened.

He leaned close until their cheeks were almost touching. "We could go to the peach orchard," he whispered.

"Oh!" Instinctively, Sina pulled back. The small cry escaped her throat before she could stop it.

"Just to talk," Henry said matter-of-factly.

His suggestion sparked a civil war in Sina's mind. On the one side were her parents armed with words of caution about the peach orchard. On the other side was Henry—dear, sweet, lovable Henry, whom she adored—and his suggestion that she go there with him. Her parents' objective, of course, was to keep her from the orchard for obvious reasons. Henry, on the other hand, wanted her to go with him to the peach orchard just to talk.

She believed him; why shouldn't she? So, then, why was she hesitating to accept his invitation? She knew the answer, of course. Her parents. What if they found out she went with a boy to the peach orchard?

But this wasn't just any boy! This was Henry Klyn!

Then it came to her. She had it all wrong. This wasn't a battle between her parents and Henry at all! The battle was between her parents and the peach orchard's silly reputation! What if it were anyplace else? Would they object? No! Had her parents ever objected to her sitting with Karel on the bluff beside the house? No! And Karel was a boy, wasn't he? So why would they object to tonight? Instead of Karel it was Henry; and instead of a bluff it was a peach orchard that had a silly reputation due to some silly people who had made silly decisions—not like her and Henry at all!

Sina mustered the sweetest smile she could and said, "I'd love to go to the peach orchard with you, Henry." Then, thinking how that sounded, she blurted, "But just for a short time—and just to talk."

Her answer appeared to startle Henry at first. But his surprise was soon overshadowed by joy. The smile that creased his bronzed, gorgeous face melted any last bit of hesitancy Sina might have harbored.

He stood and offered her his arm. Neither of them spoke a word, none were needed. They were saving their words for the peach orchard.

7

It was Christiaan's turn to quake, as all eyes in the courtyard looked to him expectantly. He had done nothing to evoke this attention, and he certainly didn't want it. Yet, regardless of his wishes, he now found himself the unwilling subject of scrutiny.

Most disturbing was the *way* the way men looked at him. A phrase came to his mind, "like sheep without a shepherd." Wasn't that in the Bible somewhere? But sheep did not have the disagreeable temperament of these men, and Christiaan certainly did not want to be their shepherd.

Pfeffer nudged him. "Stand up and say something!"

"I don't want to say anything!" Christiaan replied with a sharper edge to his voice than he'd intended. However, he didn't apologize. This was all Pfeffer's doing in the first place.

"Speech! Speech!" the crowd began to chant.

Christiaan smiled and tried to wave them off.

"Indeed, Christiaan!" Oloff Klyn yelled over the din. "Deliver to us some of your golden words that Pfeffer has seen fit to value as deeply as the Bible."

"That's not what I said!" Pfeffer shouted unexpectedly to Klyn. Leaning toward Christiaan, he cried, "That's not what I said!"

The chanting continued. "Speech! Speech! Speech!"

There was no indication they were going to let up until Christiaan addressed them.

"Just talk to them," Pfeffer begged.

Christiaan ignored him.

With a grunt of disgust, Pfeffer stood. Grabbing Christiaan's arm, Pfeffer tried to pull him to his feet. "Stand up, man! Talk to them! I did it. It's not that hard." Apparently he had already forgotten the fear that had paralyzed him.

Christiaan hadn't forgotten. He could feel the same fear creeping into his knees, rendering them useless. All around him a wall of human faces was chanting his name, urging him to stand, to speak.

Slowly, reluctantly, as though his pockets were weighted with rocks, Christiaan stood.

"Up here! Up here!" Pfeffer coaxed him to stand on the bench as he had done.

Christiaan shook his head. "Adriaan, no, I can speak from . . ."

Pfeffer insisted. With one hand under Christiaan's arm and the other on his lower back, he tried lifting Christiaan up onto the bench. Christiaan felt ridiculous, but the easiest way for him to resolve this awkward dilemma was to stand on the bench. So he did.

A cheer erupted from the crowd as Christiaan's head and shoulders broke the surface of the sea of heads. The chanting continued. From his elevated stance, Christiaan was taken aback once more by the number of men that were packed into the courtyard. And the number seemed to be growing. Younger men and a few ladies joined the fringes of the crowd as the young people's singing festival broke up.

"I . . . I really don't have anything to say," Christiaan mumbled.

Shouts of "Louder!" and "Shut up and let him speak!" were heard all across the square. Just as it had for Pfeffer, so now the courtyard grew ominously quiet. Until now Christiaan hadn't realized how closely crowds and noise were associated; a silent multitude was eerie, unnerving. The scene ached for noise. And Christiaan was expected to be the one to make it.

"I said"—Christiaan spoke louder—"I really don't have anything to say. I'm humbled at Adriaan's faith in my judgment. But really, I don't have anything more to say." He shrugged and tried to step down.

The crowd wouldn't let him. A roar of questions thundered from among them, echoing, reverberating off buildings and trees and the cupped mountains. Below him, the crowd pressed in, not giving him any room to step down.

"What about the British?"

"What should we do?"

"Should we revolt?"

"Will you fight?"

Hands that were used to holding plows and guns reached toward him pleadingly. Eyes glazed over, some from late-night weariness, others from too much drink. These were frontier men, even at a festival, with dirt rings around their necks and earth jammed under their fingernails. Men whose days began in the dark and ended in the dark. Who always kept their guns within reach. Whose destiny was determined by the annual rainfall. Who were fighting a two-front war with Xhosa assegais aimed at them from one side and British legislation aimed at them from the other. And they were hard-pressed to know which of the two fronts was more deadly.

The crowd about him had pressed too closely. Christiaan wove from side to side with its ebb and flow. He felt someone pulling on his arm.

It was Pfeffer. He cupped hands around his mouth and shouted, "Just speak your mind!"

Christiaan could barely hear him.

Something had to be done. The situation had escalated beyond personal preference. Christiaan raised both hands over his head to quiet the crowd. They were heavy with reluctance, but he raised them anyway. The response was frighteningly immediate.

"I don't know what you want from me," he said.

From his left a voice cried, "Tell us what we should do!"

From his right, "We need a Moses!"

Christiaan found it easy to answer that one. "I'm no Moses," he said emphatically. "If you're looking for a Moses, you'll definitely need to look elsewhere. And as for telling you what to do, I can't do that either. Each one of you must decide for yourself what is best for you and your family."

"Then tell us what *you're* going to do!"

Christiaan smiled sheepishly and shrugged again. "I'm going to go back to my wagon, kiss my wife good night, and go to sleep."

The courtyard rippled with response. Laughter. Groans. Renewed calls for revolution.

A voice came from behind Christiaan. He recognized it. Oloff Klyn.

"Should we fight the British?" Klyn shouted.

Turning, Christiaan discovered that Klyn too had mounted a bench. They stood opposite one another, knee-deep in a tide pool of humanity.

By standing on a bench, Klyn had changed the dynamic of the entire gathering. No longer was it Christiaan addressing a crowd; the situation had changed to a confrontation between two men before hundreds of spectators.

"Answer me, if you can," Klyn shouted. "Should we fight the British?"

The crowd hushed, waiting. The question had plunged the gathering of settlers into the refiner's fire, separating the metal from the dross —those who favored revolution and those who opposed it.

"Unless British troops attack my house," Christiaan said, "I will not take up arms against them."

Instantly the square boiled with reaction.

Klyn raised a hand, signaling for order. After a measure of it was restored, he shouted at Christiaan, "Your wise counsel is that we do nothing while the Xhosa kill our families and the British legislate us to death?"

Before he could respond, Christiaan had to wait for a surge of noise to die down just from the reaction to Klyn's question. "I am a man of peace," he cried. His statement quieted many. He continued: "If my family is threatened, I will indeed fight, but only if there is no other way."

His statement brought the crowd to a boil again.

"When my father and I first came to the frontier . . ."

As the noise lessened, a shout from the edge of the crowd asked Christiaan to begin again.

He obliged. "When my father and I first came to the frontier, we came to live in peace. We left Cape Town behind us along with a plantation that had been in my family for over a hundred years. Just before we left, I remember how my father stood me on the porch of that beautiful house. He told me to take a good look at what I saw—the house, the orchards, the land, the cattle. He said, 'Son, where we are going has nothing as fine as this plantation. Indeed, there will be only dirt, bushes, hard work, and danger. But I want you to take a good look at what you see, because all of this is temporary. One spark and a good wind could destroy it all. Or greedy men with guns or the law on their side can wrest it away from us.'

"And I remember saying, 'But we won't let them, will we? We'll get our guns and kill them!'

"To this day I can remember the disappointment in my father's eyes. He said, 'But what if they kill you? Or your mother? Or me? Or Punga? Or Jama? Are you telling me that losing any one of these would be worth it, just to keep someone else from having that tree?'

"At that point my father placed his scarred, weathered hand on my chest—I remember how it covered my entire chest. He said, 'Son, you are worth more to me than a hundred plantations. If anyone tries to harm you, I fight them and kill them if necessary. All of this'—he waved his hand to encompass the plantation—'can be replaced. But you'—he patted my chest—'I could never replace. And that is why we are journeying to a new land. And there, together, we will build a new plantation as beautiful as Klaarstroom.'"

Christiaan paused. He was surprised to discover he was no longer shaking. For reasons he couldn't fathom, the telling of the story had had a calming effect on him. It also strengthened his resolve.

"In keeping with my father's dream," he concluded, "I have

attempted to rebuild Klaarstroom on the frontier. Despite the fact that the British have doggedly followed us here, I believe that with patience and understanding we can peacefully coexist with them. The same is true for the Xhosa. I believe that there is land and cattle enough for both our peoples. I know that most of you don't agree with me"—he nodded in the direction of Klyn—"but you asked my opinion, and so . . . well . . . there it is."

Christiaan tried to step down, but the men were still pressed in so tightly around him that he couldn't.

"I agree with him!" Klyn thundered.

His words stunned Christiaan and apparently the crowd as well.

"In truth, I agree with him, at least the part about fighting the British. This land isn't worth it. I say let the British and the Xhosa have it! As for me and my son . . . well . . . I, too, trekked here from Cape Town with my family, as did most of you. Trekking is in our blood, and I say let the British and the Xhosa squabble among themselves over this land, for just across the Great River there is land for the taking!

"You've heard the reports. The land beyond the Great River is lush, verdant, and unoccupied. The grasslands of the high veld are far superior to the shallow covering we have here. Christiaan is right—this land is not worth fighting over. Like the Israelites of old, a good number of us have decided to journey together, leaving behind this oppressive government, and go to a promised land where we can govern ourselves!"

Like a school of fish changing direction with one synchronized motion, the attention of the courtyard swung from Christiaan to Klyn. Question after question was fired at him. When was the party leaving? What else could he tell them about the land beyond the Great River? What about the Zulu tribes in that region? And on and on.

All of a sudden, Christiaan found it easy to descend from his bench. He did so gratefully. He slapped Pfeffer good-naturedly on the back. "Let's go back to the wagons," he said. "I don't know about you, but I'm exhausted."

"Whatever you say," Pfeffer replied.

With empty coffee mugs dangling on their fingers, the two men walked side by side.

"Adriaan," Christiaan said, "you're a good friend. But don't ever do that to me again."

"What did I do?" Pfeffer asked innocently.

Leaving the well-lighted clearing behind them, Sina and Henry walked arm in arm into the darkness in the general direction of the peach orchard. Other couples walked in close proximity to them, sheering off one direction or another to return to their wagons. From among those who continued toward the orchard came an increasing number of hushed giggles and stifled whispers.

Sina was aglow. She wasn't walking, she was floating. Silently, hanging on Henry's arm, she reveled in his closeness. Tall and erect, he had shortened his stride to match her more dainty pace. He would wordlessly glance down at her, and she met each glance with an uplifted smile as the skeletal shapes of peach trees emerged from the darkness.

Her best dreams paled in comparison to this night. The imagined dialogue, the way she had envisioned he would look at her, touch her—none of it compared to this evening. It was perfect in every way. Nothing could possibly happen to make it . . .

"*Sina van der Kemp!* Where do you think you're going!"

The voice startled her and Henry both. It caromed through the peach trees ahead. It turned every head in the vicinity, including Henry's.

Sina felt his arm stiffen as they came to an abrupt halt.

Behind them, Karel closed the distance at a rapid pace with Deborah trailing in his wake. "Where do you think you're going?" he demanded again, shooting a hateful glance at Henry.

"Karel! How dare you shout at me like that!" Sina cried.

Henry scoffed. "Who do you think you are, De Buys? Her father?"

Hands angrily on his hips, Karel leaned toward Sina. "You were going to the peach orchard with him, weren't you?"

"To talk! Just to talk!"

"Is that what he told you?" Karel stepped between Sina and Henry. Facing her, he said, "You're going back to your wagon."

Henry pushed him aside. "Leave her alone, De Buys! She's with me!"

By now Deborah had caught up with Karel. She looked wickedly at Sina. "My, my," she said. "Who would have thought it? Sina van der Kemp and Henry Klyn going into the peach orchard together!"

"Just to talk!" Sina insisted.

Obviously Deborah wasn't convinced, but neither did she seem interested in pursuing the matter. She grabbed Karel by the arm and tried pulling him away. "Come on, Karel," she whined, "if they want to do unspeakable things in the peach orchard, you can't stop them."

Karel shrugged her off. "Yes, I can!"

With the speed of a striking snake, Karel's hand lashed out and grabbed Sina's arm. It was a grip with authority, and it brought tears of pain to her eyes.

"Let go of me, Karel!" she cried, trying her best to pry his fingers free.

"Karel, leave her alone," Deborah wailed. "Come with me."

"Get your hands off her!" Henry yelled.

The next thing Sina knew, Karel was wrenched free. Henry had jerked him away. Karel spun about wildly from the force. He stopped, facing the three of them.

It was an odd alliance—Sina, Henry, and Deborah van Aardt aligned against Karel, who stood puffing, his fists clenched.

Just then, Kootjie could be heard in the distance. "There she is!"

At the sound of her younger brother's voice, Sina rolled her eyes.

Henry stared at her. "Who else can we expect?" he cried.

Kootjie ran up to them. Conraad Pfeffer was with him.

"Sina! There you are!" Kootjie burst out. "I've been looking all over for you." His eyes wandered behind his sister, and he seemed to realize that they were standing a few hundred feet from the infamous peach orchard. "Sina!" he exclaimed with a twisted grin on his face.

"Kootjie, what are you doing here?" Sina shouted angrily. Her voice trembled. She was on the verge of tears. Her perfect evening was ruined, first by Karel and now by her brother. She would never survive the embarrassment. Never.

At least for the moment getting over his fascination with finding his sister next to the peach grove, Kootjie said, "You have to come to the wagon now!"

"Has something happened?" Karel asked.

"British guards!" Kootjie cried. "They were at our wagon. They gave Father a some . . . some . . . a something."

"Summons," Conraad said, glad to help out. He grinned and shrugged at the second of attention it earned him.

Every time Sina saw Conraad, she thought, he looked more and more like his father, only smaller and a little thinner.

"That's it," Kootjie said. "A summons. It means they're going to put Father on trial!"

"For what?" Sina cried.

Kootjie shrugged. "I don't know. It was in English."

Sina looked at Henry. "I have to get to the wagon."

"I'm going with you," Karel said.

"Oh, no, you're not!" Deborah protested.

Karel led Deborah to one side. They spoke in forced whispers.

"Will I see you tomorrow?" Sina asked Henry hopefully.

Henry nodded. But there was no smile, no seeming regret, no warmth at all. Just an acknowledgment. It made Sina want to cry.

She turned to leave, then swung back again. "Your news!" she reminded him.

"News?"

Stepping closer, she whispered, "The news you couldn't tell me with everyone around."

"Oh, that," he said mildly. "My father and I are trekking north after Nachtmaal, that's all."

"You're moving away?" Sina shouted. His announcement hit her with the force of an elephant gun. It was compounded by the easy, matter-of-fact way in which Henry had delivered it.

"Soon," he replied.

"Henry!" Sina could hold back the tears no longer. She had been stopped shy of an unforgettable night of confidential conversation with him, and now she learned she was going to lose him forever. It was too much. The tears came in a downpour.

Karel guided her home. She hated every step of the journey because she was furious with him, but she had no choice. Her tears flowed so heavily that she could barely make out images directly in front of her.

Upon reaching the wagon, they learned that indeed Christiaan had been summoned to court to stand trial. By the time Kootjie had retrieved Sina, they had found someone who could read English. A crowd gathered around the van der Kemp wagon, and the summons was read aloud. Christiaan was accused of beating a former Khoi worker and depriving him of his lawful property. He was required to answer these charges shortly after Nachtmaal.

The next morning, under instructions from his father, Kootjie and Karel rode back to the settlement to get Jama. If Christiaan was going to convince a British court that he was innocent, he would need Jama to do it.

8

An unforgiving sun beat down upon his black head. Beads of perspiration formed, merged, then cascaded down his temples through gorgelike wrinkles and into his eyes, stinging them. It was a steadier flow than the river passing in front of him.

With the drought in its fourth year, the Great Fish River struggled in vain to live up to its name. Jama knelt and scooped a handful of water, lifting it to parched lips. Its foul odor announced the taste that followed. Brackish. Gritty. His nose wrinkled in disgust as the residue crunched between his teeth. Spitting the water back into the river, he slumped to the ground at the water's edge.

On the ground next to him a fish flopped pitifully in a canvas sack. His only catch of the day. It was a small fish at that, with dull scales. When he first pulled it out, he couldn't help but feel he was pulling a bit of life from a stream that was gasping to survive. He feared he was contributing to the river's demise.

The Great Fish River had seen better days. So had he. Jama had witnessed days when the river overflowed its banks, its waters rushing madly by in a hurry to get to the sea. Other times he had reclined at the stream's edge when the water was serene and its taste was sweet. Then there were days like today with the water level low, when it seemed as though the river were struggling just to flow downstream.

A rustle to his right caught Jama's attention. Noiselessly he reached for his gun, which was lying in the dirt next to him.

He heard the sound again. A faint rustle.

Jama lifted himself into a crouching position. He widened his eyes to take in more of the landscape, ready to snap them in the direction of the slightest movement. His ears opened wider as well as he strained to hear the softest sound.

There! A bush limb low to the ground moved. Leaves rustled. A brownish snout pushed past the branch, sniffing the earth. A wild dog.

An instant after Jama spotted the dog, the dog caught wind of Jama. He froze, looking up without lifting his head. When he spotted Jama, his chops curled into a snarl.

Jama swung the muzzle of the musket in the direction of the dog.

He glanced about, looking for others, knowing that Cape dogs traveled in packs, often using their numbers to their advantage. He had seen packs employ crafty techniques for tackling large prey such as buffalo. But that was unlikely the case here. This dog had been startled to see him. Besides, there were no signs of any other dogs in the vicinity.

The dog lifted his nose and sniffed. His eyes looked cautiously in the direction of the sack holding the fish.

"So that's what attracted you," Jama said.

At the sound of his voice, the dog forgot the fish and stared at him.

"Are you alone?"

The dog growled.

"Stay there," Jama said firmly. Without lowering the gun, he edged toward the sack. Balancing the musket with one hand, he reached into the bag and pulled out the fish. With a quick flip, he flung it at the feet of the dog.

The dog jumped back instinctively but didn't run. He sniffed at the fish, which was by now quite dead and covered with dirt. Then, realizing his good fortune, he snatched the fish and trotted off to a safe distance, glancing over his shoulder in case for some reason Jama changed his mind and wanted it back. Dropping the fish to the ground, he stared at Jama. He cocked his head. Bewilderment? A moment later a fish fin protruded from the side of his mouth as he chewed dinner.

Jama settled into a sitting position and watched him. "Where are the others of your pack?" he asked aloud.

The dog ignored him, concentrating on the fish.

Jama chuckled. "Did they go off to Nachtmaal and leave you behind too?"

It had been more than ten years since Jama had traveled with the van der Kemps to the Nachtmaal celebration. Sina would barely remember Jama's last journey to the religious festival. Of course, Kootjie couldn't remember it; he had been only two years old at the time. Jama's remembrance of the trip was pleasant enough—at least the journey to Graaff-Reinet. It was time spent with family.

And now that he pondered it, he couldn't remember a time when he hadn't enjoyed himself with the van der Kemps. They *were* family.

Jama had always been close to the van der Kemps. His family and theirs had intertwined since the early days of Cape Town colony. As the story was handed down to him, Jama's ancestor Ding, a slave on the van der Kemp plantation at Klaarstroom, demonstrated great bravery and loyalty when the plantation came under attack by renegade trekboers led by one of the van der Kemp sons. The way the story went, Ding risked his own life helping the van der Kemps hold off the attackers until military help arrived.

For his bravery, Ding was granted his freedom. He married, had children, and they became one of Cape Town's first free black families. Ding was determined not to squander his precious freedom, so he labored diligently to establish his own farm. It was an impossible task.

Because the prevailing prejudice in the colony was against blacks owning their own farms, Ding had to work twice as hard as any other farmer. He was forced to pay twice the price other farmers paid for seed, animals, supplies, and equipment. Unable to afford help, Ding struggled for two years on his own and, despite all the hardships imposed upon him, was able to eke out a meager subsistence for his family.

Then, in his third year, the land itself betrayed him. The rains didn't come. No amount of courage or determination could make up for the lack of water. His crops failed. With inadequate reserves, Ding's family soon went hungry, and he was on the verge of losing his farm.

That's when Jan and Margot van der Kemp rode onto his farm for a visit and a proposal. They proposed a joint venture that would mutually benefit both families. According to the plan, the van der Kemps would be in charge of purchasing and supplies for both farms; Ding and his family would be in charge of the labor force that would work both farms. In return, the families would enjoy the fruit of both farms equitably.

Ding agreed to the terms. No documents were signed. No papers were filed with company officials at Cape Town. The only things exchanged between the families were a pledge and a handshake. It proved to be an agreement that blessed both families for generations.

And then the British arrived. Not without great difficulty did the two families manage to weather the storm of the first British occupation. Still, Britain handed control of the colony back to the Netherlands, and for a while it seemed as if everything would return to normal.

But the Boers were not that fortunate. When the British seized the colony a second time, remaining even after Napoleon's designs on Europe were thwarted, the endless stream of stifling regulations and decrees and laws and judgments was more than the two families could stand. Rather than stay in the colony and fight a battle they knew they could not win, they turned their eyes eastward.

Leaving their beloved Klaarstroom behind, Marthinius van der Kemp and Punga, who had inherited and sustained their families' working agreement, trekked east, skirting the Great Karroo and driving their cattle before them. The two men took with them their sons, Christiaan and Jama.

The trek proved to be a costly one early on. In a hot and sandy ravine, Marthinius lost his wife and newborn infant during childbirth. Punga had lost his wife to fever a year previously, so now there were only four of them left—a father and a son from each family.

As Marthinius stood beside his wife's wilderness grave, he stretched an arm around his boy. Referring to the words of the shepherd psalmist, he likened the frontier to the valley of the shadow of concealed death. Continuing to draw from the psalm, he reminded his son and Punga and Jama that God would see them through the valley and lead them to a place where their cups would overflow.

Then, with tears streaking his dusty and weathered cheeks, he made a vow. Marthinius van der Kemp swore that nothing short of death would stop him from establishing a new farm for his son and Punga's son, one that would someday rival Klaarstroom.

Punga made a similar vow, as did Christiaan and Jama, who at the time were old enough to know what they were saying but young enough not to realize the price they would have to pay to realize their dream. For each of them it was a defining moment, the kind that shapes and directs a man's existence until his dying day.

The two men and their sons completed their trek without further loss, settling due east of the fledgling city of Grahamstown on land that stretched over rolling grass downs dotted with patches of bush. Here they hoped to build their dream based upon the three things that had built such grand plantations in the west—a vast amount of land, a plentiful supply of labor, and freedom from outside interference.

They found the land of the Zuurveld rugged and unforgiving but tamable. Local Khoi tribes proved a ready source of labor, and early relations with the Xhosa were amiable. Most important, though, the Boer farmers once again governed themselves through an appointed *landdrost* at Graaff-Reinet.

As more farmers emigrated to the area, however, the frontier government grew increasingly unstable. Britain's solution was to send colonial regiments, appoint a governor, and annex the region.

The van der Kemps were once again under British control.

With nowhere else to go—the Xhosa occupied the land east of the Great Fish River, and other tribes including the notorious, warlike Zulus, lay beyond that up the coast—the refugee families settled into their frontier homes and hoped the British penchant for control might be somewhat relaxed this far from Cape Town.

The year 1815 began with promise for the van der Kemps. Having wooed the feisty Johanna Linder the previous year, Christiaan married her at Nachtmaal. The impact of Johanna's bombastic female personality on the van der Kemp farm was immediate and greatly welcomed. For the first time since they arrived, laughter and gaiety bloomed all around the homestead like wild flowers in spring.

Christiaan knew of no one who didn't like Johanna. His own father fawned over her to such a degree that Christiaan jokingly wondered aloud which of them loved his wife more. In his heart he doubted that it was possible for any man to love a woman with greater intensity than that with which he loved Johanna. The mere thought of losing her in the manner in which he had lost his mother caused him to descend into a black mood that might not lift for days. So he tried not to think about it.

As for Punga and Jama, there was no question that Johanna had won their hearts too. To Jama, she was a sister-in-law. And although Punga treated her with detached respect at first, he warmed to her considerably when Johanna began calling him Oom Punga—Uncle Punga.

The wedding of Christiaan and Johanna created an air of expectancy to life on the frontier. A new branch had been grafted into the van der Kemp genealogical tree, and with it came the promise of offspring before year's end when Johanna announced she was with child.

The year that had begun with promise, however, was not destined to conclude that way. As 1815 drew to a close, Christiaan meditated mournfully on life's seasons as described by Solomon—for everything there is a season—a time to laugh, and a time to mourn. To him, it made sense. Just as there was a winter and a spring and a summer and a fall, there were seasons of life—good times, bad times. And the year that had begun with goodness of such great magnitude couldn't end without equally great tragedy to balance it.

On the very night Johanna announced her pregnancy, Oom Punga was shot to death. A storm had arisen with the wind blowing so hard that rain fell horizontally. Having secured the workers in their housing, he was staggering against the wind to get to the house when he spotted Oloff Klyn's prized horse, a filly with an unmistakable white diamond between her eyes.

Punga's first thought was to shelter the horse until the storm blew over. But then he got to thinking that if Klyn knew the horse was missing, he might be out looking for it. Against the advice of Marthinius, who enjoyed the thought of Oloff Klyn stumbling around in the driving rain, Punga decided to return the horse that night. That was the last time any of the van der Kemps saw Punga alive.

Oloff Klyn shot him dead midway between the houses. Christiaan found him the next morning, face down in a ditch. When the horse was discovered corralled at the Klyn farm, Marthinius demanded an explanation—to which Klyn said, "Oh, was that one of your slaves? I caught him stealing my horse."

Klyn claimed he didn't know the man he'd shot was Punga, since he'd shot the horse thief from a distance, and, because it was dark and the weather was so poor, he hadn't bothered to check on the black man's identity.

Klyn never showed remorse over the fact that he'd killed a free black man who had been his neighbor. And he never adequately explained why he thought the man with his horse was a thief when he was heading toward the Klyn farm, not away from it.

Ordinarily, the mishap would have caused a greater stir among the Grahamstown settlers, but news from Slachtersnek came three days later and quickly overshadowed Punga's death.

The balancing of the van der Kemps' happiness with tragedy continued when word reached them that Johanna's father was among those killed in the rebellion.

Marthinius himself was not well at the time. His lungs had constricted, and he was quickly winded. This malady was aggravated by a rib-rattling cough. When he talked of attending the trial, Christiaan and Johanna urged him to stay home. But he wouldn't listen. It was his neighbors on trial, and he needed to be there for them.

On the night of the hangings, Marthinius raged against the barbaric legalism of the British system. In the midst of his tirade he began to cough uncontrollably. It was as though an invisible pair of hands gripped his airway. He fell to the floor and died.

For two days Christiaan refused to be consoled. He was such a big man that, when he wept, his massive shoulders shuddered so violently even the staunchest mourners were moved to tears by the man's grief.

During the funeral service, the *predikant* remarked that bad things often come in threes and that the van der Kemp family was testimony to this belief. He cited the death of Punga, and of Johanna's father, and now of Christiaan's father.

However, the preacher was soon proved wrong. Tragedy was not yet finished with the van der Kemps. In the waning fragment of the year 1815, Johanna's pains increased intolerably as she went into labor. Everything went wrong from the start. She bled profusely. The baby had not turned. The cord was wrapped around his neck.

For the better part of the day Johanna held death at arm's length, praying for strength to fend him off long enough for her to deliver the baby. Those who attended her gave her little chance of winning the battle. They whispered among themselves as to which of them would tell Christiaan, when the time came, that he had lost both his wife and child, knowing full well that he had lost his mother in similar circumstances.

Death snatched Johanna's infant from her arms. But whether it was her love for Christiaan that kept her alive or pure stubbornness, he would claim only one life that day. In the midst of her grief, Johanna refused to give death a double victory.

It was the mountainous highs and cavernous lows of the year 1815 that knit the souls of Christiaan, Johanna, and Jama together. Theirs was a bond like no other on the frontier. They enjoyed a shared strength, knowing that if they could survive 1815, they could survive anything. During all the intervening years, Jama had firmly believed that.

Now, as he sat on the banks of the Great Fish River and watched the wild dog devour the river's meager bounty, he wasn't as confident as he once was. Like a burrowing beetle, doubt was eating away at the roots of his relationship with the van der Kemps. Jama was not unaware of doubt's infestation; he did all within his power to drive it away. But despite his effort, the pesky disquiet returned. Gnawing. Chewing. Eating away at the roots of a friendship that had meant so much to him for as long as he could remember.

With a sudden jump, the wild dog leaped, slipped, recovered, then ran into the bushes, leaving behind unfinished scraps of fish. Its sudden movement pricked Jama's senses alert. What had caused the dog to act like that? A predator?

Jama spied the threat. Across the river.

Armed Xhosa. Four of them.

Not as swift as the dog, Jama was spotted before he could slip behind cover.

The Xhosa rushed to the river's edge. With raised spears they pointed at Jama and shouted and hopped from side to side.

Jama didn't move. Nor did he reach for his gun.

9

Jama was well within striking range of the Xhosa spears. He was relieved somewhat by the fact that they had not yet launched their weapons at him. Had they done so when the dog first sensed them, he would be pinned to the ground by now. Maybe they just wanted to scare him off. He wasn't about to argue with them. The depleted brown river wasn't worth it.

Jama raised a friendly right hand. With the other, he reached slowly for his gun to leave.

Whoosh!

With a distinctive thud, a spearhead embedded itself in the earth next to the musket. Jama recoiled instinctively, looking for more spears to follow. There were none.

On the far side of the river, one of the Xhosa pushed his way to the front. Holding a spear horizontally at his side, he stared at Jama. His bare chest glistened with sweat in the sunlight. Other than sandals and a necklace made of hyena teeth, he wore only a loinskin around his hips. Speaking over the river's rush, he said, "You're the Kemp slave. The one who knows Xhosa truth."

"I'm no one's slave," Jama said from his squatting position.

The Xhosa looked at the men beside him. "Kemp slave," he said with a grin.

"I'm a free man!" Jama cried.

The spears were lowered, and it was then that Jama recognized the Xhosa chief. From a distance and without his feathered headdress and shield, the man looked different from when he stood outside the van der Kemp house.

"Is your food supply so plentiful that you feed the animals of the wild?" the chief asked.

Jama glanced at the fish remains on the ground. The wild dog had not returned for them. "He looked hungrier than me," Jama said. The tension in his limbs relaxed somewhat as all the Xhosa except the chief turned their attention to the river. "I hope the river yields more fish to you than it did to me," Jama shouted.

The chief grunted. "The whites have destroyed the river's natural abundance."

Jama shook his head. "The whites aren't responsible for the condition of the river. It's the lack of rain."

The chief stared at him with a puzzled expression. "You wear the skin and hair of a Xhosa, yet inside you are white. Why is that?"

Jama grimaced.

It was true, his skin was black, and his hair was like black wool—like Xhosa hair, not like the tight, peppercorn hair of the Khoi. And the white settlers, over the years, had at every opportunity made clear to him that he was black while they were white.

There were some concessions on their part. He could wear their clothes. He could work their land. He could talk their language. But that's where any similarity ended. He clearly was not one of them. As long as he walked among them, his would forever be a borrowed freedom, a unique standing based on his relationship with the van der Kemps.

It was as though his freedom were on loan. And it came with restrictions. He could raise their food but not eat with them in public. He could worship their God but not in their churches. He could attend Nachtmaal as long as he observed the proceedings from an appropriate distance. He could stand among them, but he would never be one of them.

The chief's words had struck at the heart of Jama's dissatisfaction with his social standing among the settlers. His comment about Jama's being white inside poked painfully at a festering wound.

"I am Nguni like you," Jama said emphatically. "My forefathers were Nguni, forerunners of the Amaxhosa, the Xhosa people."

"So you learned the Amaxhosa language from your father!"

Jama shook his head. "My father did not know the Amaxhosa language. I listen," he said. "When I listen, I learn."

"And our wise sayings? How do you know them?"

"I listen," Jama repeated. "I have heard your people talking by the river. I have the ability to understand and remember words of many languages, both words that are spoken and words that are written."

"A good ability!" the chief cried. He seemed impressed. "Other than the language of the settlers and the Amaxhosa, what languages do you speak? Do you speak Khoi?"

Jama nodded.

"Do you know the language of the English?"

"A little."

The chief was intrigued. "The Zulus?"

Jama hesitated. "A little. I have not had much chance to listen to the Amazulul."

"That is your good fortune," said the chief without intending any levity, Jama was sure.

By now the other Xhosa men had wandered downstream in search of a better place to catch fish. The chief remained behind. He seemed more interested in Jama. He squatted on his side of the river.

"Do you not find the clothing of the Boers hot and unsuitable for hunting?" the Xhosa asked. He squirmed, as though uncomfortable at the mere thought of wearing the clothing of the settlers.

Jama grinned. He looked down at his shirt and pants. His feet were encased in leather shoes. The broad-rimmed hat of a settler lay nearby on the ground. Having been raised with the Boers, Jama hadn't ever given his appearance much thought. But now that he did, he supposed, compared to what little the Xhosa men wore, his clothing *was* restricting and hot.

"I've grown accustomed to it," he said. The chief's open curiosity amused him. It wasn't often a Xhosa sat down with a settler to chat, and the chief seemed as enthusiastic about this opportunity to learn more about settlers as Jama was about the chance to practice the Xhosa language.

"You are a black man," said the chief. "Do you worship the white men's gods?"

Jama was impressed—and threatened—by the question. He only wished he had a ready answer for it. Bible reading and prayer were daily events in the van der Kemp household, events in which Jama was included. But while he knew about the settlers' God—the covenant God of Abraham, Isaac, and Jacob—Jama's relationship with Him was different from theirs. The same uneasiness he felt around the Boers socially crept into his feelings regarding their religion.

Their ceremonies, their Bible reading, their prayers, their Nacht-maal festival all served to remind them that they were God's chosen people—and indirectly that he was not. They were the people of the covenant. For Jama and the rest of the world, the only hope for securing the favor of their God lay in association with the covenant people.

"I have heard about their God," Jama said to the chief. "I do not pray to Him myself." He left it at that.

The chief seemed to sense an underlying disturbance. He nodded solemnly. "And what about a woman?" he asked. "Do you have wives? Are some of them white women?"

"I have no wife," Jama replied curtly.

This visibly surprised and intrigued the chief. He leaned forward. "You have no woman? And why is this? Are you forbidden? Or will no woman have you?"

Jama searched for words to explain his lack of marital attachments. The truth of the matter was that he was a social oddity on the frontier. There were no free black women that he was aware of who were available. As for white women, they were forbidden to him even if he felt an attraction, which he didn't. That left black slaves and Khoi.

He had no interest in the short, heavy Khoi women, and on the two occasions he managed to work up courage to visit socially two black slave women, he found them slow-witted and uninteresting. That's when he came to a depressing realization. What made him think he would find an articulate, witty, stimulating woman among those who had no more chance to grow in these things than the cattle he daily herded?

Besides, if Jama wanted a wife, he would have to buy one. This condition for finding a woman who would be uniquely his often prompted sly winks and crude jokes among the men who owned the slaves. One farmer went so far as to proclaim that Jama had an advantage over Boer farmers: if Jama didn't like a woman he took as his wife, he could easily rid himself of her by selling her again.

Even worse was the owner of one slave who confided to Jama that he had already "tried her out," comparing her to a spring filly and promising Jama he would get a lot of enjoyment from her.

"Few women are available to me," Jama told the Xhosa chief.

The Xhosa stared at Jama as though he were studying a rare species of animal. "Maybe you have been hunting on the wrong side of the river," he said. His words were laid out delicately, like bait for a wild animal. The chief paused, as though waiting to see what Jama would do with them.

To Jama the suggestion was intriguing—even tantalizing—though he wasn't sure exactly what the chief had in mind. "Interesting," was all he said.

"More than interesting," the chief replied. "It is wise. After all, you are more like us than you are like them."

The chief's comment struck Jama hard. *You are more like us than you are like them.* He had never entertained such a thought before. The Xhosa had always been that troublesome tribe on the other side of the river, while he had always been one of the frontier settlers, one of the van der Kemps. But how much like the van der Kemps was he?

They alone counted him as a settler. And if something were to happen to Christiaan van der Kemp, would the other Boer farmers still accept him? Not likely. Take away the broad-rimmed hat, the shirt, and the shoes, and what did you have? A Nguni. Just like the man sitting on the shore opposite him.

"The look on your face," the chief said, "tells me you see the wisdom of my words."

Jama neither confirmed nor denied the chief's conclusion.

"This Kemp family," the Xhosa continued, "in truth, do they treat you well?"

"I spoke the truth to you when we first met," Jama replied. "Christiaan van der Kemp and I are like brothers."

"How many other settlers are your brothers?"

The answer came easily to Jama's mind. *None.* Some might consider him a friend. Possibly the Pfeffers—and Sina's friend Karel. But the unpleasant truth was that the majority of settlers were more like the intolerant Oloff Klyn.

"My friends are few," Jama concluded aloud.

"You are to be pitied," the chief said. He stood and stretched contentedly.

Jama felt anger rising inside him. Standing to match the chief's posture, he cried, "I want no man's pity!"

"Nor should you," the chief replied. "My comment was merely an observation from what you have told me. You live among a people who do not honor you. You have no god of your own to worship. You have no woman to give you comfort or pleasure. You walk among the settlers like a leprous man, only your leprosy is nothing more than black skin. Now tell me, is not such a man to be pitied?"

Before Jama could answer, something behind him caught the chief's eye, prompting him to reach for his spear. As Jama swung around he could hear the pounding of horses' hooves approaching rapidly. Riding in front of a cloud of dust were Kootjie and Karel.

Agitated grumbling came from beyond the river. Alarmed, the other Xhosa men had returned. They hopped from foot to foot, anticipating trouble.

"They are no threat to you!" Jama yelled. "They are but boys!"

The Xhosa men were not appeased. Spears were weighed in their hands in preparation of being launched.

"Xhosa chief! You have my word, these boys are no threat!" Jama's eyes locked with those of the chief in silent communication.

The Xhosa chief extended a hand toward his men. The spears were lowered.

The threat ended, Jama ran toward the approaching riders.

Both boys wore uncharacteristic expressions of deep concern with a generous portion of fear mixed into the younger boy's face.

"Jama!" Kootjie cried. "You must come with us to Graaff-Reinet! Father is being held for trial!"

"It's true!" Karel said. *"Mynheer* van der Kemp sent us to get you."

"Just the two of you?"

Gulping air, Karel nodded. "We had to travel quickly. The trial will have started by the time we can get back there."

"We rode as hard as we could!" Kootjie's voice cracked. "Honest, we did!" He was tired and close to tears.

Jama took charge. "Let's go to the house. You can tell me what happened at Graaff-Reinet along the way."

Karel offered Jama a hand and lifted him onto the back of his horse. The exhausted animal complained at the extra weight.

"Are we going to ride out tonight?" Kootjie asked.

"Let's get back to the house, then we'll decide," Jama said.

"We *have* to ride out tonight!" Kootjie cried. "Father needs us!"

Jama met his eyes. "You'll be no good to your father if you fall out of your saddle from exhaustion halfway there."

"But I won't—"

Jama cut him off short. "First, tell me exactly what happened; then, we'll do what must be done."

Karel pulled his horse around and rode away from the river as Kootjie began to babble excitedly. Jama couldn't resist taking one last look backward.

While the Xhosa men made their way up the riverbank, the chief stood at the water's edge, watching Jama ride off. The chief's words echoed in Jama's head: *You are more like us than you are like them.*

10

The room in which Christiaan's trial was held was too shiny for a frontier man. All the polish and glare created an unsettled feeling in the pit of his stomach.

He preferred the earthy quality of his standard habitat—dust-coated grass, rough log benches, the gritty feel of dirt beneath his boots, outdoor odors, and a horizon line that stretched so far it strained his eyes to look at it.

From his first step on this glassy wooden floor—upon which he slipped—it was clear to him that he had nothing in common with the men who occupied this burnished universe. Had they lived where he lived, they most assuredly would have insisted upon polishing the dirt from the leaves, sanding the logs, and scenting the air.

It was unnatural. Luster and shine served only to mask an object's true nature.

On the frontier, things were what they were. There was something trustworthy about its naturalness. A man could trust the frontier to be hard, unforgiving, even dangerous. He understood these things, even respected them. He also knew that if he met the frontier on its own terms, matching its forthrightness with a determination and toughness of his own, the frontier would respect him for it, and each could learn to adapt to the other's peculiarities.

In this room nothing was natural. Everything was glossed over. All was polish and pretense. How could he expect the men who inhabited it to be any different?

With Johanna at his side, Christiaan surveyed the layout of the room. It was wider than it was long and had a large mullioned window at the opposite end, stretching floor to ceiling. Immediately in front of the window sat a massive mahogany table of deep reddish brown with intricately inlaid scrolls and shells adorning its sides and extending down its legs. This was the magistrate's table.

Matching mahogany cabinets, also with inlaid scrolls and shells, flanked the window. Their shelves displayed a fine array of white porcelain plates, mostly of blue Oriental design, some with the restrained flair of a Chinaman's red brush. From what Christiaan had been told, the plates were the magistrate's private collection. For unknown reasons, he had chosen to decorate his courtroom with them.

As for seating, there was a single mahogany chair behind the table. It had a high back and was easily the largest chair in the room. Three chairs with arms were positioned behind a lesser table on the left side of the room. It nearly closed the gap between the magistrate's table and the five rows of spectator chairs that faced it.

Less than a handful of the spectator chairs were occupied. Those who occupied them gave no indication that they were there for any particular purpose. On the left side a bespectacled man with disheveled gray hair peered intently into the open pages of the *Graaff-Reinet Journal*. A woman of considerable bulk had positioned herself in the center. Turned to one side in her chair, she methodically wiped the face of a squirming child next to her, who offered token resistance with muffled grunts. In the back row right, a man of unknown age had scooted forward the chair in front of him to give his legs room to stretch out. With arms folded, he reclined in his seat. His head dangled at an awkward angle over the chair's back. The man's broad-brimmed hat covered his face.

Christiaan didn't recognize any of them. For all he knew, they had wandered into the courtroom for no other reason than to rest their feet following another Nachtmaal celebration.

Skirting the edge of the chair arrangement, Christiaan walked to the front row seats. His boots and Johanna's shoes clicked on the hardwood floor in accompanying rhythm and echoed against the walls, the sound of which served to announce their presence. The man reading the paper glanced up. He was distracted but for a moment. Without expression, he returned to his columns of print. The woman, too, glanced their direction, without pausing in her attack on the dirt on the child's face. The man beneath the hat was undisturbed by their passing. He snored softly.

Christiaan selected a seat four chairs from the end. Johanna crossed in front of him and sat down. The instant Christiaan settled into the wooden chair he was reminded of the room's unnatural condition. The chair was so polished it was as slippery as ice. He couldn't lean back, for if he did he would slide right out of it and onto the floor. Only after a few moments of experimentation did he discover that if he bent forward slightly he could balance himself and counter the chair's slickness.

Johanna leaned over to him. She whispered, "Nervous?"

"I can't get comfortable in this chair."

"You were expecting to be comfortable at your own trial?"

Christiaan's lips stretched with a wry grin. "That's not what I meant. It's this chair. It's so polished I can't . . ."

The look on Johanna's face stopped his whining. Her eyes sparkled with humor. Her mouth formed a teasing smile. She was goading him.

Christiaan thought of the summons he'd received but couldn't read because it was written in English. "Did you bring the paper?"

Johanna showed him the summons, scrolled in her hand.

He acknowledged it with a nod. Until this moment, he hadn't realized how nervous he felt. The thought of his immediate predicament amused him, however. Here he was on trial, and for the last several moments he'd been fighting with a chair—and losing.

"Do I really look that nervous?"

The teasing smile remained on her face, unchanged. It was answer enough.

Christiaan took a deep breath and sighed. He patted his wife's arm. "I'm just glad you're on my side," he said. "You know me too well. If you were my judge, I wouldn't even attempt a defense. I'd cry, 'Guilty,' and plead for mercy."

Johanna's smile grew wider. "Hm. An inviting thought, I must say."

The legs of the empty chair next to Christiaan squealed against the floor. Turning, he found himself staring into the weathered face of Oloff Klyn.

"Oloff! I thought you had packed up and moved on."

The old man stared down at his chair and scowled as his bottom slid from side to side. "Someone has to come to your rescue," he said dryly. "Besides, we're in this together. If they can do this to you, they can do it to anyone. And if we don't stop it here, we'll have another Black Circuit on our hands."

The Black Circuit. Only Slachtersnek could raise more instant ire among the Boers. More than two decades earlier, in an attempt to strengthen British rule over the Boers, Sir John Cradock established a circuit court in Graaff-Reinet. It became a riotous road show that lumbered through the district, intent on blackening the Boers' reputation through a series of prejudicial trials. Every farm on the frontier buzzed with tales of its excesses. The political traveling circus stirred Afrikaner indignation to fever pitch.

The slightest accusation against Boer farmers was encouraged. Khoi and blacks alike flocked forward with complaints of maltreatment. Gleeful workers were eager to take advantage of the opportunity suddenly given them. It was their chance to get a measure of revenge on their bosses. To level a charge cost them nothing. The potential reward, should the court decide in their favor, was cattle or property or both. Even in spite of a court that was greatly disposed to favor their accusations, many charges were thrown out as nothing more than false, malicious, cooked-up accusations.

The Black Circuit, as the traveling court was called, was a hunt, and the Boers were the game. And though a fair amount of animosity arose between hunters and hunted, the greatest enmity was reserved for those who had organized the hunting party—the British.

"Like I said—if you ask me, they targeted you specifically," Klyn said.

"Why do you think that?"

"Think about it!"

Christiaan hated when Klyn did that. He seemed to take delight in making people feel stupid. However, Christiaan had learned that if he said nothing, Oloff would eventually enlighten him. So he said nothing.

"With your good reputation in the district," Klyn explained, as Christiaan knew he would, "you're the elephant! The biggest target! If they can bring you down, none of the rest of us is safe! Even you can understand that, can't you?"

"I understand what you're saying," Christiaan replied. He gave a half chuckle. "But I've never really thought of myself as an elephant."

Klyn didn't catch the humor. He wasn't listening. His mind had already prepared his next thoughts and laid them on his lips. "Do you know who is bringing the accusation against you?" he asked.

"No idea."

"It wouldn't be your black friend, would it? Mamba?"

"Jama," Christiaan corrected with irritation. "And no, it wouldn't be Jama. In fact, I sent Kootjie and Karel to let him know what is happening and to bring him here." Christiaan craned his neck toward the back door. "That was several days ago. I was hoping they'd be here by now."

"What if they can't find him?" Klyn asked.

"What are you saying?"

With a twinkle in his eye as though he knew something Christiaan didn't, he said, "What if he's already here? With the prosecutor and the magistrate?"

Color rose in Christiaan's neck. "I told you, Jama wouldn't do that to me!"

"Don't know why you'd want him here anyway," Klyn said. "He can't do you much good." He sighed and looked at the door through which the magistrate would appear. "Whoever they have, they must feel confident they can make the charge against you stick."

A commotion rumbled through the back door. It was the sound of an army of boots as a flood of Boers poured through the opening.

Each one wore a stern expression. Each one, as he entered, nodded at Christiaan. In a matter of moments the chairs were full. Still, they kept coming. They lined the walls two and three deep when the last of them were inside. Some of the men Christiaan recognized, including his neighbor Adriaan Pfeffer; some of them looked vaguely familiar from the courtyard gathering; many of them he did not recognize at all.

Klyn punched Christiaan in the arm. "Looks like we got reinforcements."

Just then Christiaan caught site of Sina. She had lagged behind to finish the chores at the wagon and had apparently arrived just before the deluge of men hit the doorway. She was seated in the back row. To Christiaan's displeasure, Henry Klyn was beside her.

Sina was busy making eyes at Henry. Laughing too readily. Smiling too broadly. Her giggle could be heard above the general commotion of the burgeoning roomful of men.

Had Oloff Klyn not announced his intention to trek north with the Louis Trichardt party, Christiaan would have made it a point to speak to her about the boy. He had considered telling her outright that she could no longer see him. As it was, he was providentially spared the confrontation. Henry and his father would soon be gone, and the problem would resolve itself.

The opening of the magistrate's door drew the attention of everyone in the room. An eerie hush fell upon the gathering as four men emerged.

"Dikkop!" Johanna cried, turning to her husband.

Christiaan nodded. He should have known. The first man through the door, a former Khoi worker of his, had been nothing but trouble since the moment he set foot on the van der Kemp farm.

Dikkop was small of stature, as were the others of his race. Also in keeping with his people, he had protruding hindquarters, which caused him to totter as he walked. His skin was brown and thick with a yellowish tint to it. His eyes, too, were yellow, whereas most people's were white; prominent red veins spread from the corners like streaks of lightning. His clothes and arms and legs and bare feet and peppercorn black hair were dusted with dirt. It was a light dusting. Someone must have attempted to clean him up for the trial.

Behind the soft padding of the Khoi's bare feet against the hardwood floor came the distinct clicks of civilized heels. The man immediately trailing Christiaan's accuser was as tall as the Khoi was short. He had to duck slightly to clear the doorway. The man's clothes draped on him as they would on a coat rack. His skin was pasty white, his nose flat and curved like a beak, and he had no lips—at least none that were readily discernible. After coming through the doorway, he stepped to Dikkop's side and, placing a hand on the Khoi's shoulder, guided him to the prosecutor's table as he would a child.

The third man to enter wore a white powdered wig. Sir William More, the magistrate. Although Christiaan had never seen the magistrate before, he recognized him from descriptions of those who had. He'd heard the man was bald—bright, shiny bald was the actual description that had been given Christiaan. And now that he saw the man himself, Christiaan readily believed the report, for even though the magistrate's baldness was covered by a wig, the action of the wig itself revealed the truth of the description. With nothing for the peruke to adhere to, it slid side to side, front to back, whichever way the magistrate tilted his head. To keep it from falling off completely, the magistrate had to dedicate one hand solely to the task of holding the wig in place.

Thus, with one hand on top of his head and the other toting several books, the magistrate made his entrance. He was a man of medium height; his build was something of a mystery since it was covered by a black robe. However, Christiaan guessed the man to be portly by the way he waddled as he walked. His nose and cheeks and chin looked like those of a man who had at one time been choked by the neck until his features bulged and then, for some unexplained reason, stayed that way. The short distance from the doorway to the center table colored the magistrate's orbed cheeks tomato red.

The last person to appear also wore a white powdered wig. Christiaan assumed this was the prosecutor since he followed Dikkop and the man with no lips to the prosecutor's table. Of medium stature and weight, he strode purposefully with a stack of papers tucked under one arm, like a man on a mission. Black, bushy eyebrows converged at the bridge of his nose. Normally, the eyebrows might not have caught Christiaan's attention, but, set in contrast to the curls of his powdered wig, the brows took on a humorous characteristic. Every time the man scowled—which was frequently—his eyebrows met. They looked like two caterpillars kissing. The image amused Christiaan. But before a grin could completely form on his face, the prosecutor shot him a murderous glance that withered Christiaan's grin instantly.

The man's eyes had an animal quality about them. Black. Menacing.

Only once before had Christiaan seen a gaze as threatening as this one. He had been on commando patrol alone when he stumbled upon a leopard, perched on a rock, ready to pounce. It wasn't hunting skill that saved Christiaan from the beast. It was instinct. In a fraction of the time it took him to later describe what happened, he turned and swung his musket at his attacker. Just as the beast leaped at him from the rock, he managed to squeeze off a shot. Unbalanced, Christiaan was knocked from his horse by the blast and found himself on the ground. His musket had fallen several feet away. Beside him in the dirt was the leopard, still alive but rendered immobile by his wound.

Both lay with their cheeks in the dirt. Their faces separated by less than a foot, they stared at each other as their chests heaved in simultaneous rhythm. Christiaan never forgot the look in the leopard's eyes at that moment. The animal couldn't move. He lay motionless, reduced to staring, dying. Still, there was killing in his eyes.

The same look that Christiaan now saw in the eyes of the prosecutor.

11

Christiaan van der Kemp! Stand and face the charges that have been brought against you." The magistrate's bulging eyes scanned the room for the man whose name he had just read from the court papers that lay before him on the mahogany desk.

In the magistrate's string of words, Christiaan recognized only his name. English was the official language of the court, a language Christiaan could neither speak nor read.

At the prosecutor's table, Dikkop leaned toward the pasty-skinned man, pointed at Christiaan, and whispered in the man's ear.

The pale man nodded. To Christiaan he said in Afrikaans, "The magistrate demands that you stand and face the charges."

Christiaan glanced at Johanna before standing. Their eyes met.

For nearly twenty years he had gazed into this woman's eyes, longer if you counted their courtship. He had seen them sparkling with youthful gaiety and impish pranks; brimming with pride as they surveyed their farm at sunset; glistening with rowdy tears from late night foolishness; saturated with pain during the travail of childbirth; shining with joy as she held her newborn babies; charged with fury over stupidity and laziness; wide and humbled in worshipful awe; half closed with sleep at the end of a bone-weary day; devoted, inspired, fearful for her life and the life of her family. But at this moment when Johanna's eyes met his, Christiaan saw in them a deep assurance that she believed in him and that no magistrate or prosecutor would ever change her mind.

Christiaan would remember that look in Johanna's eyes until his dying day.

"I am Christiaan van der Kemp," he said, standing tall.

The magistrate leaned on his desk toward Christiaan. His wig slipped forward. He caught it, pulled it back into place, and with furrowed brow spoke words to Christiaan that the frontiersman did not understand.

Christiaan glanced from side to side. He felt dumb, helpless.

The magistrate spoke again. Louder. This time his remarks did not seem directed at anyone in particular, but how was Christiaan to know?

Was he being told to sit down? Come forward? Offer a defense? Unsure, he began to take his seat.

With an exaggerated upward motion of his hands, the magistrate bellowed. The man's tomato-red complexion took on an overripe hue. This time his words were clearly directed at Christiaan.

The prosecutor rolled his eyes heavenward in exaggerated fashion. Dikkop wore a malicious smirk. Christiaan was sure the Khoi didn't understand English either, but he didn't have to understand English to enjoy watching his former employer's obvious discomfort.

Christiaan stood again on uncertain legs.

Another flurry of unknown words issued forth from behind the mahogany table.

Taking a step forward, Christiaan said meekly, "I don't understand what you're saying. I don't speak—"

Two words were shouted at him by the magistrate, accompanied by a plump, pointing finger.

The sound of a chair scraping against the floor came from the lesser table to Christiaan's left. The pale man stood. Walking around the end of the table, he approached Christiaan. In a cool voice he said, "The magistrate wants to know if you understand the charges that have been brought against you."

Before answering, Christiaan took a closer look at his interpreter. The man's pasty complexion was even whiter than it appeared at a distance. His skin was baby-smooth. Even on his chin and jowls, where most men show some amount of stubble, there was not a hint of hair. When he blinked, large eyelids fell mechanically over muddy-brown eyes like shields descending from his brow, then retracting.

"Who are you?" Christiaan asked.

The man gave Christiaan a look a teacher would use on a pupil who had spoken out of turn. His head bobbed undecidedly. When he spoke, he spoke to the magistrate in English.

The magistrate issued a curt reply.

"My name is Edward Grey. I'm a missionary with the London Missionary Society. Against my will, the magistrate has ordered me to serve as your interpreter."

"Against your will?"

"Most definitely. For three years I have ministered to the outcasts of your society. I have witnessed the abuse you Boers have showered upon the Khoi, the San, and the Xhosa. Make no mistake about my presence in this courtroom. I am not your friend. If I were magistrate, I would have you flogged for what you have done to *Mynheer* Dikkop and who knows how many countless others."

"I have not injured Dikkop in any way!" Christiaan protested.

Shieldlike eyelids lowered halfway. "I know differently," he said.

Since their arrival, the British missionaries—philanthropists, as the Boers called them—had been a thorn in the side of the farmers. Their disdain for the Boers was unmistakable. Their allegiance was to the British, naturally, and their passion was to convert the heathen, namely the indigenous African tribes. The Boers, being neither British nor indigenous, did not fall under their umbrella of compassion. In their zeal to reach the natives, the missionaries were quick to believe anything the indigenous people said against those who had been their masters.

For the remainder of the trial this missionary was to serve as Christiaan's interpreter? It would be an uneasy alliance.

From behind Christiaan came Oloff Klyn's loud whisper. "Who *is* that scarecrow?"

Turning halfway to him, Christiaan answered, "A missionary. He'll interpret for me."

"A philanthropist?" Klyn cried. "They're putting you on the spit to roast you!"

The magistrate pounded the table and shouted. His patience had expired.

Grey translated for him.

"I will not allow your ignorance of the language of this court to slow these proceedings any longer!" he thundered. "Do you understand the charges that have been brought against you?"

Christiaan turned toward the back door, hoping to see Jama standing there. The doorway was crowded with Boer farmers who understood as little of the proceedings as he. Facing the magistrate, he said, "I know that I have been called to answer charges, but until now I did not know who was bringing them; and even now I do not know what they are."

The magistrate looked at the prosecutor. "Sir Thatcher, kindly inform this man of the charges against him."

The prosecutor stood. His eyes narrowed on his prey. "Christiaan van der Kemp," he said, "you have been charged with willfully withholding property that rightfully belongs to *Mynheer* Dikkop. Furthermore, you are charged with grievous infliction of injury upon his person."

Upon hearing the allegations, Christiaan looked at the one bringing them. Dikkop returned his gaze with the wide eyes of an innocent, abused victim.

Christiaan knew he had never physically mistreated Dikkop or any of his workers. Not that the practice was unheard of among the Boer farmers—it was common knowledge that some owners were harsh with their former slaves, now workers; sometimes even cruel. But when it came to motivating his workmen, Christiaan saw cruelty as counterproductive. Besides, it was Jama who managed them. For the most part, the workers on the van der Kemp farm were less troublesome than those on other farms, maybe because the skin of their overseer was black.

"With God as my witness," Christiaan said, "I have never abused Dikkop or any of my workers. As a matter of fact, it has been my policy—"

Grey cut him off with an uplifted hand. "You will get a chance to defend yourself at a later time."

"But if I can convince the magistrate that the charges are unfounded, we can all go home!" Christiaan said.

"It won't be that easy for you," Grey replied in a low voice before relaying Christiaan's not-guilty plea.

The magistrate ordered Christiaan to sit down. Johanna was forced to move over one seat as Grey came to sit between them. Once again, Christiaan cast a longing look behind him. Still no Jama.

Mynheer van der Kemp promised me that for taking care of his cattle he would give me fifteen of his best cows and a bull." Dikkop stood in front of the prosecutor's table as he spoke. His hands were clasped in front of him. Only when answering a direct question did he look up; the rest of the time he seemed to be addressing the slick hardwood floor.

"Fifteen? Or ten?" missionary Grey prompted him.

Dikkop's mouth fell open momentarily. His eyes turned crafty in thought, then softened again to the look of a victim. "I know I told you ten," he replied, "but in truth it was fifteen."

The magistrate leaned forward to look directly into the eyes of the short Khoi. "Which was it? Ten or fifteen?"

The Khoi appeared flustered. After assurances from Grey, he said, "It was fifteen. I said ten earlier because I didn't think even the British could make *Mynheer* van der Kemp give me fifteen cattle even though that is what he promised me."

"You underestimate the power of the British legal system," the prosecutor said to Dikkop.

The missionary translated.

A grin formed on the Khoi's thick lips.

"Continue," said the prosecutor.

Dikkop looked helplessly at his missionary advocate.

"Tell them how *Mynheer* van der Kemp beat you," Grey urged. To the magistrate, Grey said, "You should have seen him when he first came into the compound. Never have I seen a man so—"

"Let him tell it," ordered the judge.

Grey conceded with a nod. "Tell them," he said to Dikkop. "Don't be afraid. *Mynheer* van der Kemp can't hurt you here."

Blinking his eyes several times, Dikkop hesitated, then said, "When I completed my task I asked *Mynheer* van der Kemp to do what he promised—to give me my cows."

"And what did *Mynheer* van der Kemp do?" the prosecutor prompted.

Dikkop bit his lower lip. "He refused to give me my cows. He ordered me off his land."

"What did you do then?"

Raising his head and looking squarely at Christiaan, he said, "I told him that I did my part and now it was time for him to do his part." He turned to the magistrate. "I didn't want to work for him at first, because I heard what a hard man he was. But he wanted me to work for him. I am the best cattleman in the land. He told me that when he asked me to work for him. He said, 'I've heard you're the best cattleman in the land.'"

Christiaan shook his head. It was a lie.

"But when I asked him for my cows, he would not give them to me. Then he tried to force me from his land. I refused to go. That's when he beat me."

"Did you resist?" the prosecutor asked.

"Resist?"

"Did you fight back?"

A horrified look crossed Dikkop's face. "Of course not!" he cried. "That would be an uprising! He would kill me if he thought I was uprising against him."

"If I might add something here . . ." Grey offered after translating the Khoi's last sentence.

The red-faced magistrate held up a hand. To Dikkop he said, "Is there anything more you would like to say?"

"Only that after *Mynheer* van der Kemp beat me, he called five of his biggest, strongest workers and told them to throw me off his land. They carried me down to the Great Fish River and hit me and kicked me and then threw me into the water. I can't swim, and, with all my bruises and sores, I nearly drowned. That is all I have to say about this horrible incident in my life."

While the missionary stood in front of his chair, translating for the Khoi, Christiaan looked past him to his wife. Johanna nodded encouragement to him. The charges were ludicrous, and she knew it. It was comforting to know that at least one person in the room believed that.

The magistrate nodded to Grey.

"I simply want to confirm this poor man's story," the missionary said. "It was hard for me to comprehend the depth of man's depravity when I saw how horribly beaten he was. And the poor innocent would most assuredly have drowned had not one of my associates fished him from the river and carried him to the compound!"

Christiaan turned to the back door. Where were Jama and Kootjie? They should have arrived long before now.

Grey continued. He spoke with impassioned tones, at times lapsing into a preachy cadence. "For years the Boers have forced into slavery the indigenous dwellers of this good land. Those who refused have been driven to take up arms in order to defend themselves. Originally, it was not this way. When the Boers first came to the Zuurveld, they dwelt with the natives in peace. Their flocks grazed on the same hills; their herdsmen smoked together out of the same pipes; they were brothers—until the herds of the Amaxhosa increased so as to make the hearts of the Boers sore with greed. What those covetous men could not get from the natives for old brass buttons, they took by force. But the natives are men like any other men. They love their cattle; their wives and children live upon milk. They fought for their property. And who can fault them when they learned to hate the colonists who coveted their all and aimed at their destruction?

"The Boers descended upon the land like locusts. They made commandos to drive the natives out of the Zuurveld. They forced them across the Great Fish River, telling them that they wanted nothing more.

"But that is a lie! The Boers will not be satisfied until the natives of this land have been utterly destroyed! The Boers will not rest until they have taken the last cow. And without milk, the wives and children will perish. Can we fault them then when they follow the tracks of their cattle into the colony? These people are fighting for their lives! Yet they have nearly lost all hope! Their people are starving while the Boer colony is still after everything they hold dear!"

A puzzled expression squeezed the magistrate's eyes until they were mere slits. "Excuse me," he said, "but what does this have to do with the matter at hand?"

"Forgive my passion," Grey said, "but if you could only see the things I see at the compound every single day. In response to your question, it has everything to do with the matter at hand. For I believe that *Mynheer* van der Kemp's behavior toward this poor indigenous soul is merely one example of an epidemic of Boer abuse of the natives of this land. I wish that with a single ruling we could stop the abuse. That would not be realistic, but let me hasten to say that if we have to do it farmer by farmer, then so be it. And may God give us strength and resolve to do it."

The missionary sat down between Christiaan and Johanna. He looked neither to his left nor his right. Maintaining an impassioned expression on his face, he stared straight forward.

"Prosecutor," the magistrate said, "do you have any more witnesses?"

"No other witnesses are available," the prosecutor said, "and understandably so."

"How so?"

With a sly grin, he said, "A man like *Mynheer* van der Kemp is well practiced at striking terror into the heart of those who work for him. Naturally, those who might have seen the event are reluctant to testify against him for fear of what might happen to them following these proceedings."

The magistrate nodded in understanding.

The room fell silent while the prosecutor took his seat and the magistrate wrote something on the papers before him.

Then the magistrate looked up at Christiaan. "*Mynheer* van der Kemp, do you wish to offer a defense before this court passes judgment?"

Before Christiaan could respond, Oloff Klyn was on his feet. "I would speak in defense of Christiaan van der Kemp," he boomed.

"And you are . . ."

"Oloff Klyn."

The magistrate nodded and wrote something down.

Although Christiaan was grateful that someone was willing to speak on his behalf, he didn't know if he wanted it to be Klyn. His doubts increased when he saw the look on the prosecutor's face. It was twisted with deadly pleasure.

12

Christiaan van der Kemp is not the one who should be on trial here," Klyn began.

The magistrate's wig rose with his eyebrows. "And who is it that should be on trial, *Mynheer* Klyn?" he asked.

"You!" Klyn cried. "And the whole British government!"

The room thundered with Boer response, drowning out the missionary's interpretation.

Johanna looked angrily at Klyn. Because of the din, Christiaan couldn't hear her words, but he was able to make them out as they formed on her lips. She said, "Not now, Oloff! Not now!"

Neither did Klyn hear her—as though it mattered. He wouldn't have heeded her advice had he heard.

When the magistrate finally succeeded in restoring order and finally got to hear the translated words that had ignited the outburst, he warned Klyn sternly to keep a civil tongue and to confine his remarks to the matter at hand.

"I *am* addressing the matter at hand!" Klyn insisted. "Were it not for your ridiculous laws that bind the hands of good men like Christiaan van der Kemp, we would not be here today. How can you expect an honest farmer to survive when you give his property away to heathen? When you deplete his workforce and put lazy Khoi on the streets and not in the fields where they belong? What right do you have to tell us how we should run our farms? We left Cape Town to get away from you once, but you followed us here! Now you're forcing good men like Christiaan van der Kemp to flee their homes once again because of your unreasonable, repressive, and ridiculous laws that favor the heathen and prosecute God-fearing men!"

Again the room erupted with noise. Had it not been for the fact that his future was being weighed in the balance, Christiaan might have found the whole thing humorous, especially the missionary's part. The way he wrinkled his beaklike nose as he translated Oloff Klyn's message clearly indicated he found the man's words distasteful.

"If I may be of assistance with this witness . . ."

The prosecutor was on his feet, attempting to get the magistrate's attention. His was one voice against nearly a hundred, and not until the magistrate succeeded in quieting the room a second time was he recognized.

"If I may be of assistance . . ." the prosecutor said again.

After warning those in the room against further outbursts, the magistrate gave the prosecutor the floor.

"A question or two for you, *Mynheer* Klyn," the prosecutor began.

Klyn faced the man squarely.

"Do you employ workers at your farm, *Mynheer* Klyn?"

"What kind of foolish question is that?" Klyn replied. "Of course I do."

"And do you find it necessary at times to discipline your workers, *Mynheer* Klyn?"

"Of course I do."

"And how do you discipline your workers, *Mynheer* Klyn?"

Christiaan stood. He saw where the prosecutor was heading. And although he was sure Klyn was now aware of it too, he knew that Oloff was not shy about speaking his mind on the subject.

"Excuse me, Your Honor," Christiaan said, "but if you don't mind . . . I am the one on trial here, not my friend *Mynheer* Klyn."

Oloff waved him off. "I don't mind answering this fool's questions," he said.

The magistrate said, "Let the man speak. Sit down, *Mynheer* van der Kemp."

The prosecutor repeated his question. "And how do you discipline your workers?"

"With whatever necessary means it takes."

Christiaan was astonished. A diplomatic answer from Oloff Klyn? For a moment his hopes rose. But only for a moment.

"Necessary means," the prosecutor echoed. "Tell me, *Mynheer* Klyn, exactly what are necessary means?"

"It means that I do whatever I deem necessary in a given situation."

"Does that include flogging?"

"Sometimes."

"With a stick?"

"Sometimes."

"With a whip?"

"Sometimes."

"*Mynheer* Klyn," the prosecutor pressed, "so you admit to beating your workers. Are you unusual in this regard?"

"Unusual? Of course not. Every farmer has to beat a worker now and then. It's the only thing some of them understand."

Christiaan grimaced.

"The only thing they understand," the prosecutor repeated with a grin.

"You have to put the fear of God in them," Klyn replied. "You get more work out of a slave when he has the fear of God in him."

"*Slave?*" the prosecutor cried.

"Force of habit," Klyn said, unruffled. "Worker, if that suits your taste better."

The prosecutor nodded philosophically. "And you say every farmer you know beats his workers."

"Don't see how they'd get a lick of work done without it."

"Including *Mynheer* van der Kemp?"

Klyn looked at Christiaan. "Can't say that I've ever seen him . . ."

"But you said that every farmer beats his workers." The prosecutor leaned with his knuckles on the table.

"I'll not contradict myself, if that's what you're trying to get me to do," Klyn replied.

"No, *Mynheer* Klyn—" the prosecutor grinned "—I wouldn't want you to contradict yourself."

The prosecutor was finished with Oloff Klyn, and the magistrate ordered Klyn to take his seat, even though the farmer tried to say more.

"*Mynheer* van der Kemp," said the magistrate, "what would you offer in your behalf?"

Christiaan was tempted not to say anything.

It was clear from the set of the magistrate's jaw that he had reached a decision in the matter. Missionary Grey was nodding warmly at Dikkop, who grinned. The prosecutor sat back, arms folded, with the satisfied look of a predator that had just eaten following the kill.

However, Christiaan couldn't bring himself to act like one of his cattle and be content to be led around at someone else's whim. He stood and looked the magistrate in the eye.

"In my own defense," he said, "all I can say is that for some reason Dikkop—"

"*Mynheer* Dikkop!" the prosecutor insisted.

The magistrate nodded his assent.

"For some reason," Christiaan began again, "*Mynheer* Dikkop has woven together a story of lies in hopes of depriving me of my property. I have been sitting here trying to think of a way to convince you that nothing that he has said in this matter is true. But how can I convince you, other than to say that he is lying?"

The missionary translated and waited for more.

Nothing was forthcoming. Christiaan took his seat.

The magistrate leaned his forearms on the table. "Are you saying *Mynheer* Dikkop was never one of your workers?"

Christiaan stood to reply. "That part is true. But nothing else."

"Then you did not seek him out to herd your cattle?"

"No, he came to me looking for work. Against the advice of several other farmers in the area, I took him on."

"They advised you against giving him work?"

Christiaan nodded. "They told me he was a troublemaker."

"And did you promise to give him fifteen cattle for his work?"

"No, I did not."

"When he left you, did he leave amicably?"

Christiaan hesitated. "I don't understand 'amicably.'"

"On friendly terms," the magistrate explained.

"I wouldn't know," Christiaan replied. "He ran away."

The magistrate looked at Dikkop, then back at Christiaan. "And you say you never beat him?"

"I do not beat my workers."

From the looks on the faces of the magistrate, the prosecutor, and the missionary, it was clear they didn't believe him.

The magistrate asked him, "Is there anyone who can give direct testimony that you do not beat your workers?"

"My wife," Christiaan offered.

The magistrate shook his head. "The testimony of a wife would carry little weight in this courtroom," he said. "Anyone else?"

Christiaan looked to the back door and saw nothing but a sea of white faces. "No," he said, "no one else." Having resumed his seat, he waited for the magistrate to render his verdict.

Completely oblivious to the throng in the room, the official bent over this papers and wrote for several minutes, occasionally having to forestall his wig from falling onto the pen. When he was finished, he ordered Christiaan to stand.

"Having carefully weighed all the evidence at hand," he said, "I'm afraid that I must side with *Mynheer* Dikkop in this matter. The weight of evidence is clearly in his favor. *Mynheer* van der Kemp, you are an enigma to me. You do not strike me as a man given to rash actions; nor do you strike me as a violent man. However, I have observed unhappily and all too frequently that a man's behavior in a courtroom is at times altogether different from his behavior in his own home. Therefore, unless there is anyone who can speak direc—"

"I can speak on his behalf."

The voice came from the back of the room. The words were spoken in accented English.

Christiaan turned. It was Jama. Kootjie and Karel were by his side.

"And you are . . ." The magistrate seemed intrigued by the black man's English.

"Jama."

"And your relationship with *Mynheer* van der Kemp?"

"I am his partner."

"*Partner?*" The magistrate was clearly taken aback. "You mean you work for him?"

"I mean I work *with* him. We have agreed to work our farm together. I am the one in charge of the workers, therefore I have direct knowledge regarding Christiaan's—*Mynheer* van der Kemp's actions in this matter."

The magistrate ordered Jama to approach the table. "And what has kept you from coming forward until now?" he asked.

"I was not in attendance at Nachtmaal," Jama replied. "When word reached me that *Mynheer* van der Kemp was on trial, I came as quickly as I could."

The missionary returned to Dikkop's side now that he was no longer needed to translate, and Jama took his vacated place beside Christiaan.

"May I speak with *Mynheer* van der Kemp for a moment?" Jama asked.

The magistrate granted his request, then watched in rapt fascination as the two men conversed. His interest escalated when Johanna handed Jama the summons and the black man studied it.

"Do you understand what that says?" the magistrate interrupted.

"Not all of the words," Jama replied, "but many of them."

After a few more moments of consultation, Jama stood to speak.

With a schoolboy grin on his face, the magistrate prepared to listen.

"*Mynheer* Christiaan van der Kemp is the most Christian man I know," Jama began. "Would that all the other settlers were like him. I consider him my brother."

At this the magistrate's wig flew backwards. "And you feel the same way about *Mynheer* Jama?" he asked Christiaan.

"With all my heart," Christiaan replied.

"Go on," said the magistrate.

"If there are charges to be made regarding worker treatment at the farm, they should be directed at me, for that is my responsibility," Jama stated. "As for this man—" he pointed to Dikkop "—he is a disreputable dog."

The prosecutor was on his feet objecting to Jama's characterization of Dikkop.

The magistrate warned Jama to refrain from calling people names.

"All I am saying," Jama continued, "is that this man did indeed work for us for a while. We treated him well. I do not know why he would make up these stories about *Mynheer* van der Kemp, but I do know how he received his beating."

"Can you prove what you are about to say?" the magistrate asked.

"I can," Jama replied. "The reason I was delayed in arriving was so that I might bring these people with me."

Jama motioned to the back of the room. Standing among the farmers were two Khoi, a male and a female.

"This is Dikkop's brother and his brother's wife," Jama explained. "Dikkop's brother beat him severely when he caught his wife and Dikkop in the bushes together."

The magistrate looked at Dikkop.

The murderous look the Khoi leveled at his brother indicated that what Jama was saying was true.

13

Christiaan found himself hemmed in by well-wishers, all of them eager to express their congratulations to the man who had beaten the Black Circuit. There were so many pats on his back he had trouble standing upright. So many men spoke at once he couldn't understand what any one of them was saying. It mattered little. At this point, individual words were unnecessary to express the Boers' feelings. The celebratory din expressed it well enough. The Boers had won one against the British/philanthropist coalition.

On the losing side, Sir Lawrence Thatcher, angrily gathering his papers from atop the prosecutor's table, cast one final predatory glance in the direction of his prey. Christiaan felt like a rabbit that had somehow managed to escape the leopard's jaws.

In a corner of the room stood the tall, beak-nosed missionary, Edward Grey. He looked doubly tall standing by two squabbling Khoi—Dikkop and his brother. Wedging himself between the men, his bony arms and legs in constant motion—holding back one, then the other—he probably would have been more successful trying to keep two waves from crashing into each other. When he thought he had them separated, he allowed himself a sigh for the briefest instant. His shoulders slumped. His eyes closed wearily.

It was a mistake.

Dikkop saw his chance. Catapulting himself past the missionary, he knocked his brother to the floor. While the missionary did his best to pry them apart, they rolled and punched and cursed each other. The commotion attracted the interest of several Boers standing nearby. As they crowded around the grappling threesome, Christiaan lost sight of them.

He acknowledged a few more congratulatory remarks as he searched the room for his family. The sudden rush of well-wishers following the magistrate's verdict had quickly separated Johanna from him. He spotted her at the far end of the courtroom. Her head bobbed determinedly as she spoke to two other women, her hands providing visual emphasis. He didn't wonder what his wife was saying. He would hear it soon enough, accompanied by the same gestures.

Sina and Henry were not in the room. That bothered him. Given Sina's emotional vulnerability when it came to that boy and the fact that Henry was leaving, he didn't want the two of them wandering off to be alone. He looked for Kootjie, to tell him to look after Sina and Henry. The boy was nowhere to be found. He never was when Christiaan needed him.

While searching for Kootjie, something caught Christiaan's attention that brought a grin to his face.

Jama had somehow managed to find himself on the magisterial side of the large mahogany table talking to the wigged magistrate. Christiaan couldn't imagine how he had gotten there unless for some reason the magistrate had invited him—which was likely the case, considering the pleasant reception the court official seemed to be giving Jama.

The magistrate's arms were folded in front of him. While one hand repeatedly raced to the top of his head to halt the erratic slide of his powdered wig, he carried on what seemed to be an enlightening conversation with Jama. From the official's ready grin and the constant nod of his head—which always sent the wig sliding, first forward, then backward—the magistrate seemed enthusiastic over Jama's comments, though Christiaan couldn't make out a single word that passed between the two men.

The brassy grating of a voice close to his ear caused him to wince involuntarily. It pulled his attention back to his immediate vicinity.

"No need to thank me."

The words needed no face for Christiaan to identify their speaker. He turned toward Oloff Klyn.

"I said, 'No need to thank me!'" Klyn shouted again.

"I heard you," Christiaan shouted in reply.

"I would have done the same for any one of our neighbors," Klyn continued. The stern line of his mouth and his unemotional eyes confirmed the statement. He wanted to make clear that his testimony was in no way to be interpreted as a personal favor to Christiaan. "It's a war," he said. "Us against them. God delivered us from the hands of evildoers because we are more righteous."

Klyn's statement brought a grin to Christiaan's face. He tried to suppress it but failed. What amused him was that Klyn's account had placed Jama—a black man—in the role of the deliverer, something he doubted Klyn had intended. But before Christiaan could relay this to Klyn, the older man had turned and elbowed his way out of the room.

The magistrate offered his hand.

Jama clasped it.

94

"It's been a pleasure," said the magistrate. His eyes sparkled with boyish joy. "I've met a lot of men in the course of my life. But not until today have I met a man who surprised me as much as you."

"Is that good?" Jama asked.

"It's wonderful!" the magistrate boomed. His wig lopped crazily to the side. After having fought it all afternoon, he grabbed it by the fistful and pulled it off with a muttered curse. "My apologies—but, yes! My comment was meant as a compliment!"

"Thank you." Jama looked at his hand. In the magistrate's enthusiasm, he had not released it yet, though Jama's hand had gone limp.

"Do you realize . . ." The magistrate looked around him, then stepped closer and spoke in confidence. "Do you realize," he said, "that you put these Boers to shame?"

"How so?"

"With your linguistic skills, son!"

"It has never been my intention to put anyone to shame with my learning."

"Of course, it hasn't!" the magistrate replied. "I'm just not sure you comprehend your situation. You are an intellect living among buffoons!"

"If you say so, sir." Jama looked with concern at his hand, which still had not been released.

"It is God's truth," said the magistrate. "And the real tragedy is that they are too ignorant to recognize the fact themselves."

"It's kind of you to think that, sir," Jama replied. "May I ask you a question?"

"Certainly!"

"May I have my hand back?"

The magistrate looked at their clasped hands with an astonished expression. Color rose in his face as he boomed a good-natured laugh, releasing his grip.

"Thank you, sir," Jama said.

"Just one more thing," said the magistrate.

"Yes?"

"Do you speak Latin?"

Jama shook his head. "I've never been exposed to it."

"Exposed to it . . ." The magistrate listened to the phrase as he repeated it. "That's how you learn? By *exposing* yourself to languages?"

"Yes, sir."

"Interesting . . . Tell you what, Jama—you can come visit me at any time, and I'll expose you to Latin—and Greek and French, if you so desire!"

"That's very generous, sir."

"Not at all!" cried the magistrate. "So you'll come?"

"It's unlikely that I'll be able to take you up on your generous offer."

The magistrate scowled. "Would that van der Kemp fellow object?"

"No! Not at all," Jama said quickly. "It's just that . . . well, I imagine we'll be returning home tomorrow, and it's unlikely I'll be in Graaff-Reinet again anytime soon."

"I see," said the magistrate. "Your voice has a tone of finality about it."

Jama lowered his eyes. "I have some decisions to make."

The magistrate acknowledged his statement with a slow nod. "When you make those decisions," he said, "don't forget what I've told you. You have a remarkable mind. I'd hate to see you waste it."

"Again, thank you, sir. You've been most kind."

With his index finger extended and shaking, the magistrate said, "If ever you need assistance, get a message to me. As I said, you are the proverbial serendipitous treasure in a barren field. Never underestimate yourself."

"I'll remember that, sir."

With a hearty slap on Jama's back, the magistrate passed him by and disappeared through the doorway. Jama found himself standing alone behind the mahogany desk with a grin on his face. What an unexpected invitation! Imagine, being invited to study Latin and Greek with a British magistrate!

The feeling the thought stirred was bittersweet, for he knew he would never be able to accept the magistrate's generous invitation.

Surrounding him, and bouncing from wall to wall, were inarticulate, barbaric whoops and guffaws and shouts. The courtroom was alive with Boer bodies whose faces were drunk with exuberance, mouths hung wide with yellow-teethed laughter. Bodies covered by coarse cloth were pressed closely together. It was a typical Boer celebration. Just as he remembered them.

The only available space in the room was behind the mahogany table, where he stood. There was no rush to occupy it, although he did lose some space as jostling bodies were shoved against the far edge of the table. They scooted it toward him an inch at a time, claiming the territory that had once been the realm of Jama and the magistrate but that now belonged to Jama alone.

Whenever Jama had attended Nachtmaal with the van der Kemps in the past, no one seemed eager to greet him or talk to him. If he initiat-

96

ed a greeting, the Boers usually responded—though often no more than with a grunt. If he struck up a conversation, it was always a brief one. Responses were limited to single-syllable words, quickly followed by an excuse of pressing matters that served to cut the conversation short.

Even now, though he had helped to secure the victory that was the basis for their celebration, few men in the room acknowledged his presence. Those who did, did so with quick looks and not so much as a nod. He received no greetings. No congratulations. No friendly smiles. Just glazed-over glances. The kind of glance a wild animal on a leash would get from them. They didn't want to get too close. Nor were they comfortable as long as he was in the room. He was cut off from the only two people in the courtroom who cared anything for him.

Christiaan was surrounded by well-wishers six deep. And their numbers continued to grow. Jama chuckled to himself. Christiaan hated crowds. He knew his friend had one thought on his mind and that was to escape. From the way things looked, that would not happen for a good while. Even then, he doubted that Christiaan would find any peace until their wagon pulled out of Graaff-Reinet.

Johanna, likewise, was surrounded by her own gender. She, on the other hand, was enjoying herself. Both her hands and her mouth were blurs of motion. At times a belly laugh erupted from her that equaled any man's.

Meanwhile, Jama stood alone. He was reminded anew of why he no longer attended Nachtmaal celebrations. After several years of absence, his reasons had been reduced to logic. There was nothing there for him, he told Christiaan year after year. But now, standing here again, his logic was reacquainted with its companion emotion. It was a hollow feeling. An unplumbable void. In a room crowded with people, with all the noise, all the celebration, Jama felt like a shade dwelling among a throng of humanity.

Wordlessly he made his way through the crowd to the back door. Being invisible, even nonexistent, would not have been as painful. Fully aware of his presence, the Boers parted before him like the Red Sea before Moses—and with as much human affection as those ancient waters. Not until he stepped into the sunlight did Jama feel any warmth.

Maybe it was his imagination, but it seemed that the festive noise coming from the building increased the moment he departed. Jama tried to convince himself it didn't matter to him.

He made his way to the wagons. At present, they were mostly inhabited by slaves, both black and Khoi. He recognized several of them. Two of the black women he had courted, albeit briefly. None spoke to him without his speaking first. When they did, they addressed him as "Sir." They were careful not to look him in the eye, nor did they presume to make casual conversation with him.

Physically, he was one of them. In every other way, he was no more part of them than he was part of the Boers. Here, too, he was alone.

Jama made his way to the van der Kemp wagon. He busied himself with tedious tasks. Stirring the slumbering fire to life. Feeding the horses. Spotting his canvas bag, which he had thrown hastily against the wagon wheel in his haste to get to the trial, he snatched it up and tossed it near a three-legged stool. It hit the ground with a flat thud. He moved to the stool and methodically opened the bag. He removed clothing, food, and utensils.

In the distance a hearty cheer could be heard coming from the courthouse. As still as a cat ready to strike, Jama listened.

Then he pitched the canvas bag mindlessly with all his might.

On her back, Sina stared at the canvas covering and sulked. From her reclined position it appeared to entomb her. She thought it appropriate now that Henry was gone and her life had ended.

The canvas that stretched from rib to rib was yellow with age. It quivered and shuddered with every rock and rut encountered by the wagon's wheels.

Sina's brow rippled as a word lay at the edge of her memory, just beyond its grasp. It was Kootjie's word. One that he learned during his studies. She remembered how at the time she was revolted by it, but somehow now it seemed fitting. What was that word?

For days he had tried to frighten her with it. He would pop up from a hiding place, his eyes squinting, his fingers curled, his voice straining to achieve a ghoulish effect. But what was it he said? What . . . was . . . it?

Then it came to her. She rolled her eyes at the remembrance, especially since the memory served to remind her of her brother's obnoxious pranks. But the word was appropriate, if not its meaning—*sarcophagus*. Or, as Kootjie would say with fingers curled and snarling lips, flesh eaters.

Morbid. But that's what this wagon was to her. It was her sarcophagus. A sarcophagus on wheels. On the other side of these canvas walls people were alive. They had something to live for. Not Sina. Not since yesterday, when Henry's wagon turned north toward the high veld. She had watched his wagon grow smaller until there was nothing to see. Not even a column of dust rising from the horizon. And with each passing minute, life drained from her wounded heart, leaving her empty, bereft of all feeling, all hope.

Warm pools formed atop her eyes and spilled over, streaming down her temples. And when her canvas sarcophagus lurched violently to one side as the wheels slid into a rut, she sobbed uncontrollably.

"What's that sound?" Christiaan asked.

From the wagon seat Johanna turned and squinted into the dark interior of the wagon. "It's Sina," she said. "Weeping again."

Christiaan sighed the frustrated sigh of a father who wanted to do something but who knew there was nothing he could do. "How long before she gets over Henry's departure?"

An incredulous expression formed on his wife's face. "Do you want the exact hour, or is the day close enough for you?"

"She is going to recover, isn't she?"

Johanna shrugged sadly. "She has no choice."

Christiaan started to say something. He interrupted himself long enough to shout at Kootjie, who was supposed to be leading the oxen. The boy was daydreaming again, and the wagon was headed for a deep rut in the road.

After they cleared the rut, he commented, "You say she has no choice. It almost sounds like you're sad the Klyn boy is leaving. You weren't hopeful for the two of them, were you?"

"What's to be hopeful about? A Dopper for a husband? And a Klyn at that? Don't be ridiculous. I'm just sad for Sina."

"What if I sent Kootjie to retrieve Karel? Do you think De Buys would let the boy travel with us for a day or two?"

"Karel has his eyes set on the van Aardt girl."

"I wasn't trying to match them up," Christiaan replied. "Karel has always had a way of lifting Sina's spirits." He nodded his head in self-affirmation. "That's what I'll do. I'll have Kootjie ride out to find the De Buys wagon. They should be four, maybe five, hours behind us, don't you think?"

"Karel's not with them," Johanna said.

"He's not?"

Johanna shook her head. "He's traveling with the van Aardts."

Christiaan sighed heavily. "So what do we do now?"

"I'll go back and sit with her," Johanna said. "And you can go talk with Jama."

Christiaan's face scrunched up with a puzzled expression. "We just broke camp a couple of hours ago. I talked with him then, and he didn't have much to say."

"You chatted with him; you didn't talk."

"Chat, talk—what's the difference?"

Looking away in exasperation, she said, "You really don't know, do you?"

"Know what? That there's a difference between chatting and talking?"

Muttering more to herself than to him, Johanna replied, "The more I live the more I'm convinced God made men's heads so thick just to test the patience of women." To Christiaan she said, "Something is troubling Jama. Talk to him. Find out what it is. Find out if we can help."

"Troubling him? Really? I hadn't noticed."

Johanna started to say something, then stopped herself. She pursed her lips as though to hold the words in until they dissolved on her tongue. Then she said, "Just talk to him."

With a nod, Christiaan called to Kootjie and had him bring the wagon to a halt. The two of them climbed down from the seat. While Johanna clambered into the back of the wagon, Christiaan mounted a trailing horse and rode out to catch up with Jama, who was riding ahead.

14

With a horse under him, the cloudless blue sky overhead, and plenty of space all around him, Christiaan felt at ease for the first time in days. This was where he belonged. Not in the middle of a courtyard throng. Not in a packed courthouse. Out here where the air was fresh and there was plenty of room.

As he thought back on the events of Nachtmaal, even now they seemed like something he'd dreamed. It had felt so unnatural for him to be the object of everyone's attention, first at the night meeting—thanks to Pfeffer—and then at the trial. He shuddered at the remembrance. He promised himself that the next Nachtmaal would be different. No more sitting in the middle of the courtyard—he would stay on the fringes. And no more—well, there was nothing he could have done to prevent the trial. He simply prayed he would never be in the center of a controversy like that again.

The wind rushed past him as his horse galloped in easy rhythm. He felt content to be out of Graaff-Reinet. Too much Nachtmaal was not a good thing.

Jama came into sight; turned, saw him coming, and reined his horse around to wait for Christiaan to reach him. Was it Christiaan's imagination, or was Jama slouching on his mount? Maybe Johanna was right. Maybe something was troubling him. Christiaan thought back over the last few days. Had he said or done something to offend his friend? After a moment's reflection, he couldn't come up with anything.

He and Johanna had thanked Jama for his part in the trial. At the earliest possible moment they broke away from the revelry at the courthouse and went in search of him. Finding him alone at the wagon, they literally gushed over him until he begged them to stop. So that couldn't be what was troubling him.

A man who was not given to emotional displays, Christiaan couldn't help but get emotional when it came to Jama. If something was indeed troubling his friend, he wanted to know about it. Maybe Klyn or one of the others had said or done something to offend him. No, Christiaan dismissed that thought too. Jama was not the kind of man who would readily say something about an offense. But then neither was he one to brood over it either.

As Christiaan approached, the mere presence of his friend warmed him. It wasn't something he felt every day when he saw Jama. But for some reason, at this particular moment, all of their years together, all of their experiences, their conversations, their common struggle, their laboring side by side, the long night hours together on commando watch —all these things coalesced into one feeling that Christiaan defined as true friendship. He could never have asked for a better partner than Jama. And he certainly couldn't imagine what life would be like on the frontier without him.

"Anything wrong?" Jama asked.

"Just thought I'd ride with you awhile. That all right?"

There was an uneasy hesitation in Jama's eyes. Then he said, "This is as good a time as any." Pulling his horse around, he set off toward home.

So Johanna was right. Jama's cryptic reply indicated he had something on his mind. Christiaan rode beside his friend, allowing him the time he needed to formulate his thoughts into words.

The horses plodded across a bush-strewn veld, down a small ridge, and paralleled a stream. For an hour they rode. Then half an hour more. Not a word was spoken between them. Even for a man of few words, an hour and a half was long enough to think of a beginning sentence.

Christiaan cleared his throat. "Did Johanna and I tell you how grateful we were that you came to Graaff-Reinet?" he asked.

Jama gave him a look that seemed to question his mental faculties. "Repeatedly," he replied, his voice heavy with concern.

Christiaan tried not to notice. "I just wanted to make sure you knew we were grateful."

"You made yourselves clear."

"Good." They rode a few steps, and he repeated, "That's good. We just didn't want you to think . . ."

Christiaan never finished his sentence.

Fifteen minutes passed.

"That reminds me," Christiaan said with half a laugh. "I keep meaning to ask you, then forget . . ."

"What's that?"

"How is it that . . ." He stopped, thought for a moment, then began again. "In Graaff-Reinet. At the trial. When you showed up with Dikkop's brother and his wife, how was it that you knew Dikkop was the one bringing charges against me? I didn't even know who it was until the trial started."

Jama smiled craftily. It was a good sign. A glimpse of the old Jama.

"When Kootjie and Karel first arrived . . ." Jama paused. The smile faded from his lips. His eyes darted from side to side, as though he had been distracted by a thought or a memory. When he took up again, the smile didn't return. "When Kootjie and Karel first arrived, my thought was to assemble some of the workers. To take them with us to Graaff-Reinet to testify on your behalf. Naturally, they asked questions about the nature of the charges against you. I told them as much as I knew, saying that I didn't know who had made the charge."

The grin returned.

"They knew exactly who was bringing the charges. I learned it from them."

"No!" Christiaan exclaimed. "How?"

"Do you remember Chinde, the worker who came to us six months ago from the van Doorn farm?"

With a nod, Christiaan indicated he remembered.

"Chinde has a sister who lives at the missionary compound. The way Chinde tells it, Dikkop was going all around the compound, boasting of the charges. Said he was soon to be a rich man with many cattle."

"So why didn't Chinde come to me—to us—with this information?"

Jama looked askance at Christiaan. "You don't want to know."

"What do you mean, I don't want to know? Of course I do!"

Shrugging, as if to say that any pain attached to the knowledge was invited pain, he said, "They heard about Dikkop's beating. They thought you did it."

"*Me?*" Christiaan shouted. "When did I ever beat any of them?"

"Never."

"Of course, never. So how can they come to such a conclusion?"

It was elementary for Jama. He seemed surprised that Christiaan couldn't figure it out. "You're a baas," he said simply. "It's commonly known that baases beat workers. It was easy for them to believe Dikkop's story."

"As it was easy for that missionary, Grey, to believe it," Christiaan concluded. "So how did you find out the truth?"

"I pressed them to find out all I could about the charges and Dikkop's life after he left us. One of them remembered Dikkop saying he was going to live with his brother on the edge of the Xhosa village. So I took a chance that a short side trip to visit Dikkop's brother might prove profitable. It did."

Christiaan grinned and shook his head. "I've got to tell you, I'm certainly glad you're on my side. I'd hate to think of what might have happened to me had you sided with the British, or, worse yet, if you were the prosecutor!"

Christiaan laughed alone, his comment having the opposite effect on Jama. Any trace of his good nature drained from his face. With eyes set steadfastly forward, Jama forded the stream.

On the far side, they waited for the wagon. Not until it had safely forded did they ride on ahead. A half hour passed before either of them spoke again.

"You know how women are," Christiaan said. He waited for a response. There was none. "Johanna thinks something is troubling you."

Jama gave no indication he heard.

"Of course, I told her that if something was troubling you, I'd know about it because you would tell me." His sentence was thrown out like a fishing line, hooked and baited. It came back empty. Christiaan concluded he had no recourse but the direct route.

"Did something happen back at Graaff-Reinet that I don't know about? Did Klyn say something to you?"

Jama pulled his horse to a stop. For a long moment he studied Christiaan. Finally he said, "No . . . well, yes, Klyn said something to me."

"I knew it!"

"But"—Jama cut him off—"that's not what is troubling me." He spurred his horse forward.

Christiaan caught up with him. "Tell me what it is! Maybe I can help."

"You can't. And I'm reluctant to tell you."

"Reluctant? Why?"

"Because it will hurt you. And Johanna, and Kootjie, and Sina."

"Hurt us? That's ridiculous. You would never intentionally hurt us."

"That's my dilemma," Jama said soberly. He looked like a man bearing a great weight that, if he did not unload it soon, would crush him. "I don't want to hurt you," he said softly, "but I cannot go on this way any longer."

Christiaan leaned over and took his friend by the arm. In his doing so, the two horses bumped together as they walked, pressing the men's legs between them. But Christiaan had learned through raising his children that sometimes a touch was needed. There was something about physical contact that created a link that could not be as easily ignored as words or a stare.

"Jama," he said, "if something is troubling you, I want to know it. Friend to friend. Then we can deal with whatever consequences might come."

Jama looked into his eyes, testing them for sincerity. Apparently he found in them the assurance he needed, for he said, "I'm leaving."

Two words. Little did Christiaan realize the power of two simple words until now. With two words his whole life was threatened. Two words and he was about to lose his closest friend.

"Leaving? Where? For how long?" The questions were a reflex action, for he knew the vexing answers to his questions before he even asked them.

With the issue finally out in the open, there was nothing left for Jama to do but speak his mind. His words flowed quickly, clearly, giving every evidence of having been rehearsed a hundred times. "I have no wife," he said. "I have no God of my own to worship. I live among a people who do not honor me—naturally, your family being the exception," he quickly added. "I walk among the settlers like a leprous man. I simply can't continue on this way any longer."

Christiaan's mind raced, searching for answers. Wife. God. Honor. Leper. He desperately wanted to believe that if he could somehow come up with adequate answers to each of these things, Jama wouldn't go away.

"Well . . . a wife would be easy," he stammered. "There are plenty of young women on the nearby farms—and, naturally, Johanna and the children would welcome her into the family."

"Slaves," Jama said. Ignoring the current law that designated them as workers, he called them what they really were. "Slaves, whose only concern is the shine on their baas's shoes, or plucking the baas's chickens, or feeding the baas's pigs. What kind of a mate is that? I want a mate I can converse with, confide in, argue with. Take Johanna, for instance—would you have been attracted to her if she didn't have a single worthwhile idea in her head?"

"It's the ones that find their way to her tongue that vex me," Christiaan said with a chuckle. Then, seeing the earnestness on Jama's face, he hastily added, "I can see your point, but surely there are women—"

"Not here," Jama said. "Not in the colony."

"Then where?"

Jama pulled his horse to a stop, giving evidence that what he was about to say was not going to be pleasant for Christiaan to hear. "On the other side of the river."

"The Fish River?"

Jama nodded.

"But what are you going to find there? There's nothing but—" Jama's intent hit him like a musket ball. "You're going over to the Xhosa?" Christiaan cried.

"They are from Nguni stock," Jama said. "Just like me."

"But they're the enemy!"

Jama's eyes hardened, as though he'd just seen something he didn't want to see. "The enemy?" he exclaimed. "The enemy? For years you have been telling everyone they're people just like us. That we can learn to live with each other. And now I discover you have always thought of them as the enemy?"

"I didn't mean it like that! All I meant was—"

"I understand exactly what you meant," Jama said, his voice hard and cold.

"Jama, listen to me—"

"Let me tell you about your enemies," Jama said. "Your enemies treat me like a human being. Your enemies accept me for who I am. It's your friends who act like I don't exist, who don't want to be in the same room with me, who are threatened by the fact that I have abilities they don't have. I'll tell you about your enemies! In that courtroom in Graaff-Reinet, only one person had the decency to speak with me—the British magistrate! Did you know that he invited me to return and study Latin and Greek with him? Of course, you didn't, because you were too busy surrounded by your friends, who will never accept me no matter what I do or what I say."

Jama's outburst left Christiaan speechless. A dam of emotions and thoughts had burst, and there was no stopping the outpouring until it had run out.

"Furthermore," Jama continued, "while you were at Nachtmaal, I carried on a conversation with the Xhosa king."

"He came back?" Christiaan cried with alarm.

"Only to fish at the river. Do you want to hear something funny? He pities me!"

"Pities you? Why?"

"Because of all the things I told you. He made me realize that I have nothing . . . nothing!"

Now Christiaan's ire was raised. "What do you mean, nothing? You have—"

"Everything I have is because of you, not me. Do you think the other farmers would let me stay on the land if it wasn't for you? Do you think the merchants would sell to me if it wasn't for you? Do you think for a moment that our good neighbors come calling on me? Of course not! They come calling on you! You have a wife. You have the family. You have your precious covenant with God, and even in His eyes I'm only acceptable because of my relationship to you!"

"Now wait just a minute—"

But the emotions had not even begun to slow. "Like I said, I don't want to hurt you or Johanna or Kootjie or Sina. But I have to make my own life. I can't continue to live among people who see me as the enemy."

With great effort, Christiaan held back his own emotions. It would do no good for two dams to burst at the same time in the same place. "All right," he said, "you've spoken your mind, and I can understand how you must feel. And now that it's out, we can talk about it and see if we can come to some mutual—"

"There's nothing to talk about," Jama said with great resolve. "This has nothing to do with you. This is my life. It's my decision, and it's been made."

"Jama, don't be foolish. The Xhosa—"

"Are my people. They will respect me."

Christiaan nodded patronizingly. "I can understand why you might think that—"

"Give my love to Johanna and the children," Jama said.

"Wait! You don't mean you're leaving right now?"

"Good-bye, friend."

Jama spurred his horse to a gallop and was soon out of sight.

For the remainder of the journey home it was as though a great cloud of gloom hung over the van der Kemp wagon. Christiaan thought of a hundred and one different ways to convince Jama to stay, but he never had a chance to use any of them.

By the time they reached their house, Jama was already gone.

15

Pfeffer was late. That made Christiaan nervous.

Tardiness was uncharacteristic of the man. There were few things you could say about Pfeffer, so nondescript was he. The man could walk into a nearly empty room, and no one would notice. Yet, if anyone took the time to notice, he would always be found there. He was quiet. A good husband and father. Hardworking. These were attributes of Adriaan Pfeffer, as was punctuality. In all the years Christiaan had ridden commando with him, he had never known Pfeffer not to be there before him. Tonight Pfeffer was late. And it set Christiaan's nerves on edge.

He tried not to make too much of it. Thinking too much on things had been his problem of late. His head hurt from thinking too much. But then there had been a lot of things to think about—too many things at once for a man.

Jama's leaving, for instance.

Things had not been the same since he left. And no amount of effort on Christiaan's part to establish a normal routine seemed to ease the pain of Jama's absence. A day did not go by but that, for no apparent reason at all, Christiaan's chest would hurt, as though an invisible hand had reached inside and squeezed his organs together. The pain was of sufficient strength to pull him away from his work. When it did, Christiaan found that if he stood straight, took several deep breaths, turned his thoughts toward God, and reminded himself of God's remaining blessings, the pain would eventually go away.

Temporarily. It always returned. Three, four, sometimes five times a day. Sometimes the ache was so strong he would think it wouldn't go away this time. But it always did, just as assuredly as he could count on its always returning.

As for the work itself, Kootjie was doing his best to assume some of the farm responsibilities that once belonged to Jama. But though his body was nearly that of a man, he was still just a boy. He couldn't possibly do the work of Jama. No one could.

The workers mourned the loss of Jama as well. Several of them had left to find work on other farms or in Grahamstown. Much of Christiaan's day was spent hiring and training new workers to replace them. It was a task for which he felt ill suited. He hadn't done it for years. This had been one of Jama's jobs.

As much as Christiaan missed his friend during the day, night was even worse. At supper. During evening Bible reading and prayers. And especially when the inevitable comments were made: "Do you remember when Jama said . . ." and "How about the time Jama . . ." With each remark Christiaan would smile and nod. It was good for Johanna and Sina and Kootjie to talk about Jama. He tried not to let on that every one of their fond reminiscences felt like a stake being driven into his chest.

The latter portion of each evening, during the hour or so it took Johanna and Sina to complete their after-dinner chores, had been a time of casual conversation for Jama and Christiaan. Sometimes they sat in the light of the house's front door; other times they walked under the stars. That time of day had always been a special time, a time of personal revelation, of laughter, of dreaming, not too dissimilar from the special sharing that married couples do while lying in bed in the darkness just before they go to sleep.

Now Christiaan had no one to talk to after dinner.

The first week following Jama's departure, Kootjie made an effort to fill Jama's chair. But few words were exchanged between father and son; awkward comments were answered with equally awkward replies. Christiaan didn't know which was worse, the painful attempt at conversation or the uncomfortable silence that separated each attempt.

By the second week Kootjie began excusing himself after supper, at first sporadically, then regularly. Christiaan didn't say anything to him. In fact, he was relieved. There was nothing for them to talk about. Kootjie was still a boy.

Now he watched the moon crest the eastern horizon like a great china plate, its light coating bushes, trees, rocks, and ground with silver dust. At night the frontier took on an ominous quality, both beautiful and deadly. With light at a premium, night travelers grew more dependent on auditory warnings of danger.

To survey his surroundings, Christiaan first cocked an expert ear. A slight wind rustled the bushes, nothing more. It was almost too still.

Atop his horse, which was growing increasingly skittish, Christiaan twisted first to one side, then the other. Straining his eyes, he peered into the night. Still no sign of Pfeffer. He let out an exasperated grunt. His emotions were teetering between concern and alarm. Should he ride toward the Pfeffer farm? No, not yet. If Pfeffer was coming from a different direction and had been delayed, Christiaan's presence would alarm Angenitha unduly. He decided to wait a little longer.

As he waited, his mind turned to Sina. She was another problem that had been causing him to think too much. It had been nearly a month since they returned from Nachtmaal. Yet the Sina that had gone with them to Nachtmaal was not the Sina who returned. The person who did return was a brooding, irascible twin. This new Sina was civil toward no one and outwardly malicious toward her brother. Her mother was ready to toss her down the well, and some nights Christiaan was tempted to assist.

It was beyond his reasoning ability to understand how such a transformation could have taken place in such a short period of time. She couldn't still be upset over the departure of the Klyn boy, could she? Yet, he had no other ready explanation for her behavior. What about the trial? It surely must have been difficult for her to see her father subjected to all the venomous darts thrown his direction.

Christiaan nodded as he pondered that. He'd have to discuss it with Johanna to see what she thought.

Just as he was about to let the matter drop—for he was thinking too much again—another thought occurred to him. Maybe something had happened to Sina at Nachtmaal of which he was totally unaware! Something emotionally devastating.

The more he considered this latest idea, the more he loathed it, for it spun a variety of wicked scenes in his mind, each succeeding scene worse than the previous one. Collectively, the images deposited a fermenting anger in his belly that, if they were true, demanded some form of retribution. At first, the images involved a faceless perpetrator. Gradually, however, features began to appear. All of them belonged to Henry Klyn.

Now the images in his mind took on different settings and themes. Confrontation, first with Sina, then with Henry and his father, if he had to track the two of them all the way to the Nile River. Then whipping, scourging, retribution, revenge for what that boy had done to his daughter.

The more Christiaan thought on these things, the more the leavenish lump of anger grew inside him. First thing in the morning, he would discuss this with Johanna. Then with Sina. He would find out the truth.

The snorting of a distant horse announced an approaching rider. Frontier instincts instantly banished all other thoughts in Christiaan's mind. The snort had pricked his senses to heightened awareness, giving priority to the auditory, while the others tingled in anticipation, ready to jump to the forefront should they be called upon.

There was no haste in the sound of the hooves. Probably Pfeffer. Still, Christiaan didn't relax. The number of approaching hooves was wrong. At least two horses. He was expecting only Pfeffer. What was more, they were not coming from the direction of Pfeffer's house.

He turned toward the sound and peered into the darkness. Two shadowy figures emerged. The black shape of one of the riders resembled that of Pfeffer, wide at the hips, shoulders slouched. But who was with him? His son, Conraad? No, the second rider had the bearing of a man, tall, slender, with a shoulders-back confidence that suggested a sense of authority.

Frontier wisdom dictated caution, and Christiaan placed his hand on his musket.

"Christiaan!" Pfeffer's voice hailed him heartily.

Guardedly, for he still did not know the identity or intent of the second rider, Christiaan returned the hail. "You're late," he exclaimed, keeping his eyes trained on the unknown man.

"I'm to blame for that," said the stranger.

It was a voice Christiaan did not recognize. Deeper than Pfeffer's, with a note of authority in it. Christiaan's fingers rubbed the smooth wood of the musket stock as he watched the two riders draw near.

"I brought someone along to help us pass the night," Pfeffer said cheerily. "He wanted to meet you, and when I mentioned that I ride commando with you, he asked if he could come along. I hope you don't object."

Keeping his eyes fastened on the unknown horseman, Christiaan did not reply.

The riders halted a few feet away. The stranger's eyes and nose were concealed deep in the shadow of his broad-brimmed hat. A short dark-brown beard, with gray streaks highlighted by the moon's silver light, extended from ear to ear.

Probably sensing Christiaan's reticence, the stranger said, "Name's Retief, Piet Retief from Winterberg."

"He's the field-commandant there," Pfeffer added.

"I've heard of a Retief from Grahamstown," Christiaan said.

"One and the same," Retief said.

Most men on the frontier had heard of the trials of Piet Retief. A man of Huguenot descent, he had grown up on a wine farm in Stellenbosch. Like so many farmers, he left the Cape Town region for the frontier to get away from British rule, only to have it follow him like a pesky, unwanted dog.

In Grahamstown, Retief made a name for himself as a man of letters who also possessed superior manual skills. He became a widely discussed topic of conversation among the farmers when, having contracted to build the magistrate's offices in Grahamstown, he suffered one setback after another and was bankrupted. This was soon followed by several clashes with the British authorities, with Retief defending the right of the farmer against the intrusive actions of the missionaries and courts in what became known as the Black Circuit. Yet, through his personal tragedy and adversity, Piet Retief had remained in general esteem a man of unquestioned integrity.

"Forgive me if I'm intruding," Retief said, "but I wanted to meet the man who lays no claim to being Moses." A half grin stretched beneath the shadow of his hat.

Christiaan felt his face growing warm. "You were in the courtyard," he said.

Retief's hat brim rose and fell as he nodded. "And in the courtroom. God was looking down on you. If it had not been for your black friend, I'm certain the outcome of the trial would have been different."

Others had made the same observation, with the difference that they usually stopped with God's blessing and failed to mention Jama's part in the trial. Somehow, coming from Piet Retief's mouth, the observation took on added significance. Here was a man who had been through similar trials. Better than anyone else, he could understand what Christiaan had been through.

"Tell me," Retief said, "is there any chance of meeting your black friend here tonight?"

The request stung, an unintentional jab at an open wound.

Christiaan looked to one side lest his face betray his pain. "Not likely," he said softly. "Jama has chosen to strike out on his own." He offered no further explanation.

Pfeffer, knowing the full story of Jama's departure, pursed his lips as though to keep from offering explanation of his own. He did not presume to tender commentary on a matter that clearly was Christiaan's personal concern.

Pfeffer's silence was appreciated by Christiaan.

Retief, too, seemed to sense the sensitivity of the question. He changed the subject. "Shall we ride?" he suggested.

The three men rode quietly into the darkness beside the Great Fish River, night sentries keeping watch for any intrusion of the Xhosa on Boer lands. A heavy mist snaked upriver, filling the valley and spilling over the edges onto the high ground, covering it like an undulating, milky carpet. Eddies of mist swirled around the horses' hooves as the riders passed through it, keeping a sharp eye out for any movement. Once again, tensions on both sides of the river were charged and unstable, prompting renewed patrols of night commandos.

Except for river sounds and an occasional howl of a dog, the night was quiet. Retief and Christiaan rode next to each other, speaking in hushed tones. Pfeffer seemed content to ride in silence and listen.

"After having suffered the capricious attack of the missionaries firsthand," Retief said, "do you still think there is a place for us here?"

Christiaan had no idea what *capricious* meant, but he understood enough of the sentence to formulate an answer. "When I was young, my father and I stood on the hillock next to where we were to build our house. My father was a practical man, not given to outward displays. Maybe that's why I remember this particular incident so well. There was a stiff breeze that day. He stood into the breeze, his eyes closed, his face lifted toward the sky, and his arms spread out like eagle's wings. I remember his shirtsleeves flapping in the wind. Maybe it was my youthful imagination, or just the fact that my father was doing something that was so unlike him, but I would not have been the least surprised had the wind picked him up from atop that hill and lifted him into the clouds.

"With a strong voice he said, '"Lift up thine eyes round about, and see: all they gather themselves together, they come to thee: thy sons shall come from far, and thy daughters shall be nursed at thy side. Then thou shalt see, and flow together, and thine heart shall fear, and be enlarged; because the abundance of the sea shall be converted unto thee . . . and they shall show forth the praises of the Lord. All the flocks of Kedar shall be gathered together unto thee, the rams of Nebaioth shall minister unto thee: they shall come up with acceptance on mine altar, and I will glorify the house of my glory."'"

The hooves of three horses beat time in the mist while Retief and Pfeffer waited reverently for Christiaan to conclude. It was one of those personal sacred moments that should never be rushed, and they seemed content to wait for it to play itself out.

In hushed tones, Christiaan said, "My father was claiming the land. For him. For me. For all generations of van der Kemps to follow. It will take more than a few skirmishes with the Xhosa and the British to make me forsake that claim."

16

When she stepped outside the house, Sina didn't pause to take a last look at the place that had been her home all her life, so strong was the pull to journey northward and join Henry. With a bundle of clothing and food for several days under one arm, she stole away into the night's dark shadows.

God was favoring her plan, she thought, as she ran under cover of fynbos bushes and outcroppings of rock. With Jama gone, her escape was made possible. Father was on commando, Kootjie was tending the herd, and a short time ago a frantic-eyed worker had appeared at their doorway, appealing for a helping hand with some disturbance at the workers' quarters. No one was there to help except Mother, so she went to handle the crisis.

Sina concluded that God must have stirred up a little mischief among the workers to facilitate her escape. After all, God alone knew of her plans.

The idea to join Henry was conceived during the ride home from Nachtmaal. Riding in the back of the wagon, jostled from side to side, immersed in a black well of despair, Sina tried to imagine life without Henry. The longer she dwelled on that unbearable thought, the deeper she sank in the well until she was so low she could sink no further. It was in the blackness of her despair that she came to a sudden realization.

She was in hades!

The realization came as no surprise. How else could life without Henry be described? This cruel separation from the man she loved was condemning her, for the remainder of her days, to dwell on earth as the walking dead, beyond feeling, beyond hope, bereft of anything good or pleasurable.

However, if comprehending her lot in life came as no surprise, the resulting feeling did. There was no sense of panic. No feeling of dread, or injustice, or anger. In fact, there was no feeling at all. The moment she realized her isolated destiny, a gray dullness washed over her. She became numb. Unfeeling and uncaring. It was a strangely comforting sensation.

As she was adjusting to her emotionless existence, the wagon came to a halt. Her mother climbed down from the front seat and joined her in the back.

Sina closed her eyes. She didn't want to acknowledge her mother's presence. All she wanted to do was luxuriate in the emotionless gray sea that had enveloped her. For the first time in days her head didn't feel as though it was going to burst from the buildup of anger and frustration.

"Sina, dear . . ." her mother said softly.

Warm fingers touched Sina's arm. The touch was an annoying sensation. To Sina it was a confirmation of the incompatibility of her new existence and the world of the living.

"I know you're grieving," the voice from the other world said, "and I think I know why."

There was a pause. Sina made no attempt to acknowledge or communicate with the other side.

"You may not believe it now," said the voice, "but this is all for the best."

Like a thorn, the words reached between the realms and pricked Sina. Anger, which had been laid to rest, stirred.

"There will be other boys."

Another prick.

Sina tried to ignore it. But try as she might, the second jab caused her anger to take on new life. It fought to rise to her defense. She held it back.

"You know," the voice chuckled, "your father and I are somewhat relieved. We were a little concerned that you were attracted to Henry, him being a Dopper and all. Believe me, this is for the best. In a few days, the aching you feel will start to fade. Give yourself some time. Someone better will come along. You'll see."

Fully awake, fully charged and ready to do battle, Sina's anger selected barbed words to use in her defense. What did an old woman know of love? It was beyond her mother's ability to understand the depth of her love for Henry! Time meant nothing to true love. Eons could pass, and her love for Henry would be as strong as it was at present.

As for someone better coming along, there *was* no one better than Henry! How dull could her mother be? Couldn't she see that her daughter had fallen into a well of hopelessness and that no one—no one!—could pull her out except Henry?

Sina's eyes fluttered. Her lips compressed. Her fingers began to draw up into fists as the barrage of defense swelled inside her, ready to burst forth in all its fury.

Then, as quickly as her emotions had escalated, they eased. Sina's hands relaxed as serenity infused her body. Her eyes closed peacefully; her peace was so complete it bordered on joy. Her lips, which had a moment earlier been pursed, not only relaxed, but she was forced to suppress a grin.

Henry alone could pull her out of this well of despair.

Henry alone.

Sina realized she had a choice. She could live the colorless life of the walking dead, or she could reach up for Henry and let him pull her back into the realm of the living.

Reach up.

Let Henry rescue her.

It was at that moment Sina decided to leave home and join Henry. She would reach up. Then, when Henry saw how much she loved him, that she was reaching out to him to save her . . .

She decided to tell no one. Certainly not her parents—they would only make it harder for her to leave. And not Karel.

This was a more difficult decision. But the more she thought about it, the more she remembered how much Karel disapproved of Henry, for reasons she still failed to understand. Besides, Karel would be concerned about her being out on the frontier alone. So, because she could not count on Karel's complete support, she decided not to tell him either.

Her plan was to sneak away at night. She would go to Grahamstown, where she would find a family that was traveling north to join the Trichardt expedition of which the Klyns were a part. Once she and Henry were together, she would send a message to her parents letting them know of her location. Her actions would finally convince them of her love for Henry.

And so the plan was born, in the back of the wagon, in silent solitude, with her mother beside her. It was carried out on the night a frantic worker appeared at their door, taking her mother out of the house and giving Sina the freedom she needed to make good her escape.

With the moon rising to her right, Sina eased her way toward the Grahamstown road. She walked close to the edge and tuned her ears to any sound of horses and human conversation. She certainly didn't want to stumble upon her father and *Mynheer* Pfeffer on commando. She tracked each approaching bush as she made her way along, ready to leap behind the closest one at the first indication someone was near.

Heightened anticipation made her jittery. Reaching inside her bundle, she felt for and found a kitchen knife, the only protection she carried with her. Not wanting to appear childishly afraid, even to herself, she had decided not to walk down the road carrying a knife but to keep it concealed in her bundle. Still, she gripped it readily, her hand buried in the folds of cloth.

At first she jumped at every movement and every sound—a mouse darting across the road, the rustle of a branch, the screech of an owl—until after only a short time she was nearly worn out by her fears. Refreshing herself with a deep breath, she instructed herself to move cautiously but to be more relaxed about it.

Sina found it next to impossible to follow her own instruction.

The moon shone brightly, providing an adequate amount of silver light for her to make her way safely. But it also deepened the shadows. Was it her imagination, or were they a deeper shade of black than she'd ever seen before? Deep enough to be a presence?

Sina cautioned herself not to give her imagination free rein. Still, she couldn't shake the feeling. The shadows were alive. They moved. And not just the shadows of the fynbos bush branches in the wind but a conscious movement. Gliding purposefully. Pausing, waiting, when she stared at them directly, then gliding again. Always purposefully, always on the fringe of her vision.

Her heart began to beat wildly. Her chest constricted, as though attempting to keep her madly beating heart from leaping from her body. She gripped tightly the handle of the knife, pulling the blade from under its cover, no longer caring if she appeared childish. The readiness of the weapon gave her little comfort. What good was a knife against a shadow?

She began to run. Forward. Toward Grahamstown. The thought of retreat entered her mind, but she couldn't go home. She'd rather die than go home.

Killed by shadows.

All of a sudden the thought struck her as humorous. Worse than childish. How does one die by shadow? What injury could a shadow cause to a person? She stopped running. Stare straight at them. *They're only shadows! What harm can a shadow do to you?*

Moving to the middle of the road, with her hands on her hips, Sina stared into the darkness toward the east. Low shadows stretched away from her, some of them swaying with the breeze. From her own feet a shadow stretched. Exaggerated. Elongated. Looking ridiculously silly with elbows jutting out and the shape of a knife blade clutched in one hand.

Sina laughed at herself and her infantile fear, watching her own shadow as she moved first one arm, then the other, then danced a silly jig.

She spun around to face the shadows to the west.

Her laughter caught in her throat.

The feeling of *presence* was strong on this side. Had she come face-to-face with a flesh-and-blood person, she would not have been as startled. The shadows here were deeper, stretching—reaching—toward her. They jerked from side to side, straining to reach her, to grab her feet, her ankles. For a moment she thought she could hear them groan with exertion.

She jumped back and pointed the knife at them.

What good is a knife against shadows?

Farther from the road the shadows grew even darker. The presence felt stronger. The shadows moved, not with the wind but with rational purpose. Gliding. Stopping. Waiting. Gliding. Southward.

Sina ran north, in the opposite direction. She stayed on the far eastern side of the road lest the reaching shadows from the west side trip her up, get hold of her, pull her into their darkness . . .

Clutching her bundle and the knife, she ran frantically. Toward Grahamstown. Her thoughts grew frenzied. Multiplying. Conflicting with one another. Cramming her head with fears, real and imagined. Rational and irrational.

She couldn't run all the way to Grahamstown, could she? Certainly she could. What was the alternative? If she slowed down, the shadows would catch up with her. But she would have to run all night. Not a problem. Her running was fueled by her fear, a commodity of which there was no present shortage of supply.

Sina pulled up short—not wanting to, but she had no choice. A large tree, one of the few in the surrounding area, rose massively on the eastern roadside, casting its shadow across the entire breadth of road. To continue on, she would have to pass through its shadow.

What other choices did she have? Return home? Even in her fear, that was unthinkable. Go around it? That would mean stepping from the road. Stepping into the shadows. That thought alone caused her to feel shadows all around her legs and feet, clutching at her as though hands were reaching out of the ground.

She decided to continue forward.

To cross the tree's shadow.

If she were facing a black leopard, Sina wouldn't have approached it any more warily. Knife extended, she inched her way toward the shadow's edge. When she was within reach, she slowly stretched the knife forward, its blade alive with flashes of moonlight. The tip touched the edge of the tree shadow. With a quick thrust, she pushed the blade into the shadow and yanked it back again.

Nothing happened. Her rational thoughts rallied. *Of course nothing happened! It's just a shadow.*

Sina wanted to believe her rational thoughts. Still, she wasn't quick to enter the shadow. She crept toward it, the toe of one foot edging closer. She could see the road on the other side, basking in moonlight. One leap and she would be there. One leap.

Taking a deep breath—she didn't know why; it just seemed the thing to do—she jumped toward the moonlight on the far side. The shadow fell upon her.

Sina was in the shadow for only an instant before she emerged on the other side. Her worst fears were not realized. She had envisioned the shadowy tree arms clutching her, the shadowy branches entangling themselves in her hair, trapping her in their grip, refusing to let her go. Should that have happened, she was sure that she would have died before sunrise—maybe not from any direct physical harm the shadow might have done to her but from going insane, such was her fear of being captured by a shadow.

And although the worst she could think of had failed to materialize, she would be deceiving herself if she tried to pretend that nothing happened as she passed through the shadow. There had been a *tangible* darkness. A chilling sensation. Not just a coolness on the skin but a chill that penetrated skin and flesh and bone and marrow and touched the invisible recesses of her being, causing her very soul to shiver.

Sina backed away from the shadow and continued her journey.

A wagon path broke off from the road to the right. Suddenly, Sina realized where she was standing. Why hadn't she seen it sooner? The tree should have given it away.

The tree marked the entrance to the Klyns' old house. *Mynheer* Klyn had planted it there for that very purpose. How many times had she heard him—or Henry, for that matter—say, "Head north [or south] until you come to a large acacia tree. It marks the entrance to our farm. Then head east, and you can't miss it"?

Henry's home. Deserted, yet still it represented familiarity and safety for the night.

Sina took the wagon road east. The rising moon lighted the middle of the road, pushing the shadows aside.

17

Jumping across the threshold, Sina entered the abandoned Klyn house and shut out the shadows behind her. She stood motionless until her eyes grew accustomed to the darkness. Gradually walls became visible. They stretched and faded into inky black corners. The room—what she could see of it—was devoid of furniture. With hesitant steps, she moved further into it. The shuffling sound of her shoes against the wooden floorboards echoed all around her.

The room had a manly scent to it. Stale pipe tobacco was predominant, mingling with the heavy odor of cooking grease. Her thoughts turned to Henry and his father. It comforted her to know that she was now sheltered by the very walls that had once sheltered her beloved Henry.

Having made her way to a far corner, Sina slumped against the wall and slid to the floor next to the large stone fireplace. Compared to the van der Kemp dwelling, this house was a mansion. She drew a candle from her bundle and lit it. Instantly, the ceiling flashed with color— bright yellow wood planks supported by red stinkwood beams, just like Klaarstroom—or so she had heard.

More than once when the Klyn house was mentioned, her father was quick to point out the similarities between it and his ancestral home. Just as quickly, he would also predict that someday the van der Kemp settlement would boast of a similar house, though he never said so in a boastful way. He was merely reminding others—and himself—of his dream, as though his words were a deposit on a future certainty. In her father's mind the yellow wood ceilings and red stinkwood beams of the van der Kemp settlement already existed; others just couldn't yet see them as clearly as he.

Sina could understand his commitment to the dream. If the house he imagined looked anything like the interior of this room in the Klyn house, it would indeed be something to be proud of.

Highlights of the room danced to the flicker of the lone candle—the exaggerated texture of the whitewashed walls, the play of light against the cratered surface of the fireplace stones, the jittery dance of her overstated shadow in the corner behind her. The display of so much color and texture fascinated and frightened her all at the same time. It reminded her that she was alone in someone else's house.

She dripped wax on the floor and set the base of the candle in it until it hardened, something she never would have done had anyone still lived in the house. Then, curling up into the corner, she waited for morning to come, when a greater light would illumine the room from the outside.

In one sense, she was disappointed. She had hoped to travel much farther on the first night. But in another sense, she was proud of herself. From the moment she conceived her plan to join Henry, she had never doubted the wisdom of it, only her courage to carry it out. In her more lucid moments, she had doubted she could leave home without telling her parents. She had anguished over how she would negotiate northern passage once she arrived in Grahamstown. These were the parts of her plan that had never seemed real to her. Until tonight.

Already she had accomplished the most difficult part, that of leaving home. Having done that, she believed the rest would follow, and she would soon be with Henry. She was sure of it. All in all, it was a good start.

With a sigh, Sina snuggled into a ball, using her bundle for a pillow. She felt safe. Her legs ached, more from tension than from the exertion of the journey, she imagined. Reaching down, she pulled her toes upward to stretch the back muscles of her legs. Grimacing against the pain, she held them for a moment, then released them. It proved to be a mistake. Like a shrinking piece of wet cloth in the sun, her back leg muscles retracted and cramped into a knot.

With a stifled yelp, Sina snatched up the candle and stood. With moans and winces she hobbled about the room to work out the cramps. Gradually, the knots lessened their grip. Still, she walked the room in circles, her head lowered, looking at her legs as though the cramps would be unable to return as long as she kept vigilant watch.

When she was sure they were gone, she looked up. There was a face in the window!

Her heart froze. Her hand flew to her throat.

The image in the window mimicked her movement. Then she understood why. It was her image.

And what a sight it was—her eyes were wide with fright, her hair flew this way and that in a tangled mass, she was gripping the candle as if it were a lifeline that kept her from slipping into the netherworld.

A sheepish grin appeared on the face in the window, not only for having scared herself but because her fright revealed her lack of sophistication. She was not accustomed to glass windows and reflections. How Henry would laugh if he could see her at this moment!

All of a sudden, Sina felt a pang of unworthiness. Yes, Henry would have laughed, but would he also have been embarrassed for her? This was only a single incident. In what other ways might she embarrass him with her lack of sophistication?

She shuddered at the thought of embarrassing Henry, imagining the way he might gaze upward in a silent plea for someone worthy of him. Bemoaning her frontier upbringing, she wondered if Henry could really love someone who was so backward. She pondered ways she could teach herself to be sophisticated. Before setting out in the morning, she would wander around the Klyn house, imagining what it would be like to live in it. Then, when she arrived in Grahamstown, she would study the ladies, learn their ways, adopt their tastes, imitate their walk, copy their . . .

A grunting sound from outside intruded on her self-instruction.

Sina caught her breath. Her hand, cold as ice and equally as immobile, gripped the candle in fear. Her heart rattled her chest with each thump.

The grunt had sounded more human than animal. Loud. Half-surprise and half-moan, as though someone had been punched in the stomach. She held her breath and listened for another sound. She heard only the soft buffeting of the wind against the windowpane.

Had the noise been close to the house or far away? It was hard to tell. And the more she forced herself to remember, the further she seemed to push the memory away, until she began to doubt that she had really heard anything at all. Maybe it had been an animal. Or the slap of a bush against the house. Or even the scrape of her shoe on the floor.

Sina stared out the window, hoping to spy something that would confirm the sound. But all she could see was her own reflection, staring back at her, her features quivering with the shaking of the candle in her hands . . .

The candle!

Sina blew out the flame, berating herself for not dousing it sooner. Instantly, her reflection disappeared, and she was cast into darkness, a darkness that matched the world outside. Again she scolded herself for standing so long at the window with a lighted candle. By now, everything on the frontier with eyes had seen her!

Stepping to one side to shield herself from further exposure, Sina craned her neck to look out into the night. She must know if she had attracted anything—or worse, anyone.

Gradually, her eyes adjusted to the outside world, illumined by the lesser light of the sky. A long rectangular structure blocked her view of the land to the right. It was black and featureless, the horse stable, if she remembered correctly from previous visits. But if it had blocked her view, than it had also blocked her from view to anyone on the other side of it.

As for the rest of the frontier, she was not so fortunate. Immediately in front of her and opening up as far as she could see, the view was unrestricted. The landscape rolled haphazardly toward the horizon, furbished with random clumps of fynbos bushes, their branches waving in the breeze like hands waving—no, signaling—trying to get her attention, to warn her! But of what?

The answer followed close on the heels of the question.

Shadows! The fynbos bushes were trying to warn her that the shadows were back! They had returned! Or maybe they had never departed in the first place.

Movement caught her eye.

Stare at the shadow, and it will go away!

Sina stared at the shadow.

It stared back at her!

She jumped back from the window. Her shoulder blades pressed against the wall, she trembled uncontrollably. Involuntary whimpers escaped her lips. The shadow had eyes! It had looked at her!

Now it was in her mind. Unwanted. Intrusive. A scene captured by a single glance. Emerging from behind the stables, skulking, black as pitch, turning toward her . . . that's when she saw them! Eyes! The shadow had eyes!

Sina wanted to run. Get out of the house. Flee. But how could she? The moment she stepped over the threshold she would once again be in the realm of the shadows. Her next impulse was to curl up in the corner and close her eyes and wait for morning. Wait for the sun. Let it battle the shadows. Vanquish them. Then it would be safe to go outside again. Let them have the darkness; her ally was the light of day.

Let them have the darkness.

Sina looked around her. A frightful realization gripped her with a frigid hand. She was standing in darkness. It surrounded her! Darkness so profound that she could feel it pressing against her, uniting her with the dark world beyond the windowpane. How easy would it be for a shadow to pass through the glass from dark to dark! For all she knew, it was coming toward her right now, with only a thin pane of glass separating them. Ready to reach its dark hand through the glass and . . .

Sina jumped away from the window, instinctively holding out the candle to ward off the shadow's attack. But without a flame, the candle was nothing more than a stick of wax with a wick, a weapon without ammunition.

The tinderbox was in her bundle beside the fireplace. Could she reach it in time? Could she spark a friendly flame before the shadows came for her? How close were they?

Light the candle first, then look.

She took a step toward the tinderbox. Then stopped. That wouldn't work! When the candle was lit, all she was able to see was her own reflection. She had to look first, to check the progress of the shadows, then light the candle.

Sina didn't want to look out the window. She knew she had to, but she didn't want to. Already her legs were drained of energy. What if she saw those eyes looking at her again? Would she be able to keep from fainting?

An unnerving image came to mind. What would happen if she looked out the window and the shadow with eyes was directly on the other side of the glass staring back at her? Inches from her face?

She had to steady herself against the wall. *Don't borrow terror,* she told herself. *Just look out the window. Then get the tinderbox. Look out the window, then get the tinderbox.*

Summoning up as much courage as she could muster, she leaned toward the window. She had to look. She forced herself and braced for the worst.

At first Sina saw nothing but undefined black shapes. Her heart fluttered. Her hands trembled so violently she nearly dropped the candle. Slowly, all too slowly, indistinct shapes with blurry edges came into focus.

There was no face staring back at her. No shadow with eyes ready to grab her. What she saw, however, was much worse. Sina steadied herself against the windowsill. The danger was greater than she had imagined. Her life was indeed in danger; and not only her life but the life of everyone else on the frontier.

She stared in horror as not one, but many, black shapes materialized from behind the stables. Not shadows. Shadows would not have been as threatening. But men. Xhosa. Xhosa warriors!

They moved silently, heads low, spears protruding into the night sky. At the moment they seemed unconcerned with the house. Did they know it was uninhabited? They must, for they appeared to be using the Klyn property as a staging area. Hundreds of them. Maybe thousands! Massing for an attack.

To Sina's immediate relief, she saw no one coming her direction, and she whispered a silent prayer to God. Not only had she not been detected, but she had not lit the candle again. If she had, it would have been nothing less than a lighthouse announcing her presence.

A steady stream of warriors continued emerging from behind the stable. They must have been crossing the river at a point somewhere beyond the structure. They gathered in a gully nearby, one that could be seen from the house but hid them from the rest of the frontier. Sina thought their caution was excessive. Who would possibly see them at this time of night? Who would be out . . .

Her father! He was riding commando tonight! She had to warn him about the Xhosa!

Just then a noise came from the back of the house. It sounded like a warped door being pushed open, scraping against the floorboards, slowly, cautiously and slowly. Footsteps followed. Soft footsteps, the kind a skulker would hope would go undetected. Had a Xhosa warrior spotted her after all? Had he sneaked around back, anticipating her escape?

Sina's eyes darted from side to side, looking for a way out. There was none. She was trapped. The skulker blocked any escape out the back of the house; and she couldn't go out the front door—the bulk of the Xhosa warriors were there. All it would take was one of them glancing in the direction of the house . . .

Bouncing on the balls of her feet, her hands limp at the wrists, flapping in front of her, Sina fought her rising panic. Her body was anxious, desperate to do something, but her mind was providing it with no decisive direction. So she bounced and flapped and whimpered softly.

The footsteps in the house stopped, and her heart froze. Hearing nothing was worse than hearing footsteps. At least with footsteps she could gauge the intruder's progress. How does one gauge silence? Silence meant surprise was at hand, and, considering the circumstances, surprise would be deadly.

Sina bolted for the front door, doing nothing to muffle the sound of her steps. With all her might, she yanked it open. Hinges creaked at the sudden strain. The door crashed against the interior wall.

Then, instead of running into the night, Sina fled back into the room. She snatched up her bundle and candle and ducked into the large fireplace, tucking herself tightly into the corner closest to the door.

As she had expected, the banging door brought a renewal of footsteps, the pounding, hurried footsteps of a pursuer. They ran to the door, then out the door.

Just as Sina had hoped.

But her relief was all too fleeting.

The footsteps came back. The door slammed shut. She was alone in the room with her pursuer. She could hear his labored breathing.

Crouched in the corner of the fireplace, Sina pressed her back against the stones. Pursing her lips, she fought back the whimpering sounds that had escaped her mouth earlier. Her entire body trembled, and there was nothing she could do to stop it.

The footsteps shuffled, turning this way and that. Almost contemplative. He was looking for her!

Tears filled her eyes. She hadn't fooled him at all! She would never see Henry again. She would die in his house. Huddled in the fireplace. Run through by a Xhosa assegai.

She lamented her failed strategy. She should have known the ploy wouldn't work. There was too much space between the house and the stable or the bushes. It would have been impossible for anyone to cover that much ground in such a short time, and her pursuer knew it! What other conclusion could he come to than that she was still in the house?

His feet shuffled again. What was he waiting for?

It was then that Sina remembered the knife, and she decided she wasn't going to die without a fight. Keeping her eyes fastened on the edge of the fireplace, expecting her attacker to appear at any moment, she slipped her hand into her bundle, felt for and found the blade. Silently she drew it out and waited, its tip pointed outward. The instant he appeared, she would attack. First with the knife, then with clawed hands, her feet, her teeth—if she had to be cornered like an animal, she would act like a cornered animal.

The first movement she saw, however, was not that of a human being. It was light. Appearing through the windows. Splashing the floorboards with orange and yellow hues. Its sudden appearance puzzled her. The light was too inconstant to be the sun rising; it flickered and danced and jumped about . . . like fire!

Then the footsteps made a new sound, the hurried sound of retreat. They grew less distinct as the intruder raced to the back of the house. A door crashed open. That was the last time Sina heard footsteps.

But now there was a new danger. The firelight in the windows grew increasingly bright. Smoke began to gather among the beams, from there threatening to fill the room from top to bottom.

The odor of burning wood turned into the acrid, throat-burning pain of black smoke. It filled Sina's lungs and stung her eyes. All attempts to stifle her coughs proved futile. In a matter of minutes, she was doubled over, coughing convulsively.

She had to get out of the house. At least with flesh and blood, her knife had a chance; against smoke and fire, it was useless.

Sina scrambled from the fireplace and ran through the house, hoping that there were fewer warriors at the back of the house than there were in front. By now, every room she passed through was engulfed in smoke. She had to feel her way with one hand, while she covered her mouth with the back of the hand that still held the knife.

Having never been in this part of the Klyn house, she had no idea where she was going. She stumbled into a room thinking she might find an exit in it. Crouched low to keep her head below the billowing smoke ceiling, she felt for a doorway, scanning the edges of the floor for a threshold. There was none.

She did manage to find a window. Pressing her face toward the smoked glass, she cleared a pane, hoping to see what, or who, was waiting for her outside. To her surprise, the moonlit landscape was surprisingly clear. She saw nothing but fynbos bushes and dirt between her and the horizon.

Suddenly, a huge brown blur brushed by the window. Sina gasped. The suddenness of its appearing and its closeness startled her, causing her to take what amounted to a bite of smoke, so thick was it around her. She gagged and coughed.

The sound of horse's hooves accompanied the blur. Through watery eyes, Sina caught a glimpse of the rider.

Karel! It was Karel!

Sina tried to call out to him. His name lodged in her throat, held back by a series of bone-jarring coughs. She pounded on the window.

"Karel!" she gasped. "Karel. It's me!"

She stumbled into the hallway, choking, coughing, feeling her way. The smoke above her took a direction, picking up speed. It had found an exit! She followed the direction of the smoke. And there it was! A back door, gaping open, smoke pouring out through the top.

Sina reeled out the door. Her legs gave out just past the threshold. She crumpled to the ground but without lowering her head. Her eyes were fixed on a horse and rider, galloping away from her into the night.

"Karel!"

Her voice was no more than a whisper. He was too far away. He would never hear her. As her chest and throat constricted with one convulsive cough after another, Sina prayed in her mind, *O God, make him turn around and see me! Please, make him turn around!*

A whoop from Xhosa warriors rose nearby. They had spotted Karel. Several dozen of them took chase.

Helplessly, Sina watched as he fled before the Xhosa. He was safe, she knew. On foot, they would never catch him. But they were now between him and her, and even if he did happen to look back, even if he knew she was here, he would be unable to return for her.

Behind Sina the crackling of the fire was now accompanied by deep groans and creaks as beams began to give way. She struggled to her feet. At least Karel had drawn the attention of the Xhosa warriors away from the house.

With knife in hand and her bundle tucked under her arm, she staggered into the night. Collapsing behind a knot of bushes, she lay in the dirt and coughed and watched, helpless, as Karel rode off in the direction of her home.

18

The easterly breeze off the Indian Ocean was warm, the night pleasant. A typical December night on the frontier. Christiaan rode between Piet Retief and Adriaan Pfeffer, nodding his head contemplatively as his aristocratic visitor spoke of trekking.

"We propose to establish a settlement on the same principles of liberty as those adopted by the United States of America," Retief said.

Christiaan's head rose. He looked squarely into the eyes of the one speaking.

"It's not inconceivable!" Retief insisted. "Think of it! Our own country, based upon the truths we hold most dear. Our own men leading it. Leaders of our choosing, not magistrates who are thrust upon us by a government thousands of miles away, who know nothing of South Africa other than what the clerics and missionaries tell them."

"You have to admit, Christiaan," Pfeffer said softly from the other side, "it is an intriguing idea."

Christiaan withheld comment until he heard more.

"Unlike the colonists in America," Retief continued, "we are not attempting to wrestle land away from England. Let them have this territory!" He made a broad, dramatic sweep with his hand, as though he were brushing the land aside. "We're not advocating a revolution. We're advocating an exodus—to a promised land of our own, where we will live by the laws of God!"

"An exodus . . ." Christiaan tested the words and did have to admit to himself they sounded inviting.

"It makes sense," Pfeffer said.

"What about the Canaanites?" Christiaan asked.

Retief smiled. "You mean those who currently dwell in our promised land. The Zulus."

Christiaan nodded. "How can we be sure that we are not trading one enemy for another?"

It was Retief's turn to nod. "I understand your concern. I share it. Two things come to my mind in way of response: First, the reports that we are receiving from those who have preceded us indicate that the land is largely uninhabited, and there is plenty of room for everyone who wants to live there. Second, I will do everything in my power to see that, before we settle in a place, we sign a treaty of friendship with our neighbors. It is not our intention to displace anyone from their land."

"That makes sense," Christiaan said. "I would agree with that approach."

Pressing his point, Retief leaned forward in his saddle and spoke enthusiastically. "It does make sense," he agreed. "We despair of saving this colony from the evils that threaten it. The vagrants who once worked our fields now crowd our streets and clog our courts with fallacious charges. Nor do we see any prospect of peace or happiness for our children in a country thus distracted by internal commotions."

"That is my greatest concern," Christiaan said. "My children. There are enough natural frontier dangers to threaten them. We don't need to create more by pitting man against man."

"My point exactly!" Retief cried, visibly delighted that Christiaan was involving himself in the discussion. "Like you," he said, "I'm a man of peace. My desire is to live quietly with my neighbors and my government."

"Piet was a strong advocate of emancipating the slaves," Pfeffer offered.

"A barbarous system," Retief added. "As you know, for years many of us advocated ways of bringing about its end, such as setting all slave children free at birth. My complaint is not in the abolishment of slavery but in the vexatious laws which have been enacted to bring it about."

Again Christiaan nodded contemplatively. He found himself doing so every time the learned Retief used a word with which he was unfamiliar. This time it was *vexatious*. By the way the man spat out the word, Christiaan took it to mean bad.

"We complain of the unjustifiable odium which has been cast upon us by interested and dishonest persons, under the name of religion—whose testimony is believed in England to the exclusion of all evidence in our favor. And we can foresee, as the result of this prejudice, nothing but the total ruin of the country!"

Odium. Christiaan nodded contemplatively.

Retief paused and studied his reaction. "So you agree with us?"

The question caught Christiaan off guard. He was still trying to figure out what *odium* meant. "Agree with you?" he stammered. "In principle, I suppose I do."

"Then you'll trek with us?"

A sharp intake of air combined with a wince and a slow shake of his head indicated Christiaan's hesitancy.

"Do you still believe there is something here for you?" Retief asked.

Before Christiaan could respond, there was a cry in the night, accompanied by the growing thunder of horse's hooves. They were being hailed from a distance.

The three men pulled their horses around to face an unknown rider. Pfeffer readied his musket.

"Hold!" Christiaan said to his neighbor as he squinted into the darkness. "It sounds like Karel!"

"A friend?" Retief asked.

Christiaan nodded. "Young man. Reliable."

His terse reply signaled the instant change in mood shared by all three men. A lone rider, this late at night, pounding across the open frontier could mean only one thing—trouble.

Christiaan felt his stomach muscles tense. His breathing grew shallow as his pulse quickened. Retief's right hand worried his horse's reins. Pfeffer shifted uneasily in his saddle and hefted his gun.

"*Mynheer* van der Kemp!" Karel cried. "Thank God, it's you! And *Mynheer* Pfeffer!" He glanced at Retief but didn't acknowledge him.

"What's wrong?" Christiaan asked.

"The Xhosa are attacking!"

"How many?" Retief asked, taking charge.

Not knowing who it was who was asking the question, Karel did not answer readily. With a puzzled expression, he looked Retief over.

"He's with us," Christiaan assured the boy.

"He's a field-commandant from Winterberg," Pfeffer added.

"Thousands of them!" Karel answered. "Maybe tens of thousands!"

"Are you sure?" Retief demanded.

"Karel doesn't exaggerate," Christiaan said on the boy's behalf.

Retief nodded. "We must be sure what we're up against—whether this is an isolated skirmish or an all-out war."

"This is no skirmish," Karel replied. "They've attacked all the settlements north of here. I was sent to warn everyone to the south. The Xhosa are headed this way."

"How do you know that?" Retief asked.

This time Christiaan did not intercede for the boy. Piet Retief was clearly in charge, as he should be. He had the experience and the skill. In order to lead, he needed information that, hopefully, Karel could supply.

"I saw them myself," Karel said. If he was intimidated by the brusqueness of Retief's questioning, the boy didn't show it. "They're massing at the old Klyn place."

"The house is empty," Christiaan said.

"Maybe," Karel corrected him.

"You think someone is living there?" Retief asked.

Karel hesitated. "I don't know," he said uneasily. "When I started out, I had no intention of stopping there, because the Klyns have trekked north. But as I was riding by, I thought I saw a light in the window. So I stopped."

"Was anyone there?" Christiaan asked.

Shaking his head in bewilderment, Karel replied, "I think so, but I can't be sure."

"What do you mean?" Retief's voice was gruff. He clearly did not like ambiguous answers when lives were at stake.

"I'm confident I saw a light," Karel explained. "And when I went in the house, I think someone ran out, but I never saw them. Before I had a chance to look further, the Xhosa charged the house and set it on fire. I barely escaped myself."

Retief stroked his beard. He glanced at Christiaan as though he was reminding himself of Christiaan's earlier endorsement of the boy. Weighing the endorsement against the report, he tossed out a question for everyone. "Do you have any idea who might have been in the house?"

Neither Christiaan nor Karel nor Pfeffer could think of anyone.

"The light might have been the Xhosa," Retief suggested. He then concluded, "Well, if someone was there, either they escaped or they're dead by now." His conclusion seemed logical to Christiaan.

"Van der Kemp," Retief barked, "your house is closest, am I right?"

"My house, then Pfeffer's."

To Karel, Retief said, "You ride with Pfeffer. Warn all the houses south of here. Tell every man and boy who can carry a gun to assemble at the van der Kemp house. We'll make our stand there."

Karel looked to Christiaan.

"Do what he says," Christiaan said.

"If it's all the same to you," Karel replied, "I'd prefer to fight. How about if Kootjie rides and I stay with you?"

"We don't have time for a discussion, boy!" Retief barked, pulling his horse hard about in the direction of the van der Kemp settlement. "Do as you're told!"

Christiaan concurred. "Kootjie may not be at the house," he said in a conciliatory tone. "If he isn't, we've wasted valuable time. Get the word out as quickly as you can, Karel, then come back to the house. We can use your gun."

Karel seemed satisfied with Christiaan's advice. He and Pfeffer rode out at a gallop.

Christiaan and Retief hurried in the direction of the van der Kemp place. Christiaan's mind turned to Johanna, Sina, and Kootjie. With his horse laboring beneath him, the landscape rushing madly by, he prayed to God that the Almighty would keep his family safe for another day.

Johanna was pacing in front of the house when Christiaan and Retief arrived. Never before had Christiaan seen his wife so agitated. Her face was drawn and tear-streaked. It seemed she moved, every part of her, with no purpose other than to be doing something—her hands taking turns wringing each other; restless feet pacing or at times merely shifting her weight from side to side in what looked like a demented dance. Her arm and hand gestures were frantic, her head jerking in the direction of imagined sounds. Her lips babbled incessantly to herself, to God, to no one in particular.

When she saw Christiaan coming, she had run toward him, and that filled him with alarm. Johanna never ran, never hurried. She scoffed at people who were always in a hurry. "There's time enough for everything," she would say. "Some people will hurry themselves into early graves and then boast that they got there sooner than everyone else." Yet here was the woman who never hurried, running toward him. Laboring. Weeping. Mumbling.

"Praise be to God Almighty!" she exclaimed. "Praise be to God!"

Christiaan flew off his horse.

Retief pulled up beside him and remained mounted, scanning the horizon for signs of the Xhosa.

Had her husband not been a sturdy man, Johanna surely would have bowled him over. Burying her head in his chest, she wept uncontrollably, her words nearly unintelligible. "You all . . . dear God, I prayed . . . the workers last night . . . how can I . . . with Sina gone . . . and Kootjie . . ."

"What about Sina and Kootjie?" Christiaan cried. "Has something happened to them? Where are they?"

Johanna lost all control. Sobs rolled unhindered. Her knees buckled so that Christiaan had to hold her up.

This was not the woman he had known for all these years. Her condition unnerved him. "What about Sina and Kootjie?" Christiaan repeated, his voice louder, more forceful.

Johanna gave no evidence he was getting through to her. She trembled and sobbed, but she didn't answer.

"Let's get her into the house," Retief suggested.

Christiaan nodded. He attempted to disengage himself in order to turn Johanna toward the house. Her grip on him was fierce.

"Johanna," he said softly, "you've got to tell me what has happened. The Xhosa are coming!"

Somehow, amid the sobs and tears and gulps of air, Johanna managed to respond. "I know! I know!"

"Then you know we must prepare for them!"

A babbling litany tumbled from her lips. "First you, then the workers, then Sina and Kootjie . . . the house."

Christiaan ignored him. "Look at me!" he shouted at Johanna.

Her head remained firmly planted against his chest.

"Look at me!" Christiaan shouted again. He managed to break the hold she had on him. "Look at me, Johanna!"

This time she lifted her head. The sobbing eased.

Christiaan could see something of the familiar Johanna in her eyes. "Where are Sina and Kootjie?"

Johanna sniffed. "Gone . . ." she wailed.

With fits and false starts, Christiaan managed to extract a narrative of the night's events from his wife.

The longer Johanna spoke, the more she regained her rational thought. She told him how she was called to settle a disturbance among the workers. Word had been received from kin living among the Xhosa on the far side of the Fish River. The news was that the Xhosa were about to attack. According to the rumor, it was not going to be another of the hit-and-run raids that occurred so frequently along the border. They were planning a full-scale war.

The disturbance broke out when the workers began discussing what they would do when the Xhosa attacked. Three prominent opinions emerged, each having its own volatile spokesperson: There were those who wanted to flee before the attack. A loyal minority wanted to stay and fight alongside the settlers. A third element, composed of disgruntled rabble-rousers, advocated storming the van der Kemp house themselves and presenting the van der Kemps to the Xhosa as a peace offering. Within this last group there was a split—those who wanted to present the van der Kemps alive and those who wanted to hand over their dead bodies.

In the course of the discussion, angry words escalated into shoves, which then escalated into swinging hands and fists, which were soon replaced with farm tools used as weapons. In the past, Jama would have been called to settle similar disruptions long before they ever got this far.

However, Jama was no longer there. And the situation got out of control before anyone thought to run to the van der Kemp house for help.

The dispute turned out to be more than Johanna could handle. The moment she arrived, those who advocated siding with the Xhosa attempted to seize her, while those who remained loyal tried to protect her. If it had not been for two men who shielded her by taking blows to their own bodies, she probably would not have escaped at all.

She ran back to the house, and it was then she discovered that Sina was missing. After searching for her inside the house and calling for her outside, Johanna could only conclude that she had been abducted by some of the hostile workers, possibly even killed.

Not knowing where to find Christiaan and fearful for her life, Johanna ran to the hills where Kootjie was guarding the herd. When she told him what had transpired at the workers' compound, he became enraged. Despite his mother's tearful pleas to wait until his father returned at daylight, Kootjie mounted his horse and rode in the direction of the workers' compound to rescue his sister. That was the last time Johanna had seen her son.

Having prayed fervently the entire way home, Johanna fully expected to find Sina waiting there for her with a simple explanation for her earlier absence. But Sina was not at the house when Johanna returned. Neither was Kootjie. Instead, the doors and shutters stood gaping open, and their belongings were strewn everywhere.

No sooner had she reached the threshold than she was spotted by a band of the hostile workers. Somehow she managed to secure the shutters and barricade the door before they reached her. For the remainder of the night, she sat in the dark in the middle of her ransacked house, pointing a loaded gun randomly at the door and windows while men pounded on the house with farm tools and fists, shouting curses and muttering murderous threats. Not until the first light of dawn did they finally give up and go away.

At the time, Johanna didn't think anything could frighten her any more than she had been frightened while sitting alone in the dark under attack. She was wrong.

The silent aftermath was worse. It was maddening.

Sina had been missing all night. Kootjie should have returned long before this from his attempted rescue at the workers' compound. And Christiaan had yet to come home. Johanna knew that the longer she waited, the slimmer were his chances of ever coming home. It was an established fact that the men who rode commando on the nights of previous attacks were the first to die. The Xhosa made it a point to kill them before they could alarm the other settlers.

Johanna wandered in a daze among the ruins of her household—she saw a yellow dress that belonged to Sina; a single boot that as of spring was too small for Kootjie; Christiaan's spare hat, smashed flat in the mud, its wide brim jutting upward at an awkward angle. Under a bleak gray sky, Johanna concluded that her entire family had been killed, that she alone had survived, just as thousands of Xhosa warriors were about to descend upon the settlement.

"And then I looked up . . ." Fresh tears filled Johanna's eyes as she spoke. "At first I thought that I had lost my mind . . . that I wanted so much for you to still be alive that I was imagining you . . ." She hugged him fiercely. "But you are alive . . . you are alive, aren't you?"

"They're coming."

Retief spoke the words quietly, evenly, almost as though he were commenting on the weather. But it wasn't gray clouds that gathered on the horizon; it was a storm of black-skinned warriors on foot, arrayed in ranks, coming toward them.

Christiaan helped Johanna onto his horse. He joined her, and the three made their way the short distance to the house.

Once again the experienced field-commandant took charge. "Guns! Ammunition! Powder! Christiaan—you start loading. Johanna—see that all the windows are secured."

Christiaan shuffled through the mess of personal belongings littering the floor. Ordering guns and ammunition was one thing; finding them amid the rubble was another. He upturned mounds of clothing, pots and pans, bedding, and a scramble of papers and personal items, ever mindful that just beyond the walls the Xhosa were descending upon his house.

He could find none of the things he was charged to find, which didn't surprise him, since guns and ammunition would be the first things the ransackers would have taken. Still, he kept searching, hoping they might have missed something. When he had gone through the house once and found nothing, he began again, this time in fear that he had passed over something, not in haste but by distraction. Despite the impending attack, Christiaan found it difficult to concentrate on the task at hand. He kept thinking about Kootjie and Sina.

Suddenly three heads reacted as one to the sound of an approaching horse, and all defense preparations ceased. Ears cocked in the direction of the open door.

Johanna was the first to the doorway.

"Kootjie!"

Christiaan was right behind her. He saw two boys sharing a horse.

Karel rode in front; a battered Kootjie clung to Karel's waist. They stopped at the doorway, and Christiaan helped his son down from the horse. The boy's face was bloodied and bruised, his eyes half closed. When his feet hit the ground, he found it hard to stand. Christiaan held him up.

"I found him beside the road just beyond the workers' compound," Karel said, glancing toward the Xhosa. They had halted their march and were forming an extended line that dipped down toward the river. There was no telling how many of them lay out of sight.

"Get the boy inside," Retief ordered. To Karel he said curtly, "As for you—on your way!"

With another glance at the Xhosa, Karel said, "You need me here."

"We need a hundred more men here!" Retief shouted. "Round them up!"

"He's right, Karel," Christiaan said. "One more won't make any difference."

Still Karel hesitated. He glanced past Christiaan into the house. With a worried, pained expression he said, "Sina?"

Christiaan pursed his lips. Kootjie must have told him. Unable to find sufficient words to convey his combination of worry, hurt, and disappointment, Christiaan answered with a grim shake of his head. His voice trembling, he added, "The best thing you can do is to get help. Now go!"

Only with great reluctance did Karel ride off.

"Karel! Thank you!" Johanna yelled after him, holding Kootjie in her arms. "Bless you! And may He keep you safe!"

They assisted Kootjie into the house and onto the floor. "Workers . . ." he mumbled. "They jumped me . . . no sign of Sina."

Retief interrupted. "God willing, we'll have time for explanations later. At the moment we have the Xhosa to contend with. Christiaan, did you find any more guns or ammunition?"

"None."

"Kootjie," Retief said, "where's your gun?"

"The workers took it."

"So that leaves us two," Retief said to Christiaan. "Yours and mine."

Christiaan walked to the open doorway. He peered out at the line of Xhosa. As they had the time before, he could see them herding his cattle toward the river.

"We can't make a defense," he said. "There are too many of them."

"I concur," said Retief, silently acknowledging that the decision meant abandoning the van der Kemp house and cattle and lands to the Xhosa. "The boy can ride with me; your wife with you. Maybe we'll find the situation more favorable at the Pfeffers—"

Holding up a hand, Christiaan interrupted him. "Not yet," he said. "I hope to see someone I know. A friend. I'll be back soon."

He stepped out of the house toward the ranks of Xhosa.

"I'm coming with you!" Retief said, grabbing his gun.

Christiaan pointed at the weapon. "Leave that here." When Retief began to object, he added, "Even if we do need it, it wouldn't do us much good now, would it?"

Conceding to the logic of a hopeless situation, Retief handed his gun to Kootjie.

Addressing his son, Christiaan asked, "Can you travel?"

Wincing back the pain, Kootjie struggled to his feet. "I can fight."

"That's good to know, should we need you," Christiaan said. "But for now, I want you and your mother to take the horses in back of the house. Wait for us there. Be ready to ride."

Kootjie began to say something.

His father cut him off. "Just do as you're told! If anything should happen to us, I want you to take your mother away from here, understand?"

Hefting the gun, Kootjie said, "But I can—"

"If anything happens, get your mother away from here!" Christiaan shouted, more forcefully than he'd intended.

Kootjie nodded submissively.

"I'm counting on you, Son," Christiaan said softly. He looked to Johanna. Their eyes met. There wasn't time to say all the things he wanted to say, that needed to be said. So he didn't try; he simply looked into his wife's eyes. In that look, he expressed and received her love, and he knew she understood.

Adjusting his hat, Christiaan van der Kemp stepped toward the Xhosa ranks with a strangely quiet but steadfast Piet Retief at his side. To reach the Xhosa they had to step over the aftermath of the night before, the van der Kemps' personal belongings that littered the landscape.

As before, three Xhosa adorned with leopardskins and feathers broke ranks to meet them.

"Do you see your black friend?" Retief whispered.

"No." Jama's absence produced in him mixed emotions. On the one hand, Jama might well assist in securing a peaceful resolution to the crisis as he had done before. On the other hand, Christiaan didn't know how he would react to seeing Jama in Xhosa clothing, especially if he was dressed as a warrior.

Christiaan came to a halt opposite the Xhosa chief. The man hadn't changed from their last meeting, except for the look in his eyes. It was more confident. The look of a man with secret knowledge, a man who was about to negotiate knowing that he did so from a superior position.

"We meet again," Christiaan said.

It wasn't until that moment that Christiaan realized he had no one to translate for him! What had he been thinking? The chief gave no indication that he understood Christiaan's greeting.

Then, "Copper pot not enough this time," the chief said in Afrikaans, after which he grinned in satisfaction at his accomplishment. Clearly the phrase had been memorized. Each word was uttered individually with no inflection or understanding to string them together.

"Copper pot?" Retief said.

"A gesture of good will the last time we met," Christiaan explained.

Without waiting for a response from Christiaan, presumably because he wouldn't have been able to understand it if one had been given him, the chief launched into his next memorized sentence.

"My people starve," he said woodenly. "This our land. This our cattle."

It was clear the recital was over. No longer were his eyes rolled upward as he strained to remember the practiced words. Now they were focused—and clearly hostile.

Christiaan looked past the chief, hoping for a glimpse of Jama.

The chief said something Christiaan didn't understand. Turning, the Xhosa strode back to his ranks of warriors.

"Seems like the negotiations have come to an end," Retief observed.

"If only I could spot Jama," Christiaan said, continuing to scan the lines of warriors. But he saw nothing but angry, hungry, unfamiliar faces staring back at him.

"Let's get out of here." Retief turned to leave.

Christiaan stood his ground. "Jama!" he called. "If you're here, come out and meet me!"

His cry caused a reaction, but not the one he'd hoped for. The warriors began to stir, perhaps taking exception to the way he was shouting at them.

A hand grabbed Christiaan's arm. "I strongly suggest we leave now," Retief said.

Christiaan backed away, continuing to look for Jama, still hoping that he would emerge from the ranks. Not until they were a good distance away did he turn around and walk with Retief.

"What kind of friend would he be to do battle against you?" Retief asked.

The question made sense. It made sense that Jama wasn't here. How could Christiaan have even thought that he would be? Were he here, the chief would expect Jama to use his knowledge of the settlers to the Xhosa's advantage. Jama wouldn't do that. A friend wouldn't endanger the life and property of another friend.

Christiaan turned his thoughts to their next move. Escape.

They had no other choice. His cattle were gone. His household effects lay scattered, and there was no time to gather them. The only thing left was to flee. To leave everything he owned, everything he had labored over for years, in the hands of these Xhosa marauders.

Upon reaching the front of the house, Christiaan took one last glance inside, then another over his shoulder at the invading army behind him.

"Let's go," he said.

They ran around the house to the back. Johanna and Kootjie were waiting for them with the two horses. To the sound of whoops and shrieks and cries from the advancing Xhosa horde, the four of them galloped toward the Pfeffer farm.

They were never in any physical danger. The Xhosa on foot were no match for the horses. But like a rising tide, the warriors kept coming and coming and coming, and there seemed little Christiaan or the other settlers could do to stop them.

When they were at a safe distance, Christiaan pulled his horse to a stop long enough to look back. A pillar of black smoke rose from the house, now completely consumed by flames. Xhosa warriors ran everywhere, gathering up articles of clothing and other possessions that lay scattered on the ground. Christiaan watched as the last of his cattle disappeared over the ridge.

Behind him, clutching his torso, Johanna wept. He could feel the warmth of her breath against his neck as she whispered over and over, "Sina . . . dear God, where is she . . . my Sina, my dear, dear Sina . . ."

Just when he had seen enough, even as his hand pulled the horse's reins in the direction of the Pfeffer farm, Christiaan spotted the man.

He stared, refusing to believe what he was seeing. There, standing on a hillock, staring at him even as he was stared at, dressed in the clothing of a Xhosa warrior, was Jama.

19

At the Pfeffer house they waited for an attack that did not come. Christiaan, Retief, and Pfeffer had positioned themselves at the windows, rifles at the ready, powder horns, greased bits of cloth, and shot laid out hastily beside them on the floor.

To Kootjie's barefaced delight, he and Conraad were also stationed at windows, on the side of the house deemed least likely to sustain a frontal assault. Normally the boys would have been relegated to loading weapons for the men, but the sheer number of Xhosa warriors demanded the additional placements, at least until reinforcements arrived. It was left to the women to load the rifles. However, with only two of them, the gunmen were largely on their own.

Once again, Sina's absence was keenly felt, this time practically as well as emotionally. With the aid of loaders, a mere handful of gunmen could hold off a small horde of attacking Xhosa. However, when a man had to load his own weapon between discharges, his effectiveness was diminished greatly. It was one more disadvantage the settlers who had barricaded themselves in the Pfeffer house could ill afford.

It was now clear that Karel had been correct in his assessment of the attack. This was no ordinary skirmish, no common test of Xhosa manhood, when a young buck would raid an outlying farm to prove himself by stealing a few Afrikaner cattle. From the looks of it, the entire Xhosa nation had been marshaled for this offensive. If the settlers were to survive this one, every available man and woman would be needed—even young women such as Sina, who could sustain a firing position by loading a gunman's weapon.

It wasn't until late morning that reinforcements arrived at the Pfeffer farm. They couldn't have been any fewer in number, composed of only a single person—Karel de Buys.

The news he brought with him was not encouraging. All surrounding farms were under heavy attack. Houses were in flames; deaths were mounting. Using his superior mobility, Karel had to breach Xhosa lines just to reach the Pfeffer farm. He informed Retief that it was unrealistic for them to expect support from the other settlers.

141

An ominous silence followed Karel's report, the kind that often follows an announcement of death. With the exception of the twins, who chattered happily in a corner of the room, everyone felt the import of the news. Their bleak situation had just become bleaker still.

"What I fail to understand is the Xhosa strategy," Retief said. "Maybe I'm missing something, but it just doesn't make sense to me. Why would they bypass this house and attack the houses south of here?"

"Maybe they suspected we would take our stand here," Christiaan offered.

"Possible . . . possible . . ." Retief worked his lower lip between his thumb and forefinger as he considered the likelihood of Christiaan's suggestion. "By flanking us, they could raid the southern farms before returning to . . ." Abruptly, he pointed to Kootjie and Conraad. "Go to the back of the house," he told them. "Keep a sharp lookout. If you see any movement—*any* movement at all—you yell with all your might. Understand?"

Kootjie and Conraad acknowledged Retief's order by gathering their powder and shot and scrambling toward the house's southern side.

Retief stopped them. "Did you hear what I said? Call first—don't shoot!"

"Yes, *Mynheer* Retief," the boys said eagerly in unison. They disappeared toward the back of the house.

"Nothing else to do now but wait and see if you're right," Retief said to Christiaan.

Everyone returned to his station. Karel settled under the window the boys had vacated.

Christiaan watched him check his loaded gun and position his ammunition and powder within ready reach. Throughout the process the boy had a distracted look in his eyes. Fumbling hands made several attempts to do what an experienced Boer, even a young one such as Karel, could normally do without a second thought in the dark or at a full gallop astride a horse.

Christiaan crossed the room and sat next to him. He spoke in a whisper. "You all right?"

"Sure. Why wouldn't I be?" Karel shrugged. His voice was unwavering. It was the unsteadiness of his hands that betrayed him. Nervously repositioning his bandolier, a hide sack containing grapeshot, he spilled it. Imperfect round balls rolled crazily across the hardwood floor.

From his window post, Retief glanced over at the sound of the scattered shot, then returned his attention to the direction of the anticipated attack.

Karel jumped to his knees and, with jittery hands, did his best to corral the runaway shot and scoop it back into the leather pouch.

Christiaan stopped a few of the rolling balls and handed them to Karel without comment or expression, as though he himself had done the same thing hundreds of times.

While Karel put the last of the balls in the pouch, Christiaan propped himself against the wall and gazed casually at the room's activity. The twins sat on the floor opposite each other, preoccupied with stacking individual towers of wooden blocks. Johanna and Angenitha were propped up against the wall in similar fashion to Christiaan. The two women leaned against one another, their shoulders touching. Her eyes closed, Johanna apparently was receiving comforting words from Angenitha, who spoke softly into her ear. Johanna's cheeks glistened from moisture. At the windows in the front of the house, Retief and Pfeffer kept a steady watch.

"How much sleep did you get last night?" Christiaan asked Karel.

"I haven't slept for two days," Karel replied. "I rode commando night before last. Then last night I was just coming in from the field when we first spotted the Xhosa."

Christiaan gave a fatherly nod. "It's been a rough couple of days for you," he commented. "Lack of sleep, plus riding all night and morning . . . seeing the things you've seen today . . . all the fighting . . . houses burning . . . death . . ."

Karel didn't reply. He continued to busy himself with his preparations.

Christiaan watched him for a moment, then said, "Your uncle's a good man. None finer . . . a good man . . . a fighter if ever I knew one."

Karel checked his loaded gun a second time.

"You know, son," Christiaan said, "whatever your family is up against, I am sure, with God's help, that your uncle will find a way to get them all through it."

Karel glanced up dumbly as though Christiaan had switched languages on him and was speaking in a foreign tongue. Then, after a moment, a glimmer of understanding lit in the boy's eyes. "Oh . . . my uncle . . . yes . . ." Then, glancing about the room to see if anyone else was listening, he whispered, "But it's not my uncle that's been on my mind. It's Sina. I can't help but think . . ."

Karel's lips pursed. Grabbing a cleaning rag, he furiously polished the stock of his gun.

"Go ahead, son," Christiaan said. "Say it. It's not as though I haven't thought of it myself."

Karel clenched his teeth. He rubbed the stock so hard it squeaked. "I can't get the image out of my mind," he said. "Sina being carried off by some Xhosa warrior."

That emotionally charged image had haunted Christiaan's mind as well. Each time it did, he had been able to shove it somewhere deep down inside himself so that he didn't have to deal with it. Until now. Karel's words had somehow strengthened the image, and no amount of mental stuffing could get it out of Christiaan's mind.

He saw Sina draped over a warrior's shoulder. His thick black arms holding down her kicking, protesting legs. Her arms pushing against the back of his leopardskin clothing. Her pale hands grabbing, scratching black skin. Her brown hair dangling downward, swinging side to side . . . wildly . . . helplessly.

The image was too strong for him. Tears filled Christiaan's eyes. Spilling over, they cut fresh tracks down his face.

"Forgive me," Karel said when he saw the effect his words had on Christiaan. He wiped away tears of his own. "I should have realized . . . after all, you're her father. It's just that . . . what other explanation is there?"

Christiaan brushed the boy's apology aside with the slow wave of a hand. "Until we know more than we know now," he said, "we'll simply have to entrust her into God's care."

The two sat in silence. Christiaan glanced at the others to see if they had noticed his weak moment. The twins were still occupied with the blocks. The two women were still huddled together. Retief and Pfeffer peered intently out the windows.

Wiping away one last tear, Christiaan started to rise.

"Can we?" Karel asked. "Right now?"

"Can we what?"

"Entrust Sina to God's care."

Fresh tears came to Christiaan's eyes. The more he was around this boy, the more he liked him. Nodding assent, he closed his eyes, squeezing a few tears onto his cheeks. With bowed head and a soft voice audible only to him and Karel, he prayed, "Almighty and all-knowing God, who knows everything and is surprised by nothing, we entreat You to do for us what we cannot do for ourselves—namely, protect Sina from the Xhosa. You know where she is . . . her current condition . . . whether or not they have . . ." Christiaan's voice broke. He fought back the rising tide of emotion within him but couldn't bring himself to continue.

"Protect her and keep her safe," Karel continued the prayer for him, "as only You can. We entrust Sina into Your tender care. Keep her as a little lamb in Your arms, we pray. Amen."

"Amen," Christiaan whispered.

For the next hour little was spoken by the adults. The predominant sound in the room was the click of polished wood against polished wood as the twins stacked the blocks. There was the inevitable crashing sound as the blocks tumbled, and an occasional sibling squabble over sharing.

The men stayed at their posts until their joints ached. One by one they would stand, stretch noisily, then resume their watch. The only movement they saw outside the house was the erratic swooping of a family of snow-white cattle egrets and the businesslike dash of small ground animals running from cover to cover, going about their daily food-gathering tasks.

At midafternoon the women prepared meat and bread, which they served to the men in the front and the boys in the back. They munched silently on the dry offering as they counted more than a dozen pillars of smoke in the direction of neighboring farms. The bars of smoke extended from the ground to the heavens, hemming them in on every side like some kind of ghastly corral.

The afternoon passed in uneasy, eerie silence.

Finally, at dusk, a rider approached from the south. He was an older man with sagging jowls and white streaks in his hair that were so wide its natural brown color was nearly lost. His beard likewise was streaked, matted, and ragged. His upper lip was clean of hair but not of dirt. A streak of grit extended from his nose to his ear, evidence of a hurried swipe from a soiled sleeve. Both shirtsleeves bore bloodstains on the forearms—apparently not his own, for lack of any visible wounds—and his hands were crusty with powder stains and dirt.

Retief, Christiaan, and the others, in contrast to the rider, emerged from the Pfeffer house only slightly wrinkled. Their unsullied appearance and the unspoiled condition of the Pfeffer house and farm clearly dumbfounded the rider.

"How did you hold them off?" he cried.

"They haven't attacked here yet," Retief said.

"They haven't *attacked?*"

The thought seemed too difficult for the rider to grasp. With gruesome detail, he described the carnage and destruction he had witnessed at the surrounding farms. Entire families had been slaughtered. Houses burned to the ground. Herds and livestock driven across the river.

"They came in swarms like locusts," he said, "destroying and killing everything in sight, stripping the land bare."

"Are they coming this way?" Christiaan asked.

The rider stared at the house and the surrounding farm area as though he had never seen anything like it before. "No," he said. "They've moved on south. Nothing left for them here. Except this house. How do you suppose they could have missed it? You the owner?" He addressed the question to Christiaan.

"Pfeffer here is the owner." Christiaan motioned to his meek neighbor.

"God's been watchin' over you real good, friend," the rider said, still shaking his head in wonder. Taking one last look at the unspoiled farm, he excused himself and continued his ride north.

If it hadn't been for the somber realization that all around them their neighbors were suffering, the small gathering outside the Pfeffer house would have appeared comical. Instead of being smitten with grief, they were smitten by good fortune. For a long time, no one seemed to know what to say. But eventually, reality revisited them.

"Well, I had best be following that fellow north," Retief said, "to see how bad it is there." He slapped Adriaan Pfeffer good-naturedly on the shoulder. "God has indeed favored you and your household, my friend. Let's hope there are others like you that we haven't heard about yet."

Pfeffer was all grins from a combination of being favored by God and congratulated by a man of Piet Retief's stature. An equally pleased Angenitha moved to her husband's side. The twins, hanging onto their mother's skirt, trailed close behind her.

"I'll ride north with you," Christiaan said to Retief. "At least as far as my farm."

"As will I," Karel said.

"I'm going with you," Johanna said to her husband.

"Me too," chimed Kootjie.

Christiaan shook his head. There was still the possibility of danger, but that wasn't why he didn't want Johanna to accompany him. He had a picture in his mind that he couldn't get rid of. It was of Johanna sorting through the rubble, lifting a discarded horse blanket, and finding Sina's mutilated body.

"It's too dangerous," he said to her.

"Christiaan van der Kemp," Johanna said, "I do not appreciate you treating me like some fainthearted female who is not acquainted with the ways of the wilderness. If Sina is dead, she is dead—you cannot protect me from that fact. I'm coming with you."

Angenitha, placing a tender hand on her shoulder, tried to turn her back to the house. "Johanna, dear," she said, "stay here with us. At least until morning. Tomorrow you can—"

Fiercely, Johanna tore herself away from her friend. "I am going to my house tonight if I have to walk!" she said firmly.

Retief joined in. "*Mevrou* van der Kemp, I must agree with—"

Christiaan held up a hand, cutting him off. "My wife is right," he said. "At a time such as this we should stay together as a family. Kootjie, get our horses. You're coming too."

"Really?" Kootjie cried, clearly expecting to be the one left behind as usual.

"There are beds for you here tonight should you need them," Pfeffer said. "Angenitha will prepare a meal in anticipation of your return."

"Your hospitality is appreciated, friend," Christiaan said. "But if our house is still standing—"

"Then naturally you will stay at your house," Pfeffer said.

Christiaan nodded gratefully. "You're a good neighbor, Adriaan."

"To every thing there is a season . . . a time to kill . . . a time to mourn . . ."

The fragment from Ecclesiastes tormented Christiaan as he approached what remained of his farm. He knew the Scripture passage well enough to know that the phrases were out of order, but for reasons that became increasingly clear to him, his mind had seen fit to pluck them from their natural order and place them together as a reminder of the cruelties of life.

"A time to kill . . . a time to mourn."

A time to kill. The carcasses of several cows lay glassy-eyed on their sides. Chickens had been trampled in the dirt, their feathers scattered on the ground. Life on the frontier. Kill or be killed. Predators. Xhosa. One and the same. If one wasn't trying to kill you, the other one was.

Until now, the van der Kemps had been the fortunate ones. While other farms were visited regularly by calamity and setbacks, the van der Kemps had enjoyed a relatively adverse-free existence. Their losses over the years had been light—a handful of cattle to disease, a disappointing crop now and then, occasional trouble with a worker. But death and calamity, those malevolent twin demons, had for whatever reason passed over them.

No longer. Tragedy had struck like a whirlwind. Death was at their doorstep.

"A time to mourn . . ."

The van der Kemps were no longer exempt from misfortune. It was as though they were riding into the center of the storm. Every turn of the head brought a different scene of calamity . . . destruction . . . chaos. In one day their world had been turned upside down.

"A time to kill . . . a time to mourn . . . a time to die . . ."

A third fragment from the book of wisdom sneaked into Christiaan's mind and appended itself to the other two phrases, then supplanted them, repeating itself mercilessly like an endless litany.

"A time to die . . . a time to die . . . a time to die . . . a time to die . . . a time to . . ."

Sina.

With each gully they passed, Christiaan fully expected to see his daughter's lifeless body lying facedown in the mud. Beneath every scrap of wood, under every pile of rubble he expected to see protruding feet . . . Sina's feet. Innocent feet that used to prance carefree through the summer grass . . . feet so full of energy they couldn't be still at the dinner table despite repeated parental warnings . . . tiny feet that used to dangle and splash in the river as she sat next to her father . . .

Johanna, too, sitting behind him, scoured the debris, expecting to make a similar gruesome discovery. Christiaan could sense it. When they first set out from the Pfeffer farm, her arms stretched around him, her breast pressed firmly against his back. She clutched him tightly, fearfully, as though he was her lifeline. As they rode toward home, her head snapped from side to side—like his—searching the debris, looking for remnants, looking for signs of Sina. And, also like him, hoping for the best, yet fearing the worst.

As their journey neared its end, as the magnitude of destruction became evident, Christiaan could feel Johanna's strength and hope waning. He could feel her giving up, yielding to her worst thoughts. Her arms hung limp in his lap. She leaned against him like dead weight. Johanna's faltering hope threatened to pull him down with it. He had to fight to keep his hopes up.

It was an increasingly difficult struggle. Everywhere he looked, large sections of land were scorched black. The workers' quarters—silent and unoccupied—were gutted. The building's thatched roof was completely gone. Its whitewashed walls were smeared and streaked with soot. In some places, portions of the walls had been pulled down. Crumbling edges rimmed gaping holes, exposing the interior's charred remains.

Their house had fared no better. The walls were still standing, but the roof was gone. So were the shutters and the doors. Pockmarked and soot-charred, it looked like the carcass of an animal that had been picked clean and tossed onto a trash heap.

Everything was morbidly still. As far as the eye could see, the only movement was that of thin, wispy puffs of pale smoke rising from the scorched earth, as though the dying land was offering up its soul.

The blackened landscape was breathtakingly stark, devoid of life. Beyond dead, it was so parched of vitality that it seemed to siphon the life force from those who trespassed upon it.

Christiaan could see the life draining from all of them. No one spoke. Their faces were haggard and drawn; their shoulders sagged. He knew how they felt, for he felt it too.

He searched inside himself for one last scrap of hope, one remaining crumb of cheer to encourage him, to help him believe that something good might come of this. To his dismay, he could find none. In the dark corners of his soul there was no shred of optimism to be found. His vision of creating a frontier farm to rival Klaarstroom was as dead as the carcass of the house that lay before him.

But that was not the worst of it. While rummaging around his soul for a bit of hope that was not there, he stumbled upon something even more shocking—a second, more devastating, discovery. During his look inward, Christiaan discovered that his belief in the goodness of mankind was one of that day's fatalities.

With mounting anger, the kind that comes when a person realizes he has been played for a fool all these many years, Christiaan concluded that not all men could be trusted. Some of them were more animal than human.

It was an easy deduction for him to reach. After all, human beings didn't act like this. This was the work of animals. Jackals. This was the kind of act one could expect from unthinking, unfeeling, soulless primates who killed without thought and who, likewise, should be destroyed before they had a chance to kill again.

With mounting fury, Christiaan decided that it was time he buried his naive and childish view of the black races and saw them for who they were. And he knew exactly where to place the headstone for his childish belief.

Christiaan's lips twisted into a bitter sneer as he and Johanna rode past the small hillock beside their house, a fitting burial place for naive notions. For it was on this hillock that he had last seen Jama—his friend —standing proud, adorned in the garb of a Xhosa warrior, victoriously watching the van der Kemps flee for their lives. Jama, the man whom he had loved as a brother, the man who had betrayed that love, who had sided with the enemy—sided with the animals who killed his Sina, sided with the thieves who plundered his cattle, sided with the raiders who burned his land, destroyed his crops, and razed his house.

As he rode past the charred and smoking hillock, Christiaan swore to himself that he would never again trust a black man.

The riders dismounted and walked silently among the ruins. The only sound to be heard was the crunch and crackle of debris or the softer sound of ashes underfoot.

Out of instinct, Johanna began picking up things from the floor in a futile attempt to tidy up. Not until she had an armful, with no shelf or chest of drawers or closet in which to place them, did she realize the absurdity of her actions. Then, without so much as a shrug or grimace or sigh, she let go, and everything in her arms fell to the floor once again.

Christiaan watched her carefully. The thing that disturbed him about her was the hollow look in her eyes, as hollow as the house in which they were standing. He could do nothing to save the house; it was gone. He didn't want to lose Johanna too.

She moved woodenly toward the back corner of the house, where Sina's bed had been. Nothing was there now but charred wood and ashes. For a long time she stood staring down at the place where Sina had lain. In times past Johanna had stood in this same place, wiping Sina's feverish brow with a damp cloth, or tucking the blanket around Sina's neck to keep out the night chill, or shaking a growing young woman's shoulder as she complained that it was too early to get up.

Now all that was left was memories . . . the household routine, the special times . . . nothing but memories . . . of Sina.

Johanna held her face in her hands and wept. Kootjie and Karel and Retief watched with saddened, sympathetic expressions as Christiaan crossed through the clutter of the room and put his arms around his wife.

Karel was the first to leave. He did so at Christiaan's insistence. If the boy rode hard and cut through Klyn's abandoned fields, he could reach home shortly after dark. Retief and Christiaan watched him go as Johanna and Kootjie picked through the mess, looking for household items that might be salvaged.

It had already been decided that the van der Kemps would return to the Pfeffer farm for the night.

Christiaan chuckled. To Retief, who was standing beside him watching Karel ride off, he said, "When we were first married, during some lean years, Johanna used to quote something her grandmother used to say to her. She said, 'With a wagon, a fire, and a pound of coffee, any true woman can make a home.'"

He chuckled again as he scanned the ruins that had once been his household. "We don't have a wagon—I don't think there's anything left to burn—and as for coffee, well, that's completely out of the question. I guess I'd be asking too much of Johanna to make this into a home again."

Retief stared at him questioningly. "Just what are you saying, van der Kemp?"

Before Christiaan could answer, they were interrupted by the sound of approaching horses. It began as a low rumble and built into a small roar of hooves. A column of British soldiers appeared, led by a pig-faced lieutenant.

At first, Christiaan chided himself for judging the man. It wasn't his fault that he looked like a pig. But the comparison was undeniable. He was plump all over. His pants legs bulged at the seams; the buttons on his red coat strained to hold back a bulging belly; he had a round face with fat cheeks and a pug nose that showed too much nostril. His complexion was pinkish. Even his ears, which were small, looked somewhat pointed on top.

All these things were coincidence, of course; and Christiaan was willing to try to look past the man's appearance and judge him on his inner qualities, which, to no one's great surprise, turned out to be piggish. Christiaan was left only one conclusion: *If a man looks like a pig, sounds like a pig, and acts like a pig . . .*

"What happened here?" the lieutenant shouted in Afrikaans. The man's voice was nasal and high-pitched. He drew an intake of breath before speaking and after, almost as though he was trying to snort.

"The Xhosa happened here," Retief answered testily, apparently perturbed by the man's need to confirm the obvious.

The lieutenant reacted to the prickliness in Retief's voice. From atop his horse, he leaned forward in his saddle. With a scowl, he said, "Is this your house?"

"It's my house," Christiaan replied, drawing the lieutenant's attention.

"Your house?" the lieutenant echoed.

"Yes."

With the column of redcoats behind him, each one surveying the damage, the lieutenant maneuvered his horse in front of Christiaan. "Looks to me like your farm is pretty much destroyed, wouldn't you agree?"

Christiaan thought it an odd question, but there was no denying the indisputable.

"Worst we've seen so far," said the lieutenant. "Anyone killed?"

"My daughter's missing."

The lieutenant sniffed. "I wouldn't hold out much hope for her, from the look of things."

Retief bristled at the officer's insensitivity.

"Why do you think that is?" the lieutenant asked.

"I don't understand. Why do I think what is?" Christiaan asked.

The lieutenant harrumphed and glanced back at the men immediately behind him. "I'm not surprised," he chuckled.

They chuckled with him.

"Not surprised at all," he said. "That you don't understand, that is." He paused, snorted, then said, "Let me put it another way. What have you done to the Xhosa tribes to warrant this level of vengeance?"

"Done to them?" Christiaan shouted. "They attacked *me!*"

"And I want to know why!" the lieutenant shouted back. "Why did they attack you? What did you do to provoke them? Steal their cattle? Violate their women? Trick them out of their land? Just what did you do to provoke them?"

"I didn't do anything to provoke them!"

"Really, Lieutenant!" Retief stepped between Christiaan and the lieutenant's horse. He stared boldly up at the officer. "Where is your compassion, man? Can't you see that this man and his family have been devastated?"

The piggish lieutenant pursed his lips in an unconcerned way, indicating that Retief was wasting his time.

"The question at hand is, where was the British army when this man needed them most?" Retief yelled. "Sitting down for tea, no doubt!"

The lieutenant's snout pulled back in surprise.

"Your job is to protect these good people!" Retief continued. "And hundreds more like them! I suggest you ride a little further down the road, Lieutenant. Take a good look at what you see! Because it's shameful! Shameful, I say, the way you British take pride in your colonies, yet care little when they need your protection!"

"How dare you tell the British army its job!" the lieutenant bellowed.

"Someone has to!" Retief yelled back. "Because apparently you've forgotten!"

The lieutenant snapped his horse's reins to one side. Maneuvering around the two men directly in his path, he led his troops forward, but not without saying, "Someone sparked this uprising! And if I find out it's either of you, I'll be back for you! Do you hear me? I'll be back!"

The soldiers began to follow their leader toward the Pfeffer farm.

Christiaan stood by, looking into their faces. Without exception they looked down at him. More than that, they looked down *on* him, as though he were the enemy rather than an ally.

After the last of them had passed, Christiaan said to Retief, "Earlier this morning, you asked me if I thought there was still something here on the frontier for me."

Retief nodded.

"At the time I thought there was. Now, I'm not so sure."

The two men turned toward the ruins of the house. In the waning light of day, as the sky grew orange and long shadows stretched like fingers across the land, embracing it for the coming darkness, they walked slowly back to the remains of what had once been the sum total of Christiaan van der Kemp's life.

Christiaan asked, "When do those wagons of yours pull out? The ones headed north for the high veld?"

Retief took a long look at him.

In the course of a single day they had shared life and death. From the glimmer in the field-commandant's eyes, it was clear he was pleased at the direction he perceived the conversation was taking. If his original purpose for the visit had been to enlist Christiaan in the trek, his joy was clearly tempered by the recent events that had brought Christiaan to this decision.

Suddenly Johanna let out a gasp, an unfeminine, loud, ghastly cry that cut through the evening and sent shivers up Christiaan's spine, froze his heart still, and stopped him dead in his tracks. The first thing that popped into his mind was the worst thing he could think of—she had found Sina's body.

But Johanna wasn't looking at the ground. Her glassy eyes were fixed on something behind Christiaan and Retief. Trembling hands covered her mouth. Tears flowed freely, like spring streams, down her cheeks.

Christiaan whirled around. A single horse approached. Two riders. Karel held the reins. The other rider was temporarily blocked from his sight. Why had Karel come back? He would never make it back to his house this late . . .

Then, the rider behind him came into view. Loose brown hair swayed with the horse's stride, curling around, hitting Karel on the shoulder. Likewise, a skirt—dirty, caked with mud—flapped around their legs. Then the back rider leaned to one side, and Christiaan saw a face—*Sina!*

Before he had time to react, Johanna had already passed him, running blindly toward her daughter, calling her name over and over.

Standing next to him, Retief, the field-commandant who always seemed in control of his emotions, grinned from ear to ear. He slapped

Christiaan on the shoulder. "After all that boy has done today, I see now why you like him so much!"

Shortly before Piet Retief's party of wagons left the British colony for the high veld, an article appeared in the *Grahamstown Journal*, written by the leader of the pioneers:

> We are resolved, wherever we go, that we will uphold the just principles of liberty; but, whilst we will take care that no one is brought by us into a condition of slavery, we will establish such regulations as may suppress crime and prepare proper relations between master and servant. We solemnly declare that we leave this country with a desire to enjoy a quieter life than we have hitherto had. We will not molest any people, nor deprive them of the smallest property; but, if attacked, we shall consider ourselves fully justified in defending our persons and effects, to the utmost of our ability, against every enemy.
>
> We quit this Colony under the full assurance that the English Government has nothing more to require of us, and will allow us to govern ourselves without its interference in the future. We are now leaving the fruitful land of our birth, in which we have suffered enormous losses and continual vexation, and are about to enter a strange and dangerous territory; but we go with a firm reliance on an all-seeing, just, and merciful God, whom we shall always fear and humbly endeavor to obey.

A list of signatures followed, composed of the names of all those who quit the colony with him. Among the names listed: Christiaan van der Kemp, Adriaan Pfeffer, Louis De Buys, and Gerrit van Aardt.

20

Leather straps cut into his wrists. Jama gasped for breath. After three frantic gulps, his mouth gaping like a fish out of water, he managed to draw some air into his lungs. It was enough to satisfy him for a minute or two.

He was dangling at full length between two poles that were lodged in the ground at such an angle that they crossed over his head. His wrists were strapped to the cross at the junction. His weight pulled his arms taut over his head. His toes made circles in the dirt beneath him. The night air chilled his exposed flesh.

All was still except for an occasional bleat or low or squeak or squawk of a disgruntled animal. Booty from the raid. In the Xhosa kraal the huts were dark. Fading orange embers were all that remained of the raging victory celebration. Exhausted warriors and their families lay sprawled on the ground, some inside, some outside their huts.

Jama squirmed, short of breath. Closing his eyes, he escaped in his mind to a more pleasant time and place. He was lying on the grassy hillock alone, his arms casually cradling his head as he stared at the night sky. Quiet. Serene. Inspiring. A feeling of calm washed over his body.

The next instant, he pulled himself up with all his might. He suppressed a scream as leather thongs cut deeply into bleeding flesh. Shoulder joints burned with fire. He had raised himself just enough to swallow a large gulp of air. Letting go, he dropped, dangling wildly, his toes making wildly erratic arcs in the dust.

The leather strips tore deeper into his wrists. Jama's eyes rolled upward. Nausea swept over them like a thin white veil. He wanted to scream, but a scream would only waste the air he'd just captured. So he bit his lower lip to fight back the cry that welled up inside him to the point that he felt he would explode if he didn't allow his body this justifiable expression.

It was the only way Jama could take a deep breath. But with each attempt, he paid a price for it in pain, every breath more costly than the last. After a time the pain was so intense that the only way he could endure it was to trick himself by lulling himself into thinking of something pleasant and then pulling himself up suddenly. If he thought of the impending agony, he never would be able to bring himself to pull up.

There were other wounds—cuts, gashes, bruises—but Jama had stopped feeling them hours earlier. These were souvenirs from the Xhosa warriors, reminders of their anger. When they hanged him from the poles, they'd beaten him and thrown stones and sticks and rotten fruit and vegetables at him. Consequently, his matted hair smelled like a rotting garden; his skin reeked of stale, fermented grain and berries, which they'd spit on him. These things were now forgotten, supplanted by the superior pain of his raw and bloodied wrists—coupled with his inability to catch his breath.

Ever so slowly, he could feel his life force leaving him. He wondered if the Xhosa would be disappointed if he died before sunrise, thus depriving them of the chance to kill him.

Jama had never imagined he would die like this. He'd always thought that death would someday quietly cover him like a blanket when he was old and tired.

He'd always envisioned it happening while he dozed in a chair on the porch of his house overlooking his farm. He had been well most of his life, so he didn't picture himself dying of a fever or disease. And he respected animals and nature too much, almost to a point of reverence, so he didn't see his demise coming in the field. And he always did his best to stay out of other people's business and to avoid arguments, so he didn't count on being murdered, even though his father had been the same way and it hadn't protected him from getting a musket ball in the back.

No, for some reason Jama had always imagined death would come on a sunny day as he sat on the porch. In short, he saw himself dozing his way into the grave. So, naturally, this recent turn of events had taken him quite by surprise. It had never occurred to him that he would find himself strung up like a side of beef waiting to be butchered.

It was an inglorious end to what had once been a promising second chance at life. He remembered his feelings as he'd approached the Xhosa kraal after crossing the Fish River. He was challenged by warriors but not afraid of them. They were kin, of the same blood. Why should he be afraid?

The sight of a black man wearing Afrikaner clothing and speaking Xhosa clearly befuddled the warriors. When Jama instructed them to take him to their chief, they readily agreed. He was no threat to them, having no horse and bearing no weapons, which itself was an enigma for anyone on the frontier. Jama had chosen to leave the Afrikaners with only the clothes on his back lest anyone accuse him of taking something that was not rightfully his.

So it was without hesitation that the warriors escorted their prize to the chief, eager to share their curious discovery with their leader. Then the warriors were further dumbfounded when, upon their presenting Jama, the chief rose and welcomed him as he would a close friend.

The Xhosa chief seemed genuinely pleased to hear of Jama's decision to cross the river. It was a victory of sorts for him, similar to the prodigal's returning home after realizing the error of his ways. Only this prodigal had been gone from home for generations. And now Jama was once again among his own people where he belonged.

The chief paraded him around the entire kraal from hut to hut like a trophy. Jama was proof that, given a choice between the ways of the Afrikaners and the Xhosa, a discriminating man would choose the Xhosa. With great relish the chief told the tale of their first meeting, when Jama was used as a pawn in the white man's schemes. He told how they met again at the Fish River and conversed from opposite shorelines and how the chief convinced Jama that there was nothing for him among the Afrikaners—that he would find peace only among those of his own race.

The Xhosa people listened with eager ears, for this was their triumph too. They begged Jama to speak in Afrikaans and British, all the while shaking their heads and laughing at the strange sounds that came from his lips. They pelted him with questions. What was it like for a black man to live among the frontier people? What strange foods did they force him to eat? Did their white skin rub off like chalk when it was touched? Was it true that they worshiped a god who lived in a black book? And when they talked aloud to their god, did he talk aloud back to them? Had Jama ever ridden a horse? Had he ever made love to a white woman?

Amused at some of their strange notions regarding Afrikaners, Jama patiently responded to all of their questions. He felt strangely warmed by this interaction with the Amaxhosa. Children gathered around his legs. Young and old alike listened intently to every word he said.

The chief took it upon himself to outfit Jama with clothing and provide him with a hut. He gave him the responsibility of herding his own cattle. For the first time in his life, Jama felt accepted by an entire community. They waved at him when he came and went from the field. They went out of their way to talk to him. They gave him mats and bowls for his hut. Generally, they adopted him as one of their own.

Even the chief's youngest daughter seemed to take an interest in him. More than once Jama caught her casting a rather fetching look his direction. His first reaction was to downplay the feelings her looks stirred in him. Habit. Over the years he had convinced himself he would never know the love of a woman. He had to remind himself that, here, things were different. He began returning the young girl's glances.

Word reached him, through one of the chief's guards, that the chief too had noticed his daughter's attraction to Jama. According to the guard, the prospect of marriage between his daughter and the knowledgeable newcomer pleased the chief. The prospect of marriage pleased Jama too.

He thought of the Van der Kemps. He missed them. But there was no comparing his life then and now. Here, he had a future. He was his own man. He had the hope of marriage and a family, eventually some cattle of his own, and the respect of his peers. He was at peace with himself. What more could he ask for?

Then, suddenly, Jama's fortunes changed.

Messengers arrived from the other Xhosa chiefs. A council of Xhosa leaders was called. At the council the tribal leaders addressed the crises at hand: hunger, depleted herds, and recent Afrikaner raids into Xhosa territory. A retaliatory attack against the white settlers was proposed. Endorsement of the plan was so enthusiastic that it reached fever pitch. This would be no ordinary strike. It would be so large that, if successful, they would drive the Afrikaners and British from the western bank of the Fish River forever.

Jama squirmed to try to reposition the leather strap to a less painful position, one that didn't feel as though it was cutting into the bone.

A lion's roar echoed in the distance. The feeble bleat of a lamb was cut short. Then all was silent again. From the sound of it, a shepherd lost a sheep. He was probably asleep or, worse, drunk.

Then a movement caught Jama's eye.

Someone from the kraal was coming toward him. It was still dark enough that Jama couldn't tell who it was. But one thing was clear. The silhouetted visitor was carrying a large knife.

There was no haste in the figure's approach. His was almost a casual stroll, or was it a drunken stroll? It was difficult to tell. Jama would just have to wait for the figure to get closer. Then he recognized the build and the swagger of the approaching man.

The Xhosa chief.

"I should have let you stay behind as you wanted," the chief said from a distance. His speech was thick and somewhat slurred, but his voice carried clearly, loudly across the predawn kraal.

"You had no choice," Jama replied. In contrast to the Xhosa's deep, resounding voice, Jama's words were no more than a dry whisper. "Neither of us did," he continued. "My fate was sealed the moment the Xhosa council decided to attack. Had I stayed behind, I would have lost the respect of the Amaxhosa. By going, I was forced to do what I did."

The chief drew within about six feet and slowed to a standstill. He stared at Jama's wrists, then into Jama's eyes. A look of chagrin twisted his lips. He collapsed to the ground and sat in a position similar to the one he had used opposite Jama at the Fish River on the day they first got acquainted. With a deliberate motion he laid the knife lengthwise on the ground between them, the implication being that it would at some point figure into their conversation, but not yet.

"We both knew the day would come." The chief sighed. "The day when your loyalties would be tested."

"I did nothing to betray the Xhosa cause."

"You deprived us of cattle and sheep."

"I protected my friends . . . my family!"

"*We are your family now!*" the chief shouted, pounding his own chest. "The Amaxhosa. Your blood! Your family!"

While the chief brooded, Jama thought back to the day of battle. He remembered standing atop the hillock beside the van der Kemp house, watching as Christiaan and the others fled. Their house in flames. Fleeing for their lives. He remembered the expression on Christiaan's face when their eyes met. Pained. Puzzled. Fearful. Given the direction of their flight, Jama presumed they were going to the Pfeffer farm.

"The generals will kill you at sunrise," said the chief.

"I'm surprised they haven't done so already."

"Then you don't understand the nature of your death."

Jama said nothing, assuming the chief would elaborate.

"Executing a traitor properly takes time. Last night was a time of celebration. Today—" he paused and craned his neck eastward, where a rosy glow illumined the horizon "—today there will be plenty of time for justice."

"I am no traitor," Jama said.

"I know," the chief replied softly.

"Then you'll speak on my behalf?"

With downcast eyes the chief slowly reached for the knife. He turned it over in his hands as he spoke. "My words fell on hardened hearts."

His words had the impact of a death sentence on Jama. Upon hearing them, his body felt heavier, the leather thongs cut ever deeper, empty lungs ached for air.

He wheezed. "Why are they so insistent on killing me?"

"Some men simply enjoy killing. Their kind can be found on both sides of the river."

It was true. Jama could think of several Boer men who fit that description.

"It is these men who always find a way to sustain this conflict. So they can kill. When they learned that you had deliberately led them away from a bountiful Boer farm, you gave them all the reason they needed to continue killing for one more day. Worse, they will use your death to convince my people that even more killing is needed. And you can be sure that, when the Boers hear of your death, it will become a cause for them to raid and kill us. As long as such men are in power, there is little chance we will ever have peace on the Fish River."

"We can have peace if more men like you and Christiaan van der Kemp speak out," Jama said.

The chief agreed with a slow nod. "In time," he said, "but not today. The people's blood is hot. They thirst for revenge."

"Had I to do it over again," Jama whispered, "I would not change what I have done."

"I know," the chief said quietly. "I admire your loyalty. I respect you for it. Given the same situation, I would have done the same thing. What are a few head of cattle compared to the life of a friend?"

The chief stood, gripping and weighing the knife in his hand. "The gods have not been kind to you," he said. "I could wish that things had turned out differently. You are the kind of man I would want for my daughter. However, what's been done is done. There are forces at work which we cannot sway."

He approached Jama until their faces were inches from each other. Jama could no longer see the knife, but he was very much aware of its presence.

"What are you going to do?" Jama asked.

"The generals would kill you slowly over the course of the day, by mounting you on a pole like a pig on a spit, then by cutting your fleshy parts, careful not to hit any vital blood sources. You will wish to die, but they will not let you. Should your heart begin to fail, they will revive you. In this way, you will be a testimony to all who would betray the Amaxhosa."

"That's not what I asked," Jama said, looking into the chief's eyes. "What are *you* going to do?"

"I cannot stand by and let bloodthirsty brutes murder a man more noble than they. With a single thrust, I can take their prize from them and spare you the agony and humiliation that await you."

160

The chief paused. His face dripped profusely with sweat. His lips trembled. Hard black eyes teared with compassion.

What was he waiting for? Did he expect Jama to thank him for what he was about to do? Helpless, Jama waited to feel the steel blade slide between his ribs and silence his heart. In a way, he even welcomed it. To slip into blackness, to feel no more pain, to escape from a world that had no place for him. He closed his eyes and waited for the flash of pain that would end his suffering.

It didn't come.

There was no sound to indicate an interruption. *What was the chief waiting for?* Jama wished he would hurry. The pain of his wrists was beyond bearable. His lungs felt ready to collapse. The chief was still there. He could feel the man's warm breath against his nose and lips. Jama waited.

Still nothing.

He opened his eyes. The chief was so close to him that it took several blinks to bring everything into focus.

Suddenly, the Xhosa staggered backwards. The knife plopped in the dirt. A low, rumbling roar could be heard deep inside the man. His eyes and nose and mouth bunched together with a look of fierce determination. The roar intensified within him, growing louder, traveling up his gullet until it exploded from his mouth. He charged forward like an enraged elephant, ducking his head at the last instant, slamming his shoulder into one of the wooden poles.

The cross structure upon which Jama was hanging shuddered violently, tipped backward, but did not fall. With the impact, Jama swung back, dangling wildly, the leather thongs groaning, stretching, cutting. His feet slapped the ground; his toes raked the dirt.

The chief pulled back for another charge. This time the two-poled structure collapsed, Jama with it. He found himself staring at the fading stars, their once-black late night background now a grayish blue. He pulled his arms down, dragging the poles with them. He gasped. Mercifully, measure after measure of crisp morning air filled his lungs.

The chief leaped to his side and began untying the leather thongs, all the while shooting nervous glances in the direction of the kraal. "The men who planted these poles must have been drunk," he said. "Otherwise, you wouldn't have been able to pull them over as easily as you did."

Once the thongs were untied, the chief carefully pulled them out of the deep grooves they had cut in Jama's wrists. It was all Jama could do to keep from crying out.

Tossing the bonds aside, the chief assisted him to his feet. In his haste to send Jama on his way, he let go too early. Jama's knees buckled.

The chief kept him from collapsing. "Quickly! You must leave!" he whispered, as though Jama were deliberately being difficult.

A second attempt to stand proved more successful.

"Where will you go?" asked the chief. Then, before Jama could answer, he waved off his own question. "Don't tell me. It's better if I don't know."

It was just as well that he didn't want to know, because Jama had no idea where he would go.

A cock crowed.

"Farewell, my friend," the chief said. "I hope you will find a place of your own and a people who will embrace you."

"Farewell," Jama said, his voice still hoarse. "If such a place exists, my one regret will be that you are not there to share it with me."

Jama glanced around only once. The Xhosa chief had turned his back. Bending down, he retrieved his knife from the dirt and proceeded toward the kraal, his shoulders slightly stooped.

Running on uncertain legs, Jama pushed through fynbos bushes and stumbled down a ravine. For a time he just ran, giving no thought to direction. Since he had no destination, any direction was as good as any other. There was no wrong way. The sky grew pale overhead. The sun lay just beneath the horizon ready to make its grand morning entrance.

He splashed through a creek, then charged up the side of a hill and bounded over the crest. He found himself staring across a flat section with several prominent outcroppings of rock. His lungs, which a short time ago were collapsing for want of air, now felt as if they would burst with each heave of his chest. He hurled himself over a ridge of rock, landing on the far side just as the first rays of sun burst over the horizon.

He lay there, hurting and disoriented. Just a few minutes earlier he had mentally quit this life. Having resigned himself to death, he had stood on the edge of eternity. Now, suddenly, he found himself catapulted back into the realm of time and place. Where to go? What to do?

He didn't know!

Back to the van der Kemps? No. He would never be accepted among the Boers now that he had gone over to the Xhosa. It would be worse than before.

So then, where? Grahamstown? No, too many people knew him there. Port Elizabeth? Or possibly Cape Town? Nobody would know him, but how could he expect anything to be different for him among the

Boers and the English no matter what the place was called? They were white. He was black. It was as simple as that.

Where then? Another Xhosa tribe? It would only be a matter of time before his actions during the frontier war would catch up with him. No, it had to be far away. A place where he could live among Nguni people. Start afresh.

The Zulu!

The thought sparked a hope strong enough to cause Jama to sit up. The Zulu! It made sense. They were of the Nguni. And they were far enough north that he could leave his reputation behind and forge a new one.

It was an inspired idea but not without its dangers. The Zulus were a warrior race. For years, under the military leadership of their ruler Shaka, the very name *Zulu* had struck fear in the hearts of other tribes. But Shaka was dead now. And word was that his brother, Dingane, though still a ruthless man, did not share his brother's vision of a far-reaching military empire.

It was decided. Jama would travel to the Zulus. There, he would be far away from the frontier conflict that had led to his predicament among the Xhosa. He could start a new life, free from the old attachments.

Rising, he got his bearings from the sun. Then, on shaky legs, Jama took his first steps toward a new life.

21

Christiaan stood on the alluvial banks of the Great River and stared three hundred yards across the yellowish band of water to the other side. He felt a hand slip around his arm.

Johanna laid her cheek against his shoulder. "Our Red Sea," she said. "On the other side lies freedom."

"Do you think if Piet Retief stretches his staff over the waters, God will part them for us?"

Johanna poked him in the side. "Don't be irreverent."

"Didn't mean to be. But if God is willing, He'll get no objection from me."

Some of the men had already plunged into the river, swimming their horses and cattle to the other side. The low, rumbling rush of the water was nearly drowned out by all the whoops and hollers. The first man to reach the far bank stood triumphantly with legs apart and his face and head lifted heavenward. He shouted, "Thanks be to God! Now we are free!"

The man's words chilled Christiaan's flesh with excitement. He was sure there wasn't a man or woman standing on the banks of the Great River that day who did not share this sentiment.

"Kootjie!" Christiaan yelled. "When you're done with the oxen, get the saw from the toolbox and start cutting that willow beside the wagon."

Kootjie grinned and nodded. The boy's pace happily quickened, which amused Christiaan. Ever since the trek began, Kootjie's attitude toward work had changed for the better.

It was hardly surprising, since the boy had traded a life of farming monotony for a life of daily adventure and the unknown. Although trekking had its share of repetition and boredom, there was also the promise of new challenges and an element of expectation. One never knew what was over the next hill or around the next bend—mountains to traverse, rivers to span, game to hunt, natives to encounter. It was the perfect life for a boy such as Kootjie, who craved adventure.

His chief responsibility was the daily care and feeding of the oxen. Christiaan was pleased with the way the boy was handling the team of sixteen. Kootjie called them by name as one by one he unyoked them and led them to feed. Each one, in keeping with its ox nature, moved slowly to obey him. Blinking their big eyes at him, they ground their cud with their molars, their lower jaws moving sideways.

From the way he handled them, it was evident the boy loved the great wide-horned red oxen that were in his care. As the *voorloper,* he had guided them expertly along the slopes of steep hills, over high sandstone bumps, protruding roots, and through deep ravines with sharp bends.

Sometimes the paths had angles of forty-five degrees ascent, and Christiaan shuddered to think of what would happen if one of the long leather traces would break. If Kootjie shared his father's concern, you couldn't tell it. His brow wrinkled in concentration, he'd whipped and chided and cajoled the animals to the top and over, after which he would heartily praise them.

While Kootjie finished unhitching the animals, Christiaan cleared a space to work. Then, as the boy sawed away at the willows, Christiaan fashioned a stout raft by lashing the tree limbs together. The wagon and stores were the first to be ferried across the river. Christiaan and Kootjie piloted the craft with long poles. Next came the sheep and goats and oxen, and finally Johanna and Sina.

The mood on the far side of the river was marked by a high degree of gaiety and festivity, unlike anything Christiaan could remember at the most memorable Nachtmaal. Children ran and jumped and played games. But presently there arose a sound above that of the laughter and the deep, low rumble of the water. The clear notes of a psalm of thanksgiving rose from among the women.

The very air and sunlight seemed keener and brighter now that the settlers-turned-trekkers were no longer under British rule.

Johanna climbed into the back of the wagon, grateful for the few days they would spend beside the river. Not only would the water barrels be topped off, but it was also a break from the road dust, which, when it touched sweaty skin, made everyone look like Red Indians with strange white rings around their eyes. In the wagon, the dust covered everything and got into everything—foodstuffs, clothing, oils and creams, personal items. It wouldn't have been a trek in Africa without dust or the smells of travel.

The land itself had a dry, peppery fragrance, which mingled with the pungency of human sweat and the deep, rich odor of native workers. These smeared their bodies with fat and red ochre, which gave out a ripe, partly rancid, smell.

Johanna used to laugh at the way Europeans, when they first discovered the smell, were nauseated by it. For her, it was as much a part of Africa as were the animals and mountains and tribes.

The wagon into which she climbed was a testimony to the community spirit of the Boer people. When word spread through Grahamstown about the devastation of the Xhosa attack, relief in the form of material goods and provisions was immediate. Piet Retief was responsible for securing them a wagon for the trek.

The wagon was of typical trek design, fifteen feet long with a canopy and high wheels painted red and green. The front wheels were three and a half feet in diameter and had ten spokes, while the back wheels were five feet in diameter with fourteen spokes. The wheel size made no difference to Johanna. She remembered the dimensions only because Retief had emphasized them several times in her hearing. Johanna would not have cared if they were ten feet tall and painted bright red, as long as they were round and would get her and her family where they wanted to go.

The great bed occupied the whole covered portion of the wagon. Over the bed were hooks for Christiaan's guns, which were kept within easy reach. Under the bed was a coffinlike wagon box. This was where the clothes were stored.

A long shelf was built onto one side of the wagon, with a ledge around it to prevent things from falling off when the wagon moved. In the front of the wagon hung two small barrels. One was for water; it had a drinking cup attached to it by a chain. The other was locked and filled with brandy for use in emergencies. Overhead, in the middle of the wagon, there was a hanging lantern.

As Johanna checked their provisions, she couldn't help but be affected by the joyous sounds coming from the other side of the canvas. The laughter and joy were that of a free people on their way to a promised land. But what they seemed to be forgetting, she thought, was that the Israelites, in order to reach *their* promised land, had to first go through the hardships of the wilderness. And then, even after reaching the promised land, they encountered faith-testing trials in various forms —the walls of Jericho, the sin of Achan, the resistance of the Canaanites. Her biblical knowledge, as well as some of the rumor she'd heard, tempered her enthusiasm.

She couldn't help but wonder what *their* wilderness would be like. She'd heard travelers' tales about the arid region they were about to cross. One such tale described how a leather thong left outside for an hour in the sun had shriveled and fallen to dust when it was picked up, so hot was it.

And then there was the report about the van Rensburg party, ten men, nine women, thirty children, colored servants, their flocks and their herds. Butchered, all of them except two children. Their wagons were looted and set on fire, their corpses tossed into the flames, and the cattle driven off. As the report went, they were attacked suddenly at night by an *impi*, a regiment of Zulu warriors. The van Rensburgs fought back gallantly until dawn, when their ammunition ran out.

Johanna checked the oil in the wagon's interior lamp and polished its chimney. She told herself that it did her no good to borrow trouble from tomorrow. Maybe the Xhosa war had scarred her more than she realized. Still, she couldn't help but feel that the whole Retief party was overly buoyant regarding their prospects. She wondered, given a year from now, how much of the jubilation she presently heard outside the wagon would remain.

Sina sat beneath a willow tree, contentedly sewing. A stack of clothes that needed mending lay beside her. She watched with mild amusement the less successful attempts made by some of the trekkers to cross the Great River.

One man was so busy yelling directions to his wife on shore that he accidentally backed off the side of his raft and, with arms twirling like windmills, splashed into the river. His son—Sina assumed the boy and only other person on the raft was the man's son—stopped poling and started to rescue his father by stretching his pole toward him. But then the pilotless raft began drifting downriver.

Mid-rescue, the boy panicked, pulled his pole back and corrected the errant raft. So there he was, caught between keeping the raft on course and pulling his father from the river. After several failed attempts to do both, the boy stuck to piloting the raft. His father, who seemed to have no trouble swimming, splashed feverishly behind the raft, yelling all the way across. The man didn't catch up with his raft until it had reached the shore.

Of course, when the father caught up with his son, he gave the boy a sound thrashing, which Sina felt the youngster didn't deserve. The whole thing was the father's fault. Besides, the boy did a man's job by getting the raft safely ashore and rescuing the family's goods, and, besides that, everything turned out all right.

Sina concluded that parents tended to be overreactive and unreasonable, *especially* when things turned out all right. Take her mother, for example. It was weeks after Karel found her walking dazed near the old Klyn farm before her mother could look at her without getting angry. At first, of course, her mother was relieved that Sina had survived the attack. But that moment of motherly tenderness evaporated like a drop of water on a hot skillet, and with as much agitation and popping, the moment she learned that Sina had deliberately run away to be with Henry.

Sina had seen her mother angry before but never this furious. Her mother's entire demeanor blackened and billowed like a summer thunderhead, resulting in a storm that lasted for days. The slightest remark could set off bolts of fury and a voice that thundered and shook the walls. Everyone avoided her.

After about a week the storm localized, affecting Sina only. She was never allowed out of her mother's sight. The two worked side by side from before sunup to after sundown. The only time her mother spoke to her was to give her directions for more work. This went on for another full week. Eventually, the storm lessened, and the thunder quieted.

But even now, months later, there was still residue from the storm. Sina was not allowed to go anyplace without an escort, which often meant Kootjie. Until now, that hadn't bothered her. There had been no place to go. But now that the wagons would soon be catching up with the earlier trekking party—Henry's, specifically—an escort would be embarrassing. Worse, if it was her little brother, it would be humiliating.

"Overreactive and unreasonable," Sina muttered as she stitched. "Especially considering that everything turned out all right."

Lowering tired hands into her lap, she gazed at the broad river. So much larger than the Fish River. To think, they were in a new land. And Henry was just a few weeks away!

Everything had indeed turned out all right. She and Henry would be part of producing a new generation in a new land, with their own laws and government and leaders. Sina wondered what role her children would play in this new land. Would they be governors? Magistrates? Predicants? Judges? Or just leading citizens? She gave no thought to their being ordinary citizens, not with Henry Klyn as their father.

"Sina? Is Kootjie around?"

A broad-shouldered shadow fell across Sina's lap. She followed its length to see who was speaking to her.

"Conraad!" she said, squinting and shielding her eyes against the sun behind him.

"Oh, excuse me!" Conraad cried. He ambled around the tree. "I didn't mean to make you stare into the sun."

Turning her head, Sina followed him to the other side. "No need for apologies," she said, smiling at his genuine concern. "I haven't seen Kootjie lately. Have you been to the wagon yet? Or he might be with the oxen."

With lowered head, Conraad cleared his throat and replied, "Um . . . no, I haven't gone there yet . . . I was passing by . . . and saw you sitting here alone . . . so, well, I thought . . . I could ask you . . . since you're his sister and all . . ."

In his entire rambling reply, never once did he look directly at Sina. He looked beside her, behind her, above her, but never at her.

"Conraad!" Sina cried. "Is that a beard?"

Startled by her exclamation, Conraad jumped. Then, a self-conscious hand rose to his chin. It stroked the heavy but short growth. "Well," he mumbled, "I guess it is." He seemed as surprised to find it there as Sina had been.

Because Conraad and Kootjie had always been close friends, she tended to forget that Conraad was her age. Actually, he was nearly half a year older. But because he and Kootjie had conspired in one immature prank after another, she had always thought of him as younger. But the Conraad that stood beside her now looked more man than boy. It was a little disconcerting.

"It's very becoming," she said.

Conraad blushed deeply, still stroking his beard.

Sina suppressed a smile at his reaction. Thinking the conversation was over, she returned to her mending. She finished the stitching on her father's shirt, tied off the thread, and was lifting it to her teeth to snap off the end when she saw Conraad's huge boots. He was still standing beside her. She looked up. Although his body was facing her, his head was turned toward the river, watching the last of the river crossings.

"Is there something else I can help you with?"

"Huh? Oh . . . no . . . no . . . I was just standing here."

Sina nodded. She placed the finished shirt aside and picked up another.

Conraad didn't move.

"You mending?" he asked.

"*Ja* . . ." Looking at the stack of clothing and the threaded needle in her hand, she thought, *Did he have to ask?*

"Looks like a lot," he said.

"Enough to keep me busy awhile."

Conraad nodded seriously, as though she had said something important. He gave no indication he was leaving.

"I assume your family made it safely across the river," Sina said.

"*Ja,* they did."

"Were the twins scared crossing the river?"

"No . . . matter of fact, they liked it."

"That's good."

"*Ja.*"

Conraad didn't move. He was there but wasn't there. The body was present, but the mind seemed to wander to the river, to the bark of the willow tree, to his fingernails, to the lowering sun. After fifteen minutes of sharing the same part of the earth—for that was all Sina could conclude they were doing—Conraad excused himself.

"Like to talk more," he said, "but I have work to do."

"Aren't you going to find Kootjie?"

"Huh? Oh . . . um . . . maybe later. I have work . . . and all . . ."

He ambled away, then stopped and turned back. "Good-bye, Sina," he said.

"Good-bye, Conraad." She watched him go. When he was no longer in sight, she cried, "What was *that* all about?"

Christiaan stood with his back to the river and, staring across the high veld, pondered what the days ahead would bring them. It was indeed a land of promise. Now that he was here, he could see more clearly its potential. The land seemed to go on forever. It was impossible for a man to grasp the enormous vastness of Africa until he actually saw it for himself by traveling across it on foot, or on horseback, or by wagon.

Beyond each range of hills lay another far horizon. Always the same. Pale-brown grass and bush and thorn trees, rocky mountains, dark valleys, sunlit plains. There was no break and no order, no roads or towns, just places that, when you got there, turned out to be merely an expanse of bush or plain exactly like the landscape you just passed.

He too had heard rumors about the land. Rumors that were far different from the ones that occupied Johanna's mind. The rumors he heard were stories of the open spaces and the hunting to be done. One traveler in the course of a week was reported to have shot three elephants, two rhinos, a giraffe, and ten hippos.

But it wasn't the land itself or the abundance of game that most excited Christiaan van der Kemp. As the sun set on the Great River and campfires flickered against the canopies of more than one hundred wagons, he was most grateful for the promise of freedom. The freedom to be left alone. The freedom to be ignored.

22

The van der Kemps, along with the others in the party led by Piet Retief, caught up with the earlier group of trekkers at Winburg. A scout had made contact with the Retief company several weeks previously and had reported their crossing of the Orange River. Their arrival was much anticipated. When the first wagons came into sight, some of the earlier trekkers rode out to meet them.

Christiaan was riding beside the wagon as Kootjie urged the weary oxen forward, promising them several days' rest once they reached the other wagons. Johanna and Sina shared the wagon bench, each bundled against the chill in the air that promised cooler months ahead.

Sina leaned forward in anticipation as rider after rider approached, then passed them by with hearty greetings of welcome. Although she acknowledged each rider cheerfully, she was clearly looking for one rider in particular.

A horseman with a familiar bearing rode directly toward the van der Kemp wagon. Sina's face brightened expectantly; then, when the rider was close enough to see his face, her smiled dimmed, but only a little.

Christiaan had similar feelings when he recognized the rider, except that his feelings went from apprehension to dread. "Look who's coming to greet us," he whispered so softly that Sina couldn't hear him.

Johanna's eyebrows rose in recognition and understanding of her husband's comment. She whispered back, "Better to face the devil first thing in the morning than to dread the battle all day long."

"Van der Kemp!" the rider hailed Christiaan.

"Oloff!" Christiaan greeted the elder Klyn.

"Greetings, *Mynheer* Klyn!" Sina said excitedly.

Klyn seemed mildly surprised at the voice from the wagon, as though it had suddenly sneaked up on him. "*Mevrou* van der Kemp," he greeted Johanna first. "*Mejuffrouw* . . ."

"Sina," Johanna offered.

"*Mejuffrouw* Sina," Klyn repeated.

Sina was taken aback by the fact that Klyn had not remembered her name, but not enough to keep her from blurting out, "Is Henry coming too?"

"Henry?" Again he wore a surprised look. "Why would Henry be riding out?"

"No reason," Sina said softly. "I was just curious." Her disappointment was written all over her face. It went much deeper than Henry's failure to greet her. Klyn's response indicated he was unaware of any relationship between Henry and her. Sina folded her arms, lowered her head, and hunched over like a flower pulling in its petals for the night.

If Klyn noticed the effect his discourse had on Sina, he didn't show it. Reining his horse around, he rode beside Christiaan.

"Hear you lost your farm," he said.

"*Ja.*"

"Everything?"

Christiaan nodded sadly. "*Ja.*"

Klyn scrutinized the van der Kemp wagon. "This your only wagon?"

"*Ja,*" Christiaan said, having heard that Klyn and Henry had departed the colony with ten wagons. The average Boer family traveled with at least three to carry their possessions, foodstuffs, spare wagon parts, guns, powder, ammunition, and a lifetime of memories.

"You should consider yourself fortunate," Klyn said. "You have only the one wagon to worry about, not fifteen."

"I'd heard you left the colony with ten wagons."

"You heard wrong. Fifteen."

"For just you and Henry?"

"So you can appreciate my dilemma," Klyn said as though the problem grieved him deeply. "My worries are compounded by having to oversee the number of workers needed to keep all fifteen wagons rolling."

"I can only imagine," Christiaan said dryly. "Given the fact that you have so many wagons to oversee, I appreciate the time you've taken to come out and welcome us. We'll understand if you can't stay long."

Klyn didn't appear to catch the hint. Or if he did, he was too ornery to take it. He rode in silence, his eyes fixed steadfastly on the horizon, where a sea of wagon canopies awaited them.

Christiaan exchanged glances with Johanna. She motioned with her head toward Klyn, urging him to get it over with. *Better to face the devil first thing in the morning than to dread the battle all day long.*

"Is that a new horse?" Christiaan asked Klyn.

Klyn beamed proudly. "Finest steed I've ever owned," he said, slapping the chestnut's flank. "Bought it especially for this trek at Graaff-Reinet, knowing that I'd need a good Cape Colony horse . . ."

For more than a quarter of an hour Klyn described the events that led to the purchase of the horse, including the owner's reluctance to part with the animal, Klyn's professed superior knowledge of horseflesh, and the three days of negotiations it took to complete the deal.

Christiaan pretended great interest, prompting Oloff for details at every opportunity. He avoided direct eye contact with his wife but did not fail to notice the annoyed shaking of her head in the background.

His was a deliberate ploy. There was nothing a Boer liked to talk about more than his cattle, his dogs, his guns, and his colonial-bred horses.

The Cape Colony horses were more thickset than their European counterparts and could not draw such heavy loads, but they could go without shoeing, climb better, and do with much less fodder. They could cover sixty miles a day if they were not pushed too hard, going a good half of it at a canter, adapting their speed to the slightest pressure applied by their riders. They stood motionless while their riders fired, then galloped off again, making an impossible target for an enemy who had to rely on his own two legs and assegai. When their masters dismounted, the horses were trained to let them rest their heavy guns across their backs or necks. Many were trained for the lion hunt.

"A fine horse indeed," Christiaan said, trying to think of more questions to ask.

"If I have a weakness," Klyn said, "it's horses. This one in particular."

Christiaan smiled and nodded and purposefully kept from looking at Johanna, though he could feel her gaze on him.

"And your horse . . ." Klyn said. "I assume that is *your* horse, or did you lose your horses in the fire too?"

"One of the few things that survived," Christiaan said jovially. "Wouldn't have thought of beginning this trek without it."

The moment the words left his mouth, he knew he'd blundered.

Johanna knew it too. She let out a "Ha!" loud enough to be heard half a mile away.

Klyn recognized the opening and took it. "If I remember correctly," he said with a superior smile, "you made an impassioned speech at Nachtmaal—something about your commitment to the frontier and building . . ." he thought a moment ". . . Klaarstroom, wasn't it?"

"*Ja,*" Christiaan said weakly. "Klaarstroom."

"You said something about patience and understanding being the key to coexistence with both the British and the Xhosa. That there was enough land and cattle for everybody. Isn't that what you said, or did I misunderstand you?"

"*Ja*, that is what I said."

Klyn shrugged as though he were befuddled. "Well then, you can understand my confusion when I heard you were leaving your land of plenty for this great unknown, uncharted wilderness."

It was time to change tactics. Christiaan decided he could either let Klyn gloat the rest of the way to the wagons, or he could . . .

"I admit I was wrong," he said eagerly, enthusiastically. "You were right, Oloff! I should have bowed to the wisdom of your years, but my foolish pride prevented me from doing it. Oh, the heartache I could have saved myself and my family had I listened to you in the first place. You had the foresight I lacked, and I paid dearly for it. I only hope that in the future I will have the wisdom to see things as clearly as you see them. And let me hasten to thank you for giving me this opportunity to set the record straight, Oloff. Thank you. You are a kind and gracious man and a good friend."

Klyn sat stunned in his saddle. He obviously was struggling to think of something to say. "It takes a strong man to admit he's wrong," he murmured.

"A humbled man, Oloff. A humbled man."

Klyn straightened himself. "Well," he said, "I'd better ride ahead. A man with fifteen wagons can't afford to wander afar for long."

"God's blessings on you, Oloff," Christiaan said.

"Oh, one more thing . . ." Klyn said.

"*Ja?*"

"Your man Retief. Word has it that he will want to assume the leadership of the combined trekking parties. That would not be wise. Potgieter is the best man for the job. When the time comes for a show of support, I'm sure you'll have the wisdom to see this matter as clearly as I see it." With that, the elder Klyn urged his chestnut horse forward, the white tail of his Dopper shirt bouncing after him. It was Christiaan's turn to look stunned. His flattery tactic had backfired. How was he to know that Klyn would use the flattery as a lever to garner an endorsement for his man Potgieter, another Dopper? It was asking too much for Christiaan to support a Dopper over Piet Retief. He couldn't do it. But by refusing to back Potgieter, he would have to confront Oloff Klyn yet another time.

A wry smile spread across Johanna's face. "Dearest, I said battle the devil. That means to resist him. Dancing with the devil is a whole other matter. When you dance with the devil, someone has to pay the piper."

Christiaan slumped dejectedly in his saddle. "*Ja,* Baas," he said.

Sina pulled back the canvas and peered out excitedly in the direction of the music. The musicians were warming up. She could hear them but not see them. A fiddle laboriously ascended and descended a scratchy scale, stopping occasionally to coax a string into tune. Before the evening was over, that same fiddle would be nimbly warbling one familiar song after another. Accompanying the fiddle was the wheezing wail of a concertina and the hollow round sounds of a flute.

With a grin and a not-so-ladylike jump, Sina bounded from the wagon. A reception marked the first night together for the combined trekking parties, and she was eager to get on with it. The circled wagons. The music. The interaction with friends. It was like Nachtmaal, only better—no one ever went home.

She smoothed the wrinkles of her green silk dress. She straightened her white stockings and wiped the dust from her shoes. This was a night she would remember forever, and she wanted it to be perfect. For Sina it was more than just a celebration of the joining of two trekking parties; it was the night in which she and Henry would be reunited. Tonight would be the beginning of their forever together.

Her mother emerged from the canvas covering and, with a couple of grunts and groans, swung thick legs over the back of the wagon and climbed out. "Are you ready to go?"

Sina smoothed her dress again and nodded. "Where's Father?"

"Here," Christiaan said, coming from the front of the wagon. He was dressed all in black with a white linen shirt. "Kootjie is still with the oxen. He'll join us when he can."

Sina's heart skipped excitedly. With Kootjie presently unavailable, she would be free to meet Henry without her little brother tagging along.

"Until Kootjie arrives," Johanna said, "you'll have to stay with us, Sina."

"But—" she started to object.

Her mother gave her a stare that stopped her cold. There would be no negotiating. No appeal. No grace.

Sina's skipping heart slowed appreciably. It now trudged along, shackled by parental command. Her head lowered, her feet shuffling in the dirt, she trailed behind her parents as the concertina squeezed out a merry tune in the distance. She never thought she'd be eager for her brother to join her, but he was certainly better than having to tag along with her parents from one boring adult conversation to another.

The laager, or circle of wagons, was abuzz with activity when they arrived.

"Like Nachtmaal," Johanna observed.

"Better than Nachtmaal," Christiaan replied. "This is a gathering of free people."

Everywhere they looked, his statement was proving itself. It *was* better than Nachtmaal. The musicians seemed livelier, the celebrants friendlier, louder, more spirited. Stories were richer. Jokes were funnier. People laughed harder. Freedom was a spice that made a good celebration even better.

Everyone was having a rousing time. Everyone except Sina. She followed her parents dutifully, answered when spoken to, rarely smiled, and prayed that Kootjie would arrive soon.

The young people gathered on the far side of the compound. Sina was careful to maneuver herself behind clumps of conversing adults so that she wouldn't be spotted by any of her friends. The last thing she wanted was for one of them to come over and ask why she wasn't joining them! It was a delicate task, for while she wanted to remain hidden from her friends, she also wanted to spy on them—to see who was talking to whom, who had arrived, and who had not.

Deborah van Aardt was there, as conspicuous as ever, surrounded by her usual entourage, twittering on and on like a mindless little bird. Karel stood nearby, his hands stuffed in his pockets. Even from a distance Sina could see that he was upset about something.

Conraad Pfeffer was just arriving. He circled the group with a smile. No one greeted him, which wasn't unusual. Conraad was the kind of boy who could walk into a room without drawing anyone's attention. If he was bothered by his invisible existence, he didn't show it. Taking up a position a few feet distant from the edge of the group, he benignly looked around, presumably scouting for Kootjie.

Noticeably absent among the group was Henry. Sina methodically scanned the compound. There was no sign of him anywhere.

Part of her rejoiced that Henry hadn't arrived yet. If she could manage to get there before him, she wouldn't have to explain her tardiness. But another part of her worried over his absence. Was he coming? Had something unfortunate happened to him?

Just as the musicians announced they were going to take a short break, Kootjie emerged from between two wagons. Squinting, he surveyed the festivities. Spotting the younger crowd and Conraad, who was signaling to him, Kootjie lowered his head and ambled that direction.

Sina pursed her lips. *What is that boy thinking?* Gathering up the front of her dress, she charged after him.

"Sina!" The tone of maternal authority weighed heavily in her spoken name.

Swinging around, Sina pointed to her brother. "Kootjie's here!" she pleaded.

Her mother followed the direction of Sina's pointing finger until her gaze rested upon Kootjie. With a solemn nod, Sina was given permission to accompany him, which she did in haste.

"What are you doing?" she berated her brother the moment she caught up with him.

"I'm walking over to Conraad," Kootjie said innocently.

"You were supposed to come and get me first!"

"I didn't see you."

"You didn't look! I was watching you!"

"So then, what's the problem? You saw me before I saw you. You're here, aren't you?"

"The problem is that you were supposed to come and get me! Where were you anyway?"

"Ticks."

"Ticks?"

Kootjie nodded. "Thousands of them. Never seen so many in my life. Tiny red ones covering the underside of the oxen. When they get under your skin, they itch like mad!"

He rolled up his sleeve to reveal an arm covered with red bumps. Most of the bumps showed signs of being scratched. They were developing into sores. Accompanying the afflicted arm was a pungent odor.

"Kootjie, you stink!" Sina shrieked, shoving his arm away. "You smell like cattle!"

Her brother shrugged, unconcerned. He rolled down his sleeve. "I hadn't noticed."

"Believe me, everyone else will!"

Just then she was suddenly aware of another presence. It was the tip of his polished boots that first announced his arrival. Sina's gaze followed long corduroy pants legs up to a waistband that had neither belt nor braces, across a distinct shirt-revealing gap, to a blue nankeen waistcoat, to a strong chin, thin cheeks, and deep blue eyes.

"Good evening, Sina."

"Henry!" She could manage only the single word, and it was breathless.

177

"Kootjie." Henry acknowledged her brother. "Seems like we'll be spending some time together tonight."

"What do you mean?" Sina shot an angry look at her brother. If he had told anyone . . . *anyone* . . . that she was being punished, she would . . .

"Henry and I have watch tonight," Kootjie said.

"Oh!" Sina said, suddenly sheepish. Her embarrassment turned to envy. She wished she could be with Henry all night long. *Patience, Sina,* she told herself. *That time will come.*

"Shall we join the others?" Henry offered.

Sina responded with her sweetest, most feminine nod, expecting Henry to offer her his arm.

He didn't.

Instead, he moved to one side so that Kootjie was between them. "You smell like you came straight from the field," Henry said to Kootjie jokingly.

"I did," Kootjie replied. "Ticks."

"You too? Our cattle and oxen are covered with them!"

Sina frowned. Her great reunion with her beloved Henry was being interrupted by a discussion about ticks! She would have to do something about that. She spied Karel. Maybe she could make Henry jealous.

Quickening her step, Sina left her brother and Henry behind. "Karel!" she cooed. "How long has it been?" Throwing her arms around his neck, she hugged him.

The hug prompted several reactions. Karel drew back in surprise. Deborah scowled. Kootjie's mouth fell open, as did Conraad's. And Henry's brow furrowed with displeasure. Of all the reactions, Henry's was the only one that mattered.

Like a fisherman who had just hooked a fish, Sina proceeded to reel him in. Drawing upon her earlier observation, she took Karel by the arm and asked, "Why so glum? This is supposed to be a festive time."

Karel looked away from her. "Not now. Not here."

"Father refused to give his consent," Deborah said. A pouting lip protruded.

"Delayed in giving his consent," Karel corrected her.

"He's right," Deborah said lightly. "Father didn't say no; but he certainly didn't say yes." She wrinkled her nose impishly. "He's hoping for a better offer."

"Karel, I'm sorry," Sina said. All of a sudden, her attempts to get Henry's attention didn't seem so important. She knew how Karel felt about Deborah. For years he had talked of marrying her. Planned openly for it. Treated her with care and the kind of attention that one associates with long-term relationships. Their wedding was an event merely awaiting its time.

Karel shrugged, pretending the recent development didn't hurt.

Sina wasn't fooled. She could tell that the response of Deborah's father had cut him deeply.

"I'll just have to convince her father, that's all," he said.

"No small task," Henry said with a smirk, "considering that van Aardt has refused to let you see Deborah anymore."

Karel shot a pained look at Deborah.

"Was that supposed to be a secret? It wasn't supposed to be a secret, was it?" Wide-open, innocent eyes and batting lashes feigned ignorance.

At least, Sina *thought* she was feigning ignorance. With Deborah it was always so difficult to tell.

Karel said, "*Mynheer* van Aardt has restricted my involvement with Deborah. He didn't tell me I couldn't see her. He just thinks that other suitors will stay away if they get the impression Deborah and I are pledged to each other."

"That's right." Deborah nodded eagerly. "That's what Father said. I can still see Karel. It's just that Father wants me to try to attract other boys too."

"No problem there," Sina muttered. Her comment drew a scowl from Karel, and she wished she hadn't said it.

The concertina player wheezed one jaunty tune after another, accompanied by the finger-flying fiddler and the red-cheeked flutist. The interior of the laager swirled with color and mirth as the weary Boer trekkers squeezed out of the night as much merriment as it could hold.

The only pocket of gloom seemed to be around Sina. *Mynheer* van Aardt checked on his daughter's company regularly through the night, which meant that Karel was forced to keep his distance from her. Instead, he shadowed Sina and sulked. Kootjie, likewise, was never out of arm's reach, taking literally his responsibility to stay close to his sister. After the initial thrill of being her keeper wore off, he felt his own celebration strained, and he turned surly.

Where there was Kootjie, Conraad Pfeffer could always be found nearby. Sina noticed that ever since they had crossed the Great River he had been acting strangely. Several times she caught him staring open-mouthed at her. When she managed to catch his eye, he would blush, turn away, and grin like a fool.

Surrounded this way by male attention, Sina found it impossible to converse with Henry for any length of time, let alone find a way to get alone with him. She had dreamed of a re-creation of that night at Nachtmaal—the music, the bench, the touching, the suggestion they go to the peach orchard. Now she would settle for a few moments of private conversation with him.

As the celebration began to break up and the three-man band wound down, Sina lost all hope for the evening. Karel stood grousing next to Kootjie, who was anxious to get back to the wagon so that he could prepare himself for his first night watch. Conraad flanked Sina on the other side, doing nothing but standing next to her yet seeming to enjoy himself immensely.

Henry was in the near distance talking to Deborah and her followers. He said something that made them all laugh. Deborah laughed the loudest. As she did, her eyelids fluttered in a flirtatious way. She reached out and touched Henry's forearm, and Sina felt the color rising in her neck. She tried to tell herself that Deborah was just being Deborah and that in no way would Henry be affected by her shallow feminine wiles.

Then, to her horror, Henry placed his hand on top of Deborah's hand, pinning it against his arm. He leaned forward and gazed past Deborah's fluttering eyelids and smiled that winning smile that Sina ordinarily loved to see. Their gaze held for what seemed an eternity.

A bitter brew of anger, frustration, and panic stirred inside Sina. She could feel tears welling behind her eyes.

Kootjie stepped in front of her, blocking her view of Henry and Deborah. "Father's motioning for us to return to the wagon."

Sina didn't respond. She didn't blink. She simply continued staring. Kootjie's chest was a short distance in front of her. Had her eyes been functioning in their normal manner, all she could have seen would have been a wrinkled, slightly soiled shirt and an open waistcoat. But her eyes were not focused on the present; they were replaying that horrible scene—Deborah touching Henry's arm; he touching her hand, laughing, giving her *that* gaze, the gaze that should have been meant for Sina, the gaze that she had dreamed of seeing when she ran away from home and for mile after mile as she traveled with her family into the high veld.

"Sina? Did you hear me? We have to go home!"

Kootjie's sharp voice, with the unfriendly tone that brothers and sisters reserve for each other, broke through the memory. That and a whiff of his dirty clothes brought Sina back to the present.

"Father's waiting!" he insisted, pointing across the laager.

Sina followed his pointing finger. Her father stood next to a wagon, talking to Conraad's father. With his arm he motioned for Sina and Kootjie to join him.

The night that Sina had dreamed about had turned into a disaster.

It was beyond redemption. Her only consolation was that, now that they were traveling together, there would be daily opportunities to see Henry. But tonight there was nothing more she could do. Turning dejectedly toward her father, she started across the laager.

"Sina, thanks for being sympathetic," Karel called after her.

She managed a weak smile in return.

"Mind if I join you? My father's waiting for me too." Conraad didn't wait for an answer. He took up a position next to Sina.

She shared her weak smile with him. *Why not?* she thought sarcastically. *It's the perfect ending to a perfect evening.* Sandwiched between her brother and Conraad, she shuffled wearily toward her home on wheels.

"Sina! Wait!"

It was *his* voice! Twirling around, she saw Henry hurrying toward her.

Ignoring the boys on either side of her, he grabbed Sina by the hand and pulled her a short distance to one side. "I couldn't let you leave without saying good-bye," he said, smiling his best smile.

"You couldn't?"

"I had wished for things to be different for us tonight."

"Different? How?"

"Well . . ." Henry shrugged and looked down as though embarrassed, but his neck and cheeks didn't color. "If you'll recall, the last time we were together, we were on our way to the peach orchard. And I was hoping that tonight we could have gotten away . . . alone . . . just for a while . . . to talk."

"I would have liked that."

"You would have?"

Sina was taken aback by the question. Her feelings for Henry were so overwhelming that at times she felt as though she radiated with desire for him—so much so that anyone within a hundred yards could feel it too. But Henry had seemed not to notice. And for him to desire her company—well, it was almost too good to be true.

"Why wouldn't I?" he asked. "Don't you know that you're special to me, Sina? Tonight didn't work out, but there will be other nights."

"Other nights . . ."

"Soon."

"Oh! Please, let it be soon!"

Henry gave her that look, then turned and left the laager.

Sina floated home between her brother and Conraad.

23

Kootjie pulled his heavy jacket around him and squinted into the blackness. He sat on a rock, his back to the fire. Behind him, Henry leaned toward the flame. He clapped and rubbed his hands together to get warm.

The coolness of the rock penetrated Kootjie's moleskin pants. He shivered, not so much from the cold but because he was scared and nervous. He had looked forward to this evening. It was the first time he'd stood watch at night without his father. But until this moment he hadn't realized how much comfort came from knowing his father was close by should anything happen. Tonight was different. Tonight it was just Kootjie and Henry. Peers. Equals. For Kootjie, the added responsibility sat chilly on his shoulders.

To make matters worse, the night was inky black. It was as though a black curtain hung at the edge of the fire's light. Kootjie had moved away from the fire and kept his back to it in an attempt to adjust his eyes to the darkness. It did him little good.

It was unnerving to think that without warning any number of beasts or persons could burst through that inky curtain and be on top of them in mere seconds. Deprived of his ability to see, Kootjie shifted emphasis to his other senses. He strained his ears for any sounds of life, friendly or unfriendly. It wasn't much, but it was the best he could do. He wondered if it was possible for a man to smell or taste approaching danger.

A lion roared in the distance. Kootjie jumped and gripped his gun. An elephant answered. On the edge of the rock, he listened hard, trying to determine if the animals were on the move and, if so, in what direction. No matter how hard he strained, he heard nothing more. He couldn't decide which was worse, hearing the wild animals or not hearing them. It was going to be a long night.

"You're going to freeze over there," Henry said.

The sound of his voice made Kootjie jump again.

Henry had bundled himself up tightly with blankets so that only his face was exposed. He was reclined next to the fire against a fallen tree limb. His gun was propped up next to him. What if a lion suddenly leaped at them out of the darkness? Kootjie wondered if Henry would have time to shed the blankets and retrieve his weapon.

"One of us needs to be ready at all times," Kootjie replied. "I'll warm up when it's your turn to keep watch."

Henry sniggered at Kootjie's response. "Can't shoot if your fingers are frozen stiff."

Kootjie flexed his hands. They were stiff but not enough to prevent him from firing his gun. "I'll manage," he said.

Henry chuckled. It was an unkind chuckle, the satirical grunting a learned person makes when a novice fails to heed the voice of experience. "By the way," Henry called to him, "what was all that about tonight between you and Sina?" His voice was muffled. He'd pulled the blanket up over his nose.

"Between me and Sina? I don't know what you're talking about."

"Sure you do. You and Conraad. The two of you never wandered further than a few feet from her all night. Whenever she moved, you moved. You didn't use to do that at Nachtmaal."

"Oh, that."

"Yeah, that. What was it all about?"

Kootjie sniffed and rubbed the cold tip of his nose with the palm of his hand. Sina would be furious with him if he told Henry about her punishment, and even more so if he revealed the reason for the punishment.

"Are you going to tell me, or not?"

"Sina would kill me."

This seemed to spark Henry's interest. He scooted into a more upright position. "So then, there's something to tell."

"You won't hear it from me."

Henry chuckled his superior chuckle. "I understand your dilemma," he said. "You're young. You don't know any better."

Kootjie frowned. He didn't like the implication that he was less than grown up.

"When you become as experienced as me, you'll learn that there exists a perpetual war between men and women. Unfortunately, in this war the men are at a natural disadvantage."

"What are you talking about?" Kootjie cried.

"I'm talking about the way women share everything with each other," Henry replied. "They talk to each other all the time. Tell each other everything. Everything! That gives them an advantage over men because we tend to keep everything to ourselves. You've noticed that, haven't you? Women always talking about how men are always doing this and how men never do that?"

Kootjie nodded, though he still didn't know what this had to do with him and Sina.

"And when men get together, what do we usually talk about?"

Kootjie thought a moment. "Guns. Horses. Cattle. Wagons. That sort of thing."

"My point exactly! Why don't men talk about women? If we did, maybe we could have a fighting chance against them. The way I see it, it's your responsibility to tell me what you know—man to man."

"Makes sense," Kootjie said in a philosophical tone. He hadn't thought in those terms before. Sides had been chosen. Lines drawn. Was he on his sister's side, or was he on the side of men everywhere?

"Seems to me," Henry sniffed, "you have a decision to make. If you asked me, I'd say it's time you started to fulfill your role as a man."

Facing the darkness, Kootjie nodded. Was he a man or not? "Sina's not allowed to go off by herself," he said. "Mother won't allow it. I have to stick close to her."

"Why?"

"She's being punished."

"Sina? Punished? That's hard to believe."

"Not as hard as you might think," Kootjie said with an air of superior knowledge. "You don't know her like I do."

"And believe me, Kootjie, I deeply appreciate the fact that you are enlightening me regarding Sina. What is she being punished for?"

Kootjie relaxed. The more he talked about the matter, the easier it was for him. "She ran away. The night the Xhosa attacked. Mother was beside herself. She thought for sure the Xhosa had kidnapped or killed her. Then, after the attack, Sina shows up. The Xhosa had nothing to do with her disappearance. Come to find out, she'd run away the night before."

Henry shifted beneath the blankets. "Let me get this straight," he said. "You have to watch Sina because your parents are afraid she'll run away again?"

"There's no reason for her to run away again," Kootjie said, enjoying his role as the holder of the keys to what seemed to Henry to be a mystery.

"Then why does Sina need someone to guard her?"

"Mother says it's a matter of trust. Until she trusts Sina again, Sina has to have someone stay with her all the time."

Henry scooted up into a sitting position. The blankets dropped from in front of his mouth. "I still don't understand why she ran away from home. Where was she going?"

"To marry you."

A moment elapsed between the time the explanation hit Henry's ears and the slow, wide grin spread across his face. There was an accompanying flash in his eyes, the kind that appears when a profitable opportunity is spied. Kootjie had seen it in men's eyes at Nachtmaal as they bargained for horses or wagons or guns.

"Was anyone else with her?" Henry asked.

Kootjie shook his head.

"She set out alone?"

"Dumb, huh? Like I said, you don't know her like I know her."

Henry rubbed his chin thoughtfully. "I'm beginning to . . ." For a time he was lost in thought. Then, "You did yourself proud tonight, Kootjie. You proved your loyalty to men everywhere."

Kootjie stared into the blackness, feeling older and wiser and more experienced in worldly matters. He dismissed the sliver of doubt that set uncomfortably like an undigested bit of tainted beef. More than once he assured himself that he had done nothing wrong.

As the night wore on, he forgot about the conversation. It was eclipsed by a more important discussion regarding the Matabele.

"They have a shield covered with spotted oxhide and three types of assegai," Henry explained. "One type of assegai is for stabbing. It has a short shaft about thirty-six inches long with a twelve-inch blade. Another one, also for stabbing, has a shorter blade. Its shaft is up to forty-eight inches long. Then, there's the throwing spear. It has a six-inch blade with a much longer shaft."

Kootjie sat enraptured by Henry's talk of Matabele weapons. Eager eyes fastened on Henry's hands as each assegai size was visually demonstrated. His attention was broken only for an occasional nervous glance at the curtain of darkness that surrounded them.

"So, if the Matabele were out there right now," Kootjie postulated, "they could kill us with their throwing spears before we had a chance to react."

Henry shook his head. "Too risky for them. What if they didn't kill us but only wounded us? It would give us time to get off a shot that would warn the others. No, they'd probably sneak up behind us and club us to death with their *induka*s or slit our throats before we had a chance to react."

Kootjie gulped. *"Induka?"*

"A throwing and clubbing stick. We call them *knopkierie*s."

Kootjie gave an understanding nod.

"Did you know that their leader, Mzilikazi, was formerly one of Shaka's generals?"

"Shaka, the Zulu warrior?"

"The same. Some call him the 'black Napoleon.'"

"I hadn't heard that."

Henry gave a reassuring nod that the quote was an accurate one.

"Do they ever capture people? Or do they just kill them?"

"Sometimes they capture people."

Kootjie gulped again. "What do they do to the people they capture?"

"I've heard they impale their enemies on poles. Slice their flesh to ribbons. Sometimes they cut out their hearts. Other times they throw a still-living victim to wild animals for sport. My father says they're cannibals."

Kootjie's face twisted.

"I remember once, just before they attacked, the field was thick as fleas with black warriors! I'd never seen anything like it."

Kootjie's eyes widened appreciably. "Were you scared?"

"Of course not, horsehead! They're nothing but heathen. God's not going to let a bunch of heathen deprive His chosen people of their promised land. Don't you read your Bible?"

Henry was using his father's words, not his own. Kootjie recognized them but said nothing, taking the rebuke in silence, hoping that Henry would continue the story. In time, he did.

"Sarel Cilliers and a few other men rode within fifty yards of them. They had a Hottentot with them who could speak the language. So he was instructed to ask the Matabele why they had come to murder and rob them."

"What did they say?"

"No sooner had the question been put to them, when they sprang up as one man and roared, 'Mzilikazi! Mzilikazi! Mzilikazi!' They hurled their knobbed sticks at Cilliers and his men and chased them back into the laager. But they didn't attack yet."

"Why not?"

"Who can say? They're savages, not like us. They don't have human brains. Trying to outguess them is like trying to outguess a crazed animal. So we watched as they rounded up all the stray cattle and livestock that surrounded the laager, about eighty head in all. Then they stabbed the cattle to death, cut them up, and ate the meat—raw."

Kootjie made a face.

Henry leaned forward with anticipation. In barely a whisper he said, "Then do you know what they did?"

"Attacked?"

A slow shake of the head. "They sat about on rocks."

"That's all? They just sat down?"

"Not just. While they sat on the rocks, they sharpened their weapons and glared at the laager—sharpening and glaring, sharpening and glaring—until finally the men in the laager could stand it no more. One of them grabbed a red kerchief, held it high, and signaled them with it. Well, I don't know what a red kerchief means to them, but let me tell you, as soon as that kerchief was waved, the Matabele jumped up. They began hissing and drumming their shields, hissing and drumming, louder and louder and louder until the drumming sounded like thunder."

"And then they attacked?"

Henry nodded. "Imagine six thousand black savages running toward you! Shouting. Their faces painted. Assegais raised high. We were instructed not to fire until a signal was given. So we stayed at our posts as they came closer and closer. Shouting and yelling, louder and louder. Then, when they were a mere thirty yards away, the signal to fire was given. There was a deafening roar as all of our guns sounded at once. A dense cloud of gunpowder rose from inside the laager. Warrior fell on top of warrior as our shot found its mark. Two, sometimes three, savages fell from a single blast. Those who escaped the volley launched their razor-sharp assegais at us. The sky was thick with them. When they landed, the canvas canopies of the wagons bristled with them. Afterwards, on one of the canopies we counted seventy-two slashes!"

Henry paused in his story. His eyes played back and forth, lit by the firelight.

"Some of the savages managed to reach the laager. They grabbed at the wheels and tried to pull the wagons apart. When this tactic proved unsuccessful, they tried to climb over the canopies! I remember looking up just in time to see a snarling Matabele warrior ready to leap inside the laager. But *Mevrou* Swanpoel grabbed an ax and chopped his hand off. He fell backward."

"You're making that up!"

Henry looked shocked by the accusation. "You can ask *Mevrou* Swanpoel yourself!" he cried. "You just wait! You'll see for yourself. The Matabele are still out there. So are the Zulu, who are even worse! You'll see that everything I'm telling you is the truth."

But Kootjie wouldn't have to wait. He already believed. More than that, he longed for the day when he would see such things for himself.

"Sometimes," Henry said with a wicked grin, "when I'm lying out here in the darkness—exposed, completely vulnerable—I can still hear that hissing sound, the kind the Matabele made just before they attacked." He cupped his hands around his mouth and hissed.

"Stop doing that!" Kootjie complained. His eyes scanned the darkness, but all he could see was the inky black curtain.

Henry hissed again.

"Henry, stop it!"

"They could be just beyond the edge of light. Crouched. Waiting. Waiting for the nod of a sleepy head or a single moment of inattention. And then . . ." He hissed wickedly.

Henry slept first. Kootjie remained on watch until his eyes could no longer hold themselves open. He awakened Henry long after their agreed upon time. That had been his plan. He hoped to get himself so tired that by the time he lay down he would fall asleep easily. He didn't.

At first he couldn't get comfortable. Then, every time he dozed, Henry would move, and the sound would startle him awake. Finally, after lying still for nearly an hour, he fell into the dark hole of slumber.

"Kootjie!"

His body was being rocked back and forth violently.

"Kootjie! Wake up!"

It was Henry. His eyes were wide with fright and fixed with panic on the blackness. He kept shaking Kootjie and calling to him, seemingly unaware that he was awake.

"What is it?" Kootjie asked, shrugging off Henry's grasp.

Henry glanced down quickly and then back up, as though there was some doubt in his mind that it was still Kootjie under his hand. "I heard something," he said. His voice quivered. It had a raspy, spectral sound to it.

Kootjie was wide awake now. He knew where he was and, more important, knew what dangers lay just beyond the veil of darkness.

"There! Did you hear it?"

Up on his haunches but staying low, Kootjie reached for his gun.

"Did you hear it?" Henry asked again.

"No."

"How could you not have heard it? It came from over there!" Henry pointed into the darkness.

Everything was black. There was no reference point other than the general direction in which Henry was pointing. Kootjie aimed his gun that direction. Beside him, Henry trembled mightily, so much so that the barrel of his gun swung in erratic circles. He was slowly backing away from the direction of the noise. His back hit the fallen tree limb that had earlier served as his pillow, halting his progress.

A rustling sound emerged from the darkness. The shaking of dry leaves. Someone or something was pushing past a bush.

"Did you—"

"I heard it," Kootjie said.

"The first time I heard it, it came from over there." Henry pointed a short distance to his right.

"It could be moving," Kootjie said cautiously, "or there could be more than one of them."

A whimper escaped from Henry's lips. "More than one of what?"

The question went unanswered. The answer was obvious. Matabele.

Kootjie raised his rifle to his shoulder. "I've got this one covered," he whispered. "You aim in the direction you first heard the sound."

"I don't want to die!" Tears streaked Henry's cheeks. His hands trembled so violently his gun rattled.

"Henry, aim your gun over there!" Kootjie shouted.

It looked as if Henry was attempting to haul up an anchor, but he managed to raise the barrel of the rifle and point it in the direction of the first sound.

Kootjie called to the darkness. "Identify yourself!"

There was no response.

He tried again with the same result. "Maybe we scared them off," he said.

"Or maybe they don't answer because the Matabele don't speak our language," Henry said.

"It could just be an animal."

They waited.

No matter how hard he squinted, Kootjie was unable to increase the distance he could see by a single foot.

What to do? Two options came to mind. They could wait for whatever was out there to attack or wander away; or they could light a torch and go out to see what was making the sound. Kootjie was not overly fond of either option. A third one came to mind. Fire a warning shot. A warning to whomever or whatever was out there, it could also serve as a warning to the encampment.

At first, this third option appealed to him. A warning shot would bring his father and the others. They would know what to do. But what if it turned out there was nothing out there? What if, when they arrived, they could find no Matabele or no beast or even tracks of a beast? Kootjie dreaded the implications. His first night on watch would end in embarrassment. The entire camp would laugh at him for months. The boy who was afraid of the dark. No, he'd better make sure he knew what was out there before he did anything that would embarrass him.

"What are we going to do?" Henry moaned.

"We're going to wait."

"Wait for what?"

Another rustle answered Henry's question. Then another.

"It's coming toward us!" Henry's feet dug gouges in the ground as he pushed backwards. The fallen limb scooted in the dirt.

Kootjie stared down his gun barrel, waiting for something to emerge from behind the black veil. The end of his barrel twitched with the pounding of his heart.

Henry grabbed Kootjie by the shoulder. Kootjie looked away for just a moment. Just long enough to free himself from Henry's grasp.

That's when it appeared. For a fraction of a second. A flash of brown and white. Higher than expected. Kootjie caught only a glimpse of it out of the corner of his eye.

"A Matabele shield!" Henry shrieked. His legs shot out in panic, pushing him backwards over the limb. His gun clattered to the ground. In his terror, he grabbed at Kootjie again, getting a fistful of coat as he was falling backward.

"Shoot them!" he screamed. "Shoot them! Shoot them!"

With his hands clamped onto Kootjie's coat, Henry was pulling Kootjie with him over the limb.

Kootjie's mouth gaped in horror as he watched his gun barrel jerk skyward. His back arched over the limb, exposing his belly. An easy target for a Matabele assegai.

"Shoot them! Shoot them! Shoot them!" Henry clawed at him furiously, his hands groping, clutching at anything. One hand managed to grab Kootjie's chin, the other clamped around his neck.

At any moment Kootjie expected to feel a razor-sharp blade slip between his ribs. He didn't know how many warriors were out there, but he figured he could at least get a couple of them if he could just manage to lower his gun. Wrestling to free himself with one hand, with the other he lowered the rifle until the barrel was nearly parallel with his leg. He groped for the trigger. Henry clawed at him and screamed. The gun barrel swayed erratically from side to side.

BLAM!

The rifle's report startled Henry. He let go, falling on one side of the limb while Kootjie slumped to the ground on the other. A heavy thud sounded. It came from the same direction as the rustling noise.

From the sound of the thud, Kootjie figured he'd got one warrior, possibly two. The others would now attack. He scrambled for Henry's rifle and swung it in the direction he expected the attack to come.

All was silent. Still.

Behind him Henry stirred.

Kootjie peered anxiously into the darkness. In the distance, he could hear the alarm sounding in the encampment. Reinforcements would be there soon.

Beyond the dark veil nothing stirred.

Kootjie got to his feet to investigate. He inched his way toward the edge of the firelight, then beyond.

"Oh, no," he moaned.

"What? What is it?" Henry came up behind him. And in an instant, the quivering Henry was gone. In his place was a bold, brash accuser. "Look what you've done!" he cried. "I can't believe it! You fool!"

Kootjie stared dejectedly at the lifeless animal at his feet. Even in the dark, its chestnut color shone. As did the white diamond between its eyes.

"You shot my father's best horse!" Henry cried. "I can't believe it! You shot my father's best horse!"

A mob of trekkers streamed down from the encampment. They were greeted by Henry's cry. "Look what he did! He shot my father's best horse!"

24

It stalked him. Tirelessly. Relentlessly.

With each passing day Jama could feel the predator gaining on him. To throw his pursuer off track, he changed his route. The predator was not fooled. He changed his routine, sleeping by day and traveling by night. The predator adapted accordingly. It was determined, never deviating from its course. On the third week of Jama's journey, the predator caught up with him.

It attacked at dawn. That night Jama had slept fitfully. He arose surrounded by the blackness of the prairie night. Sitting atop a small bluff with his arms wrapped tightly around his hunched-up legs, he watched the crest of the eastern horizon as it prickled with predawn light. Everything was still. So still it was chilling. It was as though the whole world was holding its breath in anticipation of another day. There were no animal grunts or cries or howls. The birds held their song. The leaves of the bushes and trees refused to rustle. The stars hung overhead, silent in their courses. The moment was so still that Jama imagined he could hear the sunrise.

Then, when the first rays of dawn leaped over the horizon into his face, the predator pounced. It fell upon him like an icy blanket, kissing his flesh with a penetrating cold, black gloom. Jama offered no resistance. There was no fight left in him. Bone-weary and drained of hope, he succumbed to the predator—the loneliness that had dogged him since the day he left the Xhosa encampment.

It possessed him like a parasite, squeezing his heart and bowels until they ached, bruising them with pangs of anguish. It flogged his mind senseless with an invisible cat-o'-nine-tails, each blow a memory of a lifetime of injustice.

The scourging brought to the surface regrets, feelings, and thoughts Jama had buried deep inside himself long ago. He ached for the things he had never known—the warmth of a woman's breath against his neck as she lay asleep beside him; the joy of a companion's rib-bruising embrace following a long absence; the gaze of a lover's eyes; the soft warmth of infant flesh pressed against his chest, the product of his seed.

As the sun ascended over a thousand surrounding hills; as animals called to their mates; as birds scratched for food to feed their young; as families gathered around frontier breakfast tables; as friends drank to each other's health; as storekeepers opened their doors to the first customer of the day; as young ladies primped in anticipation of a chance encounter with the opposite gender; as husbands and wives stole private moments out of sight of the children, Jama lay sprawled atop a naked hill, his eyes and cheeks glistening wet in the morning sun, his insides twisted in tight knots. Exhausted. Numb. Alone.

There was no one within miles of him. And Jama never felt his isolation more keenly than he did during that sunrise, sprawled and vulnerable on the barren hill.

From that day on, loneliness was Jama's constant companion. Though he refused to allow it to gain mastery over him, neither did he attain mastery over it.

The most effective trick he learned to keep loneliness at bay—and the black depression that accompanied it—was to occupy his mind. He did this by becoming a student of nature. As he traveled north, his surroundings became his daily classroom.

He wandered from the limestone banks of the Indian Ocean shoreline up a series of escarpments into the great interior plateau that bordered the Drakensberg mountain range. The entire area was a veritable garden. On the shoreline he was surprised by the variety and colorfulness of the mollusks left in the little puddles on the rocks at high tide. He poked sea stars that were nestled between bushes of algae. He amused himself with the boldness and bravado of crabs as they protected their territory from his intrusions.

Farther inland he encountered a great many elephants. It was later he learned that the Zulus called the area *um Gungundhlovu,* the Place of the Elephant.

The first elephant he saw was an old bull, obviously thrown out by the herd, ambling slowly along the edge of a forest. As Jama approached, the elephant scarcely took notice of him but simply broke his way into the woods by pushing down a number of quite sturdy trees. A day or two later he saw two elephants swimming across a bay. Later, still farther inland, he spied on a herd of more than one hundred, old and young, on the grasslands near the forest.

His least favorite discoveries were the giant snakes that inhabited the area.

He was passing a small village when a young boy alerted the other boys of a great snake sunning itself in the road not far distant. The boys didn't seem to mind Jama's trailing after them. Just as they spotted the snake, it vanished into a hole. The boys quickly set to work digging it out with sticks. After nearly an hour of hard digging, they happened upon the snake's nesting place. With quickness and caution, the boys managed to get a rope around the snake's neck. With everyone manning the rope, Jama included, they managed to pull it out of the ground. It was twelve feet long and more than an arm's thickness. After strangling their catch, they flung it over their shoulders and carried it triumphantly back to their village.

At that same village Jama was witness to an elephant hunt. The massive animal had waded into a deep marsh, making it a prime target for the village hunters. After suffering dozens of assegai wounds, it lowered its erect trunk and fell down dead. The villagers quickly stripped off its skin to get to the fat, which in taste, color, and hardness was much like the Boers' lard. The tusks were cut off. And that night its feet were roasted—a tasty treat for the villagers.

Hunting for birds also proved successful. There were pigeons and woodpeckers and partridges and sunbirds and finches and storks and even a rare water dikkop. Most exciting to Jama was the ground hornbill, which made a humming sound when he chased it. There were a great many snipes, and for a time they became his principal meal.

As Jama roamed the grassy savanna, which was dotted with shrubs and trees and divided, it seemed, by hundreds of brackish rivers, he observed great herds of gnu, zebra, blesbok, hartebeest, eland, and other antelope grazing. Not far from the herds he could always spot the predators—the cheetahs, lions, and wild dogs.

But in all his travels, the animal Jama became most fond of was the lion. His infatuation with lions began when he discovered he could talk to them.

It was on long, sleepless nights that he started listening to them. He began to sense they had a language of their own. Sounds were repeated, oftentimes in sequence. Altogether Jama learned fifty distinct sounds, which he assumed was lion vocabulary. But what did the sounds mean? What good was it for him to know the words if he didn't know what the words meant? Then one day he received a lesson in how to talk lion.

He happened upon an elderly couple who lived at the edge of a small village. The couple invited him to stay with them for the night. Jama was grateful for the chance to have at least one night of human companionship.

It was during his visit that Jama learned of a curious relationship between the elderly couple and a lion. The old man, who was much too aged and frail to hunt, told an unbelieving Jama that a certain lion was accustomed to sharing his kill with them. Naturally, Jama was skeptical, so the old man insisted on proving his claim to his guest.

Jama followed the couple out of the hut. They had walked less than a mile when they came upon a lion who was enjoying an evening meal of eland. As the couple approached, the lion ignored them, deliberately, in Jama's estimation. Without fear, the elderly man and his wife walked up to the lion. The man shouted sounds at the beast, some of the same sounds Jama had heard lions make late at night.

The dining lion looked up at them. He gave them a disgusted look, then obligingly moved away from the fallen eland. The beast watched from the shade of a tree while the old man cut off a portion of the carcass. Then the couple saluted the lion and walked away, leaving the beast to continue its dinner.

Amazed, Jama asked the man what he had said to the lion.

The old man replied, "I called him a great hunter. Then I reminded him that it was the responsibility of great hunters to share their kill with those too weak to hunt for themselves."

"And where did you learn the lion's language?"

The old man looked at him strangely. "By listening to them," he replied, "and by observing their actions. How else does one learn?"

Indeed, thought Jama. *How else does one learn?*

From that day forward Jama watched and listened to lions, learning their language.

It was nearly a fatal mistake. The skies had been dark and the rains heavy. Jama hadn't been dry for more than a week. His days had been spent trudging through wet grass and along muddy trails, his nights spent shivering beneath an outcropping of rocks or at the base of a tree. So when the morning dawned blue and cloudless and sunny, Jama luxuriated in it. His attention was diverted to the fresh colors of the foliage, the smell of spring in the air, and the warm touch of the sun's rays on his skin. He wasn't paying attention to his surroundings. It almost cost him his life.

He stumbled upon them. Looking back on it, he found the encounter humorous. How can a person accidentally stumble upon a full-grown rhinoceros and her two calves? But that's what he did.

He was wading through a waist-deep grassy field, feeling good about being warm again. He didn't see the massive back of the black rhinoceros protruding above the grass. Her head was down, uprooting grass with her long, pointed lip, so she didn't see him either.

Her calves, one well-grown and the other small, were similarly preoccupied with grazing.

Jama and the mother rhinoceros frightened each other simultaneously. Jama jumped back, and the mother rhinoceros reared her head, her horns thrusting upward forcefully. But while Jama's expression changed from a startled wide-eyed look to one of fear, the rhinoceros's eyes changed from reflecting fright to anger. Instinctively, she swung her horns at him. Her ponderous three-toed feet plowed the ground.

Backing away slowly, Jama raised both hands in an appeasing gesture. "Sorry, old girl," he said softly, his heart pounding. "Didn't mean to intrude."

By now, three pairs of rhinoceros eyes rested on him. None of them were amused, let alone friendly.

"I'll just be on my way," Jama said, continuing to back up.

The mother snorted. She turned his direction and began inching forward.

"Stay. Stay there," Jama said, trying unsuccessfully to sound soothing. Panic tinged his words. He could hear it in his voice, and he feared the rhinoceros could sense it too.

The mother rhinoceros lowered her head. She leveled tiny eyes at him. The tip of her front horn circled menacingly.

Turning slowly, without taking his eyes off the animal, Jama positioned himself to run. "Easy now . . . easy . . . easy . . ."

With a snort, the rhinoceros lowered her head and charged. Her first steps were lumbering.

Jama ran. His feet dug into the ground and threw up small chunks of moist earth. He knew he had to put distance between them as quickly as possible. Once the rhinoceros gained momentum, he could never outrun her.

He had to find someplace safe. Quickly. Someplace sturdy or deep or high! Jama looked for a tree. There were none in the direction he was running. An outcropping of rocks, then? The field was flat. Nothing but ripples of freshly watered savanna grass stretched before him, while behind him he could hear and feel the heavy thunder of pounding rhinoceros feet.

Glancing over his shoulder, he saw the charging animal. She cut through the grass so effortlessly he could have sworn the grass was parting in front of her. Worse yet, she was gaining momentum. The distance between them was diminishing rapidly. It was difficult for Jama to conceive that something so large could move so quickly.

The thought gave him an idea. He could use the beast's weight and speed to his advantage. It was a dangerous plan, but it was the only plan he had.

Jama continued to run, but he slowed his stride. The rhinoceros was so close now, he could hear the animal huff and grunt with each stride. The ground beneath Jama's feet trembled violently. Jama waited and waited. He had to time his move just right. Not yet . . . not yet . . .

At the last second, just as the rhinoceros was about to bowl him over, Jama planted his right foot and sprang sideways, jumping as far out of her path as he could. As he had hoped, the speeding animal charged past him as he tumbled through the grass.

What happened next was not part of the plan. With great agility for such a massive beast, the rhinoceros wheeled around and prepared to charge again. Her quickness was astounding, and, given the time, Jama would have marveled at it. But there was not a moment to spare. In an instant he was back on his feet, the rhinoceros was turned around, and the chase was on again, this time in the opposite direction.

The rhinoceros was upon him quickly, and Jama had to dodge out of her path again. His timing and dexterity were his only defense. But how long could he keep it up? Already his legs were tightening and threatening to cramp.

While he and the rhinoceros trampled the field in circles, the calves romped around and chased each other, presumably thinking this was some sort of game. For Jama it was too serious to be a game, especially if he lost. If only he could convince the rhinoceros that he was no threat to her calves . . .

A thought came to him. Lions had their own language; maybe rhinoceroses had a language too. What sounds did they make?

Diving out of the path of the charging animal for the fifth time (or was it the sixth?), he tried to recall some rhinoceros sounds. His exposure to them was limited. He tried grunting loudly.

The rhinoceros appeared unimpressed.

Jama huffed and pounded his feet. It was a pale imitation of the thunder of rhinoceros feet.

A new thought came to him. Maybe he could scare the animal away. After once again diving and rolling, he roared his loudest lion roar.

The rhinoceros wheeled around. But instead of charging, she stopped. Her sides heaved mightily.

Jama smiled. He'd made contact! Cupping his hands, he roared again. The lion sound he imitated meant "Go away. This is my territory." At least that's what he thought it meant.

The sound made a definite impression on the rhinoceros. It made her angrier. With renewed fury the monstrous animal took up the charge.

"No! No!" Jama shouted as he ran. He tried yelling in Afrikaans and Xhosa. He even tried English. Nothing seemed to soothe the rhinoceros's anger.

Jama was getting desperate. His legs were cramping. His chest felt as if it was going to explode. He couldn't keep this up much longer.

The circling maneuvers had taken them to the far edge of the grassy savanna, and Jama saw two things that gave him hope. A few hundred yards away there were a couple of sturdy trees. Several hundred yards to one side of them stood two Zulu natives, a man and a young woman. They were watching the chase.

"Help me!" Jama cried to them.

They didn't respond. They didn't come to his aid. In fact, they didn't move at all. They just stood there.

"Try to divert her attention!" Jama called. He thought that if they could just get the rhinoceros's attention, that would give him time to reach the trees. The two were far enough away that they could reach the trees themselves before the animal could get to them. But they did nothing to divert the rhinoceros's attention. They did nothing at all. They stood there like stones.

Jama turned *his* attention back to the charging animal. He yelled and cajoled and ducked and dove, working his way toward the trees. Finally, he managed to get within range. With one last dive, he sprang up into the sturdiest of the trees, scrambling onto a thick limb.

The rhinoceros wheeled around, looking for Jama, but couldn't find him.

"Thought you had me, didn't you?" Jama yelled.

At the sound of Jama's voice, the rhinoceros charged. It slammed into the tree with tremendous force. The tree shook violently, almost knocking him from the branch. If he hadn't grabbed the trunk with both arms, he would have fallen.

She hit the tree again. This time Jama was prepared. The tree quaked. Jama held firm. It was a stout tree, but at this point he wasn't willing to test the strength of the tree against that of the rhinoceros. Since his taunt had prompted the latest attack, he decided to sit quietly on his branch and hope the rhinoceros would get bored and wander away.

Below him, the hulking gray beast snorted and sniffed and wandered around the tree. In the field the calves bounded about playfully. At the edge of the field, the two Zulus remained just as they had always been, standing erect and stone still.

Jama pulled his feet up onto the branch and leaned against the trunk. He waited.

A good portion of the afternoon passed before the rhinoceros wandered away. Not wanting to chance a repeat encounter, Jama decided not to be too anxious to give up his secure perch. He could wait.

He remembered the Zulus. When he looked, they were gone!

"*Sawubona*."

The word startled him. It came from directly below.

Glancing cautiously downward, Jama came face to face with the Zulu man and maiden who had stood so lifeless in the distance. They were staring up at him as though he were some kind of curious creature.

"*Sawubona*." The male Zulu repeated the word.

Jama had picked up enough of the Zulu language to be able to carry on rudimentary conversations. He recognized the greeting, which in this case was especially appropriate. Literally, it meant "I see you."

Jama responded appropriately. "*Sanibona*," he said.

They stared at each other. The man was much older than the maiden. He was probably her father, possibly her grandfather. She was definitely not his wife. Her manner of dress indicated she was unmarried. Jama cast a cautious glance in the direction in which he had last seen the rhinoceros.

"*Sondela! Sondela!*" the Zulu scolded.

Embarrassment warmed Jama's face. The Zulu had interpreted his caution as an affront, and rightly so. The rhinoceros was no longer a threat. What sort of man would endanger a young maiden in order to trick a stranger?

Jama climbed out of the tree.

Now that he was closer, the Zulus examined him again. The maiden held a delicate hand over her mouth to hide her amusement.

"What sort of man are you?" the man asked. "From what tribe? You wear the clothing of the Xhosa, the Zulu, the English, and the Boer!"

It was true. Jama's apparel consisted of a collection from his travels, showing contact with a number of peoples and allegiance to none.

"I have no tribe," he said.

At first his statement seemed to shock both man and maiden. Then the old man nodded his head wisely. "You speak the truth," he said, taking another look at Jama's conglomerate of clothing. "One who travels. And one who has not lived long enough among the *uBejane* to know her ways."

"uBejane?"

"The vicious one," the Zulu said.

The maiden lowered her head, pawed the ground with a foot, and snorted. *"uBejane,"* she said.

Her portrayal brought a grin to Jama's face. It was the most attractive demonstration of a rhinoceros he'd ever seen. However, his grin appeared to embarrass the girl. "Ah! *uBejane!*" he cried. "Rhinoceros! *uBejane!*" He lowered his head, pawed the ground and snorted in similar manner to the maiden. His imitation brought a reciprocal smile from her.

"Do you not know that the *uBejane's* eyes are bad, but her ears and nose are superior!" the Zulu cried.

Jama's eyebrows rose in acknowledgment. "Her eyesight is poor—that's why you stood still. She couldn't see you. And then, when I climbed the tree and she lost sight of me, she was bewildered until I called to her. *Then* she knew where I was!"

"What did you want to say to *uBejane?*" the maiden asked.

"Why did you roar like a lion at *uBejane?*" the Zulu man asked.

Jama couldn't help but smile. Now that the danger was past, he imagined his encounter with *uBejane* did have its humorous side. He would have laughed too had he seen an oddly dressed man flitting all over a field yelling and roaring at a charging rhinoceros.

"Sondela," the Zulu said, taking Jama by the arm. "Come. You can tell us about your roaring and your travels while we eat. Thandi is a good cook. She'll fix a meal for us."

Thandi. The maiden. Jama looked at her. The maiden's smiling eyes served to validate the Zulu's invitation.

The old man led the way, motioning for Jama to walk beside him. Thandi trailed a discreet distance behind them.

"I see you, brother," the Zulu said, launching into the standard Zulu greeting. "I see you. My eyes look upon you in peace, and my heart is at peace when I see you."

25

Sina's heart fluttered excitedly. Her feet were so happy they wanted to leap and dance. It was all she could do to restrain them to a simple walk. *Control yourself. You look like a fool.* But it was hard to control the flood of joy she felt inside. She'd waited too long for this moment.

Carrying an empty brass pot in her hands, she passed one wagon after another. A few minutes ago the pot had been filled with stew, which she had delivered to the Pfeffer wagon. Angenitha had taken ill, and Sina's mother sent the pot of stew to help feed the family.

There was a secondary reason for the visit. Johanna was concerned for her friend, and she wanted an update on Angenitha's health. For Sina that meant getting away from the wagon for a while.

It had been weeks since she had seen anyone unless somebody wandered by their wagon. But the thing that sparked her explosive joy was the fact that she was being sent to the Pfeffer's wagon alone! Kootjie, who had served so well as her annoying shadow, was in the field. For the first time since they started the trek, she was able to go someplace without an escort!

When she reached the Pfeffer wagon, Sina's good fortune continued to abound. Angenitha was too ill to receive her for any length of time. This was good news because Sina's mother expected her to sit with her ailing friend for a spell, which meant she wasn't expected home soon, which meant she had time to wander near the Klyns' wagons and possibly catch a glimpse of Henry!

Sina did her best to act carefree but not too carefree, lighthearted but not giddy, which in fact she was. She felt as though her love for Henry was written all over her face, that everyone she passed knew where she was going and why. She did her best to respond to casual nods and greetings in kind. She feared, however, that the sparkle she felt in her eyes, the wideness of her smile, and the lilt in her voice betrayed her exalted emotions.

But what did it matter? She couldn't help herself. She had never felt this happy before in all her life. Now, if only her good fortune would continue a bit longer. She prayed that, when she reached the Klyn wagons, Henry would not be out in the field.

The long line of wagons belonging to Oloff Klyn was impressive. They were almost a complete laager unto themselves. A beehive of activity surrounded them. It was well known that Oloff Klyn kept his workers busy. There were no idle hands. Nor was there idle chatter. The workers passed one another without a word, sometimes without even a glance. For the number of workers in any one place, it was strangely quiet.

Sina scanned the line of wagons. There was no sign of Henry. She looked again, this time more slowly, hoping that he would appear. He didn't. Workers fed chickens, repaired canvas coverings, tended fires, mended clothes, cooked food, herded animals, but none of them was Henry. Sina supposed her good fortune had run its course. It was asking too much to expect everything to go her way on her first day of freedom.

She considered asking one of the workers if he knew Henry's whereabouts, but that was being too forward. Besides, it would be embarrassing if word got back to Henry that she had come looking for him. At least she got to see the wagons where he lived. Being near his things made her feel that much closer to him. With a sigh, Sina started for home.

Just then, her eye caught a flash of white protruding between a man's back vest and pants. To everyone else, it was simply the look of a Dopper. To Sina, it was possibly . . . She looked again. Yes, it was Henry! He must have come from behind the last wagon when she glanced away. His hands were black with wheel grease. A worker followed him, rolling a wheel.

Henry had not spied her yet. Little did it matter to her heart. It couldn't possibly beat any faster than it was beating right now.

Then he turned. Their eyes met.

Sina's heart seized; her breath was held captive in her throat. For an instant nothing else existed, just she and Henry caught in a lovers' moment.

Then Henry smiled that precious smile of his. The world returned to its preordained course.

Signaling to the worker to continue without him, Henry walked toward her. "What a pleasant surprise," he said with a rakish bow, looking her up and down. "Did you bring me something?"

Sina had forgotten the brass pot in her hands. "Oh, this," she said, fumbling it from hand to hand. "Food for a sick friend. There's nothing left." She lifted the lid to show him, then replaced it with a clang. "Do you like stew?"

"Very much."

Sina beamed. Henry liked stew! "I'll have to bring you some."

"I'd like that."

"I would too."

A quizzical expression formed on Henry's face.

"I mean, I'd like to bring you some sometime," she stammered. "Some stew. Bring you some stew. It would be my pleasure."

Henry glanced behind her. "So, where's your brother?"

Turning to look behind her, even though she knew Kootjie wasn't there, Sina said, "My brother? Why do you ask?"

Henry grinned knowingly. "It's just that lately he's always been nearby."

"Not today!" Sina said happily.

"I'm glad."

"You are?"

Henry smiled warmly. "Can I help you?"

Clutching the brass pot against her chest, Sina shook her head. "I was just passing by when you spotted me."

"You mean if I hadn't turned around, you would have passed by without stopping to say a word?" A pained look crossed his face.

Sina's face flushed. "Do you have time to walk with me awhile?" he asked. "It's the least you can do after bruising my feelings."

"Walk with you?"

"Down to the stream. There's a secluded little spot I've been wanting to show you."

Sina felt warm inside. Henry had been thinking of her! "I don't have a lot of time . . ."

He motioned with his head for her to follow. He started walking. "It's not far," he said. "You'll love it."

Still clutching the pot, Sina joined him. Could the day get any better than this? she thought, stealing a glance at Henry beside her.

As they passed the line of wagons, he grabbed a cloth with which to wipe the grease from his hands. "How about if we leave that here?" he said.

"Leave what?"

He motioned to the brass pot.

Until that moment she hadn't realized that she was clutching it as a little girl clutches her favorite doll. "Oh, of course," she said, handing it to him. "I can pick it up on the way back."

Henry set the pot in the back of a wagon. He hesitated. "Unless it's your favorite pot, and you wanted to show it the stream?" His eyes twinkled.

"You are company enough for me." The moment she said the words, she blushed and wished she hadn't.

But Henry's warm smile put her at ease. He had not been offended by her forwardness.

Side by side, they walked down the gentle grassy slope toward the brook. They walked in silence as Henry worked the rag with his hands to remove the grease. His nearness was intoxicating. For so long she had thrived on fantasies of Henry. And now that he was actually beside her, his physical presence was nearly overwhelming. She didn't know what to say. Of course, in her dreams she was witty and lighthearted and always said the right things at the proper times. But at the moment, try as she might, she couldn't remember a single one of those witty lines!

Though there were still several hours of daylight left, the sun was low enough to cast long shadows, shadows that stretched out in front of them. Her shadow and Henry's shadow, walking side by side, in stride, perfectly, just as it should be. How natural all of this seemed to her. Walking beside the man she loved. He wanting to share a favorite spot with her. The two of them. Alone.

She remembered the peach orchard at Nachtmaal. How silly that all seemed now. She had none of the reservations she'd felt then. After all, why should she? It was the peach orchard's reputation that was the problem, not she and Henry. This was natural. It was good for two people who loved each other to want to spend time alone.

Sina heard the brook before she saw it. A soft rippling gurgle announced that they were approaching a small, quiet stream.

"It's over here," Henry said, pointing, then leading the way.

Brushing aside the thin lower branches of a tree, he led her to a little grassy clearing. Trees and bushes formed a natural amphitheater opening out toward the stream. Patches of wild flowers added color— violet, red, blue, and yellow.

"It's lovely!" she cried, clapping her hands like a little girl. "How did you ever find it?"

"It was quite by accident, but I think I was meant to find it," Henry said. "As you know, we don't have a lot of privacy on the trek. This is a perfect little spot we can call our own, a place where we can be alone."

He was saying all the right words. *We . . . our . . . alone.* Sina's head was swimming in the moment.

"Here, sit down," he said, offering her his hand.

For the most part, the grease had been wiped off. There was still grease in the crevices, but Sina didn't mind. It was attached to Henry, and that was all that mattered.

"You don't know how long I've looked forward to this day," he said.

Sina closed her eyes and reclined on the grass. She had dreamed those very words, and now he was saying them! Could this really be happening? The grass was green and cool and lush beneath them. Overhead, tree branches arched gloriously, forming a leafy canopy. The fragrance of the wild flowers swirled about them.

"Here, let me help you." He moved to her feet and began to take off her shoes.

Sina pulled her feet away. "What are you doing?" she cried.

"Taking off your shoes, silly! How else are we going to wade in the stream?"

Emotions swirled inside Sina, formulating a confusing mixture. There was something about his handling her foot that both confused and excited her. It was wrong. Or was it? He was only touching her foot! *But he didn't ask . . . he just grabbed . . . assumed . . . but it's only a foot . . .*

"It's not hard," Henry said with mock silliness. "Here, watch me." He removed his shoes and dangled his bare feet in the edge of the stream. With a mock shiver he pulled his feet out and made a funny sound with his lips and cheeks, the kind people make when bracing against a winter wind.

Sina giggled.

"Really, it's nice!" Henry said, serious now.

Sina felt foolish. What was wrong with her? Why was she acting so foolish? Gently, she extended her foot toward Henry. He smiled and slowly unlaced her shoe. A shiver traveled the length of Sina's back before her foot had even been exposed to the air.

She sighed contentedly when her feet hit the water.

"Mmm, you were right. This is nice." She closed her eyes to better feel the cool water as it flowed around her hot, tired feet. When she opened them again, Henry was staring at her chest. When he saw she was looking at him, he glanced away. Something stirred inside her. It was an uncomfortable feeling.

"You have a strange brother," he said.

"What?" The abrupt change of thought took her by surprise.

"Your brother. He's an odd one, to say the least."

How could he go from staring at her like that to Kootjie? Unless she had misread his wandering gaze. And why was she acting so defensive all of a sudden? Wasn't this what she had hoped for, prayed for, dreamed of? What was wrong with her? Taking a deep breath, she did her best to relax. She told herself to enjoy the moment. Everything was going just as she had imagined it, except for the turn in conversation to Kootjie.

"He is a bit strange," she said with a forced laugh.

Leaning back on his elbows, his feet still in the stream, Henry laughed. "A bit strange? You should have seen him the night he shot my father's chestnut horse!"

Sina didn't want to hear about it. It was all the laager had been talking about for weeks, laughing at the boy who got spooked and shot the horse Klyn had been showing off to everyone.

She splashed her feet playfully in the brook. "It's so nice and peaceful here," she said, hoping to channel the subject away from her brother and back to them.

"He began shaking the moment the sun went down." Henry smirked, ignoring or missing Sina's hint. His eyes looked upward and darted from side to side as if he remembered the night he and Kootjie stood watch. "When I asked him if he wanted to sleep first, he said"—at this point Henry batted his eyelashes and spoke in a high-pitched, frightened voice—"'You're not going to go to sleep, are you? What if something happens? Please don't go to sleep! Please!'" He paused for a dramatic review of his portrayal of a frightened brother.

Sina looked indifferently at her feet playing in the water.

"I did my best to stay awake for him, Sina. Really I did. But the night was so quiet and peaceful, I knew nothing would happen. And . . . well . . . I began thinking of you, and I guess I dozed off."

Sina's feet stopped splashing. "You were thinking of me?"

With a boyish shrug, he said, "I probably shouldn't tell you this . . ."

She turned toward him. "Tell me. Please tell me!"

Another shrug. "Well . . . I think of you often, just before I fall asleep."

A warm sensation filled Sina. It felt like liquid delight flowing from her head to her toes.

"But on that night," he said, returning to the story, "just as I was dozing off, all of sudden your crazy brother is all over me! He's shaking me and crying and yelling and pointing his gun in the direction of the horses. It was crazy! I couldn't get him off of me! He kept screaming and crying about being afraid to die. By then, my eyes had cleared enough for me to see that he was aiming at the horses. I tried to tell him they were only horses, but he wouldn't listen. He kept screaming that the Matabele were going to kill us."

Sina had heard enough of the story to be disturbed. Naturally, she had heard Kootjie's account of what happened that night. He'd claimed it was Henry's fault that the horse was shot. At the time she didn't believe him. Nobody did. But Henry's account wasn't any better.

"When I saw that he was going to shoot, I did all I could to wrestle the gun from his hands, but . . . well, you know how big your brother is—an immature boy in a man's body—and strong. Anyway, like I said, I tried to wrestle the gun away from him, but he was on top of me, and all of a sudden—*BLAM!* The gun goes off, and my father's prize chestnut plops to the ground."

"That doesn't sound like Kootjie." She didn't want to say it. She didn't want to be having this conversation at all. But Henry's portrayal of Kootjie irritated her. It just *didn't* sound like him. True, he was a nuisance and her brother, but since they started the trek she had seen Kootjie in ways she'd never seen him before—mastering stubborn oxen, hunting, assuming a man's responsibility. She couldn't imagine this grown Kootjie being frightened like a child.

"Things are different on commando," Henry said with a superior tone. "You'd have to be out there to understand. It takes a real man to survive. Give him time. He'll grow up. Tell you what I'll do. After that night together, I sort of feel responsible myself . . ." He paused, giving her time to object. She didn't. "So I'll sort of watch over him. You know, like a big brother. It's the least I can do for him."

Sina pulled her feet from the water and scooted back from the stream. She could feel the ire rising inside of her. The more she felt it, the angrier she became—and not over the shooting of some horse. She found herself angry with Henry and defending Kootjie. She was angry at herself for being so mixed up.

"I've offended you," Henry said softly. He pulled himself up beside her.

Sina looked away.

"Please forgive me." He placed a gentle hand on her shoulder. "That was not my intention. I only brought up the story because someday we're going to look back on this and laugh. I have no hard feelings toward your brother for what he did. As for my father, given time, he'll get over it too."

The warmth of his words began to melt the anger within her. She lowered her eyes. "No, it's me who must ask your forgiveness," she said. "I don't know what has come over me. Kootjie is . . . he's just Kootjie. Always has been. It's just that . . . lately, I thought I had seen some changes."

Henry laughed good-naturedly. "It has been my observation that brothers and sisters know very little about each other. Sisters think they know what their brothers are like, but once boys get away from home they are an entirely different person."

"Maybe so."

"I know so," Henry assured her. "For example, you don't know your brother at all."

She looked at him.

"Really, you don't," he insisted. "He told me something that night that he never should have told me."

"Oh? What did he tell you?"

Henry smirked. He drew himself into a sitting position. Biting his lower lip, he hesitated. "He couldn't wait to tell me, in fact," he said. "It was about you."

"Kootjie told you something about *me*? What?"

"He told me why he has been with you everywhere you go lately."

Red, warm blood rushed to Sina's face. "He didn't! He wouldn't!"

Henry nodded to affirm that he did indeed. "See? You don't know your brother as well as you think you do."

"What did he say?"

"He told me that you ran away from home on the night the Xhosa attacked."

Sina spied one sliver of salvation in this disaster. If that was all Kootjie had told him, she might be able to escape dying from embarrassment. As long as he had not told Henry . . .

"He also told me the reason you ran away."

Sina buried her head in her hands. "What did he tell you?" she said, her voice muffled.

"He told me that you ran away to be with me."

"This isn't happening," Sina muttered.

Warm hands touched the back of her hands. Fingers pried her fingers away. Her eyes remained clamped shut.

"Look at me," Henry said softly.

She couldn't. She would never be able to face him again.

"Please, look at me!" he cajoled. "When Kootjie told me that, it made me feel good. It was then that I realized that you want to be with me as much as I want to be with you."

Sina lifted her eyelids barely enough to peek. Henry's face was inches away from hers. His eyes had a soft, dreamy look in them.

He spoke softly, almost inaudibly. "Kootjie may have been wrong in telling me," he said, "but something good has come of it. Had he not told me, I might never have known how strongly you feel about me."

Her eyes opened fully now. "You want to be with me?" she asked.

"Very much!" His hands slipped down to her shoulders and squeezed them. He leaned toward her.

Instinctively, she pulled back slightly.

"It's all right," he whispered.

His cheek touched hers. It was warm and rough with stubble. Her eyes closed again to savor the sensation. She grabbed Henry's warm hand with both of hers.

"What's the matter?"

Playfully, she said, "All good things will come in time, *Mynheer* Klyn."

He inched closer, moving his free hand to the side of her face. A small gasp escaped from her lips. Still holding his one hand, she grabbed for the other and held it too.

"No use in trying to deny it, *Mejuffrouw* van der Kemp," Henry said. "You want me as badly as I want you."

"Deny it? I can hardly do that now, can I?" She giggled, holding his hands as he tried to struggle free.

Suddenly he stopped struggling. Looking at both hands, he said, "You've taken me captive. I'm your slave. What devious forms of torture do you plan to use on me?"

"I would be betraying women everywhere if I told you that," she joked. "All I can say is that it will take a lifetime for you to discover all I have in store for you."

"A lifetime?"

She nodded with a playful smirk.

"Then we'd best get started now!"

He leaned into her, knocking her off balance.

She let loose his hands to catch herself.

He pinned her to the ground. "Now who is the master, and who is the captive?"

"Henry, let me up," she said firmly.

He kissed her.

She tried to push him away. "Henry! Let me up!" A feeling of panic began to sweep over her. She went limp. "All right, all right," she exclaimed. "Have it your way. Give me your hand."

Her sudden capitulation got his attention. "I knew it," he said with a leer.

"Give me your hand." Sina used the same playful tone she'd used before.

He looked at her suspiciously.

"Your hand," she insisted.

He freed his hand and held it up to her face. He grinned. "What are you going to do with it?"

"I'll show you." She pulled one of her own hands free. Slowly, she raised it to his until they were palm to palm, barely touching. She began to swirl her hand against his in a gentle rubbing motion.

"Feel good?" she asked.

Henry's eyes closed. "Yes," he whispered.

"How about this?" With the speed of a leopard's pounce she grabbed his little finger and bent it back as far as she could.

Henry howled in agony. "Let go!" he screamed. "You're breaking it!"

But Sina didn't let go. Every time he made any effort to free himself or reach for her, she bent the finger back even farther.

"I surrender!" Henry yelled. Tears streamed down his face. He was on his back now, afraid to move.

"Will you promise to behave yourself if I let go?" she asked.

"I promise."

"How do I know you'll keep your word?"

"I will! I promise! Let go. Please let go!" he whimpered.

With one last bend backward, which prompted the loudest yell yet, she released the finger and jumped out of arm's reach.

Henry cradled his hand in his lap. "Why did you do that?"

"Why did you do what you were doing?" she replied.

"Because you wanted it."

"Not that way."

"Then how?"

"In marriage. That's how!"

"That's ridiculous. Why would I want to marry you, if you're not willing to give yourself to me?"

"I *am* willing to give myself to you—*after* we're married."

"Do you know how stupid that sounds?" he scoffed.

Sina's ire was rising again, and this time no amount of tender words would be able to soothe it. "Stupid? How can you say that?"

"Yes, stupid!" he insisted. "What farmer in his right mind would buy a cow—or, better yet, a horse—without first inspecting it?"

"*Cow?*" Sina shouted. "You're comparing me to a *cow?*"

"A horse," Henry shouted back. "I said a horse was a better example."

"Thank you for clearing that up for me," she cried. "I feel so much better now."

"Think about it," he insisted. "A wife is far more important than a horse, isn't she?"

"I'll grant you that."

"Then how much more important is it to thoroughly inspect a potential wife before you marry her?"

Sina stared at him in disbelief. "You're serious, aren't you?"

Henry sat as proudly as he could manage, given the fact that he was sprawled on the ground holding his own hand.

"Well, I have news for you, Henry Klyn," she said, snatching up her shoes. "I don't care to be inspected by you or any other farmer." She pushed aside the lower branches of the leafy canopy and fled from the clearing.

It didn't matter that the rocks and briars hurt her feet. She was too angry to stop to put on her shoes. To make matters worse, she was nearly back to her own wagon when she remembered the brass pot. Could anything else happen to ruin what had been a promising day? She whirled and retraced her steps, hoping that she could grab the pot without seeing Henry.

If that's who he really was.

She found it hard to feel about Henry as she did at the moment. That hadn't been her Henry beside the stream but a rogue, an impostor. Her Henry was polite, considerate. He would never try to do what that person beside the stream tried to do. The more she thought about it, the angrier she became—with herself, mostly.

Luckily, Henry was nowhere to be seen when she reached the Klyns' line of wagons. She grabbed her pot and wheeled around toward home, clutching the pot with one hand while her shoes dangled from the other.

Hot angry tears filled her eyes, blurring her vision. How could she have been so mistaken about Henry? Being fooled was one thing, but the thing that hurt most was the empty feeling she felt inside. It was as though someone had died.

Indeed, someone had. The good, kind Henry that she had fallen in love with had died. She would never know what it was like to be held in his arms. She would never share private moments with him. She would never realize all the dreams that had sustained her for so long. All that was left now was a cavernous, aching hole in the pit of her stomach that would never be filled.

"Sina? Sina, didn't you hear me calling to you?"

Turning, through blurry eyes she saw Karel approaching on a horse.

"Are you all right?" He dismounted and walked beside her.

Sina tried to answer. She couldn't. She barely managed a sniff.

"You've been crying," he said, stating the obvious. He peered curiously at the pot and her shoes. "Sina, what's going on?"

When she couldn't answer again, Karel pulled her aside to a log situated beneath a tree a discreet distance from the closest wagon. He set her on the log, then tied the horse's reins to a branch.

"Now, tell me what's wrong," he said, sitting beside her.

Sina looked at him, then shook her head sadly. Karel had always been such a good friend. He'd always been supportive of her. They'd never hidden anything from each other—until Henry came along. Even then Karel had been outspoken in his objections to her infatuation with Henry. Now, as it turned out, he had been right all along.

"I'm late. I have to go home," she said, starting to rise.

"No, you don't," Karel said. "Not until you put your shoes on. Look at your feet! They're bleeding."

Several red scrapes and cuts stood out against dirty flesh.

"Let me help you." Karel kneeled down to assist Sina with her shoes.

Angrily, she placed her foot against his chest and pushed him away.

Karel bounced backward in the dust.

"What is it with men and women's feet?" she shouted.

Karel picked himself up. Dusting off his trousers, he said, "I was only trying to help."

"I'm sorry," Sina said apologetically. "It's not been a good day." She started to weep openly.

"Sina, tell me what's the matter!"

It took several attempts, but between sobs she managed to say, "It's Henry."

She'd only spoken two words, but those two words brought the deepest scowl she'd ever seen on Karel's forehead.

"He has hurt you, has he?"

His question sounded like a threat. No doubt a promise of action was implied, depending upon her answer.

"He didn't hurt me. At least not in the way you're thinking."

"If he has . . ." Karel balled his hands into fists.

"He hasn't," Sina insisted. "It's just that I discovered he's not exactly the person I thought he was."

"Oh." That was it. A simple "oh" spoken solemnly, understandingly, as though Karel had known this day would come eventually and that the realization would be a great disappointment to Sina. "Is there anything I can do?"

"No," Sina said softly. "I suppose I'll get over it in a decade or two."

"Do you really think it will be that short a time?"

Sina looked at him. His face was dead serious. Then it broke into a wide grin that caused her to laugh.

"How are you and Deborah doing? Any new developments?"

Karel's face drained of all emotion. "She's seeing someone else steadily. She won't tell me who it is. But I understand her father is thrilled with the prospect."

"I'm sorry."

"I haven't given up hope . . . yet."

"Karel?"

"Yes?"

"Thank you for being here when I need you."

Karel de Buys touched the tip of his hat in response.

If Sina's day had started out as the most promising of her life thus far, it ended as the most miserable. The remainder of her walk home, she worked out the details of the lie she intended to relate to her mother. It wasn't really a lie, she told herself. It was more like an extended version of what really happened. All she was doing was implying that her visit to Angenitha took longer than it did.

But she never had a chance to tell her lie or even imply something that wasn't true. When she reached the wagon, Adriaan Pfeffer was there, speaking in hushed tones with her father and mother. One of the twins sat somberly in the dirt clutching her father's leg. The other was being held by Johanna, who busily wiped a runny nose. From the looks of it, the twins had been crying. So had *Mynheer* Pfeffer.

Angenitha was dead. She had died shortly after Sina left the wagon. Sina's delayed return had added concern to her parents' grief.

Sina's story came out. The true one.

She had seen her parents angry before. She had seen them hurt. But never had she seen them angry to the point of tears. When all was said and done, she concluded that this had to be the worst day of her life. She was wrong.

The next day was worse. Henry Klyn was spreading the story that Sina had lured him to the little grassy clearing beside the stream and seduced him.

26

Despite significant opposition, fueled by the considerable influence of the wealthy Oloff Klyn, Piet Retief was chosen to be the leader of the trek. His task was simple: lead his people to a promised land, one flowing with milk and honey. And though he agreed to do so, he insisted on one condition: Should there be any peoples currently inhabiting the land, they would settle only after a suitable agreement had been signed between the two parties.

From their recent battles with the Matabele, it was clear that the current land—although it was spacious—would not be suitable, considering Retief's condition. He had sent a letter to the Matabele's Mzilikazi seeking a bond of friendship and asking to share the beautiful and fertile country, only to suffer rejection in the form of Mzilikazi's silence and continued attacks.

In some ways it was just as well that an agreement had not been reached with the Matabele. Reports were coming to them of the land of Natal on the eastern side of the Drakensberg Mountains. If there ever was a land flowing with milk and honey, this was it. However, like most things worthwhile, several obstacles needed to be overcome if they were to possess it.

First, there was the physical obstacle. The Drakensberg range, so named because its sheer, jagged surface resembled a dragon's spine, would not be easy to cross. Retief sent out scouts to look for suitable passes. The variable harsh mountain climate only added to their problems. Rainfalls came in sudden thunderstorms, and cold snaps were possible even in the middle of summer.

Second, there was the Zulu problem. The land upon which they had placed their dreams was part of the southern portion of the Zulu tribe. Dingane, the Zulu leader, was the brother of the notorious warrior chief Shaka. Though Dingane was not as militaristic as his dead brother had been, he had the reputation of being crafty as well as cruel. If they were to settle in the land, they would have to formulate a treaty with Dingane.

And third, there was the problem of staying alive until they could locate a suitable pass through the mountains. Finding enough food and water to satisfy the multitude and holding off the hostile Matabele were daily problems.

As for the Matabele, Retief organized the men into commandos to scout the outlying areas and to warn of any impending attack. In order to facilitate the formation of the scouting groups, he used the same hometown organizations with which the men had been associated in the colony. For the most part, this was agreeable to all. The Grahamstown group was quietly disgruntled over the fact that they were stuck, again, with Oloff Klyn.

"Erasmus was not more than five hours distant from the other wagons," Oloff Klyn said. He took a swig of coffee and swished it around in his mouth before continuing.

The others sat about the fire, occupying themselves with a variety of tasks. They listened to Oloff's tale rather indifferently, all except for Kootjie, who couldn't seem to get enough stories about battles with the Matabele.

It was nearly dusk. The horizon was taking on a magnificent violet hue, tinging everything in the camp with a violet coating. Christiaan and Kootjie were cleaning their guns. Pfeffer was chewing on a piece of dry meat, while Conraad tended the horses. Karel absentmindedly tossed twigs into the fire. Henry sat on a log watching the horizon nervously. He twitched and started at the slightest sound. Louis de Buys and Gerrit van Aardt remained with responsibilities at the laager.

"He left his wagons and animals," Oloff droned on, "in the care of his servants while he went hunting. In the evening when he returned, he heard a frightful noise at his encampment. As he got closer, he saw some six hundred Matabele surrounding his wagons and butchering his servants."

"Six hundred!" Henry said in a low, trancelike voice while he continued to scan the horizon.

"His two other sons," Oloff said without acknowledging his son's comment, "who had formed another hunting party, had also been murdered. Stephanus Erasmus rode for his life to our laager."

"Six hundred!" Henry said again.

Christiaan, Pfeffer, and Karel exchanged grins.

"On his way," Oloff said, "Erasmus stopped to warn another party that had separated from the main group, the Liebenbergs. The fool! He didn't believe Erasmus. Stayed there and did nothing. When day broke, the Matabele attacked, yelling and waving their shields, assegais, and knobbed sticks. They resisted, of course, but it was futile. Liebenberg was stabbed to death, along with his three sons and several others. The Matabele swept off all his livestock and two white girls as presents to Mzilikazi."

"Makes you wonder what the pagans did to those girls," Henry said.

"We waited for an attack, but it didn't come," Oloff continued, still ignoring his son. "The next day I was one of eleven who rode out with Erasmus back to his camp." Klyn shook his head. "It was a pathetic sight. The Matabele are barbarians—dogs—and ought to be treated as such."

Christiaan glanced up at his son. Kootjie was drinking in every word spoken by Oloff, even though the old man gave the boy a sneer at every glance. He still hadn't forgiven Kootjie for shooting his horse. Probably never would. But that was past. It was Kootjie's rapt attention and seeming agreement that the Matabele were less than human that concerned Christiaan. It was a growing sentiment among the trekkers.

Christiaan felt the pull to believe it too, especially since the last frontier war. Blacks weren't to be trusted. The chances that there could ever be peace between them and the Boers were slim indeed. At times he despised Klyn's simple perception of the world—there were God's chosen people, and there were the cursed. You were either one or the other. The chosen deserved to live. Those not chosen were heathen; like all other animals they were to be ruled over.

At other times, however, he envied Klyn. The old man's perspective made life so much easier. You were either one or the other: chosen or cursed. Yet deep inside him a sliver of optimism remained despite the Xhosa attacks, despite the Matabele threat. The sliver worked on his mind in the same annoying way a splinter worked in one's hand.

"That's when we spotted them!" Oloff cried. "It was about nine in the morning. One thousand of them, massing for attack!"

"What did you do?" Kootjie asked.

Oloff sneered at the boy but continued the story anyway. "We sounded the alarm all the way back to the wagons. Formed them into a laager and waited. At first the heathen didn't attack. They'd never seen a laager before and didn't know what to make of it. But when they came, they came in waves."

He grinned wickedly. "That's when we showed them what God's army can do. The thunder of our guns drowned out their heathen cries. A single shot felled two, sometimes three of them. After it was all over, we counted more than a hundred and fifty of them dead. One thing was clear: God protected us that day. Only one boy was killed inside the laager." Another sneer, this time a smiling one directed at Kootjie's father. "Oddly enough, the boy's name was Christiaan."

Henry gasped. "Someone's coming!" He started to stand and point at the same time. His heels caught the back of the log upon which he had been sitting. He stumbled over it and sat down hard. The fall didn't keep him from pointing, though. With eyes wide with fright, his head swiveling, he shouted, "They're all around us! We're surrounded."

The reaction around the campfire was instantaneous. Each man grabbed a gun and, with his back to the fire, pointed it outward.

Henry was right. They were surrounded.

"Can't be Matabele," Christiaan said. "They're on horseback. And they have guns."

"Griquas," Oloff muttered. "Almost as bad as Matabele. The British pay them to attack trekkers. Their way of discouraging more of us from leaving."

"I've heard the same thing about them," Pfeffer added.

The Griquas were a people of mixed blood—traders and farmers mostly. The product of mixed marriages and out-of-wedlock pregnancies, they were outcasts mostly from Cape Town who fled the colony to establish a life where they were no longer treated as outcasts.

The Griquas rode to within about fifty yards of them, then stopped.

"At my signal, we fire," Oloff said.

"No!" Christiaan cried. "We don't know what they want."

"It's obvious what they want," Oloff replied. "They want to stop us from obtaining what is rightly ours. They're heathen, like the Canaanites of old. It's our godly duty to destroy them."

"Nobody fire," Christiaan said.

"Wh-wh-what are we going to do, then?" Henry cried in defense of his father. "Wait here until they decide to slaughter us?"

"I'm telling you, nobody fire until we know what they want!" Christiaan insisted. "Who's with me? Pfeffer? Conraad?"

"We're with you," Adriaan answered for both of them.

"Karel?"

"With you."

"I'm with you, Father," Kootjie said before he was asked.

Christiaan looked over his shoulder at Oloff.

"And how are we going to find out what they want?" Oloff exclaimed.

Christiaan lowered his gun. "I'm going to go ask them."

"Not again!" Oloff rolled his eyes pleadingly heavenward.

"*Mynheer* van der Kemp, let me go with you," Karel said.

Christiaan looked at the boy. He was sincere. What's more, Christiaan saw no fear in his eyes.

"I'd appreciate the company," Christiaan said.

Following Christiaan's example, Karel laid down his gun. With their hands stretched out to their sides to indicate they had no weapons, Christiaan and Karel stepped forward.

The circle of horsemen stood silhouetted against the darkening sky.

"Of all the fool . . ." Oloff muttered. "He's going to get himself killed yet."

Ignoring Oloff's prediction, Christiaan and Karel walked slowly toward the Griquas. Christiaan was unsure which of them he should speak to, but his dilemma was soon resolved.

A horseman from their right rode the circumference of the circle toward them. He pulled up in front of Christiaan and Karel and stared down at them. He made no attempt to speak.

"I hope you can understand me," Christiaan said, "otherwise I don't know how we are going to—"

"We speak Afrikaans," the Griqua said. He was a dark man with chiseled facial features, who sat proudly atop his mount. A broad-brimmed hat shadowed his eyes, making them difficult to see in the waning light. His clothes, other than carrying a day's dust and sweat, were clean and fine, not ragged as Christiaan had expected of a Griqua, for whatever reason.

"Good," Christiaan said, relieved. He remembered his disastrous attempt to communicate with the Xhosa chief without the aid of a translator. "Then let me say that we mean you no harm. We are a commando from a nearby laager of wagons. We're just passing through."

"Just passing through?" the Griqua said. "You've been here for weeks!"

Karel jumped in. "We have scouts looking for a way across the Drakensberg Mountains. As soon as they find a pass, we'll be on our way."

The Griqua studied the boy. He seemed impressed. "Is this your son?" he asked Christiaan.

"A friend of the family," Christiaan replied.

"How do I know you're telling me the truth? How do I know that you're not here to steal our land for yourselves? Convince me, if you can."

Christiaan stretched out his hands. "You can come to our laager and speak with our leader, but he'll only tell you the same thing we've told you. Other than that, you'll just have to take me at my word."

"And who are you that I should take you at your word? Are you someone important?"

Christiaan grinned self-consciously. "I'm no one important. All I can tell you is that Christiaan van der Kemp gives you his word that we are no threat to you."

The Griqua seemed to give his promise more weight than Christiaan had expected. Then his face wrinkled with concern. "Who was that who said to fire at his signal?"

Christiaan closed his eyes in frustration. Sound carried well across the veld in the twilight hours. "He is of no consequence," Christiaan said. "I'm sure I'll be able to convince him that you are no threat to us."

"Oh? And how do you know we are not?"

"I don't. But if you tell me so, I will take you at your word."

The Griqua grinned. "Van der Kemp, is it? And this is . . ."

"Karel de Buys," Karel answered for himself.

"My terms are these: If the two of you come with me, I will promise that no harm will come to your commando or your laager. But if you refuse to come, or if anyone comes searching for you, the agreement is broken, and I can guarantee nothing."

Christiaan and Karel looked at each other.

"What would you possibly want with us?" Christiaan asked.

"Those are my terms," the dark man said. "Accept them or refuse them. I don't have all night."

"You may regret having come with me," Christiaan said softly to Karel.

"We've come this far . . ." Karel replied.

To the Griqua, Christiaan said, "We accept your terms."

Christiaan and Karel were allowed time to get their horses and guns. Oloff was against the whole idea, but there was little he could do. He concluded that if the two wanted to ride off and be killed, it was their business. Christiaan made him promise that he would not allow anyone to come after them.

Kootjie wanted to join his father. Christiaan insisted the boy go home and tell his mother what had happened. He told him to assure her that he would be home in a day or two. It was a promise made without foundation, so he shored it up with a strong fatherly tone.

After one last pronouncement of doom by Oloff, Christiaan and Karel mounted their horses and rode off with the Griquas.

Not long after Christiaan lost sight of the commandos' campfire, the Griquas split up and went in various directions. Four men continued to ride with Christiaan and Karel, two flanking each side. The Griqua spokesman led the way.

They traveled a good hour. The moon had risen, showing nearly a full face. A patch of lights indicated buildings in the distance. Christiaan began to see evidences of a thriving farm. Cattle and sheep. Crops. A cluster of buildings that seemed to multiply in number the closer they came to them.

It was truly impressive. Christiaan had not seen a farm like it since passing through the Graaff-Reinet district at the beginning of the trek.

Workers met them and took their horses. The four riders left them. The Griqua who had served as spokesperson led them up a few steps onto the veranda of a whitewashed brick house of impressive size.

Christiaan and Karel were offered chairs, which they took.

The Griqua pulled a chair opposite them and tossed his hat onto a wooden table.

Christiaan and Karel removed their hats, holding them in their hands.

Immediately, a worker appeared asking the Griqua if he and his guests wanted anything to drink. He ordered drinks for all three of them, then settled back into his chair and stared at the two Boers.

The light from the door and windows of the house gave Christiaan a better view of the man who had led them here. He was indeed dark skinned with prominent cheekbones and hollow cheeks. His hair was black and wet from the ride. An impression made by his hat rimmed the man's forehead. He sat back in a relaxed manner. He acted nothing like a captor at all.

"Do you know why I brought you here?" he asked Christiaan.

"Not as hostages," Christiaan replied, "though that's initially what I thought we were to be."

A large white smile spread across the man's face. It wasn't forced nor was there any insincerity in it. From the ease with which the smile appeared, it was evident he smiled often. "Not as hostages," he repeated and laughed. "You"—he pointed at Karel—"I wanted to get to know because of the way I saw you look at him. Your eyes indicated that you trust and admire him."

"You are a keen observer of men," Karel said, "if you got that from a glance. You are also correct. I do trust and admire him."

"As for you," the Griqua said, pointing to Christiaan, "I wanted to talk further with you. It was something you said that intrigued me."

They were interrupted by the worker bringing the drinks. The Griqua served Christiaan and Karel first, then served himself. He took a long pull from his mug.

"Something I said?"

"And, hopefully, something you are."

Christiaan's puzzlement appeared to delight the Griqua.

"Forgive me for amusing myself at your expense," he said. "I only hope that what I suppose is true is indeed true."

That statement didn't make anything any more clear to Christiaan.

The Griqua set his cup aside and leaned forward, his forearms resting on his legs. "You said you were a van der Kemp."

Christiaan nodded. "Indeed, I am."

"And you came from . . ."

"Most immediately from the vicinity of Grahamstown."

The Griqua nodded. "And your ancestors. From where do they hail?"

Christiaan was perplexed by the line of questioning. What did his ancestry have to do with the trekkers crossing Griqua land? But the only way he was going to find out was to answer the questions to see where they led.

"I was born in Cape Town," Christiaan said. "When I was young, my father and I moved east to Grahamstown."

The Griqua's eyebrows shot up. He was clearly pleased with Christiaan's answer. More than pleased. He looked excited. "And how would you respond to this word—*Klaarstroom?*"

"My ancestral home!" Christiaan cried, both shocked and surprised.

The Griqua leaned back in satisfaction. "I thought as much!" He rubbed his hands together excitedly. "I'll be right back!" Jumping up from his chair, he disappeared through the front door of the house.

Karel looked at Christiaan and laughed. "What's this all about?"

Christiaan laughed with him. "I don't know. But I don't think we're in any danger."

"Clearly not," Karel agreed.

The Griqua reappeared. In his arms he cradled a vase with a white background. A pattern of blue flowers pulsated with life on its side. "Does this mean anything to you?" he asked.

Christiaan studied the vase. He couldn't remember ever seeing it before.

"It belonged to one of my ancestors," the man said.

The clue didn't help. Try as he might, Christiaan could not make any connection between Klaarstroom and the vase. "Sorry," he said, "I must be missing something."

Sighing, the Griqua seemed a little disappointed but still eager to help Christiaan put the pieces of the puzzle together. "This used to sit on the mantle at Klaarstroom," he said. "It belonged to your ancestors—Jan and Margot van der Kemp."

Christiaan's mouth fell open. How was it that this Griqua, living out here on the high veld, knew so much about his family?

"Margot gave it back to my family just before she died. It was originally given to her by one of *my* ancestors. She wanted us to have it as a memorial to him. He used to sell these to sailors on the streets of Cape Town to make a living. He used to do that before he married Rachel van der Kemp."

The fog in Christiaan's mind was clearing. "I'm beginning to remember now! Rachel's husband—he died saving Klaarstroom—was of mixed blood, so Rachel had to leave Klaarstroom. Matthew, wasn't it? Yes, Matthew!"

"Matthew Durbin," the man said proudly. "My ancestor. Only one child was born before he died—a girl, Deborah. He died without knowing that another of his seed was already growing inside Rachel. This time a boy, which she named Matthew after his father."

"Imagine that!" Christiaan said. "And your name?"

"Adam. Adam Durbin."

"Pleased to meet you, Adam," Christiaan said, extending his hand.

Durbin shook it heartily. "For many years the Durbins and the van der Kemps had a close relationship. I hope we can continue that tradition. Stay until morning?"

"It would be our pleasure," Christiaan said.

For the remainder of the evening, Adam Durbin was an impeccable host. He introduced Christiaan and Karel to his wife of twenty-three years and their seven children. Christiaan learned that they were strong Christians, having been converted through the ministry of Robert Moffat of the London Missionary Society. The work of that society among the Griquas, as Adam described it, redeemed it in Christiaan's eyes, since his only experience with them had been in court.

Adam told him how Moffat had rescued two bush babies from death when he unexpectedly came upon a funeral. Several bushmen were digging a grave large enough for a dead mother and her two live children. It was their custom that if a mother died, her children were buried along with her. Somehow Robert managed to talk them into letting him have the children instead. His wife, Mary, who loved children, raised the two as her own.

Christiaan learned that the Griquas were an autonomous, multi-racial society; that they made their living mostly as hunters and traders;

and that they had recently suffered a split prompted by the rivalry between two chiefdoms. They, too, had their troubles with the Matabele, who were constantly disrupting the Griquas' access to Cape Town colony markets.

Come morning, Adam Durbin outfitted Christiaan and Karel with provisions and gifts. He sent three workers to accompany them on the journey back to the laager. Each worker led a donkey loaded with ammunition and powder, Durbin's peace offering to the Boers for allowing him to kidnap one of their own for the night.

Christiaan and Karel rode home in triumph.

Nearly half the laager turned out to greet them, including Piet Retief himself. "Let me see if I understand this correctly," he said. "One night you ride off as a captive; the next morning you return, not only having freed yourself but also bearing gifts from your captor? From now on, whenever we are negotiating with an enemy, I want you by my side!"

"How were the twins?" Christiaan asked. He lay in the dark next to his wife. The curved canvas covering overhead was awash with moonlight.

"They miss their mother."

"Pfeffer misses her too. Rarely speaks a word."

"She's the twenty-third."

"Twenty-third?"

"Person to die from a tsetse bite. Strange, isn't it? She survived childbirth, natural disasters, Xhosa attacks, only to die because a fly bit her. I should have known." Her voice trembled. "She showed all the symptoms. Fever. Inflammation. Lethargy. I guess I didn't want to believe it. I told myself she was just tired from the journey and the twins."

"You couldn't have done anything to save her."

"I could have stayed with her. Been there for her. Instead, I sent Sina."

Christiaan turned toward his wife and embraced her. She was warm from her tears.

She sniffed. "I told Adriaan that we'd help him raise the girls. Several other wives have made similar offers. At least until he remarries."

The statement gave Christiaan pause. He chuckled. "I never thought of Adriaan marrying again. Do you really think he will?"

"A man needs a wife, especially with two little girls."

Christiaan pulled her closer to him.

She chided him without resisting. "And then you had to do something ridiculous like riding away with a band of Griquas, leaving me with

nothing more than 'Tell your mother I'll be home in a couple of days.'"
She lay in silence for a moment, then added, "I thought I'd lost you too."

Christiaan's first response was to defend his actions. He'd done the right thing. Given the same situation, he'd do it again. However, this was not the time to debate his behavior. Johanna was suffering the loss of her best friend, and she'd feared she'd lost a husband too. He cleared his throat to say, "I'm sorry to have caused you grief, Baas. I could think of no other way to relieve your fears. And I can't promise that it won't happen again."

Johanna bolted up. Propping herself on one arm, she looked incredulously through the dim light at her husband. "What are you talking about? Of course, it will happen again. It will happen tomorrow and the next day and the next!"

Christiaan stared at his wife.

"Don't you realize that I die a little every single day when you and Kootjie ride out? How do I know either of you will ever come back? Dead is dead, whether you're killed by the Xhosa or the Matabele or a lion or an elephant or a fall from your horse!"

"I would never fall off my horse!" Christiaan protested. A half-suppressed grin showed the comment for what it was, a mock portrayal of Boer male pride.

It achieved its purpose. Johanna grinned and lay down, resting her head on his shoulder. "Dying a little every day is simply my lot in life for loving you."

"Would you prefer me to stay around the wagon all day?"

Her answer was quick and definite. "No. If you did that, I'd have no respect for you as a man, which would be far worse."

"How do you handle it every day?" Christiaan asked.

"I put you and Kootjie in God's hands. What more can a woman do?"

Christiaan pulled her closer to him. There was no more talking that night, but it was the first night for as long as they could remember that they fell asleep in each other's arms.

27

Having come in from milking the cows, Jama balanced on his haunches against the wall. He watched as Thandi prepared the morning meal. Earlier, while he had taken the cows to pasture, she had spent the morning in the fields hoeing and weeding.

Her grandfather, Ndaba, had gone to the kraal of Dingane, the Zulu king, to fulfill his duties as one of the king's advisers. This he did several times a week. Sometimes he didn't return until after the morning meal, which was normally served shortly before noon. This meant that during his absence Jama and Thandi had the hut to themselves, a situation that Jama had grown to look forward to, having spent nearly three weeks with the family.

Since the day Ndaba took him in, Jama had been made to feel a part of the family. It didn't take long for him to develop a deep respect for the elderly Zulu, which seemed to be mutual. This pleased Jama. But what pleased him even more was that Thandi had taken to him. She made no pretense of pretending otherwise.

The Zulu maiden, several years past the Zulu marrying age, was not one to play coy games. She did not giggle or hide her eyes when Jama looked at her. There was bold confidence in her gaze. Nor did she hide the fact that she thought Jama deserved special treatment, a fact that appeared to surprise her grandfather but not displease him.

At first Jama was taken aback by her direct glances. He was not accustomed to being around women. But he soon warmed to it and before long found himself craving her glance.

With her legs folded under her, Thandi worked maize in a bowl, crushing it into meal. She wore a short skirt of tanned skin. A necklace made of shells dangled back and forth from the rocking motion as she worked.

Jama thought she radiated with beauty. Her skin was a deep chocolate brown. Close-cropped black hair capped a smooth oval face with a prominent forehead. She had clear brown eyes that were captivating, a small flat nose, and a full smiling mouth. Slightly shorter than Jama, she was tall for a Zulu maiden. Yet she handled her height magnificently, moving gracefully even while performing the most menial task.

Glancing up, Thandi saw him watching her. A pleased look crossed her face as she returned her attention to the maize.

Ndaba appeared in the doorway. He stood momentarily silhouetted against the daylight in the only entrance to the Zulu hut. With just a single opening, the interior of the thatched round structure was dim even during the day. This served to keep it cool during the hot months and to keep the flies and other insects to a minimum.

The man in the doorway was typical for a Zulu male—tall, slender, muscular, well built, and strong. This particular Zulu was stooped with age and gray, but his dark eyes were still sharp with intelligence. He wore a loinskin around his hips and a necklace of animal teeth. There was a ring made of fungoid growth from a tree atop his head. This head ring was never removed. It was a badge of respect and dignity, signifying that he was an elder and adviser to the king.

"*Yoh!* You are back from milking the cows already!" he said to Jama. "Good. I wish to talk with you. I think it is time I introduce you to King Dingane."

Thandi stopped her grinding. She sat up. "So soon?"

Her grandfather ignored her. His eyes and thoughts were focused on Jama. He strode purposefully across the smoothly rubbed dirt floor. "There are opportunities presenting themselves through which you will be able to impress the great Dingane."

"Opportunities?"

Thandi interrupted them. "First we eat, then we talk."

Receiving no objection from her grandfather, she spread out woven mats for herself, for him, and for Jama.

"What's this? A new mat?" Ndaba said, pointing to the one she had stretched out for Jama. It was the newest and finest of the three.

"I thought it time he had a mat of his own," Thandi said, smiling sweetly at Jama. She ignored the exaggerated wink her grandfather gave him.

They sat in the traditional Zulu seating arrangement: Ndaba, being the oldest male, sat closest to the door. Jama sat beside him, to the right of the entrance. Thandi sat in the place of the women, opposite them, to the left of the entrance. The meal consisted of toasted ears of corn, boiled sweet potatoes, and fermented sorghum porridge.

As they ate, Jama picked up the conversation again. "If I am to meet Dingane," he said, "I would like to know more about him. What sort of man is he?"

226

"Dingane is Dingane," Ndaba said. "He is not a man to understand—he is a king to be obeyed."

Thandi scowled at her grandfather but said nothing.

If Ndaba noticed her reaction, he didn't show it. "However," he said brightly, "it is our privilege to be his adviser, and this is where you can help."

"What can I do?" Jama asked. "I am but a stranger. I am not even a Zulu. What makes you think he will listen to me?"

"Because the time is ripe," Ndaba said, "and your appearance at this precise time is no mere accident."

Uneasiness settled like fog in Jama's mind. The old man's veiled response disturbed as well as puzzled him.

Ndaba seemed to sense his anxiety and to be pleased by it. Several moments passed as he studied the man before him. "There are only a handful of us on the council who are old enough to remember the legend," he said solemnly. "It is a fire that burns within us, one that will not die. Though we have spoken of the legend often, our words are not heard. Others on the council—ambitious men, some of them weak and fearful men—scoff at us for what we believe. They think that because we have wrinkled skin our minds are feeble. They are wrong. And if Dingane continues to listen to them, I fear that within a generation the Zulu people will cease to exist."

Ndaba paused as he chewed and thought. His eyes were fixed as he pondered the future—or the past. Jama didn't know which. He only knew from the old man's grim expression that the vision he saw in his mind was a frightful one.

Breaking his own trance, Ndaba gazed upward. His eyes seemed to search the roof of the hut for words to adequately convey his thoughts.

"There is a revered legend among the Zulu tribes," he said, "called the Feast of Peace. According to this legend, a supernatural being appeared one day among the warring Zulu tribes. He revealed himself to them as the Lost Immortal and announced that he would be the new ruler of the Zulu people."

Thandi recognized her grandfather's tale. Jama could see it in her. Eyes that had been bored and somewhat contemptuous when the discussion was politics now glimmered warmly. Her admiration for the old man was obvious. It created a radiance about her that Jama found attractive.

Ndaba continued. "The Lost Immortal promised to rule with justice and godly wisdom. But in order for him to do so, the various tribes of the Zulu nation had to agree to stop warring among themselves. To assist them, he captured and ate all the warring kings in a stew his three daughters and wives prepared. Immediately, all fighting stopped.

"In a grand announcement the Lost Immortal declared that he would hold a Feast of Peace. At once the people began to prepare for the celebration according to his instructions. When the day arrived, the Lost Immortal emerged from his hut and stood regally as all the military regiments passed in review.

"He was dressed as befitted a king with red feathers of royalty in his hair, wide armbands of carved ivory, a wide leopardskin sash across his broad chest, and a leopardskin kilt. The whole people rose in unison and praised him with shouts of joy.

"Now, you need to know this about him," Ndaba said to Jama. "The Lost Immortal was blind. Yet in his blindness was great insight. He knew a person's unspoken thoughts. And on that great day of celebration, he knew how much everyone in the assemblage yearned for peace. It made his heart pound with joy!

"At his signal, drums began to beat. Ten warriors appeared carrying a large stone. On the stone was an inscription that read, 'Here two great tribes spoke the oath of peace for a thousand years. All tribes are to respect this peace!'

"Thousands of people craned their necks just for a glimpse of the stone. Men lifted their children high to see it, telling them to remember forever the peace that was made on that day. Two singers stepped forward and sang the peace song. They sang that the song of war and the black deeds of war would be buried under the great slab."

Ndaba's hands began to tremble, and his eyes glazed with tears. "Then two of the bravest young soldiers stepped forward, one from each warring tribe. They were tall and handsome men. Without telling anyone, they had decided to seal with their lives, for all time, the peace that had been declared and to be buried with the great stone. They stepped bravely into the pit dug for the Stone of Peace and were immediately covered with earth. The wife of one of the men, torn with grief over her husband's actions, hurled herself into the grave onto his body. She too was instantly covered with earth from a hundred hoes."

Ndaba looked gravely at Thandi. "Like those two brave warriors, I am prepared to give my life for such a cause. It is such a small offering to make if it will bring my people a thousand years of peace."

Jama was still basking in the warm glow of Ndaba's narrated commitment to peace as they walked to the kraal of the Zulu king. It had affected him deeply, probably because he shared Ndaba's desire. Yet he was still perplexed as to what *he* could do, an outsider, to bring about such a peace among the Zulu people.

Ndaba waved aside his questions and doubts, saying that he would understand in time. That time did not come when Jama caught his first glimpse of Dingane's kraal. The sight of the expansive array of huts only made his questions and doubts multiply a hundredfold.

"This is emGungundlovu," Ndaba said with a sweep of his arm. "The great place of the elephant."

The heart of the Zulu nation lay on a gentle slope above a stream. Oval in shape, it was completely and neatly fenced in with thornbush. Within the fence, packed close to this outer wall, were perhaps a thousand beehive-type huts forming concentric rings, six deep in some places. These, Jama was told, were the barracks for the military officers. Each hut had room enough for twenty warriors. Royal shields hung on poles, giving the kraal a military appearance. Within the lines of huts was a large area fenced off as the cattle kraal.

Dingane's own quarters consisted of his council house and reception hall, situated on the highest ground. A portion of the royal enclosure housed the royal harem, where the king's multitude of wives and concubines dwelt.

Jama stayed close to Ndaba as they wove their way through the daily activity of the kraal—past officials, warriors, caretakers, animals. When people saw Ndaba's head ring, without exception they bowed slightly and made way for him. Ndaba led Jama into the reception hall. Jama was no more than two steps inside before he had to stop to take in its majesty.

The hall was twenty feet high. Its roof, plaited as finely as the finest basket, was supported by twenty-two pillars entirely and exquisitely covered in beadwork. The floor had the appearance of marble, being made of mud and dung, polished with blood and fat until it shone like a mirror. The curved walls led the eye to a triangular-shaped clay dais. A single chair, carved from a solid block of wood, served as the Zulu king's throne.

The room was alive with sound. Clutches of men were scattered across the floor as they awaited Dingane's arrival.

Ndaba led Jama to a small group of elderly men, who greeted him with friendly eyes. But before verbal introductions could be made, Dingane entered, surrounded by attendants and generals. All talking ceased. Everyone, including Jama, knelt in submission.

As the business of the day began, Jama sat cross-legged, following the elders' lead. From his vantage point he was able to observe the man who was king of the Zulus. He was an enormous man and singularly black for a Zulu. Tall, with a huge belly, buttocks, and thighs, he gave every evidence of a man with insatiable appetites. He was entirely hairless and was anointed with fat, which made him appear like polished ebony.

Of special interest to Jama was the etiquette used when addressing the king. One always approached on his knees until told to rise. A brief acknowledgment of Dingane's greatness was expected—usually with reference to an elephant or a lion, both of which were revered by the Zulus —accompanied by the royal salute of *"Bayede."* Another term of respect used frequently was *"Baba,"* which was a form of address for an honored and superior man.

Within a brief span of time it was clear to Jama that Dingane was a man of many moods. Very personable, humorous, and even musical one moment, the next he could be ruthless and treacherous. The swiftness of his mood changes disturbed Jama.

A Rev. Francis Owen was called forward.

Ndaba leaned over and whispered to Jama. "An English missionary," he explained. "He settled nearby a short time ago. He has helped Dingane on occasion as a secretary. This is the opportunity about which I spoke." He motioned for Jama to listen to what Rev. Owen had to say.

The missionary paid homage to Dingane, then proceeded to read from a letter, translating as he read. It was a letter from a group of Boers who wished an interview with the king, desiring to discuss the possibility of settling peaceably in the uninhabited parts of Natal.

Ndaba leaned toward Jama again. "Between your experience with the Boers and your linguistic abilities," he said, "you are just the person to advise the king toward a peaceful solution." Ndaba returned to his upright position.

Jama leaned toward him and whispered, "Why would Dingane even care what I—"

A scream from the entrance to the hall cut off his sentence. A woman, perhaps one of Dingane's wives, came running in. Sobbing hysterically, she threw herself at the king's feet.

"She is gone, *Baba!* Gone!" the woman wailed.

Dingane was clearly not pleased with the interruption. He seemed unmoved that one of his wives was distraught. He signaled to two guards to take the woman away.

On their first attempt, she fought them off to remain at Dingane's feet.

"The lion has returned!" she shrieked. "He has taken her! He has taken my baby!"

Whereas her distress moved Dingane not at all, mention of the lion brought rage to his face. "Witchcraft!" he cried. "How else can it be explained that this animal eludes my best warriors!"

Ndaba was standing. Jama had been so caught up in the woman's drama that he hadn't noticed. When the old man spoke, he first thought it odd that his voice was coming from such an elevated position.

"*Baba,* if it please the great elephant," he said, "there is one among us who can rid our tribe of this lion forever."

"Ndaba," Dingane said slowly with a scowl, "am I to believe that you know of someone who can kill this lion when my best warriors are unable to do it?"

"No, *Baba,* not kill. But he can rid us of the lion."

"Rid us of it? How?"

"By speaking to it."

A chill fastened itself on Jama's spine. "No," he whispered. "Don't do this!"

Dingane was skeptical. "You know a man who speaks the language of lions?"

"Yes, *Baba.* He is here beside me." Looking down at Jama, Ndaba motioned him to stand. "Get up! This is your chance to meet Dingane."

Under the circumstances, Jama didn't want to meet Dingane. But he didn't seem to have a choice. Every eye in the hall was on him, from that of the warriors to the elders. Even the hysterical wife calmed down enough to take a look at him. But the eyes that were felt most keenly by Jama were those belonging to Dingane.

"Come forward," the king commanded.

Jama looked at Ndaba, who gave him a frantic if-you-know-what's-good-for-you-you'll-go-forward-as-he-commanded glance.

Jama moved in front of the king and knelt. Following the example of the others, he said, "*Bayede,* thou that art black, thou that art frightful, thou that art like a lion . . ."

"Yes, yes," Dingane said impatiently. "Are you the one who speaks lion?"

"I have studied their language, *Baba.*"

"Say something to me in lion!" Dingane commanded.

Jama hesitated. He turned his head to look at Ndaba.

Dingane became enraged. "Don't look at others while I am speaking to you!" he screamed. "Say something in lion!"

Jama nodded. Closing his eyes, he did his best to let out a sufficient roar.

A smattering of laughter circled the hall. Dingane looked unimpressed.

"What did you say?" he asked.

"I said, 'You are a great hunter.'"

Dingane's eyes narrowed suspiciously.

Jama felt himself being weighed in the balance.

"With your lion words could you entice the lion to come into the open so that we might kill it?"

"No, *Baba*."

"No?"

"You being a great hunter yourself—if an enemy of yours asked you to come out into the open, would you do it?"

"If you cannot help us kill it, what good is your lion talk?"

Here was an opportunity for Jama to discount his own usefulness in the matter. But if he did, he would bring disgrace on Ndaba. "I might be able to persuade it to go to another territory," he said.

"Might?"

"Lions have strong wills, *Baba*. They are not accustomed to someone telling them what to do or where to go."

Dingane seemed intrigued. "Can you tell the lion to go to the Matabeles and eat Mzilikazi?"

The hall erupted with laughter. Dingane himself seemed pleased with his own humor.

After the last of the laughter died out, he issued orders to two of his warriors: "Take this man and Ndaba to the place where the lion was last seen. Let him speak to the lion. If the lion obeys him, bring them back to me. If the lion does not obey him, kill them both."

He signaled their dismissal without a word of comfort to his wife or an expression of concern for their baby.

"Over there! Quickly! Hurry! My baby!"

Whether the woman believed Jama could actually talk to the lion, he didn't know. All she knew was that someone had been sent to deal with the lion, which meant hope for her child. She grabbed his arm and pulled at his clothing to get him to move faster.

Jama didn't share her hope. He considered it unlikely the baby was still alive. From Ndaba and the two warriors he'd learned the full story of the lion. Nobody knew the secret of its lair, and it never killed twice in the same area. This lion was so cunning that the Zulus were convinced that witchcraft was involved, as Dingane had indicated.

A Zulu had watched as it carried an ox over a corral fence and dragged it into the bush. It had to be a big lion to be that strong. The lion had already killed a woman. In the pitch dark of a drizzly night it had clawed its way into her hut. With the woman in its jaws, it disappeared into the night. At dawn, hunters followed its tracks in the soft earth and found the remains several hundred yards from the village. The lion's tracks then led to a stream where the hunters lost them. It had struck several other times, taking more oxen, another woman, and a boy.

"This way! This way!" the woman urged.

She showed Jama and the others where she'd last seen her child. It was a short distance from where she had been washing clothes. She'd heard the baby whimper. When she looked up, the lion had the infant's head and arm in its mouth and was carrying the baby away. The woman ran after the lion, screaming at it, trying to get it to drop her baby girl. The lion slipped into heavy bush and disappeared.

"Do you think you can frighten the lion away?" Ndaba asked Jama.

"It's a little late to be asking that question, isn't it?" Jama replied. He looked behind him at the warriors. They were the grimmest men he'd seen in a long time. He had no doubt that, should he fail, they were fully capable of fulfilling Dingane's orders.

"Listen!" Ndaba stopped and cocked an ear.

Jama and the warriors stopped too.

"Hurry! My baby!"

Ndaba scolded the woman and placed a hand over her mouth. When she heard what he'd initially heard, her eyes grew bright with hope. It was the sound of an infant crying.

Noiselessly they traveled toward the sound. With each few steps the crying grew louder.

Slowly Jama pulled back a low branch to reveal an incredible sight. The baby sat on the ground between the front paws of a lion, bellowing with all her strength. Her right arm and head had bleeding puncture wounds from the lion's teeth. The lion was staring at the baby quizzically, cocking its head from side to side.

The warriors stepped forward, their assegais ready to strike.

Ndaba put out a hand to stop them. "If you only wound it, the lion may maul the child. Let Jama try. If he fails, you can kill the lion . . ."

The "and us" at the end of his sentence remained unspoken.

Jama stepped forward.

The lion snapped its head Jama's direction. Opening its mouth, it reached for the baby as though to carry it farther into the bush.

Jama roared. It was a low, rumbling roar.

The lion stopped. It cocked an ear.

Jama roared again. This time longer and higher in pitch.

The lion shook its mane. With a paw it scratched the side of its face.

Ndaba and the warriors watched intently. It was unclear whether or not the lion was responding to Jama's attempts at communication.

He waited a moment. Then he roared a third time with an altogether different sound.

This time there was no mistaking the lion's actions. The beast jumped to its feet and bounded toward Jama. It stopped midway between him and the baby.

The warriors raised their weapons high.

The lion roared at Jama. Once. Twice. Three times.

Jama was so close to the beast that he could feel its breath with each roar. Still, he held his ground.

Jama roared again.

The lion paced back and forth, back and forth. Finally, it went over to the baby. Before Jama or the warriors could do anything, the lion had the baby's head in its mouth again, all the way down its shoulders.

Jama's heart sank. The mother wailed in terror.

Then, just as the warriors were about to hurl their assegais, the lion turned and placed the baby on the ground between him and Jama, released it, and backed away.

Jama roared softly.

The lion wheeled and bolted into the bush. The mother rushed to her child. The warriors were transfixed, frozen in position, still ready to strike. Grinning like a fool, Ndaba slapped Jama's shoulder and congratulated him.

"What did you say to that lion?" he asked.

"I'm not sure," Jama said. "Either I told it it was a great hunter but that this was my territory, or I told it I thought it was lovely and I wanted to bear its offspring."

Ndaba laughed heartily. "You really don't know what you said to it?"

Jama shook his head. "I really don't know."

When the news was reported to Dingane, the king called Jama to appear before him. The king listened intently to everyone's version of what happened. Each time he heard the part about the lion's placing the child between them, he showed great white teeth and laughed.

"I hear you impressed Dingane," Thandi said.

She and Jama sat close to one another by the fire. In the dark reaches of the hut came soft snoring sounds from Ndaba.

234

"I was fortunate," Jama said. "It could have gone the other way."

"But it didn't. It was meant to be this way."

"I suppose."

Thandi wouldn't let it go. "There's no supposing to it. I know these things. This was how it was supposed to go, and that was how it went. The same thing is true about your coming here. You could have traveled a different direction or stopped at any number of villages and stayed for the rest of your life. You didn't, because you are supposed to be here."

Jama grinned. She was so self-assured and so lovely with the firelight flickering against her smooth skin.

Thandi saw his grin and took exception to it but without anger. "It's important that you understand that," she said.

"Important? Why?"

Picking up a twig, she twirled it gently between two fingers. "You're aware that Zulu girls marry at age fourteen or fifteen?"

"Yes, I'm aware of that."

"I'm twenty-three years old and have never been married," she declared. "Has Grandfather told you why I never married?"

Jama shook his head.

"Because I was waiting for you."

She said it without embarrassment or shame.

"But how did you . . ."

"I told you. I knew you would come."

A slow grin creased Jama's face. She was serious.

"It must have been difficult for you," he said. "The others didn't understand, did they?"

For the first time he saw Thandi's face cloud with sadness as thoughts of the past came to mind.

"At first they talked; then they gossiped. Then they ridiculed me and accused me of all manner of ugly things. Children threw rocks at me. Even the council considered forcing me to marry against my will. I go to the stream to wash our clothes after everyone else has gone. Other than Grandfather, and now you, I haven't had a conversation with anyone for more than five years."

Jama cringed. "It must have been awful."

The face that had clouded now dawned with brilliant light. "It was," she said, "but you were worth waiting for."

28

"What was that all about?"

Karel wore an amused grin. Holding the reins of his horse in his hand, he peered over his shoulder at the departing Conraad Pfeffer. The horse stared at Sina with dark eyes, appearing as interested as his master in her response.

Sina felt her face growing warm. "That was just Conraad being Conraad."

"Conraad being Conraad? What does that mean?"

"A little strange . . . a different sort."

Karel's grin widened. "Why? What did he say?"

Sina didn't want to tell. She stared down at her fingers as they rubbed each other self-consciously near her waistband.

"Tell me!" Karel urged, his grin even wider still.

"It was nothing. He just wanted me to know he didn't believe the rumors about me that Henry was spreading."

Karel's grin disappeared. It didn't fade; it vanished. One instant it was there, the next it was gone. A set jaw and clenched teeth were there instead.

"I'm still angry with you for not telling me what Henry tried to do to you. I knew something was wrong that day, but had I known . . ."

"You promised me you wouldn't hurt Henry!" Sina cried.

The grin made a slow reappearance. No longer did it show amusement but wry satisfaction. "I didn't have to do anything," he said.

"What do you mean?"

"Let's just say that Henry is a little sore this morning, and that his face is slightly discolored here and there—blue and purple and black splotches—that sort of thing. And I think it's safe to say there won't be any more rumors floating about."

"What did you do to him! You promised!"

"I didn't do anything!" Karel protested. The amused grin returned. "*He* did." With a nod of his head, Karel motioned over his shoulder.

"Conraad?"

"Knocked Henry senseless, from what I hear."

"*Conraad?* Quiet, unassuming Conraad?"

"Haven't you noticed the way he stares at you? He likes you."

The warmth returned to Sina's face. "Likes me? No . . . he's Kootjie's friend."

"That may be," Karel said. "But there's no mistaking the fact that he likes you. All he needs is a little encouragement."

"Conraad and me? That's ridiculous."

"Why not?" Karel asked. "You probably haven't noticed, but he's changed since we started the trek. And so has Kootjie, I might add. They're becoming men."

"They're just boys."

Shaking his head in disagreement, Karel said, "Conraad's older than you."

"I know that. It's just that he's always been Kootjie's friend."

"All I'm saying," Karel defended himself, "is that both of them are turning into fine men. When we're out on commando, they pull their weight. Whenever we're in a tight spot, I'm glad they're beside me. I know I can count on them. And look at how Conraad has responded since his mother's death. He's taken care of the twins like he was their mother, as well as keeping up with his own responsibilities. I have a lot of respect for him."

Sina had to admit to herself that she had noticed none of these things. Conraad had always been Conraad to her. But now that Karel pointed out these changes, she had to acknowledge that he *had* changed.

"And he's not bad-looking either," Karel said, his voice taking on a playful tone. "Broad shoulders. Thick, dark brown hair that curls at the edges. And that cute little dimple he has in his chin."

Sina laughed. "Now you're being ridiculous. You sound like a matchmaker."

His amused grin turned serious. "He's a good man. You could do worse. Take it from a friend . . . he likes you. Look what he did to Henry. He was defending your honor."

Sina smiled noncommittally.

Karel's attention was captured by riders mounting in the center of the laager. "Looks like we're riding out." He mounted his own horse.

"Wait! You haven't told me about Deborah."

"I still don't know who she's seeing. She wants to tell me, she says, but she's afraid of her father. I do know that she doesn't like the fellow."

"Do you think her father will force her to marry someone she doesn't love?"

The entrance to the laager was opened, and the other horsemen rode toward it, kicking up clouds of dust.

"I'll come by tonight. Are you allowed guests?"

Sina nodded. "Mother never believed the rumor. She was just angry that I'd put myself in a position to . . ."

"I have to go," Karel interrupted. "We'll talk tonight." He rode off at an easy canter, sitting loosely in his saddle, his feet well forward in the stirrups.

Sina watched him. As he joined the rest of the commando, her gaze was drawn to Conraad Pfeffer. He and Kootjie rode together. It amazed her how much they looked like men. The suddenness of the transformation was disconcerting. Just yesterday they were boys.

Conraad sat tall, confident, in the saddle. His shoulders were indeed broad. And it didn't take great effort to remember the way his dark hair curled slightly or to picture the cleft in his chin.

So . . . Conraad Pfeffer likes me, she mused.

They came without warning. The hills were alive with them, an undulating rippling of cowhide shields that extended for as far as the eye could see. Assegai spears beating against the shields sounded like the thunder of an approaching storm.

The commando wheeled about to warn the laager, which was still in sight. That was hardly necessary. The rolling black tide stretched the length of the horizon. The people in the laager did not need anyone to inform them they were under attack. All that was needed now was for the commando to reach safety before it was engulfed by Matabele warriors.

"We're not going to make it!" a bruised Henry Klyn cried.

"We can make it!" Christiaan shouted. "Let's go!"

The Pfeffers, Louis and Karel de Buys, Gerrit van Aardt, and Kootjie fell in behind him.

"We'll be charging right into them!" Henry protested. His horse circled nervously. Henry stared at the approaching wave of warriors and whimpered.

Oloff shouted at him. Threatened him. But the only way his father was able to get him to move was by riding off without him. More afraid to be left alone than he was to ride, Henry charged after his father and soon passed him. But they had lost precious time. Christiaan and the others were already a good distance ahead of them.

The laager entrance swung wide to receive the commandos. Men stood at the ready to close it up the moment the last commando was inside. Sooner, if necessary.

The thunder of the shields grew louder. It was deafening. Painted black warriors splashed through the little stream and were crossing the open field by the time the first of the commandos reached the laager entrance.

Christiaan rode past it and turned to wait for the others. Van Aardt was right behind him; he sped by into the laager. Next came the Pfeffers and Kootjie. Then Louis and Karel.

Christiaan looked for the Klyns. "What is he doing?" Christiaan cried.

In the distance, Henry was circling nervously again. His head was down. There was no sign of Oloff.

Standing with his hand on the door of the laager entrance, a bearded man with a worried expression stared at the oncoming hordes. "We have to close it up! Are you in or out?"

Kootjie and Conraad, still mounted, wandered back out. Karel was behind them on foot.

"What's wrong?" Kootjie asked, following his father's gaze.

"It looks like Klyn's down."

"I'll go get him!" Kootjie cried. He kicked his horse and was off as he said it.

"Kootjie! Come back here!" Christiaan shouted.

The boy didn't hear him.

"I'll go help him!" Conraad exclaimed. He too was off before Christiaan could stop him.

This time Karel joined Christiaan in shouting for the boys to come back. Their words had no effect.

The entrance guard started closing the gate. Karel stopped him. To Christiaan he cried, "I'll get my horse."

"No!" Looking at Karel with serious eyes, Christiaan said, "Take care of Johanna and Sina for me."

"Are you in or out?" the guard shouted.

"I'm out," Christiaan told him, riding off.

The guard closed the gate to the laager with Karel inside and Christiaan galloping after his son.

The line of Matabele was moving in fast on his right, their speed aided by the gentle downward slope of the terrain. Kootjie and Conraad were just reaching Henry, who was still circling in a dazed manner. Oloff was nowhere to be seen. The only conclusion Christiaan could make was that both he and his horse were down somewhere on the level field where the grass was as high as a horse's flank.

239

Kootjie and Conraad pulled up beside Henry. Kootjie was shouting something. Christiaan might have been able to hear what was said had it been any other day, but the pounding of his own horse's hooves and the thundering of the Matabele attack drowned out all other sounds.

Kootjie seemed not to be getting anywhere with Henry. Even from a distance Christiaan could see that the Klyn boy was panicked. His eyes were fixed on the approaching hordes, his jaw hung low, he looked to be sweating profusely.

Something beyond Henry caught Kootjie's attention. He rode a short distance, then dismounted. As he dropped to his knees, Christiaan nearly lost sight of him. If it weren't for Kootjie's horse, he wouldn't know where the boy was.

That gave Christiaan an idea born of desperation, but an idea nonetheless. If they could get the horses to lie still, they might be able to crouch in the grass and hide from the Matabele.

Two things about the idea bothered him: first, it was based on the hope that the Matabele would focus on the laager and wouldn't concern themselves with a handful of riders who had disappeared; and second, they would be giving up their mobility. Should the Matabele come, they'd be helpless.

Still, their only other recourse would be to ride away from the laager and seek shelter in the twisting ravine at the far edge of the field. That idea didn't set well either. It might be the wise thing to do, but he couldn't get past the feeling that he'd be running away from a fight. If something were to happen to Johanna or Sina, he'd never be able to live with himself.

Behind him, the Matabele had reached the laager. Clouds of smoke rose, accompanied by an even greater thunder than that of the enemy's shields as the Boer guns let loose with grapeshot.

Christiaan reached Henry.

Conraad had hold of the Klyn boy's reins. "I've got him," Conraad shouted. "He won't give me any trouble. Kootjie's over there. I think *Mynheer* Klyn has a broken leg."

Conraad had assessed the situation well if the confused look on Henry's face was any indication.

Christiaan rode to Kootjie.

"It's his leg," Kootjie said, bending over Oloff.

"My horse stepped in a hole," Oloff explained.

Several feet away, Klyn's horse lay on the ground. It writhed in pain, lay still for a moment, then writhed again.

"We need a splint," Kootjie said. "I've scanned the area and can't find anything."

"How about his rifle?" Christiaan asked.

"Give up the use of my gun with heathen pouring down from the hills?" Oloff yelled. "Might as well shoot me now and get it over with."

"If we can get you on a horse, do you think you can ride?" Christiaan asked.

Oloff winced and shook his head slowly. "Don't know. It's a bad break. More than one place, I'm sure of it. The pain is . . ." He didn't finish his sentence. A wince and gritted teeth and rivers of sweat coursing down the man's dirt-caked cheeks finished it for him.

Christiaan turned to check on the range of the Matabele. From his knees all he could see was grass. "If we could get the horses down . . ." he began.

"And what? Hide in the grass?" Oloff scoffed. "Better to ask God to send a legion of angels."

"What other choice do we have? There are just too few of us and too many of them to make it back to the laager."

"*Mynheer* van der Kemp! They're coming!" It was Conraad's voice.

Christiaan stood to see the boy pointing in the direction of the laager. A detachment of warriors had broken away from the main attackers and were coming toward them.

"Help me up!" Oloff shouted. "Let me see!"

With Kootjie on one side and Christiaan on the other, they lifted Oloff onto his good leg. The older man stared at the contingent of black men running toward them. "Hand me my gun," he said.

There were too many of them. Henry was no help, and if Christiaan and Kootjie held up Oloff, they wouldn't be able to fire a gun themselves.

"Lord, help us," Christiaan whispered.

From behind them came a rumbling sound. It started out low and built steadily. Christiaan's first thought was that they had been surrounded. He turned, expecting to see an entire regiment of Matabele pouring out of the ravine.

"Griquas!" Conraad shouted.

The rumbling wasn't beating on hide-covered shield but the sound of horses' hooves climbing out of the ravine. There was a steady stream of them that seemed to have no end. Their leader wore a familiar face.

"I thought you were smarter than this, van der Kemp," Adam Durbin said with a toothy grin. "Don't you know that it is safer to be inside the laager when the enemy attacks?"

241

"You're an answer to prayer!" Christiaan cried.

His exclamation pleased the Griqua. "It's not every day someone says that of me," he said. "I'll do my best to live up to that honor."

The Griquas lined up as still more of them emerged from the ravine. Their presence was enough to discourage the small detachment headed their direction. The warriors turned and fled back the way they had come.

Durbin, Christiaan, and Oloff began formulating a strategy that would get the Boers back inside the laager.

"See how they attack?" Durbin said, pointing at the Matabele. "They attack in waves. One wave goes in, while everyone else waits. Then another wave goes in. I propose we split the waves—separate those closest to the laager from the rest. We ride right down between them. We don't stop. Stopping would be fatal. The last thing we want to do is to engage the Matabele on their terms. Then, when we get to the other side, we wheel around and split the waves a second time."

"I don't see what good that will do," Oloff scoffed. "It's a fool idea."

Durbin and Christiaan exchanged glances. Christiaan started to explain Oloff Klyn to Durbin but thought better of it.

"By disrupting the waves of attackers," Durbin explained patiently, "it prevents reinforcements from reaching the lines that are closest to the laager. With no reinforcements, the number of Matabele warriors closest to the laager—and the gate, I might add—will diminish. After they've thinned out, we'll make one more pass to give you enough time to slip in behind us and inside."

Durbin waited for a response from Klyn.

"Makes sense to me," Christiaan said.

Klyn shifted his weight and winced from the effort. "It's still a fool idea," he insisted, "but it beats van der Kemp's standard approach. If we leave it to him, he'll have us lay down our guns while he goes out and prattles with them."

Durbin wore a puzzled expression.

"I'll explain when we have time," Christiaan said.

With the help of two big Griqua men, Oloff was lifted onto the back of Christiaan's horse. Likewise Henry; he shared Conraad's mount. They didn't want him meandering around aimlessly when it came time to make the dash for the laager.

While the Griquas made their first pass between the waves of Matabele warriors, Christiaan and the others readied their guns. Oloff readied a rifle even though it took nearly all his strength to stay on the horse.

"I may not be able to walk," he said, wincing, "but there's nothing wrong with my aiming eye and trigger finger."

The first pass of the Griqua troops was successful. It threw the Matabele into confusion, and a wide gap appeared between the two portions of the army. The front lines panicked, having been cut off from their reinforcements. From behind the wagons, the Boer gunners cut them down. The hillside Matabele pulled back, thinking the Griquas were attacking. Just as they were starting to regroup, the Griquas turned and made a second pass.

"It's working," Christiaan said, nodding triumphantly at Durbin.

"We're not in yet," Oloff muttered.

The number of Matabele immediately around the laager had thinned considerably.

As the Griquas wheeled to make a third pass, Durbin signaled to a select group of his men to prepare to lead the way for the Boers. "Let's hope your friends on the other side of those wagons realize what we're doing and open the gate for us," Durbin said.

"Wait! What did he say?" Oloff cried.

Durbin signaled his men. They were off.

The Griquas started their third pass, cutting off the larger force of Matabele. Charging in their wake were Durbin's selected men, plowing the way clear for the Boers. Kootjie and Conraad, with Henry clinging to him, came next. Christiaan and Oloff brought up the rear.

Christiaan rode with a double mind. Of course, there was the objective—get inside the laager. But of equal or greater importance to him were Kootjie and Conraad.

How could he face Pfeffer if something were to happen to Conraad? The man had already lost his wife. What would he do if he lost his only son too? Christiaan was determined that Conraad would make it back safely.

As for Kootjie, to Christiaan's amazement, he need not have worried.

Kootjie was every bit a man, a true Boer in every respect. As he rode, it was as though he and his horse were a single entity. They moved together in perfect rhythm—running, swerving, cutting. One would have thought that Kootjie had grown four legs and hooves. And his shooting! At a gallop the boy loaded and reloaded, firing, hitting his targets, riding through warriors' painted faces and shields and upraised assegais without fear. And it was Kootjie who had the presence of mind to begin shouting to those within the laager, "We're coming in! Open the gate!"

Those inside heard him. Without their having to break stride, the gates swung open.

Christiaan thanked God when Kootjie and Conraad passed through

243

safely. He wasn't so sure Oloff was going to make it. The pain proved to be too much for him. Klyn had gone limp. The only thing keeping him on the horse was the fact that Christiaan had the man's arm pinned around him.

As they passed through, the Boers sounded a cheer and shut the gates behind them. Outside, the Griquas, who had successfully completed their third pass, cheered too. The spectacle completely disheartened the attacking Matabele. Those who still stood closest to the laager turned and ran while the ranks on the hillside retreated.

The Boers mounted their horses to give chase, Kootjie and Conraad among them. As they stormed out of the laager, the band of Griquas joined them.

Christiaan stayed behind. Several men lifted the slumping Oloff from the horse. They led both him and Henry back toward their wagons where they could take a look at the old man's leg.

Christiaan was nearly smothered with embraces by both Johanna and Sina.

Johanna pointed after her son. "Christiaan?"

"Let him go, Baas. He's no longer a boy."

Durbin rode up, and Christiaan introduced his wife and daughter.

"And that was your son?" Durbin asked.

Christiaan nodded proudly.

"He's quite a boy."

"That he is," Christiaan replied. Changing the subject, he said solemnly, "Thank you, my friend. It was looking grim out there until you came along."

"What else could I do?" Durbin said. "We're almost family!" He grinned. It was a dazzling grin, the kind that had always been associated with Matthew, his ancestor.

"How is it that you came to show up at just the right time?" Christiaan asked.

"Spies. We got word that the Matabele would attack you today."

As Durbin and his men rode away, Christiaan placed his arm around Sina. "It is men like him that give me hope," he said. "Do you realize what he did today?"

"He risked his life and the lives of his men for us," Sina said.

Christiaan nodded. "More than that. He's Griqua, a man of mixed blood who lives among a nation of outcasts. He risked his life for the very people who drove him and his kind out of Cape Town. It reminds me of a story my father once told me about one of our ancestors."

That night Christiaan told Sina a love story, the story of Rachel van der Kemp and her beloved Matthew Durbin. But if his hopes were encouraged by the willing sacrifice of Adam Durbin, they were deflated when Kootjie returned from the pursuit.

He was hot and sweaty and aglow. In great detail and with relish he described how they ran down the fleeing Matabele. With a triumphant grin he told how he had killed one after another, hunting them down, felling them like so many antelope or zebra.

Kootjie had developed a taste for killing black men.

29

Some of the veteran trekkers believed that on the frontier victory and tragedy were opposite twins—wherever you found one, the other was not far behind. They explained that this was God's way of keeping men humble.

A woman's screams shook the late morning stillness, not because of their volume (though they were loud enough to wake a man inside his wagon on the far side of the laager) and not because of their length (though she refused to be comforted for more than half an hour). It was the anguish of her screams. Like an invisible hand her scream reached inside all who heard it and wrenched their guts.

Her scream was not a girlish scream of sudden fright. It was the herald of a catastrophic event. It gave witness to the fact that the screamer's life had been brutalized, that a piece of her serenity had been ripped away, and that she would never again be the same.

The scream came from the river. Christiaan was repairing a wheel when he heard it.

Johanna was inside the wagon sorting through laundry. Her head popped out. "Did you hear that?" she asked.

"It came from the river!" Christiaan helped her down from the wagon, then ran ahead.

He was the first to reach the woman from upriver. Several others were approaching from downriver.

They found the woman kneeling in the mud at the river's edge. Mud caked her dress and was so thick on her arms that it looked as though she was wearing brown gloves to her elbows. She clutched something with both hands. So saturated was it with mud that it was difficult to determine exactly what it was. It looked like a piece of scrap cloth. She held it against her chest and rocked back and forth as she wailed a two-word litany: "They're gone! They're gone! They're gone!"

Her voice was high-pitched and eerily disturbing, like the sound of a lonely cat howling in the darkest night.

Christiaan could see no immediate danger. He approached her and knelt. Placing a hand on her shoulder, he asked, "Are you hurt?"

Still rocking, she looked up at him with wild, vacant eyes. "They're gone! They're gone! They're gone!"

Johanna caught up with her husband. She too knelt in the mud beside the woman. To Christiaan she said, "It's Gilda van Hoorst."

Christiaan knew the woman but hadn't recognized her. Her face and front were heavily streaked with mud, and her black, thick hair, which had been pulled back, was scattered wildly and had flecks of mud in it. She had always been a sophisticated, proper woman. Her inability to have children made it possible for her to maintain a detached and elevated bearing. But sitting in the mud like this, her face screwed up in anguish, she appeared unkempt and mentally unbalanced.

"Gilda?" Johanna spoke clearly and slowly. "Can you tell me what's wrong, dear?"

"They're gone!" Gilda wailed. Then, seeming to recognize Johanna, she gripped her by the shoulders with muddy hands. One hand still clutched what now appeared to be a rag or torn piece of cloth.

"Who's gone?"

Gilda buried her head against Johanna's chest and wept uncontrollably.

By now a good number of people had gathered. They stood at a distance and gawked.

Christiaan found himself between the crowd and the two women. With each new arrival, he was questioned. Each time he repeated, "It's Gilda van Hoorst. She's beside herself with grief. We're trying to find out why."

"Johanna, how can I live knowing they're gone?" Gilda sobbed.

Johanna pulled the grieving woman off her far enough to see her eyes. "Gilda? Look at me. Who's gone?"

The woman tried to bury her head again.

Johanna wouldn't let her. "Tell me!" she insisted. "Who's gone?"

Wracked with sobs, unable to speak, Gilda van Hoorst offered up the piece of cloth. Johanna took it from her.

"What is it?" Christiaan asked.

Johanna shook her head. "I don't know," she said, "I don't . . ."

A flicker of recognition appeared in Johanna's eyes. Her mouth twisted grotesquely in horror. Tears and terror mingled in her eyes. "Dear Lord, no . . . please, dear Jesus, no!" She plunged the cloth into the river, swishing it around. When she pulled it out again, enough of the mud had washed away to reveal the color and pattern of the cloth. Light yellow with boxes drawn by thin lines, like a checkerboard with all yellow spaces.

"The twins!" Johanna cried, her voice hoarse and choked with emotion. "The twins have dresses made of this material!"

Christiaan fell to Gilda's side. On his knees, he grabbed her away from Johanna. "The twins, Gilda, are you talking about the twins?"

"Gone!" she whimpered. "I turned my back for just a . . ."

"Gone where?" Christiaan cried.

The memory seemed too much for her. Her eyes were open and fixed but vacant. She made no effort to respond to any more questions. Christiaan wasn't sure she was even hearing anything anymore.

"They must have been swept away in the river," Johanna said.

Placing Gilda in his wife's care, Christiaan instructed the men who had gathered to search up and down the river for signs of the twins. "They're wearing yellow checked dresses," he said, holding up the torn swatch for them to see.

"Van der Kemp! Over here!"

Christiaan ran the short distance to where one of the men was kneeling beside the river. He was pointing to markings in the mud.

"Crocodile," the man said softly.

Returning to Gilda, Christiaan tried unsuccessfully to ask her if she had seen any crocodiles. Her only response was a blank stare.

After scouring the riverbank, they found three other pieces of material that matched the piece Gilda held. All three were ragged, evidence that they'd been torn violently. Two of them showed evidence of blood.

"Who's going to tell Adriaan?" Johanna asked.

Christiaan and Johanna were waiting when Adriaan Pfeffer returned from the field. He and Conraad rode in side by side.

"Christiaan . . . Johanna . . ." Adriaan greeted them. From his furrowed-brow salutation, Christiaan knew Adriaan could sense something was amiss. It must have been the expression on his face—Christiaan never was good at hiding his emotions.

"We have some bad news, Adriaan," he said.

Father and son dismounted. The two men stood shoulder to shoulder. It was the first time Christiaan had noticed that Conraad was taller than his father.

"Bad news?" Adriaan repeated.

Christiaan hesitated. He'd rehearsed what he was going to say in an attempt to ease the blow to his friend. And each time he'd rehearsed it, he'd only gotten this far. Maybe he was trying to do the impossible. How can you tell a man his twin daughters are dead without its coming out as a blow to the gut?

Adriaan began to piece it together for himself. Looking past Johanna and Christiaan, he said, "Naomi? Ruth?" To Johanna he said, "They're all right, aren't they? I left them with *Mevrou* van Hoorst for the day. She had asked me so many times if she could . . ." He pushed past the van der Kemps to look inside his wagon. It was as still as a tomb inside.

"Naomi? Ruth?" Adriaan's voice trembled as he called their names.

"Pfeffer," Christiaan said, placing his hands on the man's shoulders and looking him in the eyes. Both men's eyes welled with tears. "I'm sorry," Christiaan said. "I'm afraid they're both gone."

A trickle of tears spilled out of Pfeffer's eyes. He wiped them away with the back of his hand, only to find that there was a ready supply to replace the ones he'd wiped away. "Angenitha will never forgive me!" he cried. "I promised her I'd take care of them . . . find them good husbands . . . kiss our grandchildren for her. I promised her . . . I promised . . ."

Turning to Conraad standing nearby, his eyes red and with a stunned look in them, Adriaan gripped his son fiercely. "You're all I have left, boy," he said. "You're all I have left in this whole world!"

Johanna slipped next to her husband. Christiaan put his arm around her.

"I'll put some coffee on," she said.

Christiaan nodded silently because he knew, if he tried to say anything, he'd start to cry and wouldn't be able to stop.

Several days later bits of human bone and more cloth fragments were found downstream. The entire laager turned out for the burial of what little was found of the twins' remains.

It was the strangest wedding the Zulus had ever witnessed. Under ordinary circumstances the bride would have been ten years younger, the marriage would have been arranged between kinsmen, and the fathers would have haggled over the *lobolo,* or bride wealth, which usually consisted of cattle. Thandi's wedding was anything but ordinary. The bride was older, she had arranged the match herself, and there was no *lobolo* since Jama owned no cattle. The peculiarities of her wedding fueled the gossip circles for six months.

Gossip about the wedding itself filled the balance of the year. As was the custom, everyone was invited to the father's hut, where they sat on fresh mats and drank. There was no bridal party to carry Thandi's hoe, her cooking pots, bowls, ladles, mats, baskets, and skin blankets. No one was needed to drive the nonexistent cattle. The groom arrived empty-handed; there would be no gifts given to the wedding party since there wasn't a wedding party.

Also according to custom, Thandi and Jama were taken to separate huts, where they remained alone. Normally, at this point the bride and groom's families would gather in a third hut and hurl insults, jeers, and biting comments at one another until dawn. But since the only family the bride had was Ndaba, and Jama had no family, the old man quietly lay down on his mat and went to sleep.

In the morning, the bride and groom dressed for the special occasion. Thandi wore a veil of twisted and strung leaves, reaching to her mouth and hiding her face. She dressed in a beaded leather skirt and covered her chest with beaded necklaces. Jama wore a leather kilt. Feathers were placed in his hair, and cow tails dangled on his arms and legs. When all was ready, the bride and the groom were brought together.

Ndaba approached Jama and said, "I am leaving my daughter with you. Be good to her. She is in good health. If she falls sick, let me know. If she disobeys you, speak to her as you would your own child. If you tire of her, return her to me."

To Thandi, her father repeated a prayer in a hushed voice, asking that his daughter might bring her husband many children.

At this point in the wedding, guests sang the bridal song, and the dancing commenced.

Jama and Thandi were man and wife.

Jama watched the early morning light through the hut entrance as it brightened the horizon with pale violet brush strokes. Thandi lay beside him. He felt her warmth beneath the covering, her soft skin pressed against his. It was perfect. Never had he felt contentment like this. Warm. Loved. Fulfilled.

"Are you awake?" Thandi asked in a hushed voice.

"I never went to sleep."

She rolled over and turned toward him. "What? You didn't sleep all night long? Why? Are you not well?"

Freeing his hand, Jama stroked her short hair. He wanted to kiss her, just to know what kissing felt like. Christiaan and Johanna did that often, and it looked enjoyable to them. But Zulus never kissed. Kissing was a European mating practice they found disgusting. Instead, he hugged her. She moaned contentedly. It was glorious.

"You didn't answer me," Thandi said.

"I'm feeling fine."

"Then why didn't you sleep?"

Jama shrugged. "You'll think me silly."

"No, I won't," she insisted. "Tell me! Do you find it difficult to sleep with me? Is that it?"

Jama smiled affectionately. He stroked her hair and peered into her dark eyes. "It's just that I've waited so long for you . . . all I want to do is to hold you, caress you, talk with you. I just can't bring myself to waste a single moment we have together sleeping."

30

After months of searching, a pass was found well north that would take them across the Drakensberg Mountains. It would become their portal to the promised land. Retief led his party of more than a thousand wagons to the foot of the mountains to prepare for crossing. Then he and a small contingent of fourteen horsemen and four wagons moved on in advance.

When Johanna first viewed the point of crossing, she was a little more than skeptical. "This is our portal?" she asked. "It makes going through the eye of a needle look easy."

Her assessment was accurate. Trees would have to be felled and rocks cleared; angles of ascent were dangerously steep. Many in the camp were grumbling that it couldn't be done.

However, when word reached them from Retief, who had crested the mountains, many of their fears were alleviated. From the top he described a long line of mountains whose eastern slopes rolled downward into green Natal, abundant with rivers and pastures. He wrote: "I saw this beautiful land, the most beautiful in Africa."

The entire laager was caught up with the thought of putting these mountains behind them. Their promised land was waiting for them on the other side.

When Sina arrived, all she saw was a pair of men's worn boots sticking out from beneath the wagon. They were occupied.

"*Mynheer* Pfeffer?" she asked.

"He's not—Sina?"

The boots scratched in the dirt, maneuvering their occupant from under the wagon. Conraad emerged with grease smears across his chest. His entire back was covered with dust from his hair to the back of his shirt and down his legs to his shoes. He hurriedly brushed himself off as he talked.

"Father isn't here. Can I help you with something?"

"Oh, it's nothing," Sina said, glancing down at the cloth bundle in her arms. She handed it to Conraad. "Bread. Mother was baking, and

252

she thought you and your father might enjoy a couple of—" his dark eyes distracted her "—loaves. A couple of loaves."

This was not Conraad, she mused. At least not the Conraad who used to live on the farm next to them. That Conraad was a boy. This Conraad was . . . well, he wasn't a boy, that was sure.

"Thank you," he said with a deep voice. Large hands, greasy from working on the wagon, reached for the offered loaves. Seeing how dirty they were, he pulled them back, wiped them on his pants, then reached for them again.

Sina smiled. There might still be a little bit of boy in him after all.

He peeked beneath the folds of cloth and sniffed the fresh bread. "This is great," he said. "I haven't had very much luck." He stopped short and stared at the loaves, poking one of them with his finger. "How does she get them so fluffy like that? My bread is always thick and flat."

Sina laughed. "Your bread?"

Conraad looked at her unembarrassed. "Somebody has to bake the bread."

"It's just hard to think of you baking bread," Sina said with a smile.

However, had she thought of it, she wouldn't have been surprised. The Pfeffers were coping as well as could be expected following the twins' death. And this was largely due to Conraad. Naturally, both men were affected by the deaths. Both of them had changed. Adriaan had grown more possessive of his son, wanting to know where he was at every moment. If Conraad heard his father say, "Son, you're all I've got left," once a day, he'd heard it a hundred times.

As for Conraad, the entire community was impressed with him. During the attack of the Matabele, he proved he could face crisis with a cool head. Following the loss of his mother and sisters, he proved he could face tragedy and emerge stronger for it. Sina was among those who took note of his maturing. And she remembered what Karel said about him—*"He likes you."*

"Would you like to sit down or something?" Conraad asked.

"I can only stay for a moment." She accepted a seat under the awning that stretched out from the wagon. Conraad moved a chair so that he was facing her. "Everyone is so busy preparing for the crossing," she explained.

Conraad glanced behind her at the Drakensberg range. "I love mountains," he said, his gaze working its way from the base all the way up to the snow-tipped top. "I can't wait to get up and see the whole world sprawled at my feet."

His eyes fixed on the chiseled stone face of the mountains for a few silent moments.

Sina took the opportunity to fix her eyes on the chiseled look of Conraad's jaw and cheeks. The moment his eyes left the mountains, hers left his face. She stood. "Well, I must be getting back," she said, smoothing the front of her dress.

Conraad stood with her, the bundle of bread cradled in his arms as though it were a baby. "Do you really have to go?" he asked.

Sina nodded slightly.

"At least I got to see you for a little while," he said. "I'm glad your mother sent you." His face grew red, then he added, "Not that I would appreciate it any less if she had brought it—or your father, for that matter. Or Kootjie! I don't want you to think that I'm glad your mother didn't deliver the bread. I'm glad that you . . ."

Sina held up a hand to stop him. "I know what you meant," she said with a laugh. She turned to leave, then thought better of it and turned back. "I volunteered to bring it."

An excited smile appeared on Conraad's face. "You volunteered?"

Sina's smile matched his. "So that I could thank you."

"For what?"

"For defending my honor."

For a moment Conraad looked puzzled.

"You didn't believe the rumors Henry was spreading about me, and you stopped them. Remember now?"

"Oh, that! He had it coming to him, talking about you like that."

"But you did something about it," Sina said. "And I never have thanked you for it. So I wanted to do that now. Thank you." Then she did something that surprised even her. She leaned forward and kissed Conraad on the cheek.

From the pleased look on Conraad's face, he didn't object to her act of familiarity.

As she walked back to the wagon, Sina mused about what had just taken place and how she felt about it. She felt good. Better than good. She felt warm inside, the way she used to feel about Henry, only not as jittery.

The more she dwelt on the feeling, the more she liked it. She could definitely develop a taste for it, possibly an addiction. Now, if she could only get the image of Conraad and Kootjie playing together out of her mind . . .

He knelt alone in the center of the great domed reception hall. Dressed as a Zulu. Addressed by the Zulu king.

Dingane stood. Firelight reflected on his greased black skin. He studied Jama for several minutes. The hall was crowded, yet it was quiet enough to hear the crackling of the fire. "So now you wish to be a Zulu?" he asked.

"Yes, *Baba.*"

"Yet you were not born Zulu."

"I was born Nguni, *Baba,* from which the Zulu come."

"And yet you have lived among the whites. Why is that?"

"I was born among the whites. It was all I knew."

"Then why did you leave them?"

"I was not fulfilled among the whites, *Baba.*"

"And you claim to have found fulfillment here?" Dingane looked at Ndaba as he spoke.

"Yes, *Baba.*"

"And you, who are not a Zulu, marry one of our Zulu maidens?"

"Yes, *Baba.*"

Ndaba stood. "*Bayede.* If I may . . . my daughter would marry none other."

"So I am told." Dingane motioned for Ndaba to sit down. He turned his attention back to Jama. "And having lived so long among the whites, you understand them?"

"No, *Baba.* How can you understand a people who do not understand themselves?"

Dingane roared with laughter.

The gathering followed his example.

"Well spoken!" Dingane cried. "But you do know their ways, do you not?"

"I know their ways, *Baba.*"

The bulky king stepped down from the dais. Without once removing his eyes from the prostrate Jama, he asked slowly, "And should we do battle with them, whose side would you be on? To whom do you own allegiance?"

"I am a Zulu, *Baba.*"

Dingane returned to the dais and his chair. Several of his advisers huddled around him and spoke in hushed tones. When they parted, Dingane said, "This man will be useful to me."

The crossing began. The Pfeffers and van der Kemps teamed up to help get each others' wagons over the summit. From the outset, it was clear that the journey would be a long one. Days were spent with little progress. It would be months before they would see the other side and walk on level ground again. But the promised land lay on the other side. That dream alone drove them.

They made adjustments to living on an angle. There were no flat surfaces anymore upon which to set things. If objects were not propped or anchored properly, they tumbled down the hillside. They cooked at an angle, ate at an angle, slept at an angle, walked at an angle, chopped down trees at an angle, and moved rocks at an angle.

Some of the trekkers didn't attempt to drive their wagons over the mountains. They dismantled them completely and hauled them across on oxen-pulled sleds. Once on the other side, they would assemble the wagons again. The van der Kemps and Pfeffers chose to keep their wagons intact.

Eight pairs of oxen were hitched to each wagon. Three men at a time took turns driving the oxen with whips, sometimes through gorges that were so narrow the wagons scraped on both sides.

After the second week of climbing, Sina's legs hurt as they'd never hurt before. She was tired and gritty and longed to be able to jump into a nice clear lake somewhere. She'd been thinking about that lake and how good it would feel as she followed behind the wagon (pushing when called upon). They were passing between two enormous boulders when the wagon came to an abrupt stop. Then it started creeping backward. She jumped to one side to get out of its path.

After rolling back about a foot, the wagon stopped.

"Sorry!" Kootjie called to her. "I got distracted."

"Distracted by what?"

"Come see for yourself!"

Steadying herself with a hand against the wagon, Sina trudged up the mountainside. She had to turn sideways to squeeze past the wagon, which had halted directly between the two boulders.

A rush of air met her, whipping between the rocks, nearly blowing off her *kappie*. As she made her way past the first two teams of oxen, she crested the mountain.

"Over here!" her father called.

Sina's dress flapped furiously in the wind as she made her way toward her parents, Kootjie, and the Pfeffers. They were staring in wonder at eastern South Africa, spread out before them as far as the eye could see.

Sina stood beside Conraad. "Like having the earth sprawled out at your feet," she said.

Conraad beamed down at her with an affectionate grin.

So this is what the promised land looks like, Sina thought. A lush green land lay before them, extending toward the sea, rippling ever so slightly, looking like the land of a thousand hills. Plenty of streams could be seen flowing from the mountain, promising an adequate water supply. To their left a thin waterfall cascaded over the edge of a sheer cliff, plunging through thousands of feet of nothing until the treetops hid it from view. To Sina the falls looked like a silver ribbon falling off the edge of a giant table.

Beside her, Conraad stood tall, in awe of the breadth and width and grandeur of the land. If anyone could make a go of it in the promised land, it would be Conraad. He'd been through so much, had suffered such great losses, and yet still remained resolute, strong, and good-natured.

As she stood beside him, for the first time she wondered seriously if her destiny and Conraad's were tied together. He was so much more of a man than was Henry. How could she have been so blind for so long?

As they left their lookout position, Conraad brushed by her and smiled. Something inside Sina stirred.

"Looks like it's all downhill from here!" Kootjie joked loudly.

Everyone within earshot groaned.

Taking the wagons downhill proved to be harder than taking them up. The wheels had to be removed to slow the wagons' descent. Only half a team of oxen was used. Their feet gouging the earth, the oxen strained to keep the wagons from tumbling wildly down the mountainside. Ropes tied to the wagons to steady them were as taut as banjo strings.

Just as they were beginning to make good progress, the undercarriage of the Pfeffer wagon wedged against a rock. Lines grew slack. Kootjie brought the oxen to a halt while Adriaan, Conraad, and his father examined the situation.

"It looked to me like it was going to clear," Christiaan said.

"I thought so too," Adriaan replied, bending down to get a better look. "How deep do you suppose it is?"

Conraad crawled on his belly to the obstruction. "It's hard to tell. Could be a small boulder, or it could be the tip of half the mountain."

Whip in hand, Kootjie talked to the beasts, keeping them focused on their job. The last thing they needed at this point was for something sudden to happen. Johanna and Sina stood to one side out of harm's way while the men discussed their options.

"Can we go around it?" Adriaan asked, mentally measuring the distance between the rock projection and three sturdy trees on the far side of the rock.

"One way to find out," Conraad said. He pulled a rope from the back of the wagon. They measured the width of the wagon and then the width of the space.

"At least a foot too narrow," Adriaan said.

Passing on the other side of the rock was out of the question. A foot beyond it the ground fell away at a steep angle. Then, thirty feet beyond that was another drop—a cliff that ended abruptly a hundred feet below at a stream lined by boulders.

"Seems to me our options are three," Christiaan said. "Fell the trees, remove the rock, or dismantle the wagon. It's your wagon, Adriaan. What do you want to do?"

Adriaan looked at the rock, then at the trees. "Let's back the wagon off the rock and see what we're up against. We can dig around it a little. Maybe it's nothing at all."

Conraad agreed with his father.

Kootjie manned the team while Adriaan and Christiaan each held a line tied to opposite sides of the wagon. Conraad directed the effort nearest the rock. The plan was to back the wagon off the rock, then Christiaan and Adriaan would anchor the wagon in place by tying their lines to trees. That way they could rest the oxen while the rock was removed—if it could be removed.

Sina found a chair-level rock upon which to sit and rest her feet.

Her mother joined her.

With Kootjie yelling at the oxen and the two men pulling on the ropes, the wagon groaned and inched away from the rock. Steadying the wagon with one hand, Conraad leaned over to measure its progress. He raised a hand, signaling that they were nearly to the point where they needed to be. Christiaan looked around for a tree large enough to serve as an anchor.

And then an ox stumbled.

Bellowing, it fell to one side, pulling its yoked partner down with it. The combined weight of the two oxen plus the weight of the wagon were too much for the other six. Kootjie yelled and flicked his whip, but it wasn't a matter of obedience—it was a matter of strength, and there was not enough of it. The wagon began to slide.

Christiaan, seeing what was happening, tried to tie off his line around a tree. The sliding wagon ripped the rope from his hands.

Adriaan, too, tried to anchor the wagon, but the pull was too strong. He managed to hold onto the line, but it jerked him off his feet and dragged him along the ground.

The wagon shuddered, then abruptly began sliding toward Conraad. Its sudden change in direction knocked him backward. As he tried to push away from it with his feet, his boot slipped on the wheel, and his leg tangled in the spokes.

The wagon fell against the rock. The rock stopped it—but for only a moment, the briefest of instants. Only long enough for Johanna to lift her hand to her mouth, for Sina to shout half of Conraad's name, for Kootjie to bring his whip back but not forward, for Christiaan to see the rope in front of him on the ground but not to jump for it, for Adriaan to come to a halt, and for Conraad to think how lucky he was, for if it hadn't been for . . .

The rock gave way. It had no roots. They could have unearthed it in a matter of minutes. But it took gravity and the weight of the wagon less than a second before the wagon continued its slide.

Christiaan dove for his line; it was out of reach. Kootjie whipped the oxen, then had to jump out of the way lest they be pulled on top of him. Adriaan held onto the rope, single-handedly trying to stop the wagon from going over the side. Conraad tried to pull his leg free. The wagon wheel turned. His foot was caught. He and the wagon were inextricably tangled.

The longer the wagon slid, the more momentum it gained. The back wheels skidded over the edge from a sharp decline to a sharper one. It began to tip; Conraad saw the wagon coming down on top of him.

Christiaan, Sina, and Johanna watched helplessly. Kootjie lay in the dust, watching the oxen being pulled over with the wagon. Adriaan clung to the rope, struggling to get to his feet. The wagon crashed onto its side with Conraad beneath it.

"Conraad!" Sina screamed. She bolted from the rock, her mother right behind her.

Christiaan and Kootjie struggled to their feet.

There was nothing they could do. There was nothing anybody could do. But that didn't stop them from running after the wagon and the man who was being pulled behind it. Adriaan still clung to the rope, being dragged down the mountainside with the wagon and his boy.

The wagon started tumbling, over and over. Conraad, his foot still tangled in the wheel, tumbled with it, lifelessly, tossed about like a rag doll. Everything flew from the wagon as it began to break apart. Dishes. Clothes. Tools. Dried beef. Canned goods.

"Adriaan! Let go of the rope!" Christiaan yelled. "Let go!"

The wagon tumbled faster, dragging Adriaan with it. Either he couldn't let go, or he wouldn't let go. The momentum of the rolling wagon whipped him back and forth, as though it was trying to shake itself free from the last person who could stop it from its inevitable course. With one flip it threw Adriaan against a tree, breaking the man's grip.

With nothing left to stop it, it tumbled and tumbled until it threw itself off the cliff and plummeted downward to the stream.

It was just as well that they couldn't see it smash against the rocks below. Hearing it was enough to bring Sina to her knees in tears.

While her mother comforted her, Christiaan and Kootjie ran to Adriaan. He was barely conscious, but enough to respond in pain when Christiaan checked his ribs. They were broken.

Kootjie proceeded to the edge of the cliff. Sina, her mother supporting her by an arm, followed him. Through blurry eyes, she looked over the edge, hoping for a miracle. Hadn't she read stories about men who were thrown over cliffs hanging onto exposed roots? Or possibly God sent an angel to break Conraad's fall, and she would see him standing amidst the rubble below, unharmed.

But there would be no miracle today.

Twisted awkwardly among the litter of the personal belongings of what was left of the Pfeffer family, was the body of Conraad, the man she had just come to know . . . possibly even to love. The man who, moments before, had stood tall on the mountain summit with the world spread at his feet. The man who had cared enough for her to protect her honor, even though at the time she thought little of him.

Beside her, Kootjie wept unashamedly.

Turning her away, Sina's mother led her back up the hill while dozens of curious onlookers rushed down the slope to get a look at the crash for themselves.

Later that day, Kootjie and Christiaan buried Conraad beneath a pile of rocks next to the stream. With broken ribs, Adriaan was not fit to make the climb.

The man's health was a concern to Christiaan. The ribs would heal, he was sure of that. But there was something broken inside Adriaan that bandages and medicines and time would never heal.

31

Having crossed the Drakensberg Mountains with considerable difficulty and loss, the trekkers camped at a spot called Doornkop, between the Blaauwkrantz and Tugela Rivers. There Piet Retief, with a small party, left the encampment and journeyed to Port Natal on the coast, a crude town of a few stores and houses with some thirty Englishmen on a bush-cleared site.

Establishing friendly relations with the port was part of Retief's grand strategy. Although the Boers had suffered at the hands of the British, it was not in their best interests to show enmity toward them. On the contrary, they desired free and uninterrupted trade and commerce with British merchants. However, they wanted it as a free and independent people.

Having laid the groundwork for this enterprise among the merchants at Natal, Retief next focused his attention on emGungundlovu and King Dingane. He still insisted on a path of peaceful coexistence. He sought a deed from Dingane that would grant land to the trekkers.

"I don't like it," Johanna said, plunging a needle deep into a pants seam. "Riding into the capital of the Zulus? I don't like it. I just don't like it."

She, Adriaan, and Christiaan sat in the shade beside the wagon, enjoying the sunset. Since Adriaan no longer had a wagon or a family, Christiaan and Johanna had taken him in to share theirs—both wagon and family. Adriaan accepted but insisted he would stay only until he sold some cattle and purchased another wagon.

A messenger from Retief had just arrived. Their leader was requesting Christiaan and Karel de Buys to accompany him to the capital of the Zulus.

"But Baas," Christiaan protested, "Piet Retief has expressly sent for me and Karel! How does one refuse the direct request of an elected leader?"

"You asked for my opinion, and I gave it to you," Johanna said.

"Sounds to me," Adriaan said, puffing on his pipe, "like you're asking for approval to ride into the encampment of the devil."

His hands shook as he relit the pipe. The shaking had started on the day of Conraad's death. Christiaan and Johanna had noticed other changes too. His eyes were somehow different, peculiar. They had a wild look about them. And his voice . . . it had a higher-pitched, nasal quality to it now. Between these physical alterations and his constant grousing—which was so unlike Adriaan Pfeffer—it was hard for them to believe this was the same man they'd known all their lives.

"What does Retief want with Karel? He's just a boy," Johanna said.

"Karel de Buys is hardly a boy any longer, Baas," Christiaan said. "As for why Retief wants him along, all I can say is that ever since the frontier war with the Xhosa, Retief has taken to the lad."

"And what does Louis say about this? Will he allow Karel to go?"

"Louis told Karel the decision was his, as long as I agreed to go."

"Do what you want," Johanna huffed. "The whole world has gone mad, and there's not a thing I can do about it."

Christiaan hated it when she took up that tone and attitude.

"Baas, this is our chance to formulate an agreement so we can live in peace with our neighbors. I thought you'd be pleased that I've been invited to be a part of it."

"I don't trust the Zulus," Johanna said, jabbing the pants leg with the needle. "And nothing you say is going to change my mind."

"What's to trust?" Adriaan cried. "There's only one thing you can trust the devil to do, and that is to act like a devil. If you want my opinion, we ought to drive them from the land. Then we can live in peace."

To Adriaan, Christiaan responded, "Now you're beginning to sound like Oloff Klyn."

"Maybe Oloff has been right all along," Adriaan said.

Christiaan and Karel joined up with Piet Retief on a rocky hill just outside of emGungundlovu. The Zulu capital seemed to be erected entirely in circles on a grassy slope leading down to a tributary of the White Umfolozi River. It was completely and neatly fenced in with thornbush.

As they approached, their presence was readily detected. They were escorted by Zulu warriors to Dingane's kraal.

"Sorry you came?" Christiaan asked Karel as the two rode side by side.

Karel glanced nervously at the warriors flanking them. "Ask me at the end of the day," he replied.

An audience with the king was rarely granted right away, this not being Zulu etiquette. So it was a great honor for Piet Retief and his party to be escorted into the large domed hall as soon as they arrived. There they saw a tall man with huge thighs, belly, and buttocks. His black skin glistened with grease. He wore a sumptuous robe with broad stripes in black, red, and white from top to bottom. He wore a scarlet fringe over his eyes.

Scowling generals flanked Dingane. His subjects threw themselves to the ground in his presence. They would crawl forward a distance of about two hundred yards. There they would halt and address the king only when recognized. No weapons were allowed in the room. Considering that Dingane had assassinated his half brother Shaka to get the throne, Christiaan wasn't surprised by the king's paranoid precaution.

Appearing friendly and cordial, Dingane spoke to Retief. "You do not know me," he said. "Nor I you. Therefore we must become better acquainted. You have come a long distance to see me, so you must first have rest and amusement."

At the king's signal, two thousand young warriors appeared, garbed in kilts of cattails, beads, headdresses of feathers, and ox hair tied to their calves and ankles. Each one had a smooth muscular chest and limbs that gleamed in the light. They proceeded to demonstrate the Zulu manner of beginning a battle, accompanied by yells, screams, and a deafening drumming of sticks on shields. Once the presentation started, there was no stopping it for hours.

While the warriors leaped and danced and shouted, Karel nudged Christiaan. "Look! Over there!" He pointed to a group of elderly men set off to one side. "Isn't that Jama?"

At first Christiaan couldn't locate the man to whom Karel was referring. Then he saw him. Jama. Or was it? He looked different outfitted in Zulu dress.

Just then the man turned his head, though not far enough to see Christiaan looking at him. It *was* Jama!

"I thought he was living with the Amaxhosa," Karel said.

"So did I."

But there was no mistaking it. It was Jama. Then, as though he felt Christiaan's eyes upon him, Jama turned his head. Glances were exchanged. Jama gave no physical sign of recognition. But the two men had shared life long enough for Christiaan to know that Jama had recognized him. Without so much as a blink, Jama turned his attention back to the dancers.

The last time I saw you, old friend, you were wearing Xhosa clothing and

263

my house was burning to the ground, Christiaan mused bitterly. *So we have come full circle, have we? This time I won't be so easily duped.*

Following the warrior dance, Dingane introduced them to a Rev. Francis Owen, the missionary that often served as the king's English secretary. He, his wife, and his wife's sister lived at emGungundlovu, and it was he who had penned the king's answer to Retief's correspondence.

Next, Dingane thrilled his guests with an ox dance in which nearly two hundred oxen, all without horns and of a single color, took part. The animals were decorated with fringes of hide hanging from their foreheads, cheeks, shoulders, and throats.

So ended the trekkers' first audience with Dingane. Without exception, they were impressed by the friendliness of the king. They went to sleep that night with high hopes of establishing an enduring relationship with the Zulu people. Only one of them was even slightly disturbed about the day's events.

Christiaan couldn't get Jama off his mind. What was he doing this far north? How was it that he came to be dressed as a Zulu and seated among the elders? Of one thing he was sure. Jama had abandoned him and betrayed him once. Christiaan wasn't going to let him do it again.

The next day Dingane's entertainment of his guests continued. The more mature warriors gave a dancing exhibition. It, too, was a marvelous display. On the third day, the younger warriors danced again, displaying their skill and vitality in military exercises. Dingane proudly pointed to the gyrating mass of manhood and exclaimed, "This is the *smallest* of all my regiments."

The day was hot and humid. Sweat soon poured down the bodies of the dancers. A whistling sound preceded a sham fight that built to a great climax, then turned into a kind of victory dance in a dense semicircle. The king himself at times set the tune for the songs.

Following this display, Dingane showed the trekkers his cattle herd, numbering 2,424 head. They were all alike, red with white backs. Again Dingane emphasized that this was his *"smallest* herd of oxen."

At last the king was available for more serious business. Rev. Owen was there to serve as secretary. And, to Christiaan's chagrin, so was Jama.

Retief presented his request, and after much discussion regarding mutual enemies, the king indicated he was willing to grant the country to the north, south, and west of Port Natal to the immigrants. Retief could barely contain his joy as he explained to Dingane the reason they had left the colony and their need for a land in which they could settle and expand. The Natal area designated by Dingane was perfect for their needs.

When they left Dingane's kraal, Christiaan was walking beside Retief as Rev. Owen approached. The missionary cautioned Retief that he was possibly wasting his time, for the king was utterly inconsistent. He had previously given the desired territory to the English government, but they had not accepted it.

"Please understand that we are not prepared to live under English rule," Retief said firmly, "but neither will we occupy this country by force."

"We may have another problem," Christiaan said to Retief. "The other Zulu sitting nearby during the discussion."

"The one who didn't say anything?"

Christiaan nodded. "It was Jama."

"Your friend? What's he doing here?"

"I don't know," Christiaan replied. "But I don't believe we can trust him to be favorable to our cause."

"I understand," Retief said. He thought a moment. "But until he opposes us directly or indirectly, I don't see that we have a problem. Let's wait and see what happens. Meanwhile, don't tell anyone else."

In triumph, the Retief expedition returned to the laager with a verbal commitment concerning the land. They would return in a short time to get it in writing. Retief gave an enthusiastic account of their visit, describing in detail the splendors of Dingane, his kindness, and his boundless hospitality. That night the entire laager celebrated. They were one step away from their dream.

Christiaan remained doubtful about their future. He couldn't bring himself to rejoice until he knew what role Jama was playing among the Zulus.

A part of Sina died on the day Conraad died. She didn't understand it herself, but that didn't stop her from feeling the way she was feeling. It wasn't like she and Conraad had been promised to each other. He had never courted her. And only days before his death had Sina even thought of him in terms remotely romantic.

Maybe the tragedy of his death had something to do with it. Or the fact that he'd been a neighbor for so many years. But all she could think about was Conraad, the Conraad of the last few months—the courageous Conraad, the noble Conraad, the compassionate Conraad, the Conraad who liked her, the Conraad she was finding herself attracted to.

Or maybe it wasn't Conraad at all that so depressed her. Maybe she was feeling foolish for wasting all those years pining over a version of Henry that was nothing more than the product of her own mind. All of a sudden she felt so alone. As though no one wanted her; as though she had no future. Here they were, on the edge of their promised land, but a land without anyone to share it with held little promise for her.

Sina found herself wandering away from the celebration that had been prompted by the return of the Retief party. She meandered alone to a small cluster of boulders. With the imposing Drakensberg range at her back and the verdant Natal valley before her, she reached down, plucked a wild flower, and leaned against a boulder. The pure colors of the sky and scenery stood in contrast to the grayness she felt inside. Her only comfort was that which came from brooding.

A twig snapped, startling her.

"Karel!" she cried, holding a hand against her chest. "You frightened me!"

He jumped too, evidently unaware of Sina's presence until she cried out. He had been walking with his head down and had just emerged from a small patch of woods.

"Why aren't you at the celebration?" he asked.

"Why aren't you?"

He ambled toward her and fell against the rock beside her with a long sigh. With his head lowered, he pursed and unpursed his lips several times before he could get the words out. "I've lost Deborah."

"You sound so definite," Sina said. "Has her father . . ."

"I am definite, and it's not because of her father." He looked away, struggling with his emotions.

Sina didn't press. She knew Karel. He would tell her when he could.

Blinking back tears, Karel said, "Deborah's . . ." He looked away, sniffed, and tried again. "Deborah's with child."

"Karel! No . . . I'm so sorry." Not for an instant did she think the child was his.

He continued to struggle with his emotions. Sina had expected him to feel better once he got it out. The hard part was over. Or was it?

"The father . . ." Karel said, his teeth gritting, "is Henry Klyn."

Sina was struck dumb. Then she wondered why she was surprised. An isolated clearing beside a rippling brook came to mind. She had not been the only one Henry had lured there.

"You must feel awful!" she whispered sympathetically. She placed a comforting hand on his shoulder.

For a long time they were silent. Words were not needed for two

266

people who had known each other as long as they had. Each allowed the other the freedom to mourn in his own way. Each was comforted by the closeness of a caring friend.

"And you?" he managed to say. "Why aren't you at the celebration?"

"I can't get Conraad out of my mind."

Karel nodded with understanding.

Sina twirled the wild flower between her fingers.

He stared absently at the ground. "It seems like it always comes down to you and me, doesn't it?"

She glanced over and smiled. "Almost like old times on the hillock beside the house."

"We spent a lot of time together there."

"A lot of time," she said warmly. "A lot of memories."

"And one kiss."

Sina laughed. She slapped him playfully. "You would bring that up, wouldn't you?"

They shared silent smiles as both of them relived the memory.

"You've always been there," Sina said. "Even when I made a fool of myself with Henry, you were always there. Remember Nachtmaal? When you stopped Henry and me from going to the peach orchard? I was so furious with you!"

"Furious?"

"We were just going to talk!" Sina protested. Then, considering the events that had transpired since then, she said softly, "At least that's why *I* was going there."

The subject of Henry and the peach orchard brought a painful reminder of more recent events with Deborah, which subdued the emerging laughter.

"Anyway, thank you for protecting me," Sina said.

Karel shrugged. "You never gave up on me, even though you hate Deborah."

"I don't hate Deborah!"

Karel challenged her with a sideways glance.

"I don't hate her," Sina protested. "I just don't like her very much. I don't want her to be my best friend."

"You don't like the way she acts."

"That's true."

"Or the way she dresses."

"Yes, I would agree with that. Or the way she treats you," Sina added.

267

"But you don't hate her."

"Right, I don't hate her."

Karel grinned painfully. "Well, it doesn't make any difference now, does it?"

"No, I guess it doesn't."

Turning to face her, Karel said, "Do you know how much that disturbed me?"

"What? That I didn't like Deborah?"

"That you hated her," Karel corrected, evidently unable to hold back the verbal jab.

Sina deflected it with a grin. "Why did it bother you?"

"Because I'd always hoped that the woman I married would like you. I've always imagined you and she being best of friends . . . that the four of us—me and my wife, you and your husband—would get together often, possibly even share adjoining farms."

"What a nice thing to say, Karel. I can't say I'd ever thought about it to such a degree, but I do know that I've always wanted your approval of the man I would marry."

She hesitated to tell him the rest, then decided there was no harm in it now that they were sharing. "In fact, that was one of the things that attracted me to Conraad. You approved of him. It forced me to reevaluate my view of him, and I liked what I saw."

Karel smiled warmly. "The two of you would have made a good couple."

"And now it's just the two of us."

"And now it's just the two of us," Karel echoed.

Sina turned toward him. "You've always been my closest friend," she said.

"And you've always been mine."

Karel reached out and placed his hand against her cheek. It was warm. Tender.

Acting on instinct, Sina closed her eyes. She realized she was not alone. She had never been alone. Karel had always been there. When the Xhosa attacked, he rode all the way from his farm to see that she was unharmed. It was Karel who found her after she'd run away and brought her back home. It had always been Karel.

Opening her eyes, she reached out and placed her hand against his cheek. They had always been there for each other. They would always be there for each other. She could see it in his eyes. Love that was deeper than romance. The kind of love that doesn't suffer when persons disagree. The kind of love that thinks of the other person's good above his own. He had always loved her. Always.

Karel's hand moved tenderly to the back of her head. Gently he pulled her toward him. Their eyes locked in silent communication.

They'd always been friends. More than friends. Now, much more. For Sina, it felt so right. So natural.

His arms encircled her, and she was not afraid. She knew in the depth of her being that Karel would never do anything to hurt her. It was as though scales had fallen from her eyes and she could now see the obvious. It had been Karel all along.

His lips pressed against hers. For the second time in their lives.

32

For the second visit to emGungundlovu, Retief called for volunteers to accompany him. He was disappointed when only sixty-six men came forward.

It wasn't that they didn't wish him well; it was that they didn't trust a heathen such as Dingane.

Christiaan volunteered. So did Karel and Kootjie, both of whom Christiaan quickly un-volunteered. Not very often was he adamant about having his way. This was an exception. Until he knew what Jama was doing among the Zulus, he didn't want his family—and he considered Karel part of his family—to wander far from the protection of the laager. Both Karel and Kootjie objected angrily. But Christiaan prevailed.

To the sound of cheers and gun salutes, they rode off.

The trekkers decided that upon this visit a little showmanship of their own was in order. As they approached the kraal, they announced their arrival with the traditional Boer salute of guns. Zulus poured out of the capital gates to greet them. Festivities would commence at once, and, by the king's command, the Boers were to take the lead with a dance of their own horses.

Dingane, bedecked in robes and smiling, watched with interest as the Boers staged a mock fight. Charging one another on horseback, they made the air resound with their guns. From the startled look in their eyes, Christiaan was confident the Zulus had never seen anything like this before. The natives were amazed and delighted as soon as they got over their fright of the noise. For the rest of the day there was singing and dancing in the Zulu capital.

The reception hall was stilled. An air of expectation permeated everything. Dingane sat on his throne, surrounded by his advisers. Jama was among them.

Piet Retief stood before the king and answered his questions, the same questions that had been asked at the initial audience. Why were the Boers trekking? What were their intentions in Natal? Why were they not content to live beyond the Drakensberg Mountains? How had they defeated Mzilikazi and why?

Retief patiently answered all these questions. He reminded the king that the Boers wished to come to Natal because of its beauty and fertility and that during their previous visit the king had promised to give them land.

To everyone's relief, the king nodded in approval, and a document was produced.

Christiaan glanced up. Jama was staring at him. His eyes were neither friendly nor unfriendly; they were neutral, but they were also staring. A signal? A warning? A threat? Christiaan couldn't tell.

> Know all men by this that Dingane, King of the Zulus, hereby certifies and declares that he thinks fit to resign unto Pieter Retief and his countrymen the place called Port Natal together with all the land annexed, that is to say from the Tugela to the Umzimvubu river westwards from the sea to the north as far as the land may be useful unto them for their everlasting property.

The treaty was translated word for word to Dingane, who gave his approval and signed it, his mark witnessed by three Boers. The document was then given to Retief, who received it gratefully.

Christiaan couldn't help but smile over Retief's joy. This was a great moment for him, the fulfillment of a dream. His elation was shared equally by the other trekkers.

Again, Jama caught Christiaan's eye. And again, the Zulu did nothing but stare. It was an unnerving, unnatural stare.

The remainder of the day was filled with entertainment, celebrating the signing of the treaty. Dingane was accompanied by his vast entourage. The entire area teemed with warriors, courtiers, dignitaries, praise-singers, and jesters. Sham fights and war dances went on ceaselessly as regiment after regiment performed according to the color of their shields. The earth seemed to shake under the rhythmical stamping of feet. Sweat poured off gleaming bodies. Feathers and animal skins swirled colorfully. There were far more regiments present than during the initial visit. Far more.

That night, the Boers collapsed in their tents, exhausted. Christiaan slept, but fitfully. He kept dreaming about Jama's unblinking eyes.

The next morning the Retief party was anxious to strike camp and leave, but Dingane invited them for a final and farewell display. By this time they had had quite enough of these, but because they had yet to bid the king farewell, they obeyed. As before, they left their guns and horses outside the kraal, leaving only a few servants behind to tend the animals.

A roar hailed their entry, and Dingane gave them a greeting. The men sat down on mats, and they were served milk and sorghum beer. All around them the warriors were chanting and singing. They, too, were unarmed, in keeping with the king's edict forbidding weapons in the royal kraal.

Retief leaned toward Christiaan. He had to shout to be heard. "Have you spoken with Jama?"

Christiaan shook his head. "We've exchanged glances. No more than that," he answered. He thought about expressing his concern over those glances. But considering that they were celebrating the success of the treaty, his fears seemed unwarranted.

"Have you seen him today?" Retief shouted.

Christiaan shook his head.

"If you do, let me know. I'll ask Dingane to invite him over."

Christiaan nodded agreement, though the thought of meeting Jama in this setting at this time did not set well with him.

As the milk and beer were passed round, the singing grew louder. The warriors circled in dance, their feet pounding the dusty ground. Dingane rose to join the dancing, his great thighs quivering. In spite of his size, he danced lightly, gleefully, gracefully in his splendid costume of beads.

The tempo of the music increased. The king was sweating profusely. Sticks beat against shields, creating a low, rumbling sound. Faster. Faster. Circle after circle of warriors began to blur as the tempo increased ever faster. Muscles of the dancers shook. Feet pounded. Dust rose in great clouds.

The music and beat swelled to fever pitch, growing angry. Dogs began to growl. The Boers, seated in the center of all the activity, began to stir uneasily. Shields rumbled. Bodies gyrated, circled, faster, faster, louder, louder.

And then Dingane nimbly came to a halt. Everything and everyone stopped with him. Where once were sound and music and motion, now were stillness and eerie silence.

"Babulaleni abathakathi!" Dingane shouted. "Kill the wizards!"

Before a man could rise, the warriors fell upon Retief and his followers. A sea of hands rushed at Christiaan, grabbing him, pulling him off his feet, lifting him into the air. He struggled, but it was useless. There were too many of them.

One by one the men were held up for the king to see.

Helpless, Christiaan was carried before Dingane, his feet never touching the ground. The yellowish, bloodshot eyes of the sweating king looked on him without compassion. With the others he was then dragged from the arena to the hill of execution.

Christiaan could hear the sobs and prayers and shouts of the Boers mingled with the hisses and yells of their captors. They all knew they were done for.

He thought of Johanna. Sina. Kootjie. He prayed for them. A sense of immense gratification came over him—surprisingly strong, but then he assumed that when one approaches his execution all of a man's senses are heightened. He felt gratification that he'd stopped Kootjie and Karel from coming with him. He felt a sense of peace about entrusting his family to Karel before he left. Karel was a good man. Christiaan's only regret was that Karel and Sina hadn't yet discovered each other.

He thought of Jama. Oloff Klyn had been right about him all along. Now Pfeffer too. *These people can't be trusted.* He and Retief learned it too late. Maybe his death would save Kootjie and Karel from making the same mistake.

His hands were yanked behind him and tied with leather thongs. Though many of the onlookers had fallen back, there were still too many of them. Fighting and kicking were useless.

"We're done for! We're done for!" one of the Boers sobbed.

On the hill of execution, Christiaan watched as one by one his friends and fellow trekkers were clubbed to death.

Piet Retief, his hands bound, the leather pouch that bore the signed treaty beside him on the ground, looked over at Christiaan just before he was clubbed. Their eyes met. Two of a kind. Wanting peace. Getting death in return.

With a crack, Retief fell to the ground, his skull crushed.

"We're done for! We're done for!" A shouting Boer managed to get to his feet. Shaking free from the warriors holding him, he charged down the embankment.

A distraction! Christiaan didn't waste a moment. He must break free.

Whack!

A blow landed squarely on the back of his head. A flash of white blotted out everything. He felt intense pain. Even the attempt to open his eyes was met with blinding agony. He saw images only. Blurry. Felt himself being pulled backwards. Something thrown over him. Then the world went black. Life and energy drained from his limbs. His thoughts and memories grew darker and darker until consciousness failed him completely.

The last thing Christiaan saw was a pair of eyes. Familiar. Staring. The same eyes he'd seen in his sleep the night before.

Jama's eyes.

"What on earth is that commotion?" Johanna said.

Poking her head out of the wagon she saw people everywhere, running. "Sina? Do you know what's happening?"

A spoon dangled in Sina's hand as she stood over the boiling pot on the fire. "I can't see anything. Maybe they've returned with the treaty!"

Adriaan dozed in a chair under the wagon's awning. He'd been more surly than usual this morning, and Johanna didn't want to wake him. The number of people disturbed her. Had there been only a few, she would have sent Sina to find out what was happening.

Kootjie ran up. "Why is everyone running around? Are we being attacked?"

Johanna answered. "Help me out of this wagon, and we'll go see. It could be your father's returned."

Johanna, Sina, and Kootjie had gotten no farther than a wagon's length when Karel came running toward them. He held his arms out, stopping them. His eyes looked haunted.

"Karel, what's wrong?" Sina cried.

"Let's all go back to the wagon," he said. His voice cracked. It was all he could do to get the sentence out.

Johanna looked past him. Everyone was gathered around one man. One of Retief's servants, the one that was so good with the horses. Women were wailing. Children crying. The first dawning of awareness chilled her spine.

"Karel . . ." she said. She was beginning to guess the truth.

Swallowing hard, he said, "They're dead. All of them. Retief. *Mynheer* van der Kemp. The Zulus murdered them."

33

Black pain. Throbbing. Intense. Surprising.

Dead people didn't feel pain. At least that's what he'd been led to believe. He heard himself moan. He couldn't feel his throat actually make the sound. The pain in his head washed away all other feeling.

A slight turn of his head. A flash of white. White pain. Worse than black pain, if that was possible.

Another moan. He attempted to see something, not sure if seeing was something he could still do.

The death experience wasn't at all what he'd expected it would be.

Eyelids cracked open. Dark images. Blurred. A flicker caught his attention. Orange, flickering against what looked like woven thatch. Movement. A black shape. Spirits? Death himself?

A face came into view. Short hair. Wide nose. Female. Black skin. Kindly eyes, but not friendly.

"Who . . ." Christiaan tried to speak. His throat was parched, his tongue thick and dry. The effort rewarded him with a throbbing in his temples and behind his eyes.

Something touched his lips. Warm. Dry. Preventing him from making another attempt to speak.

A noise. Somewhat distant. The female head over him turned. Then it was gone. Voices. Or what he thought were voices. They sounded as if they were far away, or underwater, or both.

Another face. Those eyes . . . he recognized those eyes.

Christiaan wanted to reach up and strangle the neck that belonged to those eyes.

Jama.

"Don't let him . . . to rest." Garbled words, fading in and out.

Christiaan tried to sit up. Hands held him down.

Angry hands. Hands that had lifted him up and displayed him to that sweating, yellow-eyed king. He struggled. They were grabbing him. Pulling him away. Carrying him up the hill. Must break free. *Whack!* The sound of skulls cracking. Men weeping. Praying. Begging. *Whack!* Must get away. No use. Too many. Must get . . . too many. Must . . .

Black pain. Then just blackness with no pain.

Something touched his lips. Smooth. Water trickled across his tongue and down his throat. Reflexively he swallowed. Choked. Coughed. More water. This time it went down easier. He felt himself being lowered.

Eyes flickered open. The female.

"Rest now," she said.

He did.

He smelled something cooking. Stew of some kind. A gentle sound of humming accompanied it. He managed to turn his head and open his eyes. The female, stirring a pot.

"Where am I?" Christiaan said hoarsely.

She looked at him and set down the stirring stick. Then she came over and helped him sit up and take a drink.

When she lowered him back down this time, his eyes remained open.

"My name is Thandi," she said. "I'm Jama's wife."

Christiaan's first thought was that she was lying. Jama didn't have a wife. His second thought was surprise.

"You speak Afrikaans?"

"A little. It is necessary when dealing with traders from Durban. And, of course, Jama has taught me some."

She went away. When she returned, Jama was with her. Jama the Zulu. He knelt beside Christiaan.

"How are you, old friend?" Jama whispered.

"You're no friend of mine," Christiaan muttered.

Jama didn't react.

Thandi scowled.

"Rest now," Jama said. "We'll talk later." He left.

Thandi remained behind, glowering at Christiaan. Then she left.

Christiaan closed his eyes and concentrated on restoring his strength so that he could escape. He fell asleep.

The next time he awoke, Thandi was bending over him. Staring at him. None too kindly. "He put our lives in danger to save you," she said bitterly.

"It won't earn him forgiveness," Christiaan said, forming the words as best he could with a dry mouth.

"Forgiveness? For what?"

"For abandoning two generations of family life without so much as a farewell. For going over to the enemy and leading the Xhosa in an attack upon us. For his part in this black plot to destroy all chance of peace between our two peoples by killing one of the most trustworthy men I've ever known."

"Jama was not part of Dingane's treachery!" Thandi cried. "Nor did he lead the Xhosa in their attack. He was unable to prevent the Xhosa from destroying your house. And when he saw you fleeing toward the Pfeffer farm, he deliberately steered the armies away from your location to spare you and your family."

Christiaan looked at her skeptically. He was surprised, though, that she knew about the Pfeffers. "Jama has undoubtedly told you something of that time," he said. "All I can say is that you weren't there. You didn't see the things I saw."

"I don't have to see them. I know my husband. He has told me the truth. And if you knew him as well as you think you do, you would know that Jama would not lie about these things."

Christiaan was unconvinced.

"Let me ask you this," she said, "since you were there and saw everything. Were all the farms in the vicinity destroyed?" Folded arms indicated she wasn't going to continue until he answered.

"Yes, they were."

"All of them *except* for . . ."

"The Pfeffer farm," Christiaan answered. "But how do you know it was Jama who was responsible for that farm being spared?"

"You think it was coincidence?" Thandi exclaimed. "It was the Pfeffer farm incident that forced Jama to leave the Xhosa. The Xhosa generals discovered his deception and tried to kill him. Before they could carry out the sentence, he escaped and traveled north, ending his journey here in this hut."

Christiaan closed his eyes. It hurt to think. However, closed eyelids did not shut out Thandi's passionate voice.

"You lived with the man most of your life," she said. "Tell me, is the man with whom you lived capable of the things you are accusing him of? Or is it more likely he would do things the way I described them?"

Christiaan clinched shut his eyes and rubbed them. "I don't know," he said groggily. "He changed."

"He has not changed," Thandi insisted. "He is the same man today. Let me tell you about my Jama. My Jama risked his life to save a child from a lion. My Jama counseled the king to make an agreement of peace with the Boers. And when Dingane, who is forever changing his mind

277

from one day to the next, announced that he was going to kill all the Boers, it was my Jama—knowing that he couldn't save all of them—who plotted a way at least to save his friend."

Her voice trembled with passion. "When the warriors fell upon you," she said, "he stayed close by. When they carried you up the hill of execution, he was right behind you. While the others were being slaughtered, he waited and prayed for a moment of confusion, the slightest of distractions, anything that would call attention away from you. And when it happened, it was he who hit you on the head. If any of the others had done it, they would have smashed your skull. Then, in the midst of the confusion and with the help of my father, he threw a covering over you and spirited you away. They brought you to this hut."

Opening his eyes, Christiaan looked at Thandi. Tears glistened in her eyes. Fearful tears.

"By rescuing you, Jama has not only placed himself in danger but everyone in this hut. If he is found out, Dingane will mount all of us on spiked poles. Now tell me truthfully, *Mynheer* van der Kemp, which sounds more like the Jama you have known many years?"

Jama appeared behind her. "Such a spirited defense from one so lovely," he said.

Thandi stood. Jama embraced her warmly.

It was difficult for Christiaan to see Jama dressed in Zulu garb, especially now after the massacre. But when he looked past the clothing and the trappings, when he looked at the man, gazed into his eyes, which were the mirrors of his soul, he saw the old Jama. The one he'd known and admired and loved for years.

With great pain, Christiaan reached upward with one hand. "Forgive me, old friend," he said. "I've wronged you and acted like a fool."

While Thandi attended to the chickens, Jama sat on his haunches next to Christiaan.

"You've never looked so happy," Christiaan said.

"I've never been so happy," Jama replied. He hastened to add, "That isn't to say that I wasn't happy when I was living . . ."

Christiaan raised a hand to stop him. "No explanation is necessary," he said with a grin. Looking to the doorway, he added, "She loves you passionately."

"And I her."

Christiaan struggled to sit up. Not much, just enough to support himself with his arms. Blood rushed from his head, and for a moment everything went hazy white. Then his vision cleared, and the color returned. "I'm afraid she doesn't think much of me, though," he said. "I haven't exactly acted like a gracious guest."

This time Jama checked the opening to the hut to see if Thandi had returned before he spoke. "It's not you she dislikes," he said. "It's the threat you bring with your presence. And I don't mean just you, although should anyone discover you were here . . ."

Christiaan nodded. "I'll be on my way."

Now it was Jama who raised a hand. "When you're ready," he said. Then he concluded his thought. "It's not just you she fears but the coming of the Boers. The entire trek."

"We came seeking peaceful coexistence!" Christiaan cried, loud enough to set his head to pounding.

Jama nodded. Pointing to Christiaan, he said, "You came in peace. And I believe *Mynheer* Retief was a man of good character who genuinely wanted peace. But what about *Mynheer* Klyn and others like him? Do you believe he wants peace?"

Christiaan pondered what Jama was saying. "And now Pfeffer, and even Kootjie to some extent," he mused. "I myself was . . ." He didn't finish the sentence. He didn't have to.

"The Zulus have men just like Klyn. Equally passionate. Equally wrong. Witness what your coming has done to Dingane. He fears you. Shaka warned him about your coming—that it would mean the destruction of the Zulu nation. Dingane knows how easily you have defeated Mzilikazi's regiments. We cannot win a battle against horses and firearms! Your very presence threatens us. Dingane has concluded that he must kill you before you kill us."

Christiaan eased himself back down onto the mat. "There are not enough of us, are there, Jama? Men like you and Retief."

"There are more of us than you think. But hate is strong. And one hateful man can poison a score of men around him. As for Thandi—" he checked the entrance one more time "—she is a good woman. She has waited for me as long as I have waited for a woman like her. We are to be parents!"

Christiaan grinned so hard it hurt. "That's wonderful news!"

"Only she fears that now everything she has waited for and longed for all her life is about to be snatched away from her," Jama said. He added solemnly, "She is an insightful woman, Christiaan. I fear she may be right."

There was something further Jama needed to tell him. Christiaan had spent too many years with the man not to know when bad news was about to be announced.

Jama cleared his throat. "Dingane will attack the Boer encampment tomorrow morning. The regiments are already on their way."

"We've got to warn them!"

"It's too late. Zulu warriors move very swiftly."

"Horses! What about the horses?"

Jama thought for a moment. "With all the regiments gone, it may be possible . . ."

"No!" Thandi cried from the entrance. "It is too risky!"

Jama rose and went to her. "It's the only way. And I'll have to ride with him."

"No!" she shouted.

"He's in no condition to ride," Jama said. "If I don't go, he'll never make it."

"No!" Thandi shouted again. "Why would you leave your wife to help a Boer?"

"He is my friend," Jama said softly. "And if I don't, I'm no better than Dingane, or *Mynheer* Klyn, or all the others."

Christiaan struggled to his feet. He had to pause several times on the way up, catching himself against the side of the hut. But he managed to stand and shuffle toward the entrance. Thandi glared at him when he walked by her.

"I'll wait outside," he said.

The last he saw of Thandi, she was clinging to Jama as though she would never see him again.

34

Sina was curled up against Karel, her head on his shoulder. He gazed down at the smoothness of her cheek, the delicate nature of her nose, and the wisps of mussed hair near her temples. Then he turned his attention to the hilly plains and ravines that stretched endlessly in front of his watch post. It was nearly daylight.

They knew an attack was coming. They didn't know when. Karel thought they'd come at night, using the cover of darkness to their advantage. As it turned out, there had been a heavy fog that night. This, too, would have aided a Zulu attack. Now, as the sun lightened the horizon, it appeared he'd been wrong. They hadn't attacked. But although he couldn't see them, he was certain they were out there. They could be hiding in any one of a hundred ravines.

In preparation for the attack, the Boers had formed their wagons into the now traditional laager shape—wagons chained to one another end to end, thorn bushes wedged between and under them; two gated openings wide enough for only a single rider at a time; and, this time, two cannon placed strategically in the direction of the inevitable assault. For this encounter, their position was strengthened by their geographical location. The laager was butted up against a steep rise, which protected them on one side. A river, deeper than the long handle of an ox whip, too deep to wade across, protected them on a second side.

Also, the night before, in anticipation of an attack they had held a religious service with prayers, psalm singing, and a sermon. Sarel Cilliers, who had been a church elder back in the Cape Colony, had written a vow, which they repeated in unison:

> My brethren and fellow countrymen, at this moment we stand before the holy God of heaven and earth, to make a promise, if He will be with us and protect us and deliver the enemy into our hands so that we may triumph over him, that we shall observe the day and the date as an anniversary in each year and a day of thanksgiving like the Sabbath, in His honor; and that we shall enjoin our children that they must take part with us in this, for a remembrance

even of our posterity, and if anyone sees a difficulty in this, let him return from this place. For the honor of His name shall be joyfully exalted, and to Him the fame and the honor of the victory must be given.

Sina stirred. Tilting her head, she looked up at Karel and smiled.

"Mmm, this is nice," she said, snuggling against him.

Karel placed his arm around her.

She repositioned herself so that they were sitting cheek to cheek.

With the dawning of day, the sky opened up to them. It promised to be a clear, bright day.

"I wish it could be like this forever," Sina said.

"I'd prefer a house," Karel replied.

She smiled and kissed him on the cheek.

"With a kitchen, so you could cook me breakfast."

"Oh, you!" She dug her fingers into his side.

"Sina, stop!"

She did. Instantly. The tone of his voice was not playful. His eyes were fixed on the horizon. Following his gaze, she saw what he saw—Zulu warriors—each regiment distinguishable by different colored shields. Regiment after regiment appeared, advancing on the laager.

"There are thousands of them!" she cried.

Karel counted thirty-six different regiments. A frightfully large number.

Christiaan felt like a helpless boy. For a Boer, riding was like walking—it was something one did without thinking. Not today. Dizzy, nauseous, it was all he could do to stay atop his horse. Even so, he feared they would arrive too late.

Twice Jama forced him to stop and rest, both times following a fainting spell in which Jama had to reach over to prevent Christiaan's falling to the ground.

They'd had to overpower two Zulus to get the horses. But there was little danger of their getting caught once they were away. The Zulus were inexperienced in riding horses.

"Don't we make an odd sight?" Christiaan said. "Anyone seeing us would double over laughing at what looks like a drunken Boer beside a Zulu on horseback."

"You have your sense of humor," Jama said. "Either you are getting better, or I knocked you silly."

His head pounding mercilessly, Christiaan said, "If this is better . . ."

Jama reined to a stop. "There they are. We are too late."

In the distance he could see the backs of long lines of Zulu regiments. Beyond them was a great cloud of dust and the muffled sound of firearms.

"You need go no farther, my friend," Christiaan said. "Return to your wife and child."

"And what will you do from here? Say to the Zulu generals, 'Pardon me, but I must get to the laager where I can get my gun and kill you'?"

"Do you think they'll let me through?" Christiaan asked. An instant later, his grin revealed the jest.

"You are sicker than I thought," Jama said.

Christiaan looked across the terrain. "Over there," he said, pointing to his right. "I'll skirt the back of the troops to there, then try to find a ravine to hide in."

"Then what? You have no weapon, and you can barely ride."

"If all goes well," Christiaan said, "if the Zulus retreat, commandos will come charging out on horseback in pursuit. Then I can come out of hiding."

"And if the Zulu are victorious?"

Christiaan looked at him solemnly. "Then Johanna and Sina and Kootjie will be dead and I don't want to live."

"I'll ride with you to your ravine," Jama said.

"No. Go home to Thandi."

"You couldn't make it half a mile without my assistance."

"Go home."

"After you are safe in the ravine."

Christiaan couldn't force Jama to ride away. So the two men continued their journey. Christiaan didn't say it, didn't even want to admit it to himself because it was so selfish, but he was glad for Jama's company.

By riding in and out of ravines, they managed to skirt the back edge of the Zulu regiments without being detected until their progress was halted by the river. Finding an unoccupied ravine, they moved closer to the laager and the fighting.

"This is as far as we dare go," Christiaan said.

The laager was in clear sight. He was pleased to see its defensive position. They watched as a wave of Zulus rushed the wagons only to be repulsed by heavy gunfire. A thick haze of acrid smoke hung over the laager like a cloud. The terrain immediately in front of the wagons was littered with hundreds and hundreds of dead and dying Zulu warriors.

Karel fired. Two Zulu warriors crumpled to the ground. Without turning his head, he handed the gun behind him. Sina replaced it with a loaded one. He fired again. The rifles had been fired so many times, and were so hot, that they were nearly untouchable.

Beside him Kootjie fought in similar manner. His lips were curled in bitter hatred. Each time he killed a Zulu he nodded in satisfaction. But the killing only seemed to increase his hatred; it did nothing to appease it.

"They're retreating!" someone shouted.

"To the horses!"

Grabbing guns, powder, and bags of shot, Karel and Kootjie turned from their firing positions to get their horses.

Sina grabbed Karel by the arm.

He embraced her. Kissed her.

"You come back to me!" she said. It wasn't a request.

"Yes, Baas," he said. "I wouldn't want you to be angry with me."

Adriaan Pfeffer joined them as they rode out. He, like Kootjie, rode and fired like a man possessed. It was as though the anger that welled up inside him was finding an outlet through his arms, into the gun barrel and out the muzzle—spitting bitterness, anger, and death.

"Good-bye, my friend," Christiaan said to Jama. "Go quickly."

The two men lay concealed up against the side of the ravine, having hidden the horses a good distance behind them where the gully was deeper.

Jama made no effort to delay his departure any longer. "May God be with you," he said.

Christiaan looked at him curiously. Jama's reference to God puzzled him. Was it simply a reference to Christiaan's God, or had Jama finally . . .

There was no time to find out—the commandos were coming. Jama turned and retraced his steps through the ravine.

Christiaan monitored the approach of the Boer horsemen. Defenseless, he didn't want to expose himself too soon.

Just then, he caught sight of Kootjie. Riding furiously. Aiming. Shooting. Reloading.

Doing his best to ignore his pain, Christiaan climbed out of the ravine. Waving his arms over his head, he yelled at his son. "Kootjie! Over here! Kootjie!"

His movement caught Kootjie's eye. The boy's gun swung around. Pointed straight at him.

"It's me, Kootjie! Me! Don't shoot!"

The boy pulled his horse to a dead stop, dumbfounded, unable to believe what he saw. He looked at his father as though he were seeing an apparition.

Suddenly a Zulu warrior appeared beside the boy. Grabbed him. Pulled him to the ground.

"No!" Christiaan cried. His hands wanted to raise and fire a gun he didn't have. He ran toward his son, his head pounding with each step. But he was too far away. He knew he could never make it to Kootjie in time.

Then a second Zulu appeared, and Christiaan knew that Kootjie was dead.

While the first attacker pinned Kootjie to the ground, the second lifted his assegai—and plunged it into the side of the Zulu warrior! A surprised look appeared on the face of the first warrior as he slumped over the boy.

Jama!

Kootjie struggled to get free. Grabbed his gun. Aimed it at Jama.

"No, son!" Christiaan shouted. "It's Jama! Don't shoot! It's Jama!"

Kootjie stared at the Zulu in front of him.

"It's me, Kootjie. It's Jama."

BLAM!

Jama's back arched violently. He fell backward into the river. His blood mingled with the blood of other warriors, turning the water red.

Adriaan Pfeffer rode past. "You're welcome, boy!" he shouted happily, as he reloaded and shot down another Zulu warrior and another. And another.

35

The Boers arrived at emGungundlovu nine days before Christmas. They found it deserted. Dingane had burned his palace and moved on.

With Karel and Kootjie at his side, Christiaan led them to the hill of execution where the remains of Piet Retief and the others still lay exposed to the elements. He bent down and picked up Retief's leather knapsack. In it was the deed granting the Boers the right to settle in Natal, signed by Dingane, king of the Zulus.

With the help of others, they buried the bodies of their dead comrades.

Later, Christiaan went alone to the hut that had once belonged to Thandi, her father, and Jama. He went inside and stood near the spot where they had cared for him. He wondered how long Thandi had waited for Jama to return before she realized her greatest fear had come true. He wondered where she was now and what she would do when the baby was born. What she would tell her child about its father. What she would tell her child about the Boers—and Christiaan.

Leaving the hut, he found Kootjie and Karel. "Let's go home," he said.

The three of them rode back to join the other trekkers as they prepared to build their homes in Natal.

The craggy Drakensberg Mountains cast an early evening shadow over the house and the two women. Johanna and Sina sat side by side, their hands busy with needles—mending for mother, knitting for daughter. Johanna paused in her work long enough to pull a sweater around her shoulders and gaze out at the portion of the land that was still bright with sun.

"I love this time of day," she said. "The deep colors set against dark, lengthening shadows."

Sina looked up. Indeed, the plain that stretched before the van der Kemp household did look greener than normal in the afternoon light. The eastern sky was a deep blue. The brightest of the stars were beginning to make their appearance.

"At times it's so beautiful it's deceptive," Johanna said.

"How so?"

"It's breathtaking, but it's still wilderness."

As if to validate her observation, the cry of a distant elephant echoed against the mountainside.

"The men ought to be returning soon," Johanna said. "They'll be hungry."

"Here they come now." Sina pointed toward the horizon.

Riding into the rays of the lowering sun were Christiaan, Kootjie, and Karel.

"What was so special about them riding out there today?" Johanna asked.

Sina smiled an embarrassed smile. "Karel couldn't wait any longer. He wants to start building as soon as possible."

"He wants to get married as soon as possible is what you mean," her mother said with a smirk.

Sina fought back a blush. "I can't wait for you to see the spot we picked, Mother. You'll love it. There is a nice clearing not far from a stream. And to one side of where the house will be there's a knobby hillock, just like at our old house. Karel said he knew that's where we were supposed to build when he saw the hillock."

Johanna turned and looked lovingly at her daughter. "Your father and I couldn't be happier for you. For years we prayed you and Karel would have sense enough to realize how much you love each other. You don't know how many nights we prayed while one or the other of you was distracted by the wrong person."

"What made you so confident we were right for each other when we didn't know ourselves?"

"It was all that time the two of you spent whispering on the hillock."

"You heard us?" Sina cried.

"Of course we heard you. Saw you, too. One night Karel kissed you. It worried us at first, but then we saw it wasn't a regular occurrence."

"You saw us kiss!" Sina cried even louder.

"We may be old, but we're not blind. Come, help me get the meal started." Her mother rose, set her mending on the seat of the chair, and walked into the house.

Sina was right behind her. "You saw us kiss!" she cried again. "I can't believe you were watching us!"

Johanna smiled. "That's what parents are for."